Demon Hunting in the Deep South

D1311112

Demon Hunting in the Deep South

LEXI GEORGE

KENSINGTON PUBLISHING CORP.

www.kensingtonbooks.com

BRAVA BOOKS are published by

Kensington Publishing Corp.
119 West 40th Street
New York, NY 10018

All Kensington titles, imprints, and distributed lines are available at special quantity discounts for bulk purchases for sales promotions, premiums, fund-raising, educational, or institutional use.

Special book excerpts or customized printings can also be created to fit specific needs. For details, write or phone the office of the Kensington special sales manager: Kensington Publishing Corp., 119 West 40th Street, New York, NY 10018, attn. Special Sales Department; phone: 1-800-221-2647.

Brava and the B logo are Reg. U.S. Pat. & TM Off.

ISBN-13: 978-0-7582-6311-7
ISBN-10: 0-7582-6311-2

First Kensington Trade Paperback Printing: August 2012

10 9 8 7 6 5 4 3 2 1

Printed in the United States of America

To my husband, David, who stressed over every page of this book with me.
I love you, Captain Underpants.

To Mama, who taught me to love the written word and saved my awful poems because she thought I had talent.

And to Letha, my biggest cheerleader.
I love you, sis.

Chapter One

Blood. There was so much blood, especially on the dead woman sprawled across her desk.

Evie stared in shock at the corpse from the doorway of her office. Death did not become Meredith Starr Peterson. She lay on her back like a broken doll, her blue eyes open and staring, her carefully painted mouth twisted in a frozen scream. The pink sheath dress she wore was hitched around her white thighs. One designer stiletto pump was missing, and her matching pink ruffle-pleat cardigan was ripped and torn. The blade sticking out of her chest didn't do anything for her, either.

Evie's heart jerked in a crazy rhythm. Oh, God, what was happening?

Pulling her stunned gaze from Meredith's body, she looked around. Outside, things at the lumber mill seemed normal. A forklift rumbled past her window on its way to the holding yard, and in the distance she heard the muted whine of the saw and the barker. But inside things were a nightmare. Her once neat office looked like a slaughterhouse. Spatters of blood stained the beige carpet and khaki walls, ran in thin rivulets down her filing cabinets, and dripped off the framed print hanging over the bookcase. There were red streaks of it on the window and splashes on her brand-new ergonomic desk chair. Crimson polka dots decorated the paperwork strewn around the room.

The room smelled of death and something else. Scents, Evie knew. Soap-making was her hobby and her passion. The rich, fruity scent of frankincense overlaid the nauseating odor of something rotten.

She swayed and grabbed the door frame, her stomach rebelling. She needed to get out of here, but she couldn't seem to move. She kept staring at Meredith's poor, tortured body. Whoever killed her had taken his time. The victim was covered in blood from dozens of shallow cuts and stab wounds. The murderer must have chased poor Meredith around Evie's office, whittling at her as she ran. Playing with her and taking his time. Enjoying her pain.

When he tired of the game, he stabbed Meredith in the chest, pinning her to the desk like a bug.

Evie shuddered. Meredith looked so small . . . so pathetic. Hard to believe this shattered thing was her nemesis since the seventh grade—the cool, popular kid who called her Fatso and the Whale.

On Wednesday, Meredith had publicly accused Evie of having an affair with her husband, Trey Peterson, the heir apparent to the Peterson timber fortune. Evie's *boss.*

And now it was Friday and Meredith was dead in her office.

The handle of the knife in Meredith's chest glittered in the early-morning sunshine. It was mesmerizing, hypnotizing. Evie took a step inside the room. No, not a knife, she realized in dawning terror as she got a better look. Meredith had been murdered with a letter opener. *Her* letter opener, the silver one engraved with her initials, a recent gift from Trey. The man she was supposed to be having an affair with.

Oh, this was not good. This was definitely not good.

She drew closer. Funny thing about that letter opener. The handle was clean. Spotless and obscene in its shininess. Not a drop of blood on it.

She wanted to look away, to run screaming from the room, but she couldn't. Some invisible force dragged her reluctant feet to the desk, like iron to a lodestone. Inside her head, she heard a chilling, relentless litany.

Touch it. Touch the knife. The evil whisper filled her mind.

Shaking with the effort to resist the compulsion, she reached for the letter opener, tears of fright and frustration dampening her cheeks.

"Evangeline, *no*."

The deep, compelling voice rang out, shattering the spell. A pair of strong arms wrapped around her and jerked her away from the desk. She caught a brief whiff of an intoxicating scent, a subtle, dizzying combination of cedar with notes of lavender and bergamot. Whoever her secret savior was, he smelled divine.

The spicy scent stirred a whisper of memory deep within her. It fractured and flew apart as she was lifted and sent spinning into nothingness. There was a brief, falling sensation, and then she was sitting on her front porch steps.

Dazed, Evie looked around, trying to focus on her new surroundings. What happened? How'd she get here? Her office at Peterson's Lumber Mill was five miles outside of town. She must be in shock. Yeah, that was it. She drove herself home but didn't remember doing so because of the trauma. There was no other explanation.

She looked around. No car. It was like she'd fallen out of the sky and onto her front porch. Oh, God, this was nuts.

Shivering, she rubbed her arms and encountered a leather strap. She still had her purse on her shoulder. With shaking hands, she reached inside, retrieved her cell phone, and dialed 911.

As she hung up the phone, a Pepto-Bismol-pink van pulled into the driveway and stopped. It was her friend, Addy, in the delivery van from her flower shop.

Addy got out and strode up the sidewalk. Her white-blond hair was pulled back in a sleek ponytail that bounced with every step. She was dressed for work in a clingy silk top and a knee-length skirt that showcased her long, sleekly muscled legs. Some of Evie's panic receded when she saw her best friend. Addy would stand by her, no matter what. Together, they'd figure this thing out. They were as close as sisters despite their obvious differences. Addy was beautiful, funny, and a smartass to her DNA, not shy like Evie.

"I came to see about you." Addy's brown eyes were wide with concern. "You all right, chicka?"

"How did you know something was wrong?" Evie felt a brief flare of hope. "Did the fairies tell you?"

"Nope. Ansgar did."

Something thrummed deep inside Evie, a tiny thrill of recognition. It happened every time she heard Addy or Brand mention Ansgar's name, which was weird since she'd never met the guy.

"Brand's brother?" She shook her head in confusion. Brand Dalvahni was Addy's darkly handsome, intimidating, demon slayer boyfriend. The guy who saved Addy from certain death at the hands of a rogue demon and put her through the Change, as Evie and Addy referred to the infusion of demon slayer essence that transformed Addy from a human being to Something Else. An immortal super chick with lightning reflexes, stealth speed, and a buttload of Dalvahni sex appeal. "How did he know about Meredith?"

Oh, God. Meredith. Evie saw again the crumpled, bleeding figure across her desk.

"Meredith?" Addy's eyes narrowed. Addy *hated* Meredith. "What's she got to do with this?"

"You mean you don't know? He didn't tell you?"

"No, he didn't tell me anything. Just showed up at the shop and started ordering me around in that arrogant way of his. You know what a hemorrhoid he is."

"No, I don't. We've never met, remember?"

Addy looked oddly flustered. "Oh, yeah. I keep forgetting. Trust me when I say he's irritating as all get-out. Anyway, he says you need me, and then he disappears. So, what's going on?"

"Oh, Addy." Evie buried her face in her hands. "Meredith is dead."

"Dead?" Addy gave her a blank stare. "What do you mean 'dead'?"

"Somebody killed her. In *my* office. I found her this morning when I went in to work."

Addy sat down on the steps and put her arm around Evie's shoulders. "Are you sure, babe?"

"I'm sure. I saw it." Raising her head, Evie shivered. "It was awful. There was blood everywhere. And she had my letter opener buried in her chest." She clasped her shaking hands together in her lap. "My office, my letter opener. Remember Meredith's little scene in the flower shop two days ago, the one where she accused me in front of God and everybody of sleeping with Trey? People will think I did it."

"The Death Starr's dead? I can't believe it."

Evie winced. Since middle school, she and Addy had called Meredith the Death Starr because of her ability to zero in on people like a super laser and annihilate them in one fell swoop. But now that she was dead, it didn't seem respectful to call her that.

"Did you touch anything?" Addy asked. "Please tell me you didn't touch anything."

"No," Evie said. "But it was close. Something was in that office with me, Addy. Something evil. It wanted me to grab the letter opener." She shivered. "I heard it talking inside my head. I was reaching for the letter opener when someone said my name."

"Who said your name, the creepy whatzit?"

"No, this was somebody else. He called me Evangeline, not Evie, which is weird. Nobody's called me that since Mama died." Evie rubbed her temples. Her head was beginning to throb. Probably another migraine; she'd had them a lot lately. "The next thing I know, I'm sitting here. Oh, Addy, I don't understand any of this. I feel like I'm losing my mind."

"Relax, Eves, Ansgar must have brought you home. I take back everything I said about him. Okay, maybe not *everything,* but the hemorrhoid part anyway."

"But why would he do that? He doesn't know me. And how did he get me home? I don't remember being in a car."

Addy snorted. "Who said anything about a car? We're talking about the Dalvahni here. Ten to one, Ansgar teleported you here."

"Teleported me?" Evie blinked in surprise. "Oh, my goodness."

"Dalvahni woo woo, chicka. Demon hunters are loaded with it." Her lips curved in a cat-in-the-cream-pot smile. "In more ways than one."

Evie felt a pang of envy. The sexual attraction between Addy and Brand was so smoking hot you'd have to be dead not to notice. You could almost see the pheromones in the air when those two were together, which was most of the time. Brand Dalvahni loved him some Addy Corwin; that was for sure.

"I wouldn't know," Evie said. "Well . . . be sure and thank him for me. It was nice of him to get me out of there." She shivered. "It was horrible, Addy. Just horrible."

"Thank him yourself. Hannah's a small town, you know. I got a feeling you'll be seeing more of him."

Addy got to her feet.

Evie grabbed her arm. "Where are you going? Don't leave me! I need you."

"Relax," Addy said. "You're going with me. We'll go get your car and bring it back here. You can call in sick. No one will ever know you were there."

"I've already called nine-one-one. The police are on their way."

"Oh, man." Addy sank back onto the step. "You are such a rule-follower, Evie Douglass."

"I know." Evie sighed. "But you love me anyway, right?"

"Shit, I reckon," Addy said.

"*Addy.*" Evie looked around. "Your mama hears you cussing and there'll be h-e-l-l to pay."

Addy's mama, Bitsy Corwin, was a force to be reckoned with. Evie loved her to pieces, but the woman scared the bejesus out of her.

"You don't have to spell it, Eves. The Bitser's not here. She can't hear me."

"Huh. That woman has ears like an elephant when it comes to your potty mouth."

"Don't I know it?" Addy was silent. After a moment, she said, "You realize that voice inside your head wasn't human."

A chill ran down Evie's spine. "Yeah, I thought about that."

"And that there's probably a demon involved? Maybe even that a demon killed Meredith?"

"Thought about that, too."

It wouldn't be the first time a demon caused trouble in Hannah. There was something very strange about their little town.

"The demon might come after you next. You'd better stay with me for a while until it's safe."

Evie snorted. "Me underfoot all the time? Won't Brand love that?"

"Brand will have to deal. You're my best friend."

"Thanks," she said, "but I'll stay here. The fairies will warn me."

Addy gave her a curious, almost hopeful look. "I thought you said you couldn't see them anymore?"

A wave of grief washed over Evie. She'd been able to see fairies as long as she could remember, although she'd only recently shared her gift with Addy. Seeing fairies wasn't something you went around talking about, not even to your best friend. Not if you didn't want people to think you were a loon.

She inherited her ability from her mother. It was a special bond they shared, a connection she treasured, especially since her mother's death. And then, inexplicably, one day not long ago, she couldn't see fairies anymore.

She swallowed the ball of sadness in her throat. "I can't see or hear them, but they rattle the wind chimes to let me know they're there. They'll warn me if something bad comes, and they'll protect me."

Addy grunted, but she sounded unconvinced. "Fairies and demons and demon slayers, oh my! Who would've thunk boring, little Hannah, Alabama, would turn out to be the supernatural Vegas truck stop of the universe."

"Hannah's never been boring, Addy. You just couldn't see it."

"Huh. Well, I see it now." Addy straightened as two cars pulled up to the curb. "Here come Chief Davis and the sheriff. What are you going to tell them?"

"The truth. What else?"

Addy groaned. "I was afraid you were going to say that."

Chapter Two

Ansgar stood beneath a sprawling oak near Evangeline's front porch, listening as she conversed with her friend Addy. Evie could not see him. As a Dalvahni demon hunter, he could make himself invisible. But he could see her.

And hear her.

By the gods, he'd missed her. He stood in the green shadows and drank in the sultry sound of her voice. Each soft, drawling utterance from her lips played upon his senses until he thought he would go mad with need.

He'd met her but a few months past, when he'd come to Earth with his brother Brand in pursuit of a group of rogue demons. It had seemed an ordinary mission, like countless others through the centuries. He and Brand would execute their task with brutal efficiency, round up the demons, and remove all trace of their presence here. Afterward, they would return to the Hall of Warriors to await their next assignment.

Such was the way of the Dalvahni warrior.

Things had quickly spiraled out of control when Brand fell under Addy Corwin's spell. 'Twas a thing unheard of in the history of the Dalvahni, Brand's unseemly affection for the Corwin woman.

Ansgar had been baffled by his brother's odd behavior. True, he had been charmed by Addy's friend, Evangeline Douglass. But he was no weakling like his brother, who'd succumbed to this peculiar affliction called "love." Bah.

He and Brand had completed their mission, capturing the

djegrali after a battle in the town square. During the fray, Evangeline had been taken by a demon. Ansgar could see her still, white-faced with terror, beseeching him to slay her, less terrified of death than of demonic possession. And with good reason. A human possessed had no will, no choice. They were the demon's plaything, under the creature's control until their body was used up and the demon discarded them for fresher meat.

Hands shaking, Ansgar had nocked an arrow in his bow and shot Evangeline through the heart. The demon had abandoned her dying body as such creatures were wont to do—a demon trapped in death with a human dies also.

Ansgar had dispatched the demon with another arrow and, taking Evangeline in his arms, he'd saved her from death, infusing her with his essence. She'd awakened, fully healed and no longer human.

And with no memory of him.

'Twas for the best, he'd told himself. He left, with no intention of returning.

To his astonishment, the months away from her—what should have been a mere heartbeat of time in the life span of the ageless Dalvahni—had been an endless agony. He'd fought his feelings for her, losing himself in the hunt and the emptying embrace of a thrall, sexual creatures designed to sate a Dalvahni warrior's physical needs and empty them of battle rage and lust. Both species found the relationship to their advantage. The Dalvahni, drained of unnecessary feelings, were unhampered in battle, and the thralls were strengthened and sustained by Dalvahni emotion.

But love? The Dalvahni did not *love*.

The Dalvahni were immortal warriors created for a singular purpose. To hunt the djegrali, demons that had slipped the confines of their own dimension, and return them to their proper place or kill them if need be. Left unchecked, the djegrali invariably wreaked havoc upon mortals.

But his struggle had been in vain. Nothing could erase his memories of Evangeline. She was always there in the back of his mind, beckoning; light in an eternity of darkness, warmth and laughter and hope after eons of bleakness and grim, unrelenting duty. She was fever and longing and need. The scent, feel, and taste of her a craving that could not be extinguished by distance, time, or the emotion-sucking clasp of a succubus sex slave.

He abhorred his hunger for her, but at long last he accepted it. He was a fool to think he could forget. Acknowledging his defeat, he'd come back, knowing she would not remember him or their brief, sweet time together. He'd told himself it was enough to be near her, to stand over her as she slept, listening to the steady sound of her breathing, each soft exhalation of air from her lungs music to his lonely soul. He appointed himself her unseen guardian as she went about her daily tasks, following at her heels like a lovesick boy.

Gods, he was pathetic. But he could not resist her. He had not the strength or the will to try.

But neither could he be with her. She was his exquisite torture, his bane, and his every desire. But she was beyond his reach. He had put her there.

She reached up and nervously tugged at a lock of her long hair, an unconscious gesture he knew well. He remembered everything about her, the arch of her slender feet, the sweet curve of her rounded bottom, the satiny feel of her skin beneath his fingers and lips.

She, on the other hand, remembered nothing of him, and it was better so. He had hurt her, brought her nigh unto death with an arrow fired from his own bow, and for that he could not forgive himself. Nor was that the least of his transgressions. He had changed her. She was Dalvahni now, although she did not know it. And because of him, because of the change he had wrought in her, Evangeline could no longer see her beloved fairies. This, too, he'd taken from her. She would hate him for it if she knew, and that he could not bear.

No, it was better this way, although keeping his distance from her was the hardest thing he had ever done. He was fated, it seemed, to spend forever longing for a woman he could not have. There was a certain irony in that.

A dark blue vehicle with the word SHERIFF inscribed in silver letters on the door eased to a stop in front of Evie's house. Close behind it was a gray automobile with HANNAH POLICE written on the side. A distinguished-looking man with silver hair at his temples got out of the gray car. Carl E. Davis, the Chief of Police in Hannah. Ansgar remembered him from his previous visit here. Davis was courting Addy Corwin's widowed mother, Bitsy. Ansgar felt sorry for the man. All of the females in that family were unmanageable, to put it mildly. And his brother, Brand, had *willingly* bound himself to one of them. Madness. Ansgar shook his head at the thought. Addy Corwin was the most annoying creature he'd ever met.

But that was Brand's affair and not his, thank the gods.

A tall, broad-shouldered man Ansgar did not recognize climbed out of the other car. The metal badge on the front of his light brown shirt glittered in the sunshine. He was much younger than Chief Davis and moved with a predatory grace that marked him as a hunter. Ansgar frowned. This man might be clad in modern raiment, but he was a warrior nonetheless . . . and dangerous. There was something different about him, although Ansgar could not say what. His protective instincts aroused, Ansgar opened his senses. He did not detect the taint of the djegrali on the human. Still, something about the stranger made him wary, and he moved closer to the porch and Evie.

To Ansgar's surprise, the man in the brown shirt turned and scanned the area as if sensing his presence. His eyes were hidden behind dark glasses, but the expression on his lean face was watchful. His gaze lingered on the spot where Ansgar stood for a moment and then moved on.

Ansgar's warrior instincts shrieked in warning. The Dalvahni had many gifts at their disposal, including invisibility, unsurpassed tracking skills, and stealth. And, yet, this man seemed to detect something amiss. A formidable opponent, indeed, Ansgar thought grimly, and one to be watched.

Evie got to her feet as the two men approached her. Her hazel eyes were wide, her cheeks and lips pale. She was frightened. Something twisted inside Ansgar. The need to comfort her was a raw, physical ache. It was all he could do not to rush to her side.

She stood on the steps, her hands clasped tightly in front of her. Her lush body was disguised by a shapeless, cotton dress; her glorious red hair was partially hidden beneath a matching kerchief. She was all woman. Full, high breasts, a waist so tiny a man could span it with his hands, and curving, generous hips. But she could not see her own beauty.

To him, she was luscious, the essence of feminine beauty, but the cruel taunts of others and the repressive demands of her now dead father had convinced her otherwise. In their once-before, the precious days they'd spent together before he left, he'd coaxed her out of her shell. She had emerged a fragile, breathtaking creature, her burgeoning confidence as thin and brittle as ice in a spring thaw. But that brief rebirth was forgotten, wiped out by a silver arrow from his quiver and her brush with the djegrali and death.

"Chief Davis." Ansgar heard a touch of relief in Evie's voice at the sight of a familiar face. "I didn't expect to see you." Next, she met the tall stranger at the foot of the steps and held out her hand. "I'm Evie Douglass. I found Meredith this morning when I went in to work and called nine-one-one. Are you a deputy?"

"This is Sheriff Whitsun, Evie," Chief Davis said.

Evie blushed. "Oh, I'm sorry. I guess I expected someone older."

"And uglier." The chief nudged the younger man with his elbow. "Dev gets that a lot. Ain't that right, pretty boy?"

Ansgar watched the human called Whitsun. In his experience, human males often interacted with one another through mockery, whether good natured or derogatory. Whitsun, however, did not react to the chief's jibe. His expression remained as impassive as any Dalvahni warrior. Most unusual and alarming.

The sheriff turned his attention to Addy. "And you are?"

Addy rose to her feet. "Addy Corwin."

A rectangular box on the sheriff's belt squawked. " 'Scuse me," he said. He pushed a button and spoke into the device. "Go ahead."

A crackling voice emerged from the contraption. "We got a homicide at Peterson's Lumber Mill, Dev. Adult white female. Multiple stab wounds."

"Lock it down and don't touch anything. I'm on my way." The sheriff clipped the device back onto his belt and turned to Evie. "I have to go to the scene. Three of my deputies are out with the stomach flu and we're short staffed. Would you mind coming to my office to make your statement?"

"No, of course not," Evie said.

"Thank you. That would be a big help. I'll have one of my men drive you to the office."

Addy bristled. "Why can't she make her statement at the police station? She knows the chief and will feel more comfortable talking to him."

"The mill's outside of town, Addy," the chief said. "This is county business."

Addy crossed her arms and looked stubborn. "Then I'm going with her."

"You're welcome to wait for Miss Douglass in the reception area while she makes her statement," the sheriff said. "I'll warn you, though. Sometimes these things take a while."

"The wheels of justice grind slowly, is that it?" Addy said in a belligerent tone.

Evie laid her hand on Addy's arm. "Addy, please, the sheriff's just trying to do his job." She gave Whitsun a wan smile that pierced Ansgar's heart. "We've been friends since elementary school, and she's a little overprotective."

"That's quite all right, ma'am. I understand." The sheriff looked at the chief. "Carl, would you mind waiting here with Miss Douglass until my deputy gets here?"

"Be glad to," the chief said. "Anything we can do to help, you let me know."

"I'll do that."

With a curt nod, Sheriff Whitsun left.

The chief took Evie by the elbow and guided her up the steps. "You look a little puny, Evie. Why don't we sit on the porch and maybe Addy can get us a little something to drink?"

"I am feeling a little dizzy." Evie gave Addy a pleading look. "There's sweet tea in the fridge, Addy. Would you mind?"

"Course not, although I don't think I should leave you alone with the Po-Po." Addy paused at the front door and scowled at the chief. "Don't you try any of that sneaky cop stuff while I'm gone, you hear? Evie, you holler if he does and I'll come running."

"Oh, for the love of—" The chief gave Addy an exasperated look. "Do you think I'd do that to Evie? I've known you two girls all your lives. For Christ's sake, Addy, I date your *mother*."

"Huh," Addy said with a sniff. "You're the Man now, Chief, and everybody knows you can't trust the Man." She started inside and took a step back. "And you'd better not let Bitsy hear you calling Our Lord and Savior out his name, or your ass will be grass and Mama will mow it."

Addy was standing at the counter in the kitchen when Ansgar materialized at her elbow.

"There is something peculiar about the human called Whitsun," he said without preamble. "I do not trust him."

Addy shrieked and almost dropped the pitcher she was holding. "Blondy, don't sneak up on me like that. Are you *trying* to give me a heart attack?"

Irritation spiked along his nerves. "As I have told you many times, my name is Ansgar, not Blondy. As for your question, I assume it was rhetorical. You are Dalvahni now. We do not suffer heart attacks or other human maladies."

Addy rolled her eyes. "Same old Blondy. About as much fun as a kidney stone. God, I'm *soooo* glad you're back. *Not*."

"My cup of joy overfloweth at seeing you as well. Tell me about this Whitsun. Who is he?"

Addy shrugged and set the pitcher on the counter. "I don't know much about him, except he's not from Hannah. Grew up somewhere out in the county. But he seems like an all right guy to me."

"He is not 'all right,' " Ansgar said. "I do not like him."

Addy gave him a shrewd glance. "You don't like anything with a pecker that gets around Evie. Why don't you stop moping around and introduce yourself? Or should I say *reintroduce*? We both know she's the reason you're here."

"A Dalvahni warrior does not mope."

"Huh. Could have fooled me. You've been following Evie around like a dog that's lost its bone."

Irksome woman. Her description of him mirrored his own gloomy thoughts, which made her remark sting all the more.

"I came back to Hannah because I was assigned to this realm," he said through his teeth. "The presence and number of djegrali in this place are most peculiar. Conall thought reinforcements necessary."

"Oh, yeah?" Addy raised her brows. "And I suppose you just *happened* to be out at Peterson's this morning when Evie got into trouble?"

"That is correct."

"Horse hockey." Addy placed the drink glasses on a wooden tray. "You've been shadowing Evie for weeks. Not eating. Not sleeping. Standing by her bed at night like a creeper."

"Who told you this?"

Addy gave him a sweet smile. "The fairies told Mr. Fluffy Fauntleroy, who told Dooley, who told *me*."

Mr. Fluffy Fauntleroy was the ridiculous moniker Addy gave the fairy cat that had inexplicably attached itself to her. Dooley was her dog, her big, yellow *talking* dog. Ansgar made a mental note to have a word with both creatures.

"Don't tell Evie about the fairies," Addy said with a frown. "It would make her feel bad."

"I would never do anything to hurt Evie."

"Hate to break it to you, Blondy, but you already have. First you shot her in the chest. With. An. Arrow. Gotta tell you, I was majorly pissed about that one. But I calmed down a little once I realized you had to do it to save her from the demon. And you did heal her, I'll give you that much. But then you left. *Pfft*. Just when I was starting to think you liked her."

Liked her? *Liked her?* Was the woman mad? He *adored* Evangeline. Not that he would admit it to Addy. His feelings for Evangeline were no one else's affair.

"I did not hurt her by leaving. She does not remember me."

"Oh, yeah? Then how come she's been walking around like something dead since you skedaddled out of here?"

Skedaddle. It took Ansgar a moment to translate the strange term. *Skedaddle: to run away, as if in fright.*

He stiffened in affront. "She is melancholy because she lost the sight. It is a great loss, but she will adjust, in time."

"Sure, she misses not being able to see the little guys." To Ansgar's surprise, angry tears filled Addy's eyes. "But that's not why she's so sad. You broke her heart, you big jerk. I know, because I felt the same way when Brand left me. Only, it's worse for Evie 'cause she doesn't *know* her heart is broken. There's a big empty space where you used to be, but she has no idea why she feels so hollow inside. She's bewildered and lost and hurt, and she doesn't know *why*. You're the only one who can help her, but you won't. Oh, no, not you. You're too busy being all noble, Mr. Big Bad Demon Hunter. For two cents I'd kick your ass all the way from here to Sunday."

Addy picked up the tray and stomped out of the kitchen.

Chapter Three

"Okay, Miss Douglass. One more time," the sheriff said. "After you found the victim, how'd you get home from the mill?"

"I told you. I don't remember. I found Meredith's body, and the next thing I know, I'm sitting on my front porch steps."

"Alone?"

"Yes."

The sheriff regarded her from the other side of the desk. He'd removed his sunglasses, and his gray eyes were unreadable. He was handsome, in a dark, lean, and dangerous way.

Men made Evie nervous. Handsome men made her practically catatonic. But Sheriff Whitsun was not just another pretty face. There was something about him, something watchful and tense. A wolf, Evie decided. If Sheriff Whitsun were an animal, he'd be a wolf. She had the uneasy feeling he could tell where she'd fudged on the details. Like how she got home.

Good grief, she was letting her imagination run away with her. It was because she was so tired.

Evie rubbed her forehead. Her head hurt, probably from lack of rest. It seemed like months since she'd had a decent night's sleep. And when she did sleep, she dreamed. Disturbing, sensual dreams of a man's hot mouth and hands moving over her body, arousing her, until she woke up panting with desire, the sheets twisted around her damp limbs.

Dreams that made her blush to remember them and that left her feeling antsy and unsatisfied.

Unsatisfied my hind foot, a sly inner voice said. *They make you plain old horny.*

She shifted in the straight-back chair, embarrassed by the direction of her thoughts. Last night, she had trouble falling asleep. Lying in bed, she'd stared into the darkness, feeling sad and miserable and achingly lonely, with no idea *why.* It was hours later when she dozed off.

This morning, her alarm didn't go off and she had overslept. Consequently, she'd rushed out of the house without eating breakfast. Now that she thought about it, she'd forgotten to eat supper last night, too.

She glanced at her watch. Almost two o'clock. She hoped Addy wasn't still waiting for her. Addy wasn't what you'd call long suffering, especially when she was hungry. And Addy was a three-meal-a-day kind of gal. She'd be gnawing the woodwork by now.

Evie sighed. Her patience was running thin as well. She'd been at the courthouse in Paulsberg since 8:30 this morning, sitting for hours in a stuffy back room while the sheriff and his men processed the murder scene. Paulsberg was the county seat, thirty miles from Hannah.

It had been past noon when the sheriff had arrived and escorted her to his office. She looked around. It wasn't much of an improvement from the glorified broom closet she'd been waiting in. Whitsun's office was small and cramped with a ground-level window that framed a scraggly boxwood on the other side. A battered desk, a dented filing cabinet, and a couple of chairs completed the furnishings. The walls were a dull gray and unadorned except for a University of Alabama football schedule. The surface of his desk was neat and uncluttered. They'd been at it more than an hour and were hashing over the details of her statement. For the third time. Sheriff Whitsun was nothing if not thorough.

He fiddled with a button on his handheld digital recorder. "You found Mrs. Peterson's body in your office, and the next thing you remember is being back at your house. But you left your car at the mill. Did you walk home?"

"Yes . . . maybe." She shook her head. If she told him the truth, he'd think she was crazy. *Um, well you see, Sheriff, I was rescued by an invisible man.* Correction, an invisible demon hunter. Oh, brother. They'd lock her up and throw away the key, if they didn't put her in jail first for murder. She didn't have to be a cop to know things looked bad. The evidence against her was circumstantial, but what if that was enough? Panic iced her veins. Oh, God, she would not do well in prison. "I don't know."

"Maybe someone gave you a ride to your house. Someone like . . . Trey Peterson, for example?"

"I told you. Trey . . . uh . . . I mean, Mr. Peterson, is out of town on business. I haven't seen him since day before yesterday."

"Trey? So you and Mr. Peterson are on a first-name basis."

Evie clasped her hands together in her lap. "It's a s-small town. We went to high school together. But I try to remember to call him Mr. Peterson at the office. It's more professional."

He looked down at his notes. "How long have you been the office manager at Peterson's Mill?"

"I started working there last October, so a year this month."

"And what is your relationship with Mr. Peterson outside the office?"

Evie felt a small surge of irritation. "Like I told you before, Trey and I don't have a relationship outside the office, unless you count singing together in the choir at the Episcopal church."

Whoa, that was borderline sassy, totally unlike her usually meek, mild self. She must be channeling Addy.

"But Meredith Peterson thought you were sleeping with her husband. You say she accused you of it."

"At the flower shop," Evie said. "In front of a bunch of people. But nobody believed it."

The sheriff sat back in his chair. "Why not? You're a beautiful woman, Miss Douglass. But I'm sure you know that."

Beautiful? Evie flushed. Was he making fun of her? Before she could decide, an animal growled in warning.

Startled, she looked around. "Good gracious, what was that?"

"Probably a dog outside in the bushes."

Evie eyed the pitiful bush through the window, unconvinced. "It didn't sound like it was coming from outside. It sounded like it was in the room with us."

"Unless you have an invisible dog, it's just you and me, Miss Douglass. So, let me get this straight. You're not having an affair with Trey Peterson?"

"No. I'm not having an affair with Trey Peterson or anybody else."

"Then why are you lying about how you got home?"

Evie stared at him. "I beg your pardon?"

"I can smell a lie, Miss Douglass. It's a talent of mine. You've told me the truth about everything except how you got home. For some reason, you're lying about that. Who are you protecting? Is it Trey Peterson?"

He was a wolf, all right; a sharp-eyed wolf with a nose for prevarication.

"Got yourself a built-in lie detector, huh?" she said. "That must come in handy in your line of work."

"It helps. Now why don't you answer my question so we can both get something to eat? Who are you trying to protect?"

Evie sighed. "Me. If I tell you the truth, you'll think I'm crazy."

"Try me. How'd you get home?"

Evie closed her eyes, dreading his reaction. "I was teleported by a demon hunter."

She opened her eyes to find the sheriff watching her. She couldn't tell what he was thinking, but she could swear his nose twitched.

"I see," he said after a moment of silence. "And where is this demon hunter now?"

"I don't know."

"What does he look like?"

"I don't know that, either. He was invisible."

"Does this demon hunter have a name?"

Evie hesitated, reluctant for some reason to implicate Ansgar in this mess. "I'd rather not say."

Sheriff Whitsun leaned across the desk. "Miss Douglass, you could be facing a murder charge."

"Don't you think I know that?" Evie gave a shaky laugh. "There's a dead woman in my office with my letter opener sticking out of her chest."

"I'll have to wait for the forensics report, of course, but I'm pretty damn sure your letter opener wasn't the murder weapon."

A wave of relief washed over Evie. "What?"

"Meredith Peterson was cut to pieces. There's no way a letter opener inflicted those injuries. It's too dull and flimsy. Judging from the size of the stab wound to the chest, the killer used a much bigger blade. Some kind of hunting knife, I think. Whoever killed her planted your letter opener in her chest to make it look like you did it. Someone's trying to frame you, Miss Douglass. I'm trying to help you, but you've got to cooperate. And telling me wild stories about invisible demon hunters isn't helping."

Evie's shoulders sagged. She was suddenly very tired. "You say you can smell a lie, so you tell me, Sheriff. Am I telling the truth?"

He regarded her thoughtfully. "Yes, or at least you think you are." He tapped the end of his pen on the desktop. "Very well, you can go. But don't take any trips."

Evie got to her feet. "I'm not going anywhere. I can't afford to pay attention, much less leave town."

She left his office and walked down the narrow, dingy hall that led to the public area of the Sheriff's Department. Pushing open the swinging door, she stepped into the waiting room. A low wall separated the receptionist's desk from the seating area. The receptionist was not at her desk.

"Evie," Addy cried, jumping to her feet. "I've been so worried!"

A dark-haired giant of a man rose out of the chair beside her. It was Brand Dalvahni, Addy's drop-dead good-looking boyfriend. Her immortal *demon hunter* boyfriend.

Evie barely noticed him. She was too busy gawking at the blond Adonis standing beside him. She realized she was staring and dragged her gaze away. It was no use. Her eyeballs kept rolling back to the guy of their own accord. Heavens to Betsy, he was so gorgeous it hurt to look at him. Hurt so *good.* She closed her eyes. Yep, she could still see him. She was pretty sure his image was burned onto her retinas.

Like Brand, he was tall and muscular, and supernaturally handsome. But, whereas Brand was handsome in a dark and deadly kind of way, the stranger was a blond Viking warrior with silver eyes, stacks of muscles, and sex appeal that was clean off the charts. Both men wore jeans and a T-shirt, the cotton tees molding to their broad chests and showing off their muscular arms. But their casual attire did not disguise the aura of danger that surrounded them.

Evie took another peek at the blond guy through her lashes. Cheese and crackers, the guy had to be a demon hunter. No human was that beautiful or exuded so much power, sensuality, and jaw-dropping charisma.

Yikes, he was looking at her. She ducked her chin and fastened her gaze on her feet. It was safer that way. Looking at him made her feel breathless and tingly and *alive,* as if she teetered on the edge of something wonderful.

Or something terrifying, a bottomless well of despair and soul-rending loss from which there was no release.

Jeez, where did that come from? She wasn't usually such a drama queen. As if a guy like that would have anything to do with her.

"You were back there for hours," Addy said, frowning. "Are you okay? Do you need a lawyer?"

"I'm fine, Adds." Evie stared at her worn sandals, feeling miserable and self-conscious. "You didn't have to wait."

"Of course I waited. You're my friend. I thought I was going to have to bust you out of here."

"Adara, I think you should introduce Evie to my brother, Ansgar," Brand said.

Bong! There it was again, that darn bell. Her head started to ache. It happened every time someone said the name Ansgar.

Wait. Ansgar? Evie's cheeks burned. *He* was the unseen,

yummy-smelling fellow who snatched her out of harm's way? Oh, no. She should thank him, but how could she? She couldn't talk to *him*. He was perfect.

"Oh, of course." Addy sounded flustered. "Evie Douglass, this is Ansgar Dalvahni, Brand's . . . uh . . . brother."

"This is a pleasure, Miss Douglass," Ansgar said. "A very great pleasure indeed. Addy has told me much about you."

Something tight and painful uncoiled inside her at the sound of his voice. Like she'd been tensed and waiting for it forever. Her head jerked up and their gazes collided. She felt the impact like a physical blow.

His big, strong body exuded a loose-limbed grace and animal fitness. His stance was relaxed, his expression impassive. He seemed calm, immovable, and dispassionate.

But his eyes . . .

His eyes when he looked at her were hot and hungry.

The room went still and airless. She couldn't breathe, couldn't look away from him. No one had ever looked at her that way. She'd never dreamed that anyone could.

Chapter Four

Evangeline's lips parted in a soft gasp of surprise. The sound was too slight to be noticed by the others, but they were not as attuned to her as Ansgar. He could hear her heartbeat and the rush of the blood through her veins. The flowery smell of her skin and hair was intoxicating, the sound of her voice a lover's caress. Not wanting to frighten her, he schooled his features in the expressionless mask of the Dalvahni warrior. It should have been easy, given his years of training. A warrior did not lose control. But seeing her like this, face to face instead of hidden in the shadows after months of wanting her . . .

A wave of desire engulfed him that left him shaking with need.

Some small measure of his feelings must have shown, because Evie's face went white with shock. Her eyelids fluttered and her knees buckled. With a muffled curse, Ansgar sprang across the room, catching her as she fell.

"What's the matter with her?" Addy cried, rushing over. "What did you do, Blondy?"

Ansgar did not answer her. He could not. Holding Evangeline in his arms again felt too damn good. By the sword, he'd been too long without her warmth and sweetness. She was like a drug, an addiction to him. How could he hope to resist her? But he had to try. He was not good for her.

And she was not good for him, he reminded himself sternly.

It was a familiar litany, one he'd recited countless times as he struggled to stay away.

With her, he became someone else. She shifted his vision of

reality, his vision of himself. For eons, he had known the universe and his place in it, his purpose and his duty.

Until Evangeline. She'd changed everything. Changed *him*.

That is why he left.

That is why he returned.

He could not stay away. Yet neither would he yield. Regret gnawed at him and guilt, another damnable and unaccustomed emotion. Over and over again, he saw his arrow pierce her body. Heard her anguished cry and saw her crumple to the ground, her life's blood pouring from the wound to her chest. The wound he had inflicted.

The image haunted him. He did not know how to make amends, how to make things right. He was terrified of hurting her again.

He lifted her against his chest. She was in danger. She needed him. For now he could hold her. This much, he would allow himself.

He carried her to a leather couch on one wall and sat down with her in his lap. Brand and Addy followed.

"I do not think he did anything to her, Adara," Brand said, looking down at them. "It would appear she has fainted."

Addy snorted. "Fainted? No way. Evie never faints." She glared at Ansgar. "You did some kind of Dalvahni mind thingy on her, didn't you, butthead?"

"Adara," Brand said. "It is unseemly to refer to a Dalvahni warrior as a 'butthead.' "

"Like I care. What did you do to her, Blondy?"

Ansgar smoothed Evie's hair out of her face. Her lips were pale and bloodless, and the pulse in her throat beat like the wings of a startled bird. "I looked at her."

Addy whirled on Brand. "You *see*? He looked at her."

Brand tugged her into his arms. "Adara, you are not making sense. You have spent the morning importuning Ansgar to give Evie his protection. He has agreed to your request. Let him be."

"You're right, babe. I know you're right." Addy's voice was muffled against Brand's chest. "It's just that she hasn't been herself these past few months. And now with Meredith's murder . . ." Her voice trailed off. "I'm worried about her."

Ansgar barely heard them. His entire being was focused on the enchanting bundle of femininity in his arms. He bent his head closer to hers. "Evangeline." He gave her a little shake, but she did not open her eyes. *"Evangeline."*

Panic sliced through him. "What ails her? Why does she not awaken?"

"Maybe she's under a spell." Addy stepped out of the circle of Brand's arms. There was a calculating gleam in her brown eyes that sent a stab of alarm through Ansgar. Such a look from Addy did not bode well. "Maybe you should kiss her."

He scowled. "To what purpose?"

"It works in the fairy tales. You whammied her. Stands to reason you're the only one who can un-whammy her."

Ansgar clenched his jaw. "This is not a . . . a fairy tale, and I did not *whammy* her. I looked at her. That is all."

Addy gave him a measuring look. "What's the matter, you chicken?"

Chicken: a domestic fowl bred for flesh and eggs. Also a term connoting cowardice.

Of a certainty, Addy did not refer to poultry. "Woman, I am Dalvahni. You do not question a warrior's mettle."

"Yeah? So kiss her already. Go on. I dare you."

She was questioning his valor. Again. The woman had no semblance of decorum.

He looked to Brand for support. "Is she serious?"

"It is sometimes difficult to tell, but 'twould seem so." Brand shrugged. "At any rate, where is the harm? Unless you think it unwise."

Unwise? Holding Evangeline nearly drove him mad. Kiss her, and he would be lost.

He touched Evangeline's cheek with the tip of one finger. Her skin was tender and soft, a white rose without the faintest blush. She lay in his arms limp and wan, a sleeping princess waiting for a prince.

He was no prince. He was a warrior, hardened by countless years of blood and battle, his hands and soul stained by death. Still, the gauntlet had been thrown, and it was not his nature to back down from a challenge.

Lowering his head, he brushed his lips across hers. They were cool beneath his, bliss after the endless days and nights of desperate longing.

"Evangeline," he murmured against the lush fullness of her mouth. "Open your eyes, sweetling."

Lifting his head, he looked down at her. To his relief, delicate color suffused her cheeks and lips, but she did not stir.

"You call that a kiss?" Addy scoffed. "Come on, Blondy. Lay one on her. I thought all you immortal super dudes had game. Don't you *like* girls?"

Aggravating creature. How Brand refrained from strangling her was a mystery.

Cradling Evangeline's head in his hands, Ansgar bent once more to the task, his mouth moving over hers. He held nothing back, pouring the months of desolation, of aching for her, of unbearable desire and loneliness, into the kiss.

Evangeline stirred. With a soft sound of surprise, she opened her eyes. The scarf that covered her fiery locks was askew. She looked dazed, confused, and utterly adorable. Ansgar's arms tightened around her. His mind told him to let her go, but his body would not obey.

"Hello," he said softly.

She gazed up at him in wide-eyed befuddlement. The color returned to her cheeks in a rush, and Ansgar winced as Evie flailed her arms and hit him in the eye.

"Easy," he said. "You are in no danger."

She scrambled awkwardly out of his lap and backed away, skittish as a colt. Round eyed, she looked from him to Addy. "What happened?"

"You fainted," Addy said. "When's the last time you had something to eat?"

Evie raised a shaking hand to her forehead. "I don't remember. I think I ate something yesterday. I haven't been hungry lately, and sometimes I forget to eat."

"Uh huh. I've noticed. In fact, you haven't had much appetite since . . . let me see . . ." Tapping her finger against her chin, Addy shot Ansgar an accusing look. "Oh, right. Since this *summer.*"

Ansgar frowned. Addy's implication was clear. Evangeline had not been eating properly since his departure. Almost as if she were in mourning. Preposterous. How could Evie mourn someone she did not remember?

Still, it was another sin laid at his door, another way he had hurt Evie. This, at least, he could remedy.

"This is unacceptable," he said. "Miss Douglass, if you would permit, it would be my honor to partake of sustenance with you."

Evie gaped at him. "Huh?"

"He wants to take you to get something to eat," Addy said.

Evie flushed and then went pale. "Oh, no, I couldn't. It's too much trouble."

"I assure you, it would be no trouble at all," he said. "Of a sudden, I am hungry also."

And not just for food, he thought wryly. His body burned for her, and his fingers itched to touch her again. So much for holding back, for staying away. He had not the strength, and he should have known it.

Evie's hands flew to her hair. "I can't. I'm a mess."

"You look lovely," Ansgar assured her. And she did, in spite of the hideous bag covering her delectable body and the scarf on her hair. Mere clothes could not disguise her beauty. "We can ride back to Hannah together with Brand and Addy. I understand there is a pub of good repute there where we can break our fast."

Addy put her arm around Evie's shoulder. "He means the Sweet Shop, chicka. If they're still serving by the time we get there. It's past two o'clock now, and they're closed from three until five."

Evie hung back. "But . . . y'all don't want to be seen in public with me. I'm a murder suspect. People will talk."

"So what if they do?" Addy's dark eyes sparkled with indignation. "People are always gonna talk about something, especially in a small town. But you can't let that stop you. You look them right in the eye and dare them to say something to your face."

"As much as it pains me to admit it, she is right, Miss Douglass," Ansgar said. "You cannot let the wagging tongues of others chart your course."

"And if they say anything about my BFF where *I* can hear them, I'll hoo doo 'em." Addy made a twirling motion with one hand. "See how they like that."

"Adara, you are Dalvahni now," Brand said. "You cannot use your powers to torment the weak. It is not our way."

"Wanna bet?"

Evie made a sound of distress. "Meredith! Oh, Addy, you gave her butt boils last summer 'cause she was ugly to me."

"You remember that, Eves?"

"Of course I remember. Why wouldn't I?"

Addy shrugged. "Nothing. Your memory has been a little patchy lately, that's all. Let's eat. I'm starved."

Evie looked around. "Darn it. I don't have my purse. I must have left it in the sheriff's office."

Addy nodded. "We'll get the van and meet you and Ansgar out front."

"But—" Evie began, sounding rattled. But Addy and Brand had already gone.

Evie slid him a nervous glance. "It's all right. You don't have to wait for me."

The thought of being alone with him, even for a moment, frightened her. The knowledge was like a punch in the gut.

"But I insist." He added a pulse of power to the words.

A human female would have melted in a puddle of feminine compliance under the strength of his spell, but Evie's eyes merely widened. She was Dalvahni now and able to resist him, Ansgar reflected with chagrin.

"O-okay," she said, looking slightly dazed. Perhaps not quite so immune after all. "I won't be but a minute."

She disappeared through the swinging door and returned a moment later with her bag.

"Here it is." Her cheeks were bright pink. "Sorry to make you wait, Mr. Dalvahni. I'd forget my head if it wasn't screwed on."

"Please. Call me Ansgar, Miss Douglass."

He was rewarded with a shy smile. "Only if you call me Evie."

He stepped closer, breathing deeply of her sweet scent. She smelled of honeysuckle and goat's milk. "Evie is the name of a frightened, lonely girl. Evangeline is a beautiful, strong woman. You are Evangeline."

Her startled gaze flew to his. "Oh, that's right! You called me that this morning at the mill when . . ." The color rose to her cheeks and she added breathlessly, "When you rescued me. Thank you."

"No thanks are necessary. I was doing my duty."

"But how did you know? I mean, what brought you to the mill?"

Because I need to be near you, pathetic thing that I am. To breathe the air you breathe. To bask in the scent of your skin and the sound of your voice. To know that you are safe.

"I was following the djegrali."

Not entirely a lie. He had sensed something evil stirring.

"A demon?" She wrinkled her brow. "Oh, I see. You were hunting. Addy's told me all about the Dalvahni. That's what you do, isn't it? Hunt demons, I mean."

"Yes."

"Lucky for me you were there this morning. Well, thanks again for helping me."

"You are most welcome, Evangeline."

She lowered her eyes. "H-how do you know my name?"

"Adara told me."

Another falsehood. He knew her name the first time he saw her. It was engraved upon his heart.

"Of course. I know it's crazy, but I feel like we've had this conversation before." She darted him a quick, shy glance. "But we've never met, right?"

The truth would not do, but neither could he stomach another lie.

"Had we met before, I assure you I would not forget you." He gave her a slow smile infused with his considerable Dalvahni charm. "I, however, appear to be less memorable."

She blinked up at him in delightful confusion. "How silly of me! Of course we've never met. I would remember, wouldn't I?"

"It pleases me to think so." He offered her his arm. "Shall we?"

She blushed and took his arm. The universe seemed to shift, and something clicked into place. After the long months of darkness, he was back at her side. It felt right.

As they started for the door, a short, plump woman burst into the Sheriff's Department and tottered up to the front desk on a pair of high-heeled boots. She wore her hair shaved close in the front and long in the back. The bristles at the top of her scalp were bright pink, fading into stringy, yellow locks that fell below her shoulders. A tight top displayed her fleshy arms and overflowing cleavage, and her stocky legs were encased sausage-like in shiny, form-fitting black breeches that ended below the knee. This vision of oddness carried a writhing furry lump under one arm. The lump was conical at one end. An alarming noise emanated from the depths of the cone, like the slathering growl of a rabid wolf.

More like a pack of rabid wolves, Ansgar decided, his warrior instincts roused.

Or a demon.

The creature swung its head in his direction, giving Ansgar a glimpse of glowing, yellow eyes. A demon, right enough, though smallish in size. But the djegrali were sly and took many forms.

He barked out a command, and his bow appeared in his hand. Readying an arrow, he stepped in front of Evie.

"Hold, demon spawn," he said in a thunderous voice. "Release the human or die."

The woman in the boots screeched and clutched the demon to her bosom. "Mothertrucker, who are you?"

The door to the ladies' room opened with the sound of rushing water, and a steely-eyed matron with a towering poof of gray hair marched out.

"What in tarnation's going on?" she demanded. "Can't a body twinkle around here without the whole place breaking out in crazy?"

"Beware," Ansgar said grimly. "That woman has a demon."

"What are you, high?" The gray-haired woman glared at him. "It's a Chihuahua. Get rid of that bow *now* before I call a deputy."

Chihuahua. A small breed of dog with large, pointed ears popular with humans.

"Oh." Ansgar lowered his weapon. "That is different."

Chapter Five

The woman with the dog rounded on Ansgar. "What is your problem, mister? You ought to be ashamed of yourself, picking on a poor, helpless little pooch."

Evie eased around Ansgar to get a better look. Pink Converse boots, the woman with the mullet from hell wore pink Converse boots. Crushed against her ample bosom was a gunmetal blue Chihuahua with an inverted lamp shade on its head. The dog's eerie golden eyes shone at the bottom of the cone, and its mouth bristled with an impressive set of gleaming, white teeth.

Helpless? Evie smothered a giggle. That Chihuahua looked about as helpless as a cornered wolverine.

"Don't you worry, Frodo, Mommy won't let the bad man hurt her widdle Precious," Mullet Woman said, cooing into the cone. "Even if he is sex on a stick and so fine he makes Mommy think about abandoning our No-More-Men-Because-Men-Are-Scum-Sucking-Low-Life-Two-Timing-Weasel-Dick-Bastards resolution. The one we made after Daddy runned off with Brittany, the husband-stealing 'ho from Loo-zee-anna."

Ansgar slung the bow across his back. "I did not realize the creature was a dog with that contraption upon its head."

The elegant weapon he carried was hand carved of pale, gleaming wood, beautiful and deadly like the man who wielded it. The bow had scarcely settled across his wide shoulders when it faded and vanished from view. *Poof!* It was gone, just like that, and the quiver of arrows with it. She darted a startled glance at the other two women. They were too busy gawking at Ansgar to notice his little magic act, thank goodness.

An image of Ansgar dressed in leather warrior garb flashed through Evie's mind. She frowned, trying to hold on to the scrap of memory, but it was gone.

A ripple of unease shook her. How could she have a memory of Ansgar when they'd met less than an hour ago?

Shaking off her disturbing thoughts, she stepped forward and gave Mullet Woman a reassuring smile. "It's called an Elizabethan collar. Isn't that right?"

"Stay back." Ansgar placed his body between Evie and the dog. "The animal is dangerous."

His sudden movement sent the dog into a renewed frenzy of barking.

"Sorry," Mullet Woman said over the noise. "Frodo hates men ever since my ex, Travis the Louse, shut the Barker Lounger on his tail. Did some serious nerve damage, although I didn't know it until later. By the time I realized it, poor Frodo had done chewed off his tail."

"Oh, the poor doggie," Evie said.

The Chihuahua threw back its head and howled.

The receptionist clapped her hands over her ears. "Have mercy!"

"Hush, Frodo, hush. For Mommy's sake, please." Mullet Woman patted the Chihuahua's minuscule rump, and the dog's yowling muted to a rumbling whine. "My bad. He does that ever time he hears the ex's name. Makes him crazy. I have to spell it out when I'm around him. T-r-a-v-i-s did a number on us both. Broke Frodo's tail and my heart, and busted my pocketbook all to pieces."

The receptionist lowered her hands. "This is the Sheriff's Department, not a vet's office. Get that animal out of here."

Mullet Woman wobbled after her, the yapping dog in her arms. "I can't leave, not until I see the sheriff. Frodo's in terrible danger." Her double chins trembled. "Somebody's trying to kill him. I need me one of them restraining orders."

The woman at the desk gave Mullet Woman a hard look. "You want a restraining order. For a dog."

"Not for the dog! For the dog stalker."

"I don't have time for this."

"Please, Miss . . ." There was a pause as Mullet Woman squinted at the nameplate on the desk. "Uh, Miss Mooneyham."

"It's Willa Dean," the receptionist snapped.

"Well, Willa Dean, if you'll just listen to me . . ."

Lowering her head, Mullet Woman launched into a spirited discussion with the receptionist.

Evie was riveted by the drama across the room. She jumped when Ansgar touched her on the arm.

"We must go," he said. "Brand and Addy are waiting."

"Did you hear that?" Evie worried her bottom lip. "Somebody's trying to kill her dog. That's horrible."

"With good reason. 'Tis a singularly unpleasant creature. We should depart. It is seldom wise to involve oneself in the affairs of humans."

"You involved yourself in my affairs and *I'm* human," Evie said. "If you hadn't been at the mill this morning, I don't know what would have happened to me."

"That is different. You are different."

"She's in trouble, same as I was this morning. Only she doesn't have a handsome demon hunter to save her."

He stepped closer, surrounding her with his spicy cologne. Coriander, she thought in dazed delight, her soaper's nose working to identify the complexity of his unique scent. *With a little cedar and amber thrown in.*

"Handsome? You find me attractive?"

Startled, she looked up at him. He had that hungry, aching look in his eyes again, the one that made her feel dizzy, breathless, and oh-so-wonderful. Like she had wings and could step off the precipice and fly, instead of going splat.

"What, are you kidding?" she said. "Have you seen yourself?"

"That is not an answer."

Evie stared at him in confusion. Was he playing with her? Teasing the fat girl, like the boys back in school? A spark of anger she didn't know existed smoldered and ignited.

She raised her chin and looked him in the eye. "You're gorgeous. Probably the best-looking guy I've ever seen. But you don't need me to tell you that."

"I will be the judge of what I need." He paused, frowning. "What do you mean *probably* the best-looking guy? Is there someone else?" She could swear little red flames danced in his silver eyes. "Are you involved with the Peterson human?"

"How do you—" she began. The sound of raised voices drew her attention to the other side of the room.

"Out." Willa Dean pointed toward the door. "Take your nasty little mutt and get out. Now."

"Evangeline." A shiver of delight coursed from her head to her toes as he placed his fingertips beneath her chin and turned her head toward him. "Are you involved with Trey Peterson?"

"Oh, for Pete's sake, why do people keep asking me that? No, I'm not involved with Trey."

"Good."

Bewildered, she watched him turn and stride across the room to Mullet Woman, who was still arguing with the receptionist.

"And I'm telling you, I ain't leaving till I see the sheriff," Mullet Woman said.

The dog responded to the tension in his mistress's voice by throwing back his head and yodeling. The cone amplified the sound like a megaphone.

Ansgar loomed over Mullet Woman. "Give the creature to me," he said. "You cannot converse whilst the thing makes that infernal noise."

Mullet Woman gazed up at him, her eyes widening in alarm. "I don't think so, mister. Frodo don't cotton to men."

Frodo confirmed this statement by trying to launch himself at Ansgar.

"Fear not," Ansgar said. "I will have a care to avoid the end with the teeth."

Mullet Woman clutched the wriggling dog tighter. "No thanks. I got enough trouble as it is."

"You have my word no harm shall come to the animal."

"It ain't the dog I'm worried about. Frodo's like a grizzly bear when he gets riled up."

"Trust me," Ansgar said in a deep-timbral purr.

Wowza, this guy was something else. Evie felt the seductive power of the Voice clear across the room. Poor Mullet Woman was standing at ground zero and looked like she'd been knocked upside the head with a two-by-four.

As for Willa Dean, Evie was pretty sure the old grump just had her first Big One in twenty years. Maybe ever.

Even Frodo the Misandrous Chihuahua shut the hell up.

"Wow." Mullet Woman gazed at Ansgar in awe. "Say something else. Anything. Listening to you talk makes my Happy Place go all warm and tingly. And I'd plum forgot I *had* a Happy Place."

"Congratulations. I am gratified to hear it. The dog, madam, if you please."

Mullet Woman sighed. "Okay, it's your funeral."

She handed him the Chihuahua. Holding the writhing dog at arm's length, Ansgar gazed into the cone. "Hear me, fiend. Sting me with thy teeth to thy everlasting regret."

To Evie's surprise, Frodo subsided with a disgruntled growl. Tucking the five-pound dog under one arm, Ansgar walked across the room and stood near the door.

"Most ridiculous thing I ever saw, that great big guy holding that itty-bitty butt-ugly dog." Shaking her head, Willa Dean picked up the telephone and pushed a button. "Sheriff, could you come out here? There's a woman here who insists on seeing you."

"What the Sam Hill's going on?" Sheriff Whitsun said, coming out of the back a moment later. "I'm trying to talk to the forensics guy in Mobile, and I can't hear myself think for the racket. Sounds like somebody's scalding a bobcat out here."

Willa Dean pushed to her feet. "This woman wants a restraining order. I tried to tell her we don't do that kind of thing, but nothing doing, she has to talk to you. Maybe you can talk some sense into her. It's time for my co-cola break."

She flounced through the swinging door.

Mullet Woman pounced on the startled sheriff in an earthquake of jiggling boobs. "You Sheriff Whitsun?"

"Yes."

"My name is Nicole Eubanks," she continued, panting a little. "And I need me that restraining order. Real bad."

The sheriff held up his hand. "One thing at a time, Ms. Eubanks. Where do you live?"

"Quit my job at the Gas 'N Gulp and moved to Hannah last week. No choice. Me and Frodo had to get outta Baldwin County. Fast, on account of we got us a dog stalker."

"Hannah? Well, now, you'll have to—" Whitsun faltered. "You got a what?"

"A dog stalker. His name is Sylvester Snippet. He's a vet in Stapleton, and he's trying to murder my dog."

"I know I'm gonna be sorry I asked," the sheriff said, "but why is a vet trying to kill your dog?"

"That Snippet feller called me a Chunky Monkey and asked me didn't I want to eat his banana."

The sheriff choked. "Are you saying your dog bit the vet because he said something *rude* to you?"

"Took off two of his fingers," Mullet Woman said. "That Snippet's a lucky son of a gun. Frodo was going for his banana." She waved her hand, indicating the Chihuahua. "There's my baby. Smile for the sheriff, Precious."

Frodo peeled his lips back, revealing a double row of foam-flecked, razor-sharp teeth.

"God almighty, that's a dog? It's got teeth like an alligator." The sheriff seemed to notice Ansgar for the first time. For a big, supernaturally handsome guy, Ansgar had a way of fading into the woodwork when he wanted to. "Who are you?" Whitsun asked.

"I am Ansgar."

"Are you with this woman?"

"No."

"Don't I wish." Mullet Woman gave a wistful sigh and shook her head. "My hootie says, *Hey, baby, you know what I like,* but my head says, *Are you nuts, Nikki? The last guy took you to the cleaners.* My hootie can talk all it wants. From now on, I'm listening to my head. Frodo and I have sworn off men but good."

The poor sheriff looked a little glassy eyed. "Uh huh," he said. "Seeing as you live in Hannah, you'll need to speak to the Chief of Police. His name's Carl Davis. He's a good man. He'll take your complaint."

"Will he give me a restraining order?"

"No, he can't do that. But he'll talk to this Snippet if he comes around and tell him to leave you and your dog alone."

"But that won't do no good! I've done talked to the man till I'm blue in the face." Mullet Woman's round face creased in distress. "I offered to pay his medical bills and everything. But nothing doing. I'm telling you, the man ain't right. He won't stop until my Precious is dead. You got to do something."

"I can't give you a restraining order, Ms. Eubanks. You'll have to file a motion in court for that. You can do it yourself or hire a lawyer to draw up the papers for you."

"But that could take months." Mullet Woman seemed to wilt. "I don't know nothing about that legal stuff, and I ain't got no money for a lawyer. I quit my job as cashier at the Gas 'N Gulp and moved here because I'm afraid for Frodo's life."

"I'm sorry, ma'am, but that's the law."

"Well, the law stinks." Evie surprised herself by speaking up. But she couldn't keep still any longer. She turned to Mullet Woman. "You looking for a job?"

Mullet Woman nodded. "Yeah, but I'm new in town and you know how that is."

No, she didn't. Evie had never lived anywhere but Hannah.

"My friend Addy runs the flower shop on Main Street," Evie said. "*Flowers by Adara.* Do you know it?"

"Yeah." Mullet Woman's blue eyes glistened with tears. "South of the funeral home and over the river bridge, ain't it?"

"That's the one. You come in first thing tomorrow morning.

I know for a fact Addy's looking for somebody to drive the delivery van. You can drive, right?"

"Are you kidding? If it's got wheels, I can drive it. Fix it, too. My daddy was a grease monkey." Mullet Woman grinned and pumped Evie's hand up and down. "You're an angel, Miss. A purentee angel. The good Lord put you here to help me, I just know it. What's your name?"

"Evie Douglass."

"Evie. That's a real pretty name." Mullet Woman glanced at Ansgar. "You got man troubles of your own, Miss Evie? Is that why you're here?"

"No, nothing like that." Embarrassed, Evie hesitated. The reality of her situation was too awful to contemplate, much less say aloud. She drew a deep breath and blurted it out. "They think I killed a woman."

Mullet Woman's eyes grew round. "Get out of this town! Did you do it?"

"No!"

"Of course you didn't. You're too sweet and good." Mullet Woman shot Sheriff Whitsun a look of reproach. "Anyone with two brain cells to rub together could figure that out. Well, Miss Douglass, you won't regret this. Me and Frodo won't let you down. You betcha bottom dollar we won't."

"Wait," Evie said with a stab of panic. "I didn't mean for you to bring the dog. I'm not so sure how Addy will feel about—"

Moving like a pink and black polyester whirlwind, Mullet Woman snatched the Chihuahua out of Ansgar's hands and blew back out the door.

Chapter Six

"Oh, man," Evie said. "Addy's gonna kill me."

The sheriff's mouth twitched. "You don't know that woman from Adam, do you? Are you always so impulsive?"

"I'm usually not impulsive at all." She glared at him. "But somebody had to help her, and it was obvious you weren't going to do anything."

Whoa, where did that come from? Shy, self-conscious Evie Douglass wouldn't say boo to a goose. Yet here she was bowing up at the sheriff.

Twice.

It must be Mullet Woman. Evie could relate to her, with her People of Walmart fashion sense and her disaster of a hairdo. No doubt people made fun of her. Evie knew what that felt like.

And Mullet Woman seemed so alone. Evie knew about that, too.

Or maybe you're tired of being such a doormat and eating that crap sandwich you've been chewing on most of your life. God, I hope so, 'cause being you blows. Big time.

Evie started. Where did that thought come from?

To her relief, the entrance door opened and Addy stuck her head in the room. "Hey, what's the holdup? Did you leave your purse in Timbuktu?"

"Sorry," Evie mumbled.

Ducking her head, she hurried out of the sheriff's office and into the hallway. For goodness' sakes, she was borderline rude to the man and she'd hired a stranger to work in Addy's flower shop. Without asking.

A stranger with a mutant flesh-eating dog.

What was the matter with her?

It had been a horrible day. That was the problem. This morning started out like any other, boring and familiar. She'd waded through the sameness to work, aware of the dull, aching weight of depression bearing down on her, a feeling of soul-numbing sorrow she could not shake. Then, without warning, her day morphed into something else. Meredith was dead. And mousy Evie Douglass, who never got so much as a conduct check in school, was a person of interest in a murder. Small wonder she was rattled.

The back of her neck tingled. Oh, Lord, Ansgar was behind her. He moved without sound. But she knew he was there. She could *feel* him, for Pete's sake.

He was a big part of why she was on edge. Being near him shattered her nerves; he was so intimidating and gosh-darn perfect.

A few minutes ago, she'd been in his arms. The thought of it made her shiver. She'd opened her eyes and found herself heartbeat to heartbeat with the most beautiful man in the world, her breasts pressed against his broad chest. He radiated heat and strength and danger. She wanted to sink into him.

She wanted to run away.

God, she was a basket case.

Cheeks burning, Evie scurried up the basement stairs and into the rotunda of the courthouse, a domed structure built in 1898. Eager for some fresh air after the hours of confinement in the sheriff's office, she darted across the gleaming expanse of marble floor and pushed open one of the brass-plated glass doors. She stepped outside into the sunshine and took a deep breath.

The air held the crisp tang of autumn, and the October sky was a brilliant, cloudless blue. Beautiful and serene. Perfect, like the endless grace of God.

Hard to believe anything bad could happen on a day like today. But it had, and in spades. A few hours ago, she'd looked upon the face of death and felt the presence of evil. Whatever malignant thing had been in the office with her this morning was still out there, watching and waiting. It had killed Meredith and liked it. It would kill again.

Addy paused on the portico beside her. "Where's the fire?"

"I'm tired and I want to go home," Evie said, hurrying down the steps.

She'd go home, fix herself a cup of hot tea, and curl up in her favorite chair. She'd try to forget the events of the past few hours. Meredith's tortured body tossed across her desk at the mill like so much messy, discarded trash. The nerve-racking wait in the tiny backroom of the sheriff's office followed by the exhausting two-hour interrogation by Whitsun himself—El Lobo in a khaki shirt with a built-in lie-detecting snoot.

Last but not least, leaving Whitsun's cramped office and running smack into Ansgar, with his bedroom eyes and velvet voice.

Don't go there, she told herself sternly. *He's a major hottie and he's not for you.*

How do you know if you never give it a try? Unbidden, the rebellious thought floated through her mind. *Flirt with him and see what happens. What have you got to lose?*

She reached the curb, flung open the back door of Addy's delivery van, and climbed in. Glancing back, she watched Ansgar walk down the worn concrete steps at the front of the courthouse. He might be dressed in modern clothes, but he moved like a warrior, all hard muscle and predatory grace. A man in a business suit shot him a startled glance and leaped out of his way, like an alarmed impala avoiding a hungry lion. Two women stopped in their tracks to gawk at him, their mouths hanging open at his masculine deliciousness.

What did she have to lose? she thought, watching him stride toward the van in all his glory, his long hair gleaming in the sun like a blond halo.

How 'bout body and soul, for starters?

★ ★ ★

The ride home was miserable. Addy drove and Brand sat beside her in the front of the van.

Well, duh, no surprise there. Brand was never far away from Addy. They were in love with a capital L. Addy had won the Trifecta of boyfriends: handsome, sexy, faithful, and adoring.

Wait. That was four. Sadly, the list went on and on. Sadly for *her*, not Addy. Addy was in hog heaven with her demon hunter.

Evie was happy for her BFF. Really. But sometimes when Brand looked at Addy like he wanted to eat her with a spoon one slow bite at a time, Evie got the teensiest bit jealous.

Okay, she was rotten with it, but she would deal.

What she couldn't deal with was the seating arrangement. Addy and Brand were in the front, which left Evie in the back of the van with Ansgar the Nordic god of Splendor. She clung to her side of the van like a suckerfish in a vain attempt to keep some space between them. It was a waste of time. He was a big guy, and the van had all the suspension of a Conestoga wagon. Every time Addy rounded a curve, Evie swayed against Ansgar's muscular thigh. She couldn't help it. There was no *oh shit handle* in the back, and gravity, physics, and her less than dainty weight were against her. She kept rolling into him like a drunken penguin.

He seemed unaffected by the contact, but it nearly sent her through the roof. She was having hot flashes from touching a guy's *thigh,* for heaven's sake. But, oh, my God, what he did for a pair of jeans ought to be a felony. The denim molded to his quads and . . . uh . . . other places.

She realized she was staring at his crotch and jerked her head up. Her gaze collided with Ansgar's, and she nearly died a fiery death right then and there. Sweet baby Jesus, he just caught her checking out his package.

And it was some package. Birthday, Christmas, and Bat Mitzvah rolled into one. All it needed was a big red bow.

Holy cow, she did not just think that!

She spent the rest of the trip back to Hannah staring out the window as if pine trees and kudzu were the most fascinating things in the world. Maybe if she wished hard enough, the floorboard would open up and she would be sucked out of the van, roll down the highway and into a ditch, where she'd lie in a roly-poly ball of mortification forever and ever. Amen.

No such luck. She was stuck in the van with Captain Pheromones.

A small eternity later, they pulled into Hannah and cruised past the Dairy Spin.

"The Sweet Shop is closed until five," Addy said. "You want a burger?"

"No." Evie saw Addy's eyes widen in the rearview mirror. Her face grew hot. She was being a rudie again. Much more embarrassment and her darn face would explode. "Uh . . . I mean, no thank you. I'm not hungry. Please take me home."

Home was a 1920s Craftsman bungalow in the heart of Hannah, an older section of town with houses dating back to the turn of the twentieth century. Addy and Evie grew up a few blocks from one another on Magnolia Street, and Addy's mother still lived in the same house.

Evie loved her home with its deep, square-columned front porch, gabled roof, and stone accents. She even loved the hopelessly outdated bathrooms and the tiny kitchen. She couldn't imagine living anywhere else. In spring, Magnolia Street was festooned with bright patches of azaleas, clumps of blue and white hydrangea, and fragrant wisteria. Summer meant the sweet smell of freshly cut grass and the steady hiss of sprinklers on manicured lawns. Neighborhood children rolled down the sidewalks on their bicycles, roller skates, and skateboards, and dads performed the age-old ritual of grilling animal flesh over barbeques in backyards.

Summer was a recent memory, and fall was now upon them. In two days it would be Halloween. The maples, dogwoods, and redbuds were aflame, and there was a crisp tang in the air, a welcome relief from the sticky heat of summer.

Evie couldn't wait to get away from Ansgar. She felt like she'd been dipped in fire ants. What was it about him that set her on edge? Aside from the fact he oozed danger and sex and was supernaturally gorgeous.

She took a deep breath and tried to calm her racing heart. She was being ridiculous. The guy was a demon hunter, for heaven's sake. He had places to go, demons to kill. He wasn't interested in a frumpy woman from an itty-bitty town at the ass end of nowhere. She was acting like an idiot.

They pulled up in front of her house, and Evie got out. She thought about hurling herself onto the sidewalk while the van was still moving, but managed to exit the vehicle with relative dignity. All in all, she was rather proud of herself.

Okay, so maybe she caught her shoe in the hem of her dress and almost fell on her head. But no one noticed. She hoped.

Addy rolled down her window. "I forgot about your car. Want me to take you out to the mill to get it?"

"Thanks, but I'm too beat. Can we do it tomorrow?"

"Sure thing." Addy's brown eyes held concern. "Try and get some sleep. You look exhausted."

Evie leaned through the open window and gave her friend a quick hug. "Thanks, babe," she whispered in Addy's ear. Tears stung the back of her throat. "I love you all the way to your gizzard."

Addy hugged her tight. "Love you more."

Addy waved good-bye and drove off. Evie stood at the end of the drive and watched the pink van turn down Maple Street and disappear. *He's gone,* she thought. Her chest felt hollow and funny.

She might not see him again. That's what she wanted, right?

But if that was the case, then how come she felt so sad? So *bereft,* like all the happiness in the world had been leeched away, leaving nothing but dreary, unrelenting grayness. She turned and staggered toward the house. The driveway blurred and the monkey grass lining the walk melted in a ribbon of green.

Blip! She was at her front door. It was like she flew or something.

She fumbled with the key through her tears. At last, the lock turned and she stepped inside. The curtains were partially drawn, the living room dim. A large shape passed in front of one of the windows, blocking the late-afternoon sun.

"Ah, there you are," a deep voice said. "I have been waiting for you."

Chapter Seven

Evie shrieked and stumbled back, slamming her heels against the door.

"Forgive me," Ansgar said. He towered over her, seeming to take up all the air and space in the room. "I did not mean to startle you."

"What are you doing here?" She sounded breathless and giddy. But how could she help it when her heart sang and her skin tingled with little bursts of gladness? He was *here*. He didn't leave. "How did you get in my house?"

"Mortal locks are not effective against the Dalvahni." A frown marred the perfection of his chiseled features. Lifting his hand, he brushed a tear from her cheek. "You are weeping. What has happened to distress you? Is it Meredith?"

Evie wiped the back of her hand across her wet cheeks. "No, I thought . . ." Her throat tightened. She shook her head, unable to continue.

How could she tell him the truth? That she was crying because she thought she'd never see him again. Which made no sense at all. How do you miss a person you've just met?

Hunching her shoulders, she tried to step around him.

He blocked her. "Why are you crying?" he demanded gently. "I must know."

She shook her head again, her eyes on the floor. "It's nothing. Really."

"It is not nothing if you are distraught. Tell me."

"Please," she whispered. "Let me go."

"Not until I know what troubles you." He tilted her chin. It was impossible to think straight when she was surrounded by his enticing scent, like clean linen and evergreens touched with frost. "Look at me."

Three little words, but they throbbed with power. His sorcerer's voice made her drunk with longing. Fire and ice, shadow and light, steel wrapped in velvet.

Silken. Sensual. Compelling.

She felt her defenses crumbling beneath the seductive onslaught. *Oh, for crying in the beer, tell the guy how you feel. Aren't you sick of the shrinking violet routine? So what if he laughs at you. You should be plenty used to that by now. Throw it out there and see what happens.* She was suddenly feeling rebellious.

Summoning her courage, she lifted her gaze to his and stepped off the ledge. "I was sad, because you left. I-I thought I might not see you again."

She braced herself for his rejection.

"Evangeline."

His cool voice held a husky note, and his silver eyes turned smoky gray. He cupped her face in his hands. Heat poured off his big body, and his touch made her shiver with longing. She wanted him, all of him. She wanted his strong, long-fingered hands on her body and his mouth upon her skin.

He bent his head closer. "Evangeline, I . . ."

Brand materialized in her living room. "There you are, brother. You exited the vehicle with such haste that Adara was worried. We feared something untoward had happened. But you seem to have things well in hand. Adara will be delighted to hear you are keeping your promise." He raised his dark brows. "And with such *fervor*."

Ansgar dropped his hands and stepped back. A muscle twitched in his jaw. "Evangeline was upset. I was endeavoring to soothe her."

"Ah, is that what you call it?" Brand's eyes held a sardonic gleam. He seemed to be enjoying Ansgar's discomfiture. "I will leave you to it then. I bid you good day."

He disappeared.

"What promise?" Evie demanded.

"I told Addy I would keep you safe."

She scuttled away from the door. She needed distance from Ansgar in order to think. Being around him made her brain shut down and got other parts going. Why'd he have to be so gosh-darn beautiful and smell so good? And, to top it all off, he had a voice like liquid sex. It put an ordinary girl at a serious disadvantage.

She clasped her hands in front of her, trying to remain calm. "That's sweet. It really is. I appreciate the offer, but that won't be necessary."

"You misunderstand. You have no say in the matter."

"Addy put you up to this. She is such a worrywart, but you don't have to stay. I promise not to tell her if you leave."

"No."

Her jaw sagged in astonishment. "What do you mean *no*?"

"I will not leave you. The thing that slew Meredith is still out there. You are in danger. It is my duty to protect you. I will stay with you until the matter is resolved."

"You can't stay here! This is a small town. People will talk."

Ansgar propped his shoulder against the door and crossed his arms. "Let them talk. Would you rather be dead?"

"You don't know that thing is after me. Maybe it'll go away."

"Do not be a fool. I was there this morning. I felt the creature's presence, its evil intent. The kill today has but whetted the beast's appetite for blood. It will strike again."

Fear iced Evie's skin. Ansgar was right. The thing that killed Meredith enjoyed bloodshed and inflicting pain. She'd sensed it. But stay alone in the house with Ansgar? She'd melt into a pool of frustrated hormones.

"I'm sorry, I appreciate your concern, but you can't stay in my house. It's out of the question."

"Why not?" He looked around. "I see no impediment."

"Because I don't want you here," Evie said, goaded beyond good manners. "Is that plain enough? You're too good looking, too tall, and too dad-blamed *hot* to be around. You make me a nervous wreck."

She groaned and put her hand over her eyes. "I'm sorry, that was rude. I'm not acting like myself today. But so help me, you could irritate the shingles off a house. Go away."

"Very well."

Blip! He disappeared. Evie looked around. No super sexy demon hunter. Gone, just like that. One minute he was lecturing her about danger, duty, and the evil monster on her trail, and the next he vamoosed.

In spite of an abundance of furniture, including a faded couch, a coffee table, and several overstuffed chairs, the room seemed empty without him.

Or maybe not.

Her skin tingled with awareness. Gone my hind foot, she thought. She wouldn't get rid of him that easily. She'd been around Brand and Addy long enough to know the Dalvahni were bullish in their determination to get their own way. Alpha males with an overabundance of testosterone, to put it mildly.

"You might as well show yourself," she said. "I know you're still here."

Ansgar reappeared. "I went away. Was that better?"

"No, it most certainly was not. Making yourself invisible is not the same as going away."

"Why not?"

"Because you're still here, that's why!" Evie sighed in resignation. "You're not going to leave no matter what I say, are you?"

"I cannot. Something might happen to you."

"So? What do you care? You hardly know me."

"It is Addy," Ansgar said with perfect seriousness. "She has threatened me with bodily harm if you are hurt. She is a most intimidating female."

Evie chuckled. "Liar. I don't think you're afraid of anything."

"You are wrong."

"Oh, yeah? What are you afraid of?"

"Perhaps one day I will tell you." He gave her a narrow-eyed glance. "But, at the moment, I require sustenance. As do you, I suspect."

Food, he wanted food. He was a big man. No doubt he had an equally big appetite. And she hadn't been to the store in weeks. What on earth was she going to feed him?

"I'll see what I can find."

She hurried through the dining room past the antique oak cabinet that held her grandmother's china, and into the sunny kitchen at the back of the house. This was her favorite room, the one that held her happiest memories from when her mother was alive.

Before the dark times. Before death and her father's descent into alcoholism.

Afternoons baking cookies with her mama and evenings spent doing her homework at the small table in the corner where they ate their meals. The bank of windows surrounding the square kitchen table looked out on the backyard, where Evie kept an herb garden for her soaps and a profusion of flowers for the fairies. Roses, sweet peas, and snap dragons, to name a few.

The state of her larder was worse than she feared. She opened the refrigerator first. Nothing there but diet soda and a half-empty pickle jar. The freezer compartment contained two frostbitten Lean Cuisines and a bag of green peas. Rubber peas, her daddy called them. Not exactly tempting provender for an oversized, hungry demon hunter.

A search of the cabinets turned up a few canned vegetables and a box of stale crackers. Pitiful. She hadn't been hungry lately. When *was* the last time she went shopping? Thinking back, she realized with a sense of shock that her last real trip to the grocery store had been months ago, not weeks. Granted, she and Addy went to lunch once or twice a week, but what had she been living on?

"You are disquieted," Ansgar said from the doorway. "Is there something I can do to help?"

Evie slammed the cabinet shut. "I'm sorry, I wasn't expecting company. There's not much to eat in the house. I'm afraid the best I can offer you is a fluffernutter sandwich."

"I am not familiar with this concoction."

"It's peanut butter and marshmallow cream spread between two pieces of bread." She glanced at the basket on the counter. Empty. "Oh, shoot. I'm out of bread, too. Guess it's going to have to be the Dairy Spin, after all." She made a face. "But my car is still at the mill."

"It is of no moment. Go and take your bath. That always improves your spirits."

"How do you—"

She gave a startled squeak as he streaked across the room in a blur of movement and lifted her into his arms.

"Addy told me." He smiled down at her. "How else?"

Evie's brain went mushy. He was strength and calm and steadiness, an unyielding rock in a sea of chaos. For the first time today, she began to relax. She was safe. Nothing bad could happen to her, not with Ansgar around.

She came to her senses as he strode out of the kitchen. "Ansgar, put me down!" Her face burned with mortification. She was no tiny miss like Meredith. "You can't carry me."

"I cannot?"

"No. I'm too big. You'll pull a muscle or something."

He chuckled. "Do not be absurd. You are light as thistledown."

"A silo full of thistledown, maybe," she muttered.

He stopped abruptly and looked down at her, his eyes gleaming in the dark hallway.

"You are all woman, Evangeline, not the anemic version of what passes for feminine beauty in this reality. You have curving hips and plump breasts that make a man itch to test the weight of them with his hands and his cock sit up and pay attention. You are many things, including delectable and succulent as a ripe peach. But you are not—I repeat *not*—fat. And if you say so again in my hearing, I will turn you over my knee and spank your luscious little bottom. Is that understood?"

"Oh." Evie stared at him in shock. No one had ever described her bottom as *little*. It was by far the nicest compliment she'd ever received. "You mustn't say c-o-c-k. It's not nice."

He kicked open the bathroom door and set her down on the

tile floor. "I am a demon hunter. I was created to hunt and kill. I am not 'nice.' Take your bath. When you finish, we will eat."

"Wait," she said as he turned to leave. "There's something I need to know."

"Yes?"

Her heart thundered in her ears. She couldn't believe she was doing this. But today seemed to have cracked open a hidden reservoir of boldness she never knew existed.

"That thing you said about me being a . . . a peach." Taking a deep breath, she blurted out the question foremost in her mind. "Do you eat peaches?"

"Yes, I do," he said from the doorway. The look in his eyes made her feel hot and shaky. "And once I start eating them, I find it difficult to stop."

Chapter Eight

D*o you eat peaches?*

Evie groaned and slid deeper into the clawfoot tub, letting the scented water lap at her chin. Did she really ask him that?

Did she?

Yep, bold as you please. It was like somebody took over her body, some brazen hussy she didn't recognize.

What must he think of her? She practically *threw* herself at the guy, for heaven's sake. She'd never been so bold with a man.

Her daily soak usually soothed her, but not today. Today, everything in her was coiled tight. *Aware.* She couldn't relax, not with *him* around. Heck, she couldn't relax knowing the guy was on the same planet, much less in the same house.

He made her jittery and on edge, filled her with anticipation and excitement. After months of living under a dull cloud of despair, she felt alive. Like she was stretching and waking from a long sleep, shedding the husk of her former self and becoming someone else.

Thank goodness. She was sick to death of being a good little doormat. She'd been a doormat all her life and look where it got her. A big, fat nowhere.

She wanted to be bad. With Ansgar.

So be bad already, her willful self said. *There's nobody to stop you. Your parents are dead. Your sister's dead. It's not like there's anybody around to shake a finger if you have a little fun.*

Except for Addy and Bitsy, of course. But Bitsy wasn't here

and Addy wouldn't mind. Addy was always after her to cut loose and live a little.

But after a lifetime of being a stick in the mud, old habits were hard to break.

"Besides," she muttered out loud, "in what reality do you think you'd have a chance with him?"

She replayed the moment in her mind. *You are many things, including as delectable and succulent as a ripe peach.*

Wow.

She hugged the words close, savoring them. Wicked, sexy words that made her quiver with longing. No one ever said anything like that to her, especially someone like Ansgar. Who was she kidding? She'd never met anyone like Ansgar, with his big, hard body and his mouth made for sin.

That sensuous mouth promised untold pleasures. Set above a stubborn chin and unyielding jaw, it was the crown jewel set in a face so handsome it was like something straight out of a fairy tale.

Prince Charming, eat your heart out. Ansgar the Magnificent makes you look like dog poop. She giggled to herself at the thought.

Smiling, she closed her eyes and imagined his mouth on her, kissing her, nibbling her. Her heartbeat sped up. The fantasy was so real she could almost feel his hands lifting her breasts, the satin stroke of his tongue on her nipples.

She shifted in the tub, aroused and embarrassed by the direction of her thoughts. A fragment of memory stirred of a man moving over her, of the exquisite pressure and slide as he drove his body into hers, his deep, smoky voice urging her on.

Let go, Evangeline. Let me pleasure you.

She sat up so fast water sloshed over the edge of the bathtub and onto the black and white tile floor. Ansgar. She'd know that seductive whisper anywhere.

But that was impossible. She couldn't have memories of Ansgar. It was wishful thinking, her imagination working overtime.

She leaned back. So she had fantasies about Ansgar? Who could blame her? The guy was off-the-charts sexy. Totally understandable, but she needed to get a grip.

The jangle of metal on metal drew her gaze to the bathroom window. The wind chime hanging from the dogwood branch swayed violently, though not a leaf on the tree stirred.

Fear trickled down her spine. The fairies were trying to warn her about something?

Dark smoke swirled against the outside of the drafty window, pushing and nudging against the glass as if seeking entrance. A searching finger of mist found the crack at the base of the warped sash and seeped into the room, solidifying into a hideous nightmare creature of claw and fang.

The temperature in the room plummeted, and ice frosted the water in the tub and the puddle of water on the floor. A suffocating sense of malevolence pervaded the tiny space. She couldn't breathe, couldn't think. As she watched in helpless terror, the demon reached for her with clawed hands.

The wind chime clanged again, breaking the evil spell.

Evie screamed.

Ansgar closed his eyes. Leaving Evie to her ablutions, he'd retreated to the kitchen, but he could not escape the sounds from down the hall. The Dalvahni had excellent hearing. The gentle slosh as Evie eased into the tub, the splash and trickle of the heated water caressing her skin, swirling over her beautiful breasts and thighs—he heard it all.

Sweet torment.

He cursed himself and his weakness. He was not good enough for her. She deserved better. He'd deluded himself in thinking he could resist her. She was a flame-haired enchantress, and he was her helpless captive.

A sharp sound, like the tinkle of breaking glass, made him open his eyes. A wiggin hovered at the end of his nose; a fairy gardener, caretaker of root, moss, bracken, and bramble. No bigger than the palm of his hand, the wiggin was naked but for a few strands of cobweb. It had skin the color of old leaves. Brown, lacy wings delicately veined with streaks of silver-green fluttered rapidly from the fairy's slender shoulders. The tiny creature regarded Ansgar with hard, dark eyes from a face like carved bark. Having gained Ansgar's attention, the fairy flitted in agitated circles around his head, a stream of high-pitched, frantic chatter issuing from its tiny mouth.

"You must speak more slowly, little one," Ansgar said. "I cannot understand you."

With an impatient huff, the fairy flew closer. *"Danger!"* the wiggin chirped in his ear.

At the same time, the wind chimes in the garden rang in discordant warning. Ansgar opened his mind and located the threat, seeing with his inner eye the malignant shadow on the other side of the house. The patch of darkness oozed up the wall and through the bathroom window.

Evangeline; the djegrali had found her. And he, blinded by misery and unthinking lust, had neglected to strengthen the shield spells around the house, leaving her vulnerable.

Evie screamed. Quicker than thought, the fairy darted across the room and down the hall. Ansgar was faster. Lifting his hand, he burst the door off the hinges and streaked into the bathroom. Evie sat in the tub, encased in a solid sheet of black ice. Jagged icicles rimed the walls and window casing, and sprang like glittering knives from the chamber floor. A barrier of greenish-gold light separated her from the furious demon. Fairy magic, no doubt. Poisonous spells hung in the air, detritus from the djegrali's frustrated attempts to break through the shield.

"Ilsann," Ansgar said.

His bow of Gorthian yew appeared in his hands. He nocked an arrow and fired. With a venomous hiss, the djegrali fled, shattering the window in its haste to escape, and Ansgar's arrow hit the wall in a shower of harmless sparks.

Dropping his bow, Ansgar kicked a path through the ice daggers and bent over Evie. She cried out and shrank back.

"Easy, sweetling," he said. "You are safe."

With a blow of his fist, he shattered the ice surrounding her.

"D-demon." She was shaking with cold. "T-through the window."

"Shh." He lifted her out of the tub. "The djegrali is gone."

She wrapped her arms around his neck and let her head

droop against his shoulder. Something twisted inside him at the gesture of helpless trust. He closed his eyes, shaking with relief. He had failed her again. If something had happened to her, if the fairies had not protected her . . .

The very thought drained the strength from his limbs. He was a warrior, accustomed to combat and strife, danger and pain. Thousands of years of battle, injuries beyond counting, and never had he reacted like this. Never had he needed anyone like this.

He was becoming as weak as an old woman because of her. This is what he had feared. This is why he'd left, this uncontrollable need for her.

But leaving had made no difference, had done nothing to lessen his need. Indeed, absence made him crave her more.

The detached warrior of old was gone. He had changed. Briefly, he contemplated this new reality.

So be it.

He pressed her closer to his chest, trying to infuse her quaking flesh with his warmth. A human would have suffered frostbite or worse from the demon's attack. But she was Dalvahni now, thanks to him, and already recovering. Beneath his watchful gaze, her shivering lessened and the smooth skin of her thighs grew warm against his palms. He carried her out of the bathroom and into the living room. He started to lower her feet to the floor, and she tightened her arms around his neck.

"No," she said, burrowing her face against his neck. "Warm."

" 'Twill be but a moment, sweetling. Just long enough for me to wrap you in a blanket. You are unclothed."

She stiffened against him. "Unclothed? Granny Moses, you mean I'm *naked*?"

"Evangeline, wait," he said as she tried to fling herself from his grasp.

Once, in a distant place and time, Ansgar had gone into a bog after a young shoat. Rescuing the frantic animal had been a slippery business, but holding on to an armful of wet, humiliated woman proved far more challenging. And infinitely more interesting, Ansgar thought, suppressing a groan as Evie twisted in his grasp, her breasts grazing his chest as she slid to the floor.

Plucking a blanket off one end of the couch, Evie scampered away from him in a tantalizing dance of womanly flesh. She grabbed the blanket and wrapped it around her.

He swallowed a smile. She thought to hide her lush form from him with a meager scrap of cloth. Not knowing, never dreaming he already knew her body, had committed each curve and hollow to memory. Knew the taste and scent of her, the measure and weight of each high, full breast, had traced every inch of her satin skin with his lips and tongue.

"Ohmygoodness," she said. The words came out in a rush, interrupting his lascivious thoughts. Her face and the upper swell of her bosom bloomed with color. "I am *so* sorry. In a lifetime of embarrassing moments, this one takes the cake. I don't know what to say."

"Why do you apologize?"

"For *this*." Tucking the edge of the blanket in the deep cleft between her breasts, she waved her free hand to indicate her state of undress. "You think I parade around naked as a jaybird in front of strangers every day of the week?"

"I should hope not. At any rate, I am not a stranger." He took a step toward her, and she sidled farther away. "And I like you naked. If I had my way, you would be in a permanent state of undress."

Her lovely mouth sagged in shock. "Oh! You mustn't say such things."

He stalked closer. "Why not?"

She edged away from him. "Because you don't mean them. You can't. And it's cruel of you to tease me."

She came up against the front door and stopped, squeaking in surprise as he caged her between his arms. Wide eyed, she gazed up at him.

"I am not teasing you," he said.

Her pulse fluttered in her throat. He wanted to kiss her there, to taste her petal-soft skin and feel the throb of her heartbeat beneath his tongue. Her scent was intoxicating, an ever-changing delight, sometimes lavender, sometimes lilac, wisteria, or tuberose. Today, she smelled of something dreamy and sweet, like ripe grapes. He wanted to ravish her, to gorge himself on her innocence, to make her remember, though he'd sworn not to, though she would hate him for it.

Lifting his right hand from the door, he trailed his fingertip down her perfect little nose, across her lush bottom lip to the plump swell of her bosom. He let his fingers linger there, lightly caressing the tops of her breasts, enjoying the rapid catch of her breath and the look of pure astonishment on her face.

"You are a beautiful woman," he continued, "though you do your best to disguise it. But your efforts are misspent, for you cannot hide your beauty from me."

He brushed her nipples through the cloth with the back of his hand, enjoying the way her lips parted in a little hiccup of surprise.

"You think I'm beautiful, really?" He saw the wistfulness and doubt in her eyes. "You're not just saying it?"

"I am not just saying it."

He tugged her away from the door and kissed her. He'd thought of little else since that afternoon. The taste of her, the softness of her lips, the feel of her in his arms. He wanted more. He was like a famished beggar standing before a bakery window, and she was light and warmth and sustenance.

He was hungry for her, ravenous with need.

But she was timid and shy, he reminded himself. She did not remember him. He must go slowly, else he frighten her.

And so he tamped down his raging desire and kissed her lightly, a slow, sensuous brush of his lips against hers, nothing more. She sighed and leaned into him. The blanket parted and fell to the floor. She did not seem to notice, but Ansgar did. She was naked in his arms, his for the taking. This is what he'd dreamed of through the long, lonely nights, desperate with the wanting of her but determined to stay away.

He'd lost that battle, but he would not lose this one. He was Dalvahni. Disciplined; the master of his baser self. Not a frenzied animal. He would rein in his rising lust and proceed with caution and patience.

He would not lose control.

Evie arched her back and lifted her knee, pressing the warm center of her womanhood against his crotch.

Ansgar forgot everything, restraint, self-control. He was on fire, his cool warrior brain at war with his raging lust.

Lust won.

Chapter Nine

Ansgar tangled his hands in Evie's damp hair and gave her a ravaging kiss. Evie took him in, suckling, lapping, teasing him with lips, teeth, and tongue. Each damp caress of his tongue sent little waves of sensation to her breasts and belly, and lower to the place between her legs.

She swayed against him, her head spinning. A distant, shocked voice whispered she was acting like a slut, but she didn't care. She should be dying of embarrassment, trying to hide her naked body behind the nearest piece of furniture. Instead, she clung to him without shame, reveling in the sensation of her breasts pressed against his hard chest.

Reveling in the sheer masculine strength of him. He made her feel feminine and desirable for the first time in her life.

It felt natural to be in his arms, like she'd been here before. No bashfulness. No hesitation. Twenty-eight years of inhibition and insecurity out the window. He awakened something in her, something wild and daring.

She didn't want it to end. Now that she'd had a taste of it, she wanted more.

More? She wanted it all. She wanted *him*.

Don't stop, she thought. *Just a little longer, a few more minutes of wonderful . . .*

"Evangeline," he murmured, pressing a trail of burning kisses down her neck.

She cried out as he slid his hands under her bottom and lifted her against the front door. She wrapped her legs around him and held on. The wood felt cool against the bare skin of her back and buttocks. But everything else was hot and burning for him. Her breasts ached, her skin felt too tight, and her head buzzed with desire.

She was like an animal in heat, sexually charged, jittery, and jumpy. She'd never known the pull of sexual desire, never dreamed it could make her feel this way. Hot and shaky and trembling with need.

And the biggest miracle of all? He wanted her, too. The evidence was hard to ignore. The rough denim of his blue jeans scratched her inner thighs, and the hard bulge of his erection nudged the pulsing place between her legs. She wanted him inside her, the consequences be damned. So what if she hardly knew the guy? So what if it wouldn't last, couldn't last, because he was sex on two legs and probably had a dozen girls in every dimension?

When would she have another chance like this? Never; that's when. He would leave and she would go back to being plain old Evie, the incredible shrinking woman. Stand back and watch her disappear.

But not now; right now he was here, the most scrumptious guy on the planet. And he was coming on to her.

Maybe her luck was finally turning. Maybe—

The doorbell rang. The *front* doorbell, she realized, coming slowly out of her Ansgar-induced-sex-crazed fog. Someone was on the porch.

On the other side of the door, the same door she had her naked butt cheeks smushed against. The door of Almost Sex with Ansgar.

Oh, God.

Evie's eyes flew open, alarm streaking through her. "Let me go." She shoved her hands against his shoulders. "Someone's here."

He released her at once, and she lowered her feet to the floor. Cheeks burning, she bolted into the hall and pressed her back to the wall, her arms crossed over her breasts. She felt naked and vulnerable. Well big duh. She *was* naked. As for the vulnerable part, Ansgar had swept into her life with the force of a hurricane. Small wonder if her psyche was a bit battered.

She heard voices and took a cautious peek around the corner.

"Welcome, Mistress Viola," Ansgar said, opening the front door. "It is good to see you again."

Huh? The only Viola she knew was Viola Williams, who owned and operated the Sweet Shop Café and Grill with her husband, Delmonte. What the heck was she doing here and how did Ansgar know her?

The tramp of feet through the house sent her scrambling for her bedroom. Throwing on a clean dress, she followed the sound of voices into the kitchen, where she found Miss Vi setting out food.

Ansgar looked up when she came into the room. "Mistress Viola has brought us a bite to eat. That was gracious of her, was it not?"

Miss Viola plunked a platter of steaming ribs on the counter and gave Ansgar a playful scowl. "Most folks wouldn't call it a bite, but then most folks ain't seen you eat." She smiled at Evie, a wrinkle of concern marring her caramel forehead. "You all right, sugar? I heard about Meredith. That musta given you a turn, finding her this morning." She shook her head. "Lord knows she was a pill, but she didn't deserve that."

"No, she didn't." Evie's bewildered gaze moved around the kitchen. A gallon jar of sweet tea sat on the stove, and a pie rested on the counter beside the fragrant heap of ribs. She eyed the pie with interest. Sweets were her downfall. Coconut, lemon, or chocolate? she wondered. Impossible to tell for the thick layer of meringue on top, but it didn't matter. Whatever flavor, it would be yummy. Miss Vi was known for her pies—flakey, homemade crusts filled with rich, artery-clogging goo, topped off with lightly toasted, sugary meringue that melted on your tongue.

There was more food on the little table by the window. Platters of fried chicken and catfish, steaming bowls of collards, rutabagas, green beans with bits of ham hock, mashed potatoes, and a basket heaped with hot corn muffins.

"Miss Vi, what's this about? There's enough food here for a dozen people."

"I been worrying about you all day, ever since I heard the news," Miss Vi told Evie. "I was at the restaurant getting ready for the evening crowd when Addy and that good-looking feller of hers knocked on the back door and asked me to bring you something to eat."

"That was mighty nice of them, but this is too much." Evie shook her head. "My goodness, we'll never be able to eat all this."

"Huh," Miss Vi said. "Soon as I heard it was Brand's brother keeping an eye on you, I knew I'd better load up the van." She winked at Ansgar. "Them Dalvahni boys can eat. Ain't that right?"

"We do enjoy a good meal," Ansgar said. "And you, Mistress Viola, are well versed in the kitchen arts."

The warmth in Ansgar's glacial eyes when he looked at Miss Vi surprised Evie and made her feel the teensiest bit jealous. If the way to a man's heart was through his stomach, Miss Vi had bush-hogged a trail to Ansgar's ticker and paved that sucker flat.

Ansgar pulled a bunch of twenties out of a leather pouch. "Allow me to recompense you for your trouble."

Miss Vi flashed Evie a wide smile. "Ain't he something? I could listen to him all day. And not 'cause of the way he talks, all nice and formal, though I like that, too." She sighed. "It's that *voice*. It does things to a person, if you know what I mean."

Evie knew exactly what she meant. Ansgar Dalvahni was a sexy beast. Tall. Built like a freaking god. Inhumanly gorgeous and dripping testosterone. The kind of guy who made females swoon and ordinary men want to commit seppuku.

As if he didn't already have enough advantages, the cosmos gave him a honey and whiskey, dreamy smooth, sexy bedroom voice that would make an old maid schoolteacher dry-hump a bedpost.

Miss Viola seemed to collect herself. "Well, I'd best be getting back to the restaurant." She waved a hand at the table. "Ya'll enjoy. I would've brought more than one pie, but Addy was mos' particular about that. Said one oughta knock things loose, but two might cause trouble. Whatever that means."

Ansgar tried to hand Miss Vi the money again. "You must let me pay you."

She shooed him away. "No, no, that brother of yours has already taken care of it. Dang fool tried to give me a thousand dollars. A thousand dollars! He's a purty thing, but he ain't right, you know. No money sense a'tall. Kept handing me bills out that wallet like there ain't no tomorrow. Good thing I'm a Christian woman, or I could've took him to the cleaners." She pointed a finger at Ansgar's pouch. "And here you go trying to tempt me some more, you devil. Now, y'all eat 'fore it gets cold. Don't worry about the dishes. Evie can bring them by later."

Evie thanked her profusely and showed her to the door. She stood in the living room for a moment after the older woman left, her mind gnawing on Miss Vi's comment about Brand's never-ending wallet. There it was again, that eerie feeling of déjà vu. She seemed to be having those a lot lately. She frowned, concentrating on the shard of memory.

Something about a leather pouch like the one Ansgar had. A pouch that glowed

and . . .

The image dissolved and swirled away. Shaking her head, she wandered back into the kitchen, feeling dazed and disoriented. Her head throbbed. Too much had happened, too fast. She couldn't take it all in.

Ansgar stood by the table, waiting for her. There were plates and silverware on the table and glasses of iced tea. Mr. Gorgeous had been busy while she was gone. She didn't stop to wonder how he found everything. He was a supernatural hunter. Locating flatware and everyday dishes in a strange kitchen would be a piece of cake.

Her stomach fluttered. God, he made her nervous. What could she possibly have to say that would be of interest to a guy like him? She would bore him out of his skull.

Of course, he was more of a *doer* than a talker, wasn't he? She ought to know. A few minutes ago, she'd been naked and at the point of no return with a guy she hardly knew.

Soooo unlike her.

How was she going to sit across the table from him and make small talk?

Isn't this a lovely meal? Aren't the rutabagas delish? Oh, and by the way, thanks for almost doing me against the front door. That was the bomb. Best almost-lay I've had in . . . um . . . uh . . . let's see . . . EVER.

She had butterflies in her stomach the size of basketballs. Eating alone with him at her parents' table felt so intimate.

Oh, for Pete's sake, get over it. The guy practically did a lube job on you. How much more intimate can you get?

She shot him a timid smile that he did not return. And a good thing, too. His smiles turned her brain to goop. His voice turned her brain to goop, too. And his kiss, and . . .

Ratchet down the hormones and get a grip, sistah, or else it's Hoochie Mamas Anonymous, for you. Hello, I'm Evie Douglass and I'm a slut.

He pulled a chair out for her and took a seat opposite her.

"So, how do you know Miss Vi?" she asked. "I assumed this was your first time in Hannah."

"You assumed wrong. I have been here before with Brand in search of the djegrali."

"Really?" Evie frowned. "That's funny. You'd think we would have run into one another, huh?"

"Yes."

Yes what? she wanted to ask. Yes, we've met before, which would explain her maddening feelings of déjà vu, or yes, you'd think we'd have met. She opened her mouth to ask him exactly what that "yes" meant, but got sidetracked when he reached across the table, took her plate, and began to fill it.

She stared in alarm at the growing heap of food on her plate. "Whoa, slow down. I can't eat that much."

He handed her the plate loaded with chicken, catfish, and vegetables. "You need nourishment."

She unfolded her napkin and placed it in her lap. "If I eat all this, I'll blow up like a balloon. Besides, I'm not hungry."

"You will eat or I will feed you myself. You are too thin." He handed her a small bottle across the table. "Here, I almost forgot. This is for you."

"Texas Pete!" Removing the stopper from the bottle, she dumped hot sauce on her food. "I love—" She caught herself just in time. Good grief, she'd almost said *I love you.* Talk about sending a guy running for the hills. "I mean, I love it. I eat Texas Pete on almost everything. How did you know?"

"Mistress Viola told me." He pointed to her plate. "Now, take a bite of something. It matters not what."

"Bossy," she muttered, lifting a fork full of food to her mouth without looking at her plate.

The sharp, peppery taste of rutabagas flavored with bacon tickled her tongue. Miss Vi cooked only the best, freshest produce, and she never loaded her vegetables with sugar like some Southern cooks.

Suddenly, Evie was ravenous. She took a bite of the fish. Salted, dredged in cornmeal, and fried hard. The flaky, white flesh beneath the crust was piping hot. Yum.

She took another bite and then another. She was too thin. Ansgar said so. Too thin! She was going to eat, and for once her brain could shut up and let her mouth rejoice.

She finished the fish and picked up a chicken leg. Golden-brown crust seasoned to perfection, and beneath all that crunchy goodness, tender, flavorful dark meat. She alternated bites of chicken with the mashed potatoes. No instant taters for Miss Vi. Her mashed potatoes were the real thing, made with butter, whole milk, and a touch of mayonnaise to make them extra creamy.

She buttered a corn muffin, sprinkled it with Texas Pete, and gobbled it down. It tasted so good she ate another. What the heck. Then she moved on to the collards, spiced up with Creole seasoning, a splash of apple cider vinegar, and more Texas Pete. Belatedly, she realized she hadn't tried the green beans. Heaven forbid that she insult the green bean god. She shook some Texas Pete on the beans and ate them, too. She couldn't remember the last time she'd eaten so much.

Funny thing, she didn't feel full. Better stop anyway or she'd be miserable in thirty minutes.

She dabbed her mouth with her napkin and sat back. To her shock, the food on the table was gone. Nothing left on the platters but a few chicken bits and a sprinkling of cornmeal crumbs. She checked out the rib tray. Empty except for the bones. Nada in the vegetable dishes, either, unless you counted a smear of mashed potatoes and a couple of lonely green beans swimming in a pool of pot liquor. A few strands of greens slimed the side of the collard bowl. No bread in the bread basket. The bottle of Texas Pete had been drained.

She jumped to her feet. "What happened to all the food?"

Ansgar wiped his hands. "We ate it. It was delicious, was it not?"

Evie stared at her plate. Good Lord, there were *six* chicken bones on her plate and the skeletons of *four* whole catfish.

The pile of leavings on Ansgar's plate was much bigger. But he was a warrior with warrior-size muscles. Blink his eyelids a couple of extra times and he'd burn a zillion calories. But she wouldn't. One dive into the ice cream container and she gained weight.

Stunned, Evie sat back down. She'd just consumed her caloric intake for a week. A cow couldn't eat as much as she had, and a cow had four stomachs.

Of course, a cow wouldn't eat chicken or fish . . . unless it was a carnivorous cow with big pointy teeth.

But that was beside the point. She'd pay for this little binge for months. Nothing but twigs and leaves from now on chased down with a little water. Nothing but—

"Dessert?" Ansgar said, offering her a slab of pie as big as her head.

She started to shake her head and hesitated. It was chocolate pie, her favorite. She could smell the sugar. The layer of meringue on top was a thing of beauty, a light brown swirl of deliciousness, like toasted marshmallow.

She wanted that pie. She wanted it something ferocious.

Was it her imagination, or was there a twinkle of amusement in Ansgar's eyes? Like he knew she had a weakness for sweets, darn him.

To heck with it. She'd tote her butt around in a wheelbarrow if she had to.

She was eating her some pie.

Chapter Ten

Evie took the plate from Ansgar, the scents of chocolate and sugar teasing her nose. She sliced off the pointy end of the triangle of pie with her fork and put the first bite in her mouth. The meringue was lighter than air and melted in her mouth. Beneath that, a sinfully good, dark chocolate filling and firm crust. All that chocolate-wonderfulness shot to her brain and bathed her whole body in feel-good. Serotonin City; the bottoms of her feet tingled and little goose bumps popped out on her skin.

This wasn't pie. This was a mini mouth orgasm. Hot damn, this pie was *good,* worth every fat-inducing, thigh-enlarging calorie.

She took another bite, savoring it. Man-oh-man-oh-man. Bliss on a fork. She felt better already. She felt drunk off that pie. All her cares and troubles drifted away, leaving her feeling light as a feather, brimming with joy and good cheer.

She loved pie. She loved everybody and everything.

"It is good, is it not?" Ansgar said, sucker-punching her with a smile.

The combination of that sexy smile and the pie made her giddy. "It's wonderful. The most wonderful-est, splendid-est pie ever. I love it."

"I thought you would like it. You look a little woozy. Are you sure you are feeling well?"

"I feel fi-nah." The words came out in a drawl. "Better than fine, actually. I feel hornier than a four-balled tomcat." She giggled and slapped her hand over her mouth. "Oops, did I say that out loud?"

"Yes, you did." He regarded her across the table with eyes like molten silver. "I can help you with that."

"Help me with what?" She looked down at her plate. No more pie. "It's gone."

"Evangeline?"

She blinked at him across the table. "Yes?"

"Come here."

She got up from her chair, went around the table, and sat in his lap. Hard to believe her temerity, but who could resist that bedroom voice?

He put one hand around her waist and the other on her thigh. She could feel the heat of his skin through his jeans. In her haste to get dressed, she'd put on a sundress with a deep square neckline and no sleeves. A garment she wore to work in the garden but never in public because it showed too much cleavage.

She wasn't wearing a bra, she remembered suddenly. It made her feel wicked and sensuous, instead of self-conscious. Evie Douglass, wild woman. Her skin seemed more sensitive, and she was intensely aware of the brush of her nipples against the cotton bodice of her dress, the solid, unyielding granite of Ansgar's powerful legs beneath her, the tickle of her still damp hair across her shoulders.

He bent his head close to hers. "Kiss me," he said in his silk and smoke voice. "And you can have the last piece of pie."

"What if I don't want any more pie?"

"Kiss me anyway, Evangeline. Please."

She shouldn't kiss him, she really shouldn't. She knew better. Kissing Ansgar made her brain shut off and her hootie fire up.

She did it anyway. He *did* use the magic word, and good manners should be rewarded.

He tasted hot and fragrant with spices, better than any dessert. His tongue brushed hers and she shivered. She ran her hands across his powerful shoulders, thick and ropey with muscle. He was so strong, his muscular body hard and unyielding as sculpted stone. She wanted to rub herself all over him like a cat. Kiss and lick him from head to toe.

He muttered something rough and guttural, and dragged his mouth down her neck in a lingering trail of openmouthed kisses. She leaned back, offering herself to him. He nuzzled her nipple through the fabric of her dress, and she went still, her breath hitching in her throat. The heat of his mouth, the pull of his lips and tongue against the wet fabric, sent fluttering waves of sensation to the pit of her stomach. He slipped his hand beneath her dress and caressed the sensitive skin between her thighs. Little swirls of temptation that made her go boneless with longing.

His hand crept higher, to the edge of her panties. She tensed, breathless, waiting for his fingers to push aside the worn elastic of her plain cotton briefs and touch her *there*.

Except she wasn't wearing any panties, granny or otherwise, she realized with a dim sense of shock.

No bra *and* no panties? What the heck was the matter with her? She'd never gone commando in her life. After twenty-eight years of strapping the girls down and girding her loins, how did she all of a sudden forget to put on her drawers?

"Open your legs," he murmured against her breast. "Let me touch you."

The old Evie would never let a guy she hardly knew touch her hoo hah. The old Evie wasn't on speaking terms with her inner slut, but now they were best buds.

She opened her legs, wanting him, eager for him. His hand slid closer to the throbbing place between her thighs. Not there. Not yet, but close . . . so close. He was teasing her, and it was downright cruel.

She arched against him, pushing against him, seeking release. His fingers flicked the sensitive flesh, and she shattered.

She floated back from rapture to the sound of Ansgar calling her name.

"Evangeline."

She opened her eyes. She was still in his arms. Her head lolled against his shoulder and her dress was hiked up. She blushed and tugged the sundress down to her knees. Shameless.

He looked down at her, a gleam of satisfaction in his eyes. "We have company. And whoever it is, they are most insistent."

"What?" Evie sat up and pushed the hair out of her eyes. It was hard to think through the *"oh, my God, I just came, and man, oh man, was it great"* fog that clouded her brain, but gradually it dawned on her that someone was pounding on the front door. "I guess I'd better go see who it is."

"I will go," Ansgar said. He lifted her out of his lap and stood up. The insistent knocking continued from the front of the house. Someone *really* wanted to see her. "There may be trouble."

"You mean a demon." Evie shook her head in disbelief. "I seriously doubt there's a demon on my front porch."

"You can never be too careful when dealing with the dje-grali. It could be someone you know, someone you trust, who has been possessed by one of the fiends. The djegrali are very clever and take many forms."

Evie's memories of the demon attack came back in a rush, the black mist creeping under the bathroom windowsill, the suffocating mind-numbing terror when the demon reached for her. She remembered throwing her arms up to ward off the evil thing . . . and then she was in Ansgar's arms.

Why would a demon come for her? She was a nobody, no money, no family, no power. It didn't make sense.

"So, what are you going to do if it is a demon?" she asked.

"Destroy it," Ansgar said, striding out of the kitchen.

Destroy it? Evie hurried after him. She caught up with him in the dining room and stepped in front of him, barring his way.

"Wait." She placed her hand on his broad chest. "I know more about demons than you may think. My best friend's engaged to a demon hunter, remember? I know Hannah's demon central, although no one really knows *why*. I know demons sometimes possess humans, use their poor bodies until there's nothing left, and then toss them aside like so much garbage and look for another victim." She gazed up at him, trying to assess his reaction. His expression was hard as granite. He didn't get it. How to make him understand? Taking a deep breath, she tried again. "I know about the demonoids—people in Hannah who are part demon, part human."

"Addy told you this?"

"Yes, although she didn't tell me who they are. She wanted to, but I wouldn't let her. I don't want to know that about people . . . to look at them differently, to be *afraid* of them."

"Ignorance is not a shield that will protect you."

"You assume that demonoids are bad, but you don't *know* it."

"The djegrali are concentrated evil," he said. "They thrive on mischief and creating havoc. It is what they do. Their accursed offspring are evil, too. It is the nature of the beast. Conall, our leader, has ordered us to wait, else Brand and I would have hunted the vermin down and destroyed the lot of them, like the vipers they are."

"But don't you see? They can't help it, none of them can. Not the ones who are possessed or their children. I *know* these people. I know their families. So, whoever is at the door, you can't hurt them. Promise me."

"No."

"You can't go around killing people willy nilly," Evie cried. "This is a small town. These are my *friends*."

"I will do what I must to protect you."

He pushed her aside, crossed the living room, and opened the door. Sheriff Whitsun stood on the porch. He and Ansgar exchanged silent, hostile stares, two alpha males sizing each other up. The testosterone in the air was so thick you could chop it with an ax.

"What do you want?" Ansgar said at last.

Some of Evie's tension evaporated. The sheriff had passed a test, although he didn't know it. If he was a demon or a demonoid, Ansgar would skewer him with the nearest sharp object, not glower at the poor man. It was going to be okay.

"Sheriff Whitsun, what an . . . uh . . . unexpected surprise." Evie squeezed past Ansgar, who was blocking the door. "What brings you here?"

"We found a bloody knife on the front seat of your car." The sheriff held up a piece of paper. The words *warrant of arrest* danced before Evie's eyes. "Sarah Evangeline Douglass, you're under arrest for the murder of Meredith Peterson."

The heavy metal door of the Behr County Jail slammed shut behind Evie with a hollow *clang*. Panic clawed at her chest and sapped the strength from her legs, leaving them shaky and weak. Would this nightmare of a day never end? She'd been booked, photographed, and fingerprinted, and now she was about to be locked up in jail. And she wasn't wearing panties or a bra.

Oh. God.

If Addy's mother found out she'd left the house without her drawers, Evie's un-underweared behind would be in big trouble. Bitsy Corwin was a tsunami on two legs who swept over everyone and everything in her path. Elegant, soft spoken, a will of steel encased in a petite, well-dressed form. Addy and Evie—as Addy's best friend—were her pet projects, and Bitsy had been trying for years to mold them into her vision of the perfect Southern lady.

There were a lot of rules in the Bitsy universe, and a number of them pertained to undergarments. As in wear them. Lecture eighteen: *Always wear clean panties and a bra in case you get in a wreck.* And lecture eight—or was it seven?—*always wear panties and a bra.* Period.

The Rule of Proper Coverage was high on the Bitsy List, definitely in the top ten. And Evie was in flagrant violation.

"This way," the sheriff said, recalling her from her thoughts.

He marched her deeper into the bowels of the old building. The strong odor of Pine-Sol assaulted her nose, and beneath that she detected the smells of damp stone, sweat, vomit, and urine. Chanel Number 5 it was *not*. On the positive side, crime in Behr County must be down, because most of the holding units were empty.

"Been a slow week so far," he said, as if reading her mind. "Burglary, car theft, public drunkenness. Nothing exciting. Until you, that is. You've caused quite a stir."

"Gee, glad to liven things up for you."

"Yep, the whole courthouse is buzzing about the Peterson case. Sex and violence always make tongues wag."

Reading between the lines, people were saying she was a husband-stealing 'ho and a murderess. Wonderful. Another milestone for her memory book.

Several male inmates made catcalls and lewd gestures as Evie passed their cells. She slid them a nervous glance and walked faster.

A man with thinning slicked-back hair and stained teeth, compliments of Skoal, pushed his face against the bars and waggled his tongue at Evie. "Hey, sweet tits, come to Papa."

She scurried down the hall, looking back when she heard a startled grunt. The man was lifted by unseen hands and flung across the cell. He smashed into the wall and slid to the floor in a groaning heap.

Sheriff Whitsun observed this bit of strangeness without expression. "Your invisible friend has quite the temper on him, doesn't he?"

Evie did not respond. What could she say? Thanks to the little stunt Ansgar had pulled earlier this afternoon, the sheriff knew firsthand that demon hunters existed in Behr County. One moment she'd been standing at her front door, her shocked gaze glued to the arrest warrant in Sheriff Whitsun's hand. The next moment she was standing in the woods beside the river with Ansgar's arms wrapped around her.

It had been very peaceful there. The wind sighed through the leaves in gentle accompaniment to the rush and burble of a nearby waterfall. She'd been tempted to stay—oh, so tempted— or to run and never stop.

She'd convinced him to take her back, though she had a dickens of a time doing it. She had an even harder time explaining her little disappearing act to the sheriff.

Who was she kidding? She hadn't explained it at all. Who

could explain a thing like that? Sheriff Whitsun was still standing on the porch when she'd popped back into view, looking remarkably unruffled for an officer whose suspect had just vanished before his eyes.

"Let me take a wild guess," he'd said when she reappeared. "This Ansgar fellow is the demon hunter you told me about."

"Yes," Evie said, taking a lesson in brevity from a certain warrior.

"Where is he now?"

"I don't know."

"Uh huh," the sheriff said, disbelief evident on his face.

Whitsun was no fool. He bundled her into his patrol car without another word and drove her to the station in Paulsberg. He kept checking his rearview mirror every so often, though, like he knew he'd picked up an invisible hitchhiker.

Knowing Ansgar was in the backseat with her had kept Evie from dissolving into hysterics during the long drive from Hannah to Paulsberg, even though she couldn't see him.

He was here with her now, in the jailhouse, walking behind her. She couldn't see him, but she could *smell* him—the guy smelled like four kinds of wonderful—and she could feel the heat radiating from his big body.

Judging from the way the sheriff acted, he knew Ansgar was there, too. Whitsun didn't say anything, but his nostrils flared, and several times he stared directly at the spot where Ansgar stood.

At the end of the narrow, dreary hall, the sheriff opened the door to a small cell and motioned her inside. The county must have gotten a dandy of a deal on industrial gray paint, because the whole sheriff's department was one big ball of blah. Her cell consisted of more gray blah, a narrow bed, and a toilet without a lid.

Her cell. Oh, God, this could not be happening.

The hard line of the sheriff's jaw softened. "With any luck, you won't be here long."

"The bond is seventy-five thousand dollars," Evie said

glumly. "It might as well be seventy-five million. I don't have that kind of money."

"Just so you know, that wasn't my doing. All I asked for was fifteen thousand dollars."

"Thanks, Sheriff."

"Don't thank me. I didn't do it for you. I don't consider you a flight risk, that's all. The magistrate had a different opinion, for some strange reason. I couldn't convince him otherwise." His expression tightened. "There's something mighty peculiar going on here, Ms. Douglass. I searched your car myself first thing this morning, and there was nothing in it. Then, like magic, this afternoon we find a bloody knife on the front seat." His gray gaze was hard as flint. "I get the feeling somebody's dicking with me, and I don't like it. Not one little bit. And, for the record, I don't think you killed Meredith Peterson."

"You don't?"

"No, I don't," he said. "But that won't amount to a hill of beans in court, especially if that knife turns out to be the murder weapon. Can you think of anyone who hates you enough to frame you for murder?"

"No. Don't you think I'd tell you if I did?"

"Yeah, I reckon you would at that. Tell your boyfriend to come talk to me when he gets a chance. Maybe we can put our heads together and figure this thing out."

"He's not my boyfr—"

The door clanked shut and Evie was alone. At least, she thought she was alone.

"Ansgar?" she whispered.

No answer.

She sat on the edge of the lumpy cot, her knees pressed together, her hands clasped tightly in her lap, and contemplated this unlikely turn of events.

Evie Douglass, the rule follower, the perennial good girl, had gotten her first conduct check, and it was a doozy.

She was the prime suspect in Meredith's murder, and a bloody knife had been found in her car.

She might not be the sharpest crayon in the box, but she had enough sense to know when she was being set up. Mr. Malevolent wasn't satisfied with killing Meredith. He was out to destroy her as well. And doing a bang-up job of it. Why he'd zeroed in on her, Evie had no clue.

The creepy whatzit wasn't her only problem. The Petersons were probably behind the high bail the magistrate had set. They had a lot of pull in Behr County. Meredith had been a bitch walking, but she was Trey's wife and the Petersons always presented a united front.

That left her with pure evil on one side and old money on the other. She didn't know which was worse. The knowledge should have frightened her. She should be a lump of jelly now, trembling with terror, her brain locked in an endless cycle of *ohcrapohcrapohcrap.*

But she wasn't scared. She was pissed.

It took her a while to recognize the feeling. She couldn't remember being pissed before. Hurt, ashamed, embarrassed, and a full spectrum of other emotions, but never pissed. Being pissed required a certain amount of self-esteem, a confidence that you deserved better, that you mattered. How could you matter if you were invisible?

She wasn't invisible anymore, that was for sure. Talk about your coming-out parties. This one was *big.* Little Evie Douglass was going to be front-page news.

Ansgar materialized in the cell without warning. His sudden appearance startled Evie, but she was so tired she didn't jump. Murder, binge eating, sexual bliss, exhaustion, being arrested, cuffed, and hauled to jail, all in the course of one day, would do that to a girl.

He handed her a small overnight bag. "I brought you some clothes. Adara helped me with the selection. I hope they are suitable."

"Thanks." Evie checked the contents of the bag: a new toothbrush and toothpaste, deodorant, a package of premoistened face wipes, a pair of baggy sweats, clean underwear, a bra, a pair of warm socks, and her favorite ratty old tennis shoes. Score. She clutched the small case to her bosom. "Turn around, please, so I can change."

Ansgar complied. "I have checked the building and the perimeter," he said over his shoulder. "I do not sense the presence of the djegrali."

"Oh, goodie." Evie quickly undressed and scrambled into the clean clothes. There. Loins firmly girded. Miss Bitsy would be proud. She shoved her dress and sandals into the empty bag. "You can turn around now," she said, placing the tennis shoes on the floor at the end of the bed. "I'm done."

Ansgar turned back around. "Evangeline, let me help you." There was concern and a touch of impatience in his voice. He was frustrated with her, and she didn't blame him. "Say the word and I will take you from this place."

"That's sweet, Ansgar, but I'm not running."

He picked her up and sat down on the narrow bed with her in his lap. "I admire your courage, sweetling, but sometimes the wisest course is to withdraw and regroup until you better know your enemy."

"If I run, then whoever's doing this wins. That's not going to happen," she said. "Besides, Mr. Collier is my lawyer now. He'll help me."

Addy had shown up at the jail with Mr. Collier in tow as soon as she'd heard the news that Evie had been arrested. Mr. C was a lawyer and an old friend, the fiancé of Addy's great-aunt Muddy. He was also the town drunk, or had been until a few months ago. Turned out Mr. Collier had the Eye, which meant he could see demons and other supernatural creatures. For the past thirty years, he'd thought he was crazy, and drinking had been his way of tuning out the woo woo. Until recently, that is. The arrival of the Dalvahni in Hannah and the increase in demonic activity had finally convinced Mr. Collier of his sanity, and he quit drinking.

She leaned her head against Ansgar's shoulder. He was so strong and calm. After being alone for so many years, it felt wonderful to have someone to rely upon, even if only for a little while. She could get addicted to this. She could get addicted to *him*. Maybe she already was.

"Sometimes, it stinks not having a family," she said.

"Humans set great store by the familial unit, do they not?"

"Yeah. Don't the Dalvahni?"

"The Dal do not have matriarchal or patriarchal units as humans do, though our loyalty to our brother warriors is strong."

Evie processed this. "No mother or father?"

"No."

"What about a home?"

"We abide in the Hall of Warriors when we are not hunting the djegrali."

"That doesn't sound very comfy."

He shrugged. "It suits our purpose."

Evie tried to imagine what it must have been like for him and failed. No mother. No father. No real home. No love or warmth, only duty and the Dalvahni creed.

"So, you're an orphan, like me."

"Yes, I suppose you could say that." His arms tightened around her. "What happened to your loved ones?"

"My mom died of cancer when I was eleven, and my dad drank himself to death after—"

She stopped.

"After . . . ?" he urged gently.

Evie inhaled deeply. A gaping hole yawned before her, a subject so raw, so painful, she never spoke of it, not even to Addy—the thing that had broken her family to bits and changed her life forever. She'd buried the pain deep, and so had her dad. They never talked about it after her mother died. Not talking about it had been a relief. Most days she could ignore it, but she couldn't forget it. It was a little black spot, a sore, aching place on her soul that never healed.

"I had an older sister," she said. Her voice shook. "Her name was Savannah. She disappeared when she was fifteen. We never saw her again. A year after her disappearance, the Virginia police arrested a guy on kidnapping charges. When they executed a search warrant on the man's house, they found Savannah's picture among his things. He confessed to killing her."

The temperature in the room lowered abruptly, and the ghostly form of a slender blond woman solidified in front of Evie.

"Well, boo hoo for the Whale," the ghost said. "Like I give a flying monkey shit about your pathetic little life when I've been *murdered*."

Chapter Eleven

"*Meredith.*" Evie jumped to her feet. "Holy smokes, you're dead! What are you doing here?"

Meredith rocked the whole ghost thing, Evie had to admit. She looked good. Better than good. No blood or oozing stab wounds. No gore-stained clothes. The Death Starr's stylish, gray floral sheath dress was belted at the waist and topped off with an elegant cashmere sweater. Black peep-toe stiletto pumps with fire-engine red soles encased her size-five feet. Her sleek golden bob teased her jaw line, not a hair out of place. Evie glanced down at her rumpled sweats, feeling suddenly self-conscious. Good grief, Meredith was a better dresser than she was, and Meredith was *dead*.

Meredith's lip curled. "I'm haunting your fat ass, that's what. You didn't think I'd let you get away with it, did you?"

"Get away with what?"

"Killing me, you porker. What do you think?"

"I didn't kill you," Evie protested.

"Oh, yeah?" Meredith looked around. "Then why are you in jail, Lumpy? I may be dead, but I'm not stupid."

Ansgar rose to his feet with a frown. "She speaks the truth, shade. She did not slay you."

Meredith's laser-beam gaze shifted from Evie to him. "Who's the beefcake?"

"Oh . . . uh . . . this is Ansgar," Evie said, remembering her manners.

"Hmm." Meredith's predatory gaze roamed over Ansgar's hard-muscled frame. "You look familiar. Do I know you?"

"No," Ansgar said.

"Meredith was Trey's wife," Evie said, shooting the Death Starr a nervous glance. "Before . . . uh . . . you know."

"I'm still his wife," Meredith snapped. "The only one he'll ever have. You'll remember that, Lard-o, if you know what's good for you."

Ansgar rumbled something in warning, but Evie barely flinched. After more than fifteen years of Meredith's abuse, she was used to it.

"Like I told you the other day, Meredith, I am *not* having an affair with Trey."

"Liar. Every female in town wants Trey, especially you, Tubby. You've been sniffing around him for years. Like any man, especially my Trey, would be interested in such a gross, disgusting—"

"Enough." Ansgar gave Meredith a cold glare. "You will be silent."

Meredith propped her hands on her trim hips. "Oh, yeah? Make me, asshole."

"With pleasure."

Ansgar snapped his fingers and an ornate perfume bottle appeared in his hand. He removed the crystal stopper and pointed the open mouth of the bottle at Meredith. The Death Starr's body stretched, growing thin and smoky.

"Hey, *hey*," Meredith wailed. Her face sagged and her eyes melted into blue oval smears. "What do you think you're doooo—"

Her words faded to a shrill moan of despair as her wispy form was sucked into the glass container.

Ansgar slammed the stopper back in place. "There. By the gods, I despise her shrewish tongue."

Evie stared at the crystal container in his hand. "You put Meredith in a perfume bottle."

He gave her an aggrieved look. "It is not a perfume bottle.

It is a djeval flaske, a special container used by the Dalvahni to transport demons." He shrugged. "Demons and ghosts are amorphous beings, so I reasoned it should work on both. My assumption was correct, I am happy to say." He handed her the bottle. "Here, see for yourself. But for pity's sake, do not let her out. I would take a battle-ax to the head rather than listen to any more of her raving."

The bottle was made of curved blue glass bound in gold scrollwork at the rounded base. A mini Death Starr stood at the bottom of the flask. She shook a tiny manicured finger at Evie and kicked the side of the bottle with her shoe.

Ansgar looked pleased with himself. "An improvement, is it not?"

"Oh, yeah," Evie said with a slow smile.

She gave the bottle a little shake. She knew it was mean, but she couldn't resist. Meredith staggered on her high heels like a drunk on a two-week bender. It was like watching an ant do the jitterbug.

Evie giggled. "Where were you when I was in the seventh grade? I could have used one of these for real."

"A djeval flaske does not work on humans, Evangeline."

"Oh, well. A girl can dream. Think of it. Bully in a Jar. It's perfect."

Evie heard an angry buzzing noise and looked down at the bottle. Meredith had her face pushed against the glass. Her lips moved, but Evie couldn't tell what she was saying. Judging from the Death Starr's expression, that was a good thing.

"Shoot." Evie sighed. "I guess we better let her out."

"No," Ansgar said. "I forbid it. It is bad enough you insist on spending the night in this accursed jail without suffering that harridan."

"You don't have to stay with me, you know." Evie kept her gaze fastened on Mini Meredith, afraid that if she looked at Ansgar he would see how much she wanted him to stay. "I'll be fine."

Ansgar tugged her into his arms. "I will not leave you."

"I'm glad," she whispered. She relaxed against him, soaking up his warmth. "I know it's selfish of me, but I want you to stay."

"It is a good thing you want me. I would not leave you, in any event."

The bottle in her hand vibrated.

"Oh, my goodness!" Evie stepped back. "I forgot about poor Meredith."

"She is not 'poor Meredith.' She is a harpy. You are too tender hearted, Evangeline."

"I think she must be very unhappy on a basic level to be such a bitch. Besides, we can't keep her like this forever."

"Why not?"

"Because it's mean. And because she's already had a really bad day, getting murdered, and all." Evie stilled as her exhausted brain put the pieces together. "Oh, my goodness! Why didn't I think of this before? Meredith can tell us who murdered her!"

"She thinks *you* murdered her, remember?" Ansgar said.

"But I didn't! We have to try and convince her otherwise."

"Why do you care what a ghost thinks?"

"I don't. Well . . . okay, I care a little. But here's the point. Maybe, if she concentrates, she can remember something that will lead us to the real murderer."

"Doubtful," Ansgar said. "Nor do I think she will be inclined to cooperate. She is a most unpleasant creature."

"Please, Ansgar."

He sighed. "Very well, if you insist. Release the hag."

Evie removed the stopper from the bottle, and Meredith's ghost flowed out in a smoky stream and took shape.

She glared at Ansgar. "I'm going to get you for this. You'll be sorry you ever messed with me." She rounded on Evie. "That goes double for you, Jell-O Butt."

"Guard your tongue, she devil," Ansgar said, "or you go back in the bottle."

"Don't you dare! I'll suffocate."

"You cannot suffocate," Ansgar said. "You are already dead."

Meredith stiffened in outrage. "Of all the insensitive—"

Evie cleared her throat. "Uh . . . speaking of death, Meredith, we were hoping you could tell us who killed you."

Meredith rolled her eyes. "Is your head as fat as your ass, nitwit? *Helloo. You* killed me."

"No, I didn't," Evie said. "Honest."

Meredith frowned. "Then who did?"

Bing! A bell chimed and a pudgy, middle-aged man with doughy features materialized. A narrow peninsula of mousy brown hair ran down the middle of his balding head. He wore brown dress slacks, a pin-stripe dress shirt, and a pair of thick-soled, black orthopedic lace-ups. His shirt was open at the neck and his sleeves were rolled up. He held a pen in one hand and a notepad in the other.

"Who are you?" Ansgar demanded.

The ghost blinked at Ansgar from behind a pair of bifocals. "I'm Leonard Swink, a licensed professional counselor. I'm here to see Mrs. Peterson."

"Buzz off, Tinker Bell. Can't you see I'm in the middle of a haunting?"

"But we have an appointment." Swink gave Meredith a bland smile. "Don't you remember?"

"Hell no, I don't remember, you sawed-off rabbit turd. I don't need therapy. Go away."

"Foul language, denial, and hostility." Swink *tsked* and jotted something down on the notepad. "This is worse than I thought."

Meredith gave the therapist the evil eye. "What's that supposed to mean?"

"You've had a psychotic break, Mrs. Peterson," Swink said. "PTDD, we call it in my profession. You need extensive therapy, if you expect a fully realized afterlife."

"What is this PTDD?" Ansgar asked.

Swink stuck his pen in his pocket. It leaked, leaving a blue blob on the front of his shirt. He didn't seem to notice. "Post traumatic death disorder," he said. "Mrs. Peterson is a classic case. She died suddenly and violently, and is having difficulty adjusting to her new station."

"I'm *dead,* not starting a new job, dickwad." Meredith's narrow-eyed glare roved over Swink. "Your shoes are ugly."

"More hostility." Swink shook his head. "I see I have my work cut out for me. Why don't we go to my office, Mrs. Peterson? We can have our first session there."

"She can't remember who killed her," Evie blurted. "Is that normal with PTDD?"

The expression on Swink's round face brightened. "You're saying she has deathnesia? My, this *is* an interesting case." He took out his pen and scratched a few more notes on the pad. "The trauma can manifest itself in many ways, certainly, but deathnesia is unusual. Fascinating."

Meredith waved her hand in his face. "I'm right here, Tweedle Dee. Stop talking about me like I don't exist."

"Well, technically speaking, you don't exist, at least in a corporeal sense," Swink told Meredith. "You are no longer alive, after all."

Meredith rolled her eyes. "OMG, you figured out I'm dead. What a genius. I bet I can guess what happened to *you.* You starved to death from lack of patients, you lame-ass psychobabbling numb nuts."

Swink's cherubic face creased in a slight frown. "Increased manifestation of verbal abuse." He dotted something down on the paper. "Likely a defensive reaction with roots in patient's confusion and anger relating to premature demise."

"Oh, no, Doctor Swink," Evie said without thinking. "Meredith was pretty much the same way when she was alive."

"Shove it, Buffalo Butt," Meredith snarled.

Evie offered Swink an apologetic smile. "See, same old Meredith. She cusses more, that's all. I think she's frustrated."

"Frustrated?" Meredith's voice went up a notch. "You bet your plus-sized ass I'm frustrated. This morning, I had a life. I was president-elect of the Lala Lavender League. I had a husband, a nice car, a seven-thousand-square-foot home on the river, and another house at the beach." She pointed a finger at her chest. "*I* had an appointment with Jerome at Shear Ecstasy in Mobile next week. Next *week.* Do you have any idea how hard it is to get an appointment with *Jerome?*"

Ansgar frowned. "Who is this Jerome?"

"I think he must be a hair dresser," Evie said.

"Not a hair dresser, you freak. Shear Ecstasy ain't a frigging beauty parlor. It's a salon." Meredith's voice got louder. "Jerome is a *stylist.* He used to do Reba McEntire's hair. Women wait for months, for *years* even, to get an appointment with this guy. He's a freaking hair god. But he's not going to be doing *my* hair, because I'm dead."

Swink tucked his notepad under his arm. "Come along, Mrs. Peterson. The sooner we start our sessions, the sooner you can achieve self-actualization and a healthy afterlife."

"Chew me, dough boy. I'm not going anywhere with you. I don't need a therapist."

"Enough!" Ansgar scowled at Meredith. "You will go with Swink and you will cooperate in these so-called sessions. When you have recovered your memory, you will return and tell us the identity of your killer, so that we may extricate Evangeline from this coil."

Meredith's eyes narrowed to slits of pure evil. "Like I give a Technicolor fart what happens to her. I'm *dead,* and that really pisses me off."

"Heed my warning, shade." Ansgar's voice was cold as arctic tundra. "There are worse things than being dead. If Evangeline comes to harm because of your spite, I will hunt you down and rend your hateful spirit into nothingness."

Evie put her hand on his arm. "Ansgar, please. She can't help it."

Meredith bristled. "Save your pity for yourself, Jumbotron. I'd rather be dead than be you."

Swink stuck his notepad under his arm. "I cannot work in such a negative atmosphere. Mrs. Peterson, if you wish to continue this session, it will have to be in my office."

Bing! The bell chimed again and Swink disappeared.

Meredith straightened her shoulders. "I'll do it, but not because you threatened me and not to help *her*. I'll do it for Trey, because if Elephant Ass didn't kill me then whoever did is still out there, and I don't want my Treyzy Wazzy hurt." Her blazing gaze shifted to Evie. "In the meantime, stay away from my husband, you pathetic whorebag heifer, or I'm gonna make the Amityville horror look like a Disney movie."

With that final venomous parting shot, Meredith disappeared, too.

Chapter Twelve

"Good riddance," Ansgar said when Meredith had gone. "Of all the poisonous creatures I have ever encountered, she is undoubtedly the worst. Medusa was a girl in braids by comparison."

"That's why we call her the Death Starr." Evie's eyes widened as the meaning of his words sank in. "Wait a minute . . . *Medusa?* You mean the chick with the snakes coming out of her head? Are you saying she was *real?*"

"Of a certainty. She was a beautiful woman until she was possessed by one of the djegrali. I was with Perseus the day he slew her."

"You were with . . ." Evie stared at him. "How old *are* you, anyway?"

"Ten thousand of your years, give or take a few centuries." He gave her an odd look. "Addy did not tell you this? I thought you knew of the Dalvahni."

"She told me some stuff, but—" Evie stopped as a memory flickered through her mind. She was sitting at a table in the Sweet Shop. Ansgar was there, and Brand and Addy. *Ten thousand years without chocolate . . . that's harsh* she heard Addy say before the sliver of memory faded. Evie shook her head. "I recall her saying something about it, but the way I remember it, you were there. And that's not possible, is it?" She rubbed her throbbing temples. No, please, God, not another headache. "Sometimes I feel like I'm losing my mind."

"You are not losing your mind." Ansgar picked her up and deposited her on the bed. "You are weary, that is all. You need rest. Go to sleep."

She spread the thin blanket over her legs and feet. "I don't think I can. Too much has happened. My brain's going ninety to nothing." She looked up at him. "What about you?"

"What about me?"

"Are you staying?"

"Yes."

"But, you'll be uncomfortable."

"Evangeline, I have slept in the rain and snow, on rocks and sand, and in the mud. This place is warm and dry, a palace in comparison to some of the places I have stayed while in pursuit of the djegrali. I will be fine."

Some of Evie's tension evaporated. He was going to stay. She'd been afraid he would change his mind; that she'd have to do this alone. *Don't get used to it,* her wiser self warned. *He's a demon hunter and a heartbreaker. He won't be around forever.* But she was frightened and exhausted, heartsick from her roller coaster of a day. *You can pretend he's staying. Just for a little while,* she promised herself. *Just one night.*

"But the guards . . . what if they see you?"

His sexy mouth curved in amusement. "Have you learned nothing about demon hunters?"

He vanished.

"Oh, I get it." Evie clutched the blanket, feeling foolish. "You'll be invisible. But, you'll be here, right?" She sounded needy, but she didn't care. She didn't want to be alone, especially tonight. "Ansgar?"

"I am here." He spoke from the end of the bed. "Would you like me to hold you?"

Like it? Her brain screamed *yes, yes, yes,* though the best she could manage was a nod of agreement. She scooted to the edge of the bed, turning on her side to give him more room. The mattress dipped as he eased his big body onto the little cot. A pair of strong, invisible arms wrapped around her, pulling her to safety, just as they had this morning. He tugged her against him until they rested spoon fashion. His body heat enveloped her, melting the ball of stress inside her.

"I will not leave you," he breathed against her ear. "Go to sleep."

She snuggled closer and closed her eyes. She was tired, so very tired, but the events of the day kept playing over and over inside her head. The scene in her office, the malignant thing in the room with her that morning, Meredith's tortured body . . .

Her eyes flew open. "I can't. I'm too wound up."

"Then we must unwind you."

To her surprise, Ansgar began to sing to her softly in a language she did not recognize. He had a beautiful tenor, smoky and rich, full of sensual promise. His voice wrapped around her and filled the little room with swirls of color; purples, pinks, blues, and greens. He was a sorcerer, with a sorcerer's voice, full of magic and power.

His hands were magic, too. They moved lightly over her as he sang, grazing her stomach and breasts and caressing her thighs. She drifted in a dream state, untethered from her worries. He slid his hand past the worn waistband of her sweatpants and inside her panties, and touched her *there.* All her senses became centered on that one, delicious little spot, until she soared over the edge and did a freefall into bliss.

He was a man of his word, she thought, smiling as she drifted into slumber.

Unwind her, indeed.

Evie slept. For the first time in months, she *really* slept, safe in Ansgar's arms, her slumber undisturbed by hot dreams or nightmares of running through a pea soup fog in search of something she'd lost, something she *needed,* something she couldn't live without, though she didn't know what.

Ironic that it took going to jail for her to get a good night's sleep.

The next morning, she woke to the rattle of the cell door.

"Up and at 'em," a man said.

"Huh?" Evie stirred. She was warm and comfortable, and didn't want to move. "What's happening?"

"Your bond has been posted, Ms. Douglass. You're free to go."

It was a moment before her sleep-fogged brain comprehended. Jail, she was in jail, and good old Addy must have bailed her out.

Her eyes flew open. She was lying on her right side with her left leg thrown across Ansgar's powerful thighs. Her head rested on his broad chest—his broad, *invisible* chest. To the uninformed observer, it must look as though she was levitating. She sat up. The deputy, a middle-aged man in a neatly pressed uniform, stared at her from the doorway of the cell in open-mouthed astonishment.

"Yoga," she said by way of explanation, jumping to her feet. Behind her, the bed creaked and groaned, and the mattress dented in the middle as her invisible guardian rose from the bed. Evie gave the deputy a bright smile. "The county really ought to do something about these cheap mattresses, don't you think?"

Still in her sock feet, she grabbed the bag with her things off the floor and hurried out of the cell past the stunned officer. She paused at the end of the hall to slip on her shoes. The clock over the door said 6:30. Her BFF must have pulled some strings to get her released this early in the morning. Evie wanted home, a bath, and something to eat, in that order. Hard to believe she was hungry again after everything she'd eaten the day before, but there it was. What the heck. She was sick of dieting.

She reclaimed her purse from the evidence tech and stepped into the lobby. Addy and Brand waited for her there. To her surprise and dismay, Trey Peterson was there, too. He stood near the door, his gaze fastened on her with unnerving intensity. He hated her, she realized with a little stab of dismay. Well, of course he hated her. He thought she had killed his wife.

What was he doing at the sheriff's office at the butt crack of dawn? He was probably going to fire her, though why he found

it necessary to drive all the way to Paulsberg to do it was beyond her. A simple letter of dismissal would have sufficed. *Dear
Ms. Douglass, We regret to inform you your services are no longer required at Peterson Lumber Mill. We have a strict No Murderess pol-
icy, and you are in flagrant violation.*

Oh, well. She was going to quit her job at Peterson's anyway.
She couldn't go back there, not after what happened.

"Evie." Evie forgot about Trey as Addy flung her arms
around her and gave her a bone-crushing hug. "Are you all
right? I've been so worried. I didn't sleep a wink last night
imagining you in this awful place." She stepped back and gave
Evie a worried perusal. "No one . . . uh . . . *bothered* you, did
they?"

"Virtue intact, Addy." Well, sort of, Evie thought, recalling
with a blush her night in Ansgar's arms. And the day before,
when he nearly had his way with her against the front door . . .
and later at the kitchen table. Okay, it was official. Her virtue
was hanging on by a thread. "They put me in a single cell."

"Thank goodness! Did Blondy stay with you? He better
have, if he wants to keep his balls."

"Addy." Evie ventured a nervous glance at Trey. His burning
gaze was fixed on her, his expression rigid. Oh, man, he was
fixing to give her what-for. This was going to get ugly. She
hated ugly. "Mr. Dalvahni hardly knows me. He doesn't owe me
anything, and you shouldn't talk about his *parts.*"

"You're right. Gross. What was I thinking?"

Brand tugged Addy to his side. "Adara, Evie will think you
dislike my brother."

"Oh, no, I'm crazy about the big hemorrhoid." Addy made
a face. "Really. So, where is he?"

"I don't know. He was with me a minute ago." Evie's blush
deepened; she couldn't help it. "Be nice to him, Addy. He's
been an enormous comfort to me."

In more ways than one, she thought with a secret thrill of
delight.

"Huh." Addy's gaze narrowed. "Doesn't sound a thing like
him. We talking about the same guy?"

"Of course." Evie took another uneasy peek at Trey. If he was here to fire her or cuss her out or rain down promises of retribution on her head on behalf of the Petersons, she almost wished he'd get it over with. Her nerves couldn't take it. "Thanks for bailing me out," she told Addy. "You're a good friend. I'll pay you back, I promise."

"I didn't bail you out. I wanted to. I was *going* to." Addy's lips tightened. "Somebody beat me to it."

"I don't understand," Evie said. "If you didn't put the money up, who did?"

"I did," Trey said, coming over to them. "The magistrate wasn't happy being rooted out of bed so early, but he'll get over it. He was a fraternity brother of mine." He looked down at Evie. "I know you didn't kill Meredith," he said. His voice throbbed with conviction. "You could never do something like that."

"When did you get back into town, Trey?"

"Yesterday. Did you miss me?"

"Uh, sure," Evie said, feeling awkward. "Wait a minute. You posted my bond?" The husband of the woman she was accused of murdering had put up her bail money? This was the last thing she'd expected or wanted to hear. "Have you lost your mind? People will talk. They'll say—" She stopped, unable to say it out loud.

"They'll say you've been boinking your boss, and that you killed Meredith to get her out of the way." Addy gave Trey a glare of dislike. "Which is *exactly* what I told him."

"I don't care." Trey gazed at her with that strange fixed warmth in his eyes. "Let them talk. We know it's not true, much as I'd like it to be."

"Much as you'd like it to be?" Evie shook her head in confusion. "What do you mean by that?"

Trey took Evie's hands in his. "You know what it means. Surely you know how I feel about you?"

A deep, rumbling growl shook the room, as if Cerberus himself crouched outside in the hall. The main door to the Sheriff's Department burst open, and Ansgar strode into the lobby.

He must have dipped into his magic closet, because this morning he was dressed in a black henley sweater and jeans.

Criminently, he's gorgeous, Evie thought, watching him walk toward her like a warrior out of a Viking myth, his perfect masculine features frozen in a mask of glacial fury.

"Uh-oh," Addy said. "Blondy's not happy. Trey, let go of Evie and back away. Slowly."

"Adara is correct," Brand said. "It would be in your best interest to retreat. My brother guards his woman most jealously."

"His woman?" Trey dropped Evie's hands as if they were red hot. "You mean to say you're *dating* this guy, Evie? I thought he was long gone."

Of course she wasn't dating Ansgar, but he didn't have to look so dang surprised, Evie thought with a twinge of annoyance. Jeez, she might not be a Pattie Petite, but she wasn't a total troll, either.

"No, we're not dating," Evie said. "Wait a minute. What do you mean *long gone?*"

Ansgar stalked up. "It is one thing to be circumspect about our relationship, sweetling," he said, putting his arm around her waist, "but quite another to tell an untruth."

Sweetling. Evie suppressed a sigh of pleasure. If only it were true. Trey was a nice-looking guy, tall and athletically built, with light brown hair and deep blue eyes, handsome in a clean, frat-boy kind of way. But he was an anemic ninety-pound weakling next to Ansgar.

"Dating is a form of courtship wherein two persons spend time together in order to ascertain their suitability as partners, is it not?" Ansgar asked.

Addy's eyes twinkled. "That about covers it, Blondy."

"Then Evangeline and I are dating." Ansgar fastened his cold gaze on Trey. "Thank you for going to the bailiff on her behalf, Mr. Peterson. My brother and I are new to this area and unfamiliar with the workings of the sovereign entities of this domain. Trouble yourself no more on Evie's account. She is in my care. Further assistance from you is unnecessary. In fact, it will not be tolerated."

"Hoo boy, Evie. In case you don't know it, you just got marked," Addy said. "Blondy did everything but hike his leg at you."

"Addy."

Addy shrugged. "Just saying."

Trey clenched his fists. His jaw was set in a belligerent line. "You don't tell me what to do, buddy. My family owns half this county."

Addy rolled her eyes. "Oh, please. Spare us the Royal Petersons bit."

" 'Buddy' is a term humans use to indicate friendship or camaraderie," Ansgar said to Trey in a tone as glacial as his gaze. "I am not your buddy." He removed a flat leather pouch from his back pocket and tossed it to Brand. "Brother, recompense Mr. Peterson for his trouble. Evangeline and I are leaving. She is weary and in need of sustenance."

"I don't want your money." Trey's fervent gaze shifted back to Evie. "I know you've had a terrible shock. We all have. Take a few days off. I'll see you back at the mill next week, after the funeral."

Evie shook her head. "I'm sorry, Trey, but I can't work for you anymore. Too much has happened. Besides, it wouldn't be right."

"Surely you're not going to let a bunch of small-town gossips run your life?" Ignoring Ansgar's snarl of warning, Trey stepped closer to Evie, his expression fierce. "The talk will die down once you're acquitted."

"And what if I'm not?"

"You will be."

Evie regarded Trey curiously. "How can you be so sure? Your wife is dead, and they found a bloody knife in my car. That's enough to convince most people."

"I'm not most people. I know you. I know you didn't do it."

Ignoring the waves of hostility pouring off Ansgar, Evie patted Trey on the arm. "I appreciate your faith in me, Trey. It means more than I can say. But I think it's better if we put some distance between us. Think of your family. Think of the scandal. You can't have the woman suspected of murdering your wife working for you. That would be tacky, to say the least. And the gossip won't help my case, either."

Trey looked desperate. "Evie, please. I—"

"Enough," Ansgar said. "She has spoken. Evangeline is no longer in your employ." He looked at Brand. "Pay the man, brother. I do not wish to be in his debt."

"I understand perfectly, brother." Brand gave Ansgar a knowing smile. "I would feel the same, were I in your place."

Ansgar put his hand on Evie's arm. "Come. Let us depart."

"Let me give you a ride home, Evie," Trey pleaded. "We need to talk about this some more. You can't quit. Jobs are hard to come by in Hannah."

"I know," Evie said. "Don't worry about me. I'll manage. I'm used to being on my own." She turned to leave. "I'll put my resignation letter in the mail today."

Trey lunged after her. "Evie, wait. Don't do this."

With a growl of annoyance, Ansgar jerked her into his arms. Evie felt a strange pulling sensation in the pit of her stomach. The room blurred and she fell into nothingness.

Chapter Thirteen

She landed on her feet in the middle of her kitchen. The room was neat and tidy. No dirty dishes or leftover food sitting around. Some wonderful person had cleaned up the remains of the gorgefest from the day before. The room was bright with early-morning sunshine. Looking out the window, she fancied she spotted movement among the larkspur and marigolds in the garden. It made her heart ache, that brief shining flutter. She missed the fairies.

She straightened her twisted sweatshirt and turned to face Ansgar. "Aren't there rules about this sort of thing?"

Ansgar raised his brows. "What sort of thing?"

"Doing woo woo in front of humans. First the sheriff and now Trey. Or did you think Trey wouldn't notice when I vanished into thin air? People don't get beamed up around here, you know."

"I take it you refer to the Directive Against Conspicuousness. Do not be concerned. Brand will erase the Peterson human's memories."

Evie stiffened. "What about the sheriff?"

"He may yet be of use, so he may keep his memories . . . for the moment."

"That's horrible! You can't treat people that way."

"Do you think it kinder to leave them in doubt of their sanity, like Mr. Collier?"

"No, of course not. But people aren't playthings for the

mighty Dalvahni, either." She put her hand to her forehead. "Sorry. That was bitchy. I don't know what's gotten into me."

She turned and walked out of the kitchen.

He followed her down the hall. "Where are you going?"

"To take a bath and try and get in a better mood. I'm not fit company for anyone right now." She paused in the bathroom door, staring in dismay at the broken window and the shards of broken wood—all that remained of the bathroom door. There was a shower upstairs, but she preferred to soak in the tub. She *needed* to soak in the tub. "Or maybe not."

Ansgar moved her gently aside. "Do not be distressed. I will remedy this. I should have done so already, but I had my mind on other things."

He waved his hand. The splintered wood and broken glass flew back into place, and the bathroom was restored to its former state.

It was a moment before Evie could speak. "Wow, that's some trick. Definitely a violation of that directive of yours, I think. Are you going to wipe my memory now, too?"

A strange expression flitted across Ansgar's handsome face. "No, that I will not do, no matter what."

"Thank goodness. I would hate that."

He met her gaze and looked away. "You would not hate it. You would not know it."

"You're wrong. I would know." Evie touched her breast. "Right here." She surveyed the pristine bathroom. No broken window. No busted door. It was magic. "So, is there anything the Dalvahni can't do?"

"We can be injured, but we heal instantly and we are extremely difficult to kill. We can mend most things, but we are not all-powerful. The Dal cannot bend time, for instance, nor can we restore the dead to life." He turned to leave. "I will leave you to your ablutions. I will be in the kitchen finding us something to eat."

Evie straightened, remembering her empty cupboards. "Oh, dear, I still haven't been to the grocery store."

He retraced his steps until he towered in front of her. Tall and brawny. Impossibly handsome. She took a step back into the bathroom, needing to put space between her and his sheer splendor.

He followed her, his big body filling the open door. "That will not be necessary," he said. "I took the liberty of stocking your pantry. The Dal can go long periods without sustenance, but that is not to say we do not enjoy food."

"How did you—" She shook her head. "Never mind, I get the picture. More woo woo. You cleaned up the kitchen, didn't you?"

"Yes."

"Thank you. You're quite the multitasker."

"I can do several things simultaneously, if that is what you mean." His voice deepened, and the hot look in his silver gray eyes nearly scorched her in her tracks. "I look forward to demonstrating my . . . er . . . multitasking abilities most assiduously to you in the near future."

He gave her one of his rare, devastating smiles. "Enjoy your bath, milady," he said, and closed the door.

An hour later, Evie sat at the sunny kitchen table eating the breakfast Ansgar had prepared for her—a mushroom and cheese omelet, fresh fruit, and crusty bread with butter. She was wearing a loose dress of moss green cotton with long, flowing sleeves. She thought the dress was romantic, like something a princess of eld would wear while waiting for a handsome prince to come along and rescue her.

She stole a glance at Ansgar through her lashes. Definitely a fairy-tale prince—granted, a modern one dressed in jeans. He leaned against the counter watching her eat, his long legs crossed at the ankles. Granny Moses, he was handsome. Sexy beyond belief. And he could cook? Wow.

A rap at the window drew her attention from Prince Ansgar. Addy peered through the glass at them. Evie waved her inside.

"Good morning," Addy said, stepping through the back door.

She had Dooley, her yellow Lab, with her on a leash. Dooley slunk into the kitchen, the picture of misery, head low and tail tucked between her legs. Normally, Dooley was a four-legged bundle of enthusiasm, especially in the vicinity of anything edible—like the omelet Evie was eating. But the dog seemed oblivious to the delicious smells wafting in the air. Something was definitely wrong in Dooleyville.

"What's the matter with Dooley?" Evie asked.

"Evie," Dooley said in her growly voice. Dragging Addy across the kitchen by the leash, the dog laid her head on Evie's leg and looked up at her with sad, brown eyes. *"Dooley bad dog. Go house of pain."*

Thanks to a little Dalvahni woo woo from Brand, Addy's dog had the power of speech. After all these months, Evie still found it startling to hear the dog talk.

"House of pain?" Evie raised her brows at Addy. "What's she talking about?"

"She's upset because she's going to the v-e-t for her s-h-o-t-s," Addy said.

Dooley could talk, but that didn't mean she could spell.

"Stupid cat no go house of pain." Dooley flumped to the floor in a forlorn heap. *"Dooley bad. Addy mad at bad Dooley."*

Poor Dooley. She was like a toddler, petrified of the doctor. There was no way to make her understand that going to the vet was for her own good. To make matters worse, Mr. Fluffy Fauntleroy, the fairy cat that had taken up residence with Addy, didn't have to go to the vet. Dooley clearly thought she was being punished.

Evie tried to think of a way to cheer up Dooley.

"Would you like part of my omelet?" Evie asked the dog.

Dooley did not raise her head from her paws. Goodness, this *was* serious. Dooley Anne Corwin was all about the chow.

"Oh, Addy, I've never seen her like this," Evie said. "It makes me want to cry."

"I know." Addy worried her bottom lip. "I feel horrible about it, but she has to go."

"Perhaps I can help," Ansgar said. "Dooley, come here."

There was a note of compulsion in Ansgar's hypnotic voice.

Dooley obediently rose and trotted over to him. Squatting down on his muscular thighs, Ansgar looked Dooley in the eyes.

"You are a good dog," he said. His big hands were gentle as he stroked the dog's head. "And, because you are such a good dog, Addy is taking you to the House of *Treats.* When you get to the House of Treats, you will not be frightened. You will feel no pain. Do you understand?"

Dooley wagged her tail. *"Dooley good dog?"*

Relieved, Evie smiled across the room at Addy. Addy smiled back, her eyes filled with tears. Golly, Addy loved that goofy dog.

"Yes," Ansgar said, rubbing Dooley's ears. "You are a very good dog."

Dooley began to do the doggy dance. *"Dooley good!"* She pranced up to Addy. *"Addy! Dooley good dog!"*

"Yes, you are Dooles," Addy said, laughing. "Thanks, Blondy. That was nice of you."

"It is of no moment," Ansgar said stiffly.

Evie wanted to kiss him. Ansgar could pretend to be cold and uncaring until the cows came home, but he was a marshmallow inside.

Dooley rushed over and stuck her nose in Evie's crotch, a sure sign that Dooley was feeling better. *"Dooley good dog, Evie."* She sniffed the edge of Evie's plate. *"Dooley like eats."*

"Dooley Anne, don't beg," Addy scolded. "It's not polite."

"Dogs care not for human niceties," Ansgar said. "She is hungry."

"You may be right. She didn't touch her breakfast this morning," Addy said. "Probably because she knew she was going you-know-where."

Ansgar bowed. "With your permission, I will cook her some scrambled eggs with cheese."

Uh huh. Definitely a big old marshmallow.

The Lab gave Addy a hopeful look. *"Dooley like cheese."*

"You can cook, Blondy?" Addy said, raising her brows. "My, you are full of surprises."

"Oh, yes, he can cook." Evie spooned a few more raspberries onto her plate and added more tea to her cup from her mother's favorite sturdy yellow teapot. "I bet he'll fix you something, if you ask nice."

Ansgar grunted. "Then of a certainty she will starve."

"Huh," Addy said. She examined Evie's plate. "That egg stuff doesn't look half bad."

Ansgar sighed and reached for the bowl of eggs on the counter. "That, I suppose, is your version of nice."

"Pretty much," Addy said. She sat down at the table across from Evie and poured herself a cup of tea. "I'm pulling my hair out," she said. "I usually close at noon on Saturdays, but the big Halloween dance is tonight and I've got a bunch of deliveries to make, including two dozen carved pumpkins and sixteen table arrangements ordered by the Hoo Hahs."

Evie swallowed a smile. Addy looked harried, and with good reason. The Purple Hoo Hahs were a supper club of rowdy old ladies. Addy's great-aunt Muddy was a Hoo Hah ringleader. Their outrageous and unpredictable antics struck fear into the hearts of local law enforcement, and shock and awe into the remainder of the populace. Fright Night was the Hoo Hahs's annual Halloween dance at the country club. Anything involving the Hoo Hahs was sure to be a moneymaker for the flower shop and a major headache for the police. Last year, half the Hoo Hahs ended up in the Fountain of Ever Flowing Grace in front of the First Baptist church.

Addy plucked an envelope out of the wooden napkin holder. Her brows shot up when she saw the contents. "Tickets for Fright Night? You didn't tell me you're going."

"That's because I'm not. Muddy insisted I have those, even though I told her I hate that kind of thing and I don't have anything to wear, even if I was of a mind to go." Evie shook her head. "Which I'm surely not."

"You mean because of what's happened," Addy said. "I guess I can understand that. You are kind of notorious right now."

"Thanks," Evie said. "That makes me feel loads better."

"That's what friends are for. Speaking of friends, you wanna help me make some deliveries?"

"Deliveries!" Evie dropped her fork. "That reminds me. I met a woman yesterday who could use a job. Her name is Nicole. I told her to come by the shop."

Addy's expression grew wary. "Weren't you busy yesterday getting arrested? Where'd you meet this woman?"

"At the sheriff's office. She just moved to town. She's got a dog stalker."

"Come again?"

"A dog stalker," Evie said. She rushed on, breathless. "Oh, it's just terrible, Addy! This man—a vet by the name of Snippet from Baldwin County—is after Nicole's dog because Frodo bit off two of his fingers."

"Let me get this straight. You want me to hire some random woman to work at the flower shop. That you met yesterday. In jail. A woman with a vicious dog."

"Nicole wasn't in jail. She was at the sheriff's office to get a restraining order. This guy's trying to kill her dog. Think how you'd feel if someone threatened to hurt Dooley. And Frodo bit the man while protecting Nicole. This Snippet fellow put the move on her. He's what your mama would call a masher."

"I don't know, Evie. The whole thing sounds a little sketchy. Whadda you think, Blondy?"

"I think many things," Ansgar said without turning from the stove. "You will have to be more specific."

"I'm talking about this Nicole woman and her man-eating dog, of course, Captain Literal. You were there. What am I getting myself into?"

"Why are you asking him?" Evie said. "Don't you trust me?"

"With my life." Addy took a sip of her tea. "But you're a pushover for anybody with a sob story, and you know it."

Ansgar put a plate of cheesy eggs on the floor for Dooley, and the dog had at it.

"Adara is right," he said, setting a huge omelet in front of Addy. "Much as it pains me to say it. You are too sweet and kindhearted for your own good, Evangeline."

"Don't let it pucker your butt, big boy," Addy said. "Everything about you pains me." She took a bite of the omelet and smiled in ecstasy. "Except your cooking. This is the mack daddy of egg stuff, dude."

Ansgar looked down his nose at her. "Am I to presume from that bit of incomprehensible gibberish the omelet meets with your approval?"

"Oh, yeah. Presume away."

Ten minutes later, Addy had finished her omelet and Dooley was running around Evie's backyard chasing Mr. Fluffy Fauntleroy. The fairy cat had appeared without warning as soon as Dooley hit the back steps. They were a comic pair to watch, the energetic Lab and the flying fairy cat. Mr. Fluffy flitted on gauzy wings from flower to flower with Dooley in hot pursuit. The dog was singing her favorite song as she galumphed around the yard after the flying cat, a round with simple lyrics that consisted of *Cat. Cat. Stupid cat.* Dooley Anne had many sterling qualities, but songwriting was not among them.

At first, Evie had found it weird that she could see the fairy cat, but not the other fairies, until she realized that other people could see Mr. Fluffy, too. There'd been a bad scene one day in the flower shop when the fairy cat made an unexpected appearance to warn Addy that Dooley had escaped the fenced-in backyard. Again.

Miss Mamie Hall had freaked until Addy made up a whopper about Mr. Fluffy being a battery-operated flying toy.

Addy finished her omelet and dabbed her mouth with her napkin. "So, are you ready?"

"For what?" Evie asked.

"Haven't you been listening? I need you at the shop today. I've got orders out the wahzoo, and no help."

"Oh." Evie shrank back in her chair. Go to town and face people? Her breakfast rose in her throat and parked there. "I don't have a car. The sheriff impounded it. Besides, you'll have Nicole."

"Nice try," Addy said, "but you can ride to the shop with me, and you know very well I expect you to use the van to make the deliveries. Besides, who knows if this Nicole chick will even show? I need you, and you need the money. You quit your job this morning. I was there. I heard you."

"I've got a little in savings." Evie swallowed heavily. "I don't know if I'm ready for this."

"Ready for what?" Addy demanded.

"Ready for . . . you know." Evie waved her hand at the windows. "Out there."

She was a murder suspect. People would talk and point and whisper. She would be *noticed*.

Addy's jaw tilted at a stubborn angle. "When *will* you be ready?"

Evie's heart sank. Addy had that Look, the one that meant she'd made up her mind about something.

"What about Meredith's funeral? Have the arrangements been made?"

"Not yet, but I imagine it will be at the end of next week. The chief says the body hasn't been released by the medical examiner."

"I can't go to the shop, Addy. Be sensible. You're going to be slammed with orders for Meredith's funeral. People think I killed her. How's it going to look if I'm at the shop?"

"I don't give a rat's ass how it looks," Addy said. "Get off your duff and find your purse. It's after eight. I've still got to drop Dooley off at the vet's, and I should have opened the shop already."

"I don't know," Evie faltered. "I'm not sure—"

"You have to go out sometime. It might as well be today. Unless you plan to hide out here until the trial, and that could be months."

"Addy, please—"

"You're going, Eves, and that's that." Addy slammed her hand on the table for emphasis. "I won't let you cower in this house. You didn't kill Meredith. And if anyone says anything rude to you, they'll have me and Ansgar to deal with, right?"

Ansgar crossed his arms on his chest. "Right."

"See?" Addy waved her hands in triumph. "Ansgar agrees with me."

"Twice, in the space of but a few moments," Ansgar murmured. "Something of a miracle. Or else a sign that Han-nah-a-lah approaches, the end of all things."

"Don't try to be funny, Blondy," Addy said. "You'll hurt yourself." She gave him a squinty-eyed glare. "You never answered my question. What did you think of this Nicole person?"

He shrugged. "Large bosom. Demon dog. Otherwise, unremarkable."

"Men." Addy rolled her eyes at Evie. "There was a whole person there, but he only noticed the boobage."

"He noticed the dog, too," Evie said.

"Yeah, but he was kidding about the demon part," Addy said. Her eyes widened as Evie remained silent. "Wasn't he?"

"I don't think so, Adds. You said it yourself. Ansgar's not much of a kidder."

"OMG," Addy said.

Chapter Fourteen

A short while later, Evie followed Addy through the employee's entrance of the flower shop. Dooley had been dropped off at the vet's, happy as a clam to be going to the House of Treats. It was twenty minutes after eight, and the phone in the front room was ringing off the hook.

"Crappydoodle," Addy said. She picked up the receiver. "Flowers by Adara. Oh, hey, Miss Hixie. Yes, ma'am, I'll have the Hoo Hah flowers at the club by three o'clock today. You're terrified of pumpkins?" She cut her eyes at Evie and pointed to the front door. "No, I don't believe I knew that. Yes, ma'am, there will be jack-o'-lanterns . . . Made out of pumpkins, yes, ma'am . . . No, I never thought about using squash . . . Tell you what. I'll do something special for your table, something without the evil pumpkins. Just try not to look at the other centerpieces."

Addy hung up. "Apparently she was traumatized as a child. Pumpkins are evil, the gourd-ish spawn of Satan. Can you believe it? The woman is a loon."

The phone shrilled again. "Oh, for Pete's sake," Addy said, making a grab for it.

While Addy fielded phone calls, Evie bustled around the shop, unlocking the front door and flipping on the lights. Evie loved the flower shop. It had been her home away from home since the age of twelve when she started working there with Addy, who'd fled the horrors of Dead Central—as Addy called Corwin's, the family funeral parlor down the street—in favor of her great-aunt's flower shop. It was a transgression Addy's mother had yet to forgive.

Two years earlier, Addy's great-aunt had retired at the age of sixty-three and sold the flower shop to Addy. Addy changed the name from *Fairfax Flowers* to *Flowers by Adara* and remodeled, adding two open display coolers; several large worktables in the middle of the front room that allowed customers to watch their flowers being arranged; a balloon station and a number of gift items, including pewter ware, hand-thrown pottery, monogrammed stationery and linens; and a few paintings done by local artists.

Best of all, Addy gave Evie a corner of the shop to display her handmade candles, lotions, soaps, and shampoos. Evie named the line of products *Fiona,* after her mother. She had a small but enthusiastic clientele and big dreams. Right now, *Fiona* was more of a money suck than a cash cow. But her plan was to work at the mill for a few years, live modestly, and sink all her money into her business until the line grew. "Was" being the operative word.

Now that Meredith had gotten herself murdered, Evie was out of a job, and her future as a young entrepreneur looked dim.

She didn't regret quitting the mill. There was no way she could go back there, not after what had happened. But jobs were scarce in Hannah.

Of course, depending on how the trial went, she might not have to worry about that. She might go to prison.

Prison. Oh, God. The thought made her knees go weak. So, she wouldn't think about it.

Much.

She was booting up the computer when the bell on the door jingled and Addy's great-aunt, Edmuntina Fairfax, walked in. Edmuntina was the youngest of the three Fairfax girls by a good piece—only ten or twelve years older than Bitsy—and if Addy's mama was a tsunami, her aunt Muddy was a climate-changing meteorite. Seeing Muddy lifted Evie's spirits. Muddy was her hero. Cool, confident, and unafraid. Evie wanted to be more like Muddy and less like a doormat.

Nobody loved a doormat. Heck, nobody *noticed* a doormat. They wiped their feet on it and moved on.

Always picture perfect, today Muddy wore a biscuit-colored silk top, matching peach twill slacks, and a flowing, steel-blue cashmere cardigan. Her short silver hair was swept back from her forehead, accentuating her elegant bone structure. Diamonds winked in her ears, and a huge sapphire sparkled on her ring finger, her engagement ring from her beau and Evie's lawyer, Amasa Collier.

It was a pip of a ring. But, more than that, it was proof positive that all things come to those who wait. Muddy and Mr. C's love story spanned more than thirty years, and they were finally getting married. Two of her favorite people were getting their happily ever after, and Evie was delighted.

Muddy stopped short when she saw her. "Evie! Oh, shoot, I'm too late. I was hoping you were still in jail. I was gonna drive my Mercedes through the courthouse wall and bust you out of the slammer." She made a sweeping gesture with one arm. "I can see us now, driving into the sunset like Thelma and Louise."

Addy hung up the phone. "I got news for you, Muddy. The jail is in the courthouse basement and Thelma and Louise ended up dead in a ditch."

"It was the Grand Canyon," Muddy said, "which is like a ditch, only bigger."

Evie giggled. "And grander," she added, unable to resist.

Addy gave her a warning scowl. "Don't encourage her." She grabbed a clear glass container, filled it with candy corn, and set to work on an arrangement of orange roses, butterscotch chrysanthemums, and miniature carnations. "And in case you've forgotten, auntie dear, you and I have starring roles in an upcoming double wedding. Being a fugitive from the law might spoil Mama's Big Plans, and God help you if you do that. She is *consumed*." Addy added a few sprigs of salidago and autumn leaves to the bouquet, then muttered under her breath as she knocked a bunch of dried eucalyptus off the worktable, scattering them on the floor. "You know how hard she's been working to make sure everything is perfect."

"Oh, pooh," Muddy said. "I'm sick to death of the wedding. Amasa and I should have eloped. And if Bitsy was so all-fired set on everything being perfect, she wouldn't have scheduled the damn thing on a football Saturday. Nobody's going to miss the Alabama game for a wedding, for God's sake. We'll be lucky if the priest shows up."

"That's not Mama's fault," Addy said. "Brand and I set the date. We couldn't wait until spring. We're tired of sneaking around."

Evie felt a twinge of envy. Addy and her demon hunter were so madly in love. The two of them together equaled spontaneous combustion. But there were rules in the *Bitsy Rule Book* about premarital sex, so Brand and Addy snuck around to keep her mama happy. Little did Bitsy know, Addy and Brand were already married, although Evie was pretty sure Bitsy wouldn't recognize the union as valid. Months ago, Brand whisked Addy off to someplace called the "Hall of Warriors," where he wrote Addy's name in something called the *Great Book*. Addy told her all about it. It was the first time a Dalvahni warrior had ever claimed a life mate. Apparently, in Dalvahni Land that was as good as being married.

Bitsy didn't know about the *Great Book* or the life mate thing. Heck, she didn't even know her future son-in-law was a demon hunter, much less that he wasn't from Earth. Bitsy thought Brand was European. And *Great Book* or not, Bitsy wouldn't be satisfied with anything less than a church ceremony for her daughter.

A stylish, petite blonde in a pair of pleated cropped black pants, a camel wool–blend jacket with three-quarter sleeves, and black pumps sailed past the storefront window.

"Speak of the devil," Evie said, bending down to retrieve the eucalyptus. "Here comes your mama, Addy."

The bell on the door jingled.

"Hey, y'all," Bitsy said, coming in to the shop. "No news yet on the Peterson funeral. But hold on to your hats. Once the police release the body and the family makes the arrangements, you are going to be up to your eyeballs in orders. This is going to be *huge*. I've been getting scads of calls at the funeral home since it happened. I've told Shep to reserve the Magnolia Room. It's our biggest space." Evie heard a thump as Bitsy set her purse by the cash register. "I heard the news, and it's dreadful, simply dreadful. Evie, accused of murder! What can we do to help our girl?"

Evie straightened with the flowers in her hand. "Hey, Miss Bitsy. I'm all right."

"*Evie*. I thought you were in jail."

"Yes, ma'am, I was. I got out this morning."

"That's wonderful, dear. You better believe I gave the chief an earful when I heard. I wanted to get in my car and drive to Paulsberg and give that Sheriff Whitsun an earful, too, only the chief wouldn't let me. Why anybody with the sense God gave a goose would think for a moment that you killed Meredith Peterson is beyond me. I don't care how many bloody knives they found in your car. It's a setup, and that's what I told Car-lee."

Bitsy and Carl E. Davis, Hannah's Chief of Police, were an item. Miss Bitsy adored the chief, and when she said his name it came out *Car-rah-lee-hee*.

Evie blushed and ducked her head. "Thanks, Miss Bitsy. I appreciate that."

"How'd you find out about that knife anyway, Mama?" Addy said. "That's police business." She stuck a few stalks of black, curly ting into the bouquet. "I'm surprised Chief Davis told you that, even if you two are dating."

"Oh, he didn't. Car-lee is much too professional." Bitsy examined her nails. "Dan Curtis down at the station let it slip."

"Let it slip? You mean you pestered it out of him," Addy said.

Bitsy widened her eyes. "Can I help it if he told me something of his own free will?"

"Own free will my hind leg. You peck like a chicken, Mama."

Bitsy put her hand on her chest. "I'm sure I don't know what you mean."

"Huh," Muddy said. "You're the queen of the peckers, Bitsy, and you know it."

Bitsy gave a musical little laugh. Miss Bitsy even laughed like a lady. "Muddy, the things you say!" she said. "Queen of the peckers, indeed. That sounds just awful." She turned to Evie. "How *did* that knife get in your car, dear?"

"I don't know. But I didn't kill Meredith. I swear."

"Of course you didn't." Bitsy patted Evie on the hand. "But it looks bad, all the same, no two ways about it." A little line formed between her perfectly arched brows. "I don't mean to be indelicate, dear, but do you think you should still be in the wedding? It's Addy's big day, you know." She smiled at Muddy. "And Muddy's, too."

"She knows about the wedding, Mama," Addy said. "She'd have to be dead not to know about it with you around. FYI, you should ask for a refund on those sensitivity lessons of yours. You got gypped."

"Addy, you know I love Evie, but we have to be practical," Bitsy said. "Think of the scandal. *We* know our girl is innocent, but there's going to be all kind of talk. Maybe you better ask one of the other attendants to be maid of honor. Your cousin Bernadette would be thrilled if you asked her, and it would so please your aunt Pearl."

"Bernadette!" Addy looked indignant. "No way, Mama. She put my cat in the dryer. Poor Boots was never the same after that."

"Bernadette came by that honest," Muddy said. "Pearl was mean as a snake, too. I remember this one time she talked her brother into eating some elephant ears out of the yard. Told him they tasted like green jelly beans. I looked out the window and your poor uncle Pete was making laps around the house, foaming at the mouth like a rabid dog. I had to chase him down and wash out his mouth with the garden hose. It was awful. Pete's lips swelled up, and he was choking and crying, and Pearl just stood there smiling, like that horrible little girl in *The Bad Seed*." She looked around at them. "Ever see that movie? Gave me the creeps."

Bitsy's expression grew pained. "Aunt Muddy, please. This is serious."

"I am serious! Those elephant ears burned the pea-winding stew out of that boy's mouth. He couldn't eat for a week, and he had the runs. And Pearl did that to her own brother." Muddy shrugged. "The apple don't fall far from the tree, that's all I'm saying. That Bernadette is the Bad Seed's daughter. I'd think twice about having her too close to the bride, if I were you. She's still single and that Brand is a hot-tay."

Evie worried her bottom lip with her teeth, her stomach churning. The last thing she wanted to do was ruin Addy's wedding.

"Addy, maybe your mama is right," she said. "Maybe it would be better if I bowed out."

Addy set her florist's shears on the counter, the movement slow and deliberate. "Now you listen to me, Sarah Evangeline Douglass. You're my best friend in the whole wide world. You are going to be my maid of honor and nobody else." She glared at Bitsy. "Especially not that cat molester. Even if I have to get married in jail."

"Oh." Evie blinked the sudden tears from her eyes. "Well, if that's the way you feel about it."

"That's the way I feel about it."

Bitsy fanned herself. "Adara Jean, married *in jail*? You can't mean it."

"God's sake, Bitsy, relax," Muddy said. "Evie's out on bail until the grand jury meets, and that could be months. Amasa says."

Addy picked up her shears again. "So, that's it, Mama. It's settled. Evie's in, Bernadette's out, and the wedding is still on."

Brand and Ansgar materialized behind Bitsy without warning.

"I am exceedingly glad to hear it, little one," Brand said, pulling Addy into his arms. "I would be in deep despair were it otherwise."

"Brand, I missed you," Addy squealed. Flinging her arms around his neck, she kissed him like she hadn't seen him in months.

Spontaneous combustion, no two ways about it, Evie thought

wistfully, watching the two of them. It was always like that with Addy and Brand.

"Goodness, Brand, you startled me!" Bitsy said when he released Addy at last. "I didn't hear you come in." She offered Ansgar a bright smile. "And I see you've brought your brother with you. What a nice surprise! Good to see you again, Alastair."

Evie frowned in confusion. This morning at the sheriff's office, Trey had acted like he recognized Ansgar, and now Bitsy was all "nice to see you again," too. This obviously wasn't Ansgar's first time in Hannah, but how come she never met him? He was Brand's "brother," and she was Addy's best friend. It didn't add up.

Ansgar bowed to Bitsy. "The name is Ansgar, ma'am."

"Oh, yes, silly me. Are you in town until the wedding? Brand didn't think you'd make it."

"I felt compelled to leave." His silver gaze shifted to Evie. "But found I could not stay away, after all."

So he *was* here before. Had she met him and then forgotten him?

As if. Six-foot-four-inch stud muffins didn't grow on trees in Hannah. Evie rubbed her pounding temples. This was crazy. No, *she* was crazy to forget a guy like Ansgar. She struggled to put the pieces together, to make herself remember, but it was no use. Thinking about it made her head hurt and her stomach feel funny.

"Wonderful." Bitsy's brow wrinkled. "Brand, now your brother is here, I'm sure you'll want him to be your best man. Do you think your cousin Rafe will mind getting bumped to groomsman? Ansgar, we'll have to get you down to Tompkins's right away for a fitting. I just hope Tweedy can get you a tux in time. Goodness, you Dalvahni boys are all so big and handsome."

Ansgar looked a little befuddled, kind of like a poleaxed bull. Bitsy affected most people that way.

"I'll take him down there, Miss Bitsy," Evie volunteered, glad to have something else to think about. "Will this afternoon be soon enough?"

Bitsy's brow smoothed. "That would be lovely, dear. I know you're glad to have your young man back in town again." She gave Ansgar a coy smile. "I thought it was a real shame when he left. You two make such a lovely couple. I had such hopes for another wedding in the near future."

"Couple?" The floor seemed to shift beneath Evie's feet. "I don't know what—"

"Ansgar and Evie just met, Mama," Addy said, giving Bitsy a hard look. "Remember, we talked about it?"

Bitsy looked flustered. "Oh, yes. I-I remember now. I must be thinking of somebody else. Being in the funeral business, I meet so many people, you know. Why, I—"

She faltered, staring out the window with a flabbergasted look on her face. It took a lot to render Hibiscus Corwin speechless, so Evie knew right away something was up.

Something big. Something unusual.

Evie turned. A round-faced woman with blue eyes framed by a stubby halo of hot pink hair peered through the storefront window at them.

It was something unusual, all right. It was Mullet Woman, in all her glory.

Chapter Fifteen

Nicole wore a clingy zebra-patterned camisole and a matching gauzy top. Her black jeggings were stuffed into lime green yeti boots. Plastic miniature pumpkins dangled from her earlobes. A flashing jack-o'-lantern hung around her neck from a black cord, turning the deep valley between her breasts a glowing safety orange. An enormous orange and green cheetah print bag hung from one shoulder. Under her other arm she held Frodo. The demon dog was dressed to match his mistress in a zebra print cone of shame with orange and green ribbon trim.

Nicole waved at Evie and started for the door.

"What an odd person," Bitsy said, finding her voice. "And what's that she's carrying, a possum?"

"It's not a possum, Miss Bitsy," Evie said. "It's a Chihuahua."

Bitsy pursed her lips in thought. "The mayor has a pet possum. Must be some kind of fad. I don't think people should keep wild animals as pets. It's not sanitary."

Addy rolled her eyes. "It's not a possum, Mama. Evie said."

"Huh." Bitsy looked unconvinced. "What's the matter with her hair? Looks like she cut it with a weed whacker, bless her heart."

Oh, dear, Bitsy just dissed poor Nicole big time. In the South, you could say anything about another person, no matter how horrible, as long as you tacked a "bless his or her heart" on the end of it. Like, *she's so ugly, she'd make a train take a dirt road, bless her heart.* Or, *if brains were leather, he wouldn't have enough to saddle a gnat, bless his heart.*

Nicole burst into the shop and rushed up to Evie. "Please tell me I ain't too late," she said over the noise of Frodo's snarling. She gave the dog a little shake. "Hush, Precious. Mommy can't hear herself think."

The dog's snarling subsided to a low rumble.

Bitsy whirled around. Addy was fond of saying her mama's glare was an incendiary device, and Bitsy had her lasers on lock. "Too late for what?" she demanded of Addy. "What's she talking about?"

"Nothing, Mama."

"Don't you nothing me, Adara Jean Corwin," Bitsy said. "Something's going on here, and I mean to Get to the Bottom of It."

Evie's heart sank. Bitsy would give Addy hell if she hired someone like Nicole to work in the shop, someone with bad hair who mixed her animal prints and wore hairy shoes.

Addy would do it anyway—for Evie—but that left Evie between a rock and a hard place. She wanted to help Nicole, but she didn't want to tick off Addy's mama. You did *not* want to get on Hibiscus Corwin's bad side. It was a mile wide, and people had been known to stay there for years.

Oh, Lord. Nothing to do but forge ahead and hope for the best. She *liked* Nicole. Granted, Mullet Woman's hair was a Technicolor disaster and her taste in clothes might not be up to Bitsy standards, but she seemed comfortable in her own skin.

Evie envied her that. A lot.

She pretended not to notice the sparks of irritation that popped off Bitsy like embers off a burning log, and offered Nicole a reassuring smile. "You're fine."

"Whew," Nicole said, looking relieved. "I'd 'uv been here sooner, but me and Frodo couldn't get across the river, on account of there was a wreck on the bridge. A poultry truck tumped over, and there were chickens everywhere. Birds on top of cars and all over the road. That chicken farmer was beside himself, scrambling around trying to round them all up."

"Oh, dear," Evie said. "It sounds like a mess."

"It was. And that's not the worst of it. A whole bunch of

them chickens jumped off the bridge, like they knew they were done for anyway if they reached that processing plant. I tell you, it was a poultry suicide pact or some kind of chicken cult."

"Chicken cult?" Evie tried to wrap her brain around that concept. "I'm not quite sure I follow—"

"Maybe chickens ain't as stupid as people think," Nicole said darkly. "Maybe chickens are *aware*." She rested Frodo on one hip. "The ringleader 'peared to be a big buff Orpington. That rooster hopped up on the railing and let out a crow loud enough to wake the dead. Then he jumped, and the rest of them chickens followed like lemmings."

"Lemming chicken, one of my favorites," Evie murmured, struggling not to laugh.

"Chickens are like turkeys." Nicole's round face was earnest, and she didn't seem to notice Evie's wisecrack. "They can fly short distances, but they ain't got the wing power to carry 'em off a bridge. And these birds had been plumped up for the market, see? They dropped like bricks. It was terrible. The police came and the volunteer fire department, and a reporter from the newspaper. I thought this one officer was gonna have a heart attack. He kept stomping around and cussing and throwing his hat on the ground."

"Oh, my goodness!" Bitsy's scowl was replaced by an expression of alarm. "That sounds like Car-lee. I'd better go check on him. He has high blood pressure. Muddy, come with me. We can talk about the wedding."

"Vomit," Muddy said. "No thanks."

"Suit yourself."

Bitsy grabbed her purse and hurried out the door.

Nicole turned to Evie with anxious eyes. "Anyway, that's why I'm late. Is that delivery job still available?"

"I think so, but you'll have to ask the boss." Evie led Nicole and the still grumbling dog over to the counter. "Nicole, this is Addy Corwin, the owner of the shop. Addy, this is Nicole Eubanks, the woman I was telling you about."

"Nice to meet you." Addy stared at Nicole like she had two

heads. And she did—sort of—what with the pink and yellow hair. "Uh, nice dog."

Mullet Woman clutched Frodo to her bosom. "Thanks."

"Nicole, this is Addy's aunt, Muddy Fairfax," Evie said, indicating the older woman.

"Great-aunt," Muddy said, studying Nicole like a bug. "That's a pimping zebra space collar your dog's got. Where'd you get it?"

"I made it. Covered it in Duck Tape and added the ribbons myself," Nicole said proudly. "Frodo and I always wear matching outfits." She lovingly traced the black and white stripes on the dog's cone with the tip of one finger. "This is called 'zigzag zebra,' but there are lots more patterns to choose from."

Muddy nodded. "Duck Tape's the bomb. I use it to yank the hair off my legs when I can't get to the salon."

Addy wrinkled her nose. "Ew. TMI, Muddy."

"Don't use it on your face though," Muddy said. "It'll give you a mother of a hickey."

Nicole nodded as though committing this tidbit of wisdom to memory. "Duck Tape's powerful stuff."

"You met Ansgar yesterday," Evie said, finishing the round of introductions, "and this is his brother, Brand Dalvahni."

Mullet Woman started as the two warriors stepped forward, like she hadn't noticed them standing there.

Which was like not noticing a pink elephant in the room.

It wasn't Nicole's fault. Ansgar and Brand had used their Dalvahni woo woo to fade into the background. Maybe they were feeling overwhelmed by all the estrogen in the atmosphere. Whatever the reason, they'd managed to make themselves inconspicuous; quite a trick for two such lip-smackingly bonzo-gorgeous guys.

Only they weren't inconspicuous anymore. They were fully visible and dripping Dalvahni sex appeal. It oozed out of their pores and formed a nimbus of yum around them. It was like they'd dimmed their inner lights and then flashed them to bright. The effect was blinding.

"Mistress Nicole," Ansgar said in his hypnotic voice.

Brand smiled. "A pleasure to meet you, Nicole."

Thwack! The combination of Ansgar's bedroom voice and Brand's dazzling smile was too much for poor Nicole. Her mouth dropped open and her eyes glazed over like a drunk on a three-day toot.

Evie could relate. She had a hunch she wore that same wide-mouth bass expression a lot around Ansgar. In fact, she was probably wearing it right now.

She tested the hinge on her jaw. Yep, hanging wide open. Ansgar had done it again.

She closed her mouth. "Nicole?" She would have tapped Mullet Woman on the shoulder, but Frodo had lapsed back into full snarl mode and she didn't want to lose an arm. "Are you all right?"

"Jeezy peezy," Nicole cried, staggering back. "There's two of 'em." She wobbled over to a chair near a potted fern and sat down. "One's bad enough, but two? They're like twin orgasms on legs."

Muddy chuckled. "Twin orgasms on legs. Wish I'd said that."

"You will," Addy muttered.

Evie hurried over to Nicole. "You're awfully pale. Are you all right?"

"I'm fine," Nicole said, shushing the growling dog. She plunked Frodo on her lap, pulled a Kleenex out of her over-sized cheetah purse, and wiped her brow. "Having a woozy spell. Guess I'm more nervous about the job than I thought."

Evie frowned. Nicole's complexion was pasty. She'd moved to Hannah to save Frodo from Sylvester Snippet. Moving took money, and Nicole didn't have a job.

"When's the last time you ate?" she demanded.

"Oh, you know. I eat plenty." Nicole waved a hand at her generous thighs. "Look at me. You can see I ain't exactly starving."

"Uh huh," Evie said. "How many meals has Frodo missed?"

Nicole bristled. "That's different. He's my Precious."

"That's what I thought." Evie straightened. "Ansgar, would

you mind running down to the Sweet Shop and getting Nicole something to eat?"

"Oh, no," Nicole stammered. "I couldn't let you do that."

"But I insist." Ansgar gave Evie a hot, intimate look that made her heart rate speed up and kicked her hormones into overdrive. "I will go and gladly, but I will not run."

"Dude, it's an expression," Addy said. "Pick me up an order of Miss Vi's orange rolls and some Conecuh sausage while you're at it."

Ansgar scowled. "You broke your fast not an hour past."

Addy shrugged. "I'm hungry again. So sue me."

Ding! Evie rubbed her aching temples. There it was again, that dang annoying bell and that swimmy, disconcerting feeling in her stomach.

"I will accompany you, brother," Brand said. "I feel the need to stretch my legs, and I am quite fond of Miss Vi's victuals." His gaze lingered on Frodo. "Unless you think I should remain here."

"I appreciate your concern, brother," Ansgar said. "But I do not believe the creature poses a threat to Addy or Evangeline." He arched a brow at Nicole. " 'Twould be a fair assessment to say his rancor is more readily aroused by the masculine presence than the feminine, would it not?"

Nicole gaped at him. "Huh?"

"He wants to know if it's safe to leave us with the dog," Evie said, interpreting for her.

"Oh." Nicole's brain kicked back into gear with an almost audible click. "Don't you worry about Frodo. Your lady folks are safe with my lamb."

"There, brother, you see?" Ansgar said. To Evie's surprise, his gray eyes twinkled. "He is a lamb."

Brand nodded. "Then let us depart."

They walked out the door like ordinary folks, for which Evie was profoundly grateful. She didn't think Nicole could handle it if Ansgar and Brand did their Dalvahni disappearing act.

"Wow." Nicole shook her head. "Those guys are smoking hot."

Addy snorted. "Noticed that, did yah?"

"They wouldn't by any chance be related to a Rafe Dalvahni, would they?" Nicole asked. "Big, sexy redheaded feller married to a pretty little gal name of Bunny? They came into the gas station last month. Newlyweds." Nicole's expression grew wistful. "He was smoking hot, too."

"Yep." Addy put the finishing touches on the arrangement. "All the Dalvahnis are . . . related, and all of them are butt ugly, at least the ones I've met. It's a real shame."

Nicole chuckled. "Butt ugly. That's funny." She took a deep breath, which made the glowing jack-o'-lantern between her breasts do a happy little jig. "So, about that job," she said to Addy. "I'm a hardworker and a real good driver. Never had a speeding ticket in my life."

"The job's still available. Evie says you just moved to Hannah?"

"Yep, three days ago. I'm renting a trailer in Froggy Bottom that belongs to my cousin Ick Lovelace. You know him?"

"No, I don't believe I do. Look, Nicole, the job's only part-time and doesn't pay much."

Evie heard the hesitation in Addy's voice and threw her a pleading look. Nicole was good folks—a little rough around the edges maybe—but good folks, all the same.

Nicole must have heard the uncertainty in Addy's voice, too, because she squeezed Frodo so hard the Chihuahua snarled. "Part-time's fine for now," she said. "Cousin Ick's giving us a real good deal on the rent, and my truck's paid for. Frodo and I don't need much else."

"Uh huh." Addy eyed the Chihuahua. "I'm gonna be upfront with you, Nicole. Frodo is scary. Sort of like a barracuda with fur. You'll have to leave him home. Can't have him eating the customers."

"I can't leave Frodo alone. It's not safe."

"The dog stalker, Addy," Evie said anxiously. "I told you about it, remember?"

Addy shook her head. "Look, Eves, I'm not sure I can—"

"Bitch alert," Muddy announced abruptly. "Trish Russell and Blair Woodson are headed this way."

Addy groaned. "The Twats are coming here? Somebody kill me, please."

Chapter Sixteen

Ansgar stalked down the sidewalk, heedless of the curious stares of passers-by. The town of Hannah was nestled in a clump of wooded hills. Tidy shops jockeyed for attention along the tree-lined avenue called Main Street. The streets were clean, the storefront windows polished, the people friendly. On the far side of the hill, the Devil River rumbled the bass notes of a never-ending song.

There was a hint of coolness in the air, a chill warning of winter that cleared his head. It was good to get out of doors and away from Evangeline, for her sake and his.

She was in danger. The thought repeated itself like the endless tumbling chorus of the river.

But how could he protect her when his body and brain were befuddled with lust? He wanted her with an unceasing ferocity that amazed him. She was temptation itself with her fiery hair, soft, winsome mouth, and sumptuous curves. He was like a stag in rut in her presence. She made him forget duty, training . . . *everything* but being with her, sinking into her lush body and finding release after the endless months of deprivation.

He needed her. She shone like a candle in the dark well of his existence. How had he survived without her eon after eon, subsisting on a diet of violence and grim duty? No love, no laughter, no warmth, only the companionship of his brother warriors and the meaningless, perfunctory release in the arms of a thrall to sustain him through the blur of centuries.

He was a demon hunter. The hunt was all he knew, all he'd

needed or wanted. He lived for the thrill and challenge of the chase and the adrenaline rush of battle. He was very good at his job. It was what he did, what he was.

Until Evangeline.

His first encounter with her had been a severe shock. She'd opened his eyes and made him realize he was a prisoner of the darkness just as surely as the djegrali he captured and imprisoned in the bottomless well of blackness known as the Pit.

His lips twisted in self-derision. Once, he'd derided Brand for having similar feelings for Addy. He thought Brand weak, a disgrace to the Dalvahni. How far the mighty Ansgar had fallen! Always, he'd prided himself on his discipline and imperturbability, his single-minded dedication to the hunt, even among a warrior race known for their restraint and devotion to duty.

Look at him now. He was as lovesick and randy as any callow human male, as weak as Brand.

Weaker, if the truth be known. Brand was the first of their kind to experience emotions other than rage and lust. Yet, he faced the bewildering onslaught of his passion for Addy head on. He did not run from it like a frightened youth on the eve of his first battle. The mighty Ansgar, however . . .

Cool, detached, unflappable warrior that he was, he had fled.

Not that it did him any good. Being away from Evangeline was anguish, as he quickly learned.

Being apart from her was misery. Being *with* her was a firestorm of temptation and unquenchable desire.

He was well and truly stretched upon a rack of his own making, he reflected wryly. He'd taken her memories of him, telling himself it was the right thing to do, the *kind* thing to do. The poor lass was in love with him, he'd reasoned. He was leaving and would not return. It would be cruel to leave her to suffer.

As for him, he would forget her readily enough, he'd told himself. She was a pleasant interlude, a delicious memory he would look back upon with fondness, if he remembered her at all.

He'd soon found he was sadly mistaken. He could no more forget Evangeline than he could still the rush of his blood through his veins or silence the beating of his heart. It did not take him long to admit his defeat and slink back to Hannah, staying in the shadows, haunting her every move like a pathetic, obsessed stripling in the grips of his first passion.

Brand caught up with him. "Is something amiss, Ansgar? You seem . . . restive of late."

"You know very well what troubles me." Ansgar did not look at him. If Brand's expression matched the sly satisfaction he heard in his brother's voice, he would hit him. "Or perchance 'twould be more accurate to say *who* troubles me. Go ahead, brother. Spit out your words of triumph else you choke on them."

Brand chuckled. "Nay, I relish the taste of them. 'Twas not so long ago you chided me for my own peculiar affliction. Besides, 'twould be unkind when you are so obviously in distress."

"Distress?" Ansgar slammed his fist into a metal lamppost, bending it in half. "I am as randy as a Gorthian bull."

In the blink of an eye, Brand repaired the damage. "The Directive Against Conspicuousness," he murmured in admonition. "You will startle the humans."

"To the Pit with the Directive," Ansgar said savagely.

"Restive, of a surety." Ansgar heard the laughter in Brand's voice. "Can you not prevail upon Evie to assuage your . . . er . . . problem?"

"I can hardly expect her to tumble me when she thinks we met but a day ago."

He was trapped in a coil of his own making, and Evangeline with him. She'd been like a tender blossom eagerly unfolding in the warmth of the sun, and then he left her.

But no more; she did not remember him.

Worse, she did not remember herself. She was once again the shy dowd, retiring and ill at ease in her own skin.

This, too, he'd taken from her, her burgeoning confidence in her beauty and power.

"Then give her back her memories," Brand said with a shrug.

"I do not know how."

"I see your dilemma." Brand's lips twitched. "I remember your suggestion to me when I was struggling with my own . . . er . . . little problem. 'Avail yourself of a thrall,' you said. Perhaps you should heed your own advice."

Ansgar snorted. "I would hardly call Addy Corwin 'a little problem.' "

"No, she most certainly is not."

There was a wealth of satisfaction in Brand's voice. Brand adored his little problem. Worshipped it, in fact.

As did he, Ansgar reflected glumly, thinking of Evangeline. He loved her to the point of madness. He'd run from that knowledge once. No more.

"A thrall would not have eased your suffering, nor did it mine," Ansgar said. "I share your plight, I am afraid. It is Evie for me, and no other."

Thoughts of lying with her again consumed him. He could feel his iron control, forged in the heat of a thousand battles, slipping away, like sun-dried sand between his fingers. A few moments ago, he'd come perilously close to dragging her into a back room of the shop, tossing up that rag of a dress she wore, and having his way with her. Right then and there, and the others be damned.

And the hell of it was she would have let him. Her mind might not remember him, but her body did. The knowledge that she wanted him, was his for the taking, was fuel tossed upon the fire of his already enflamed senses. Honor compelled him to resist her. She would not thank him for his selfish indulgence if she regained her memory. But he did not know how much longer the fractured joints of his already weakened willpower could last.

And 'twas Evie's hand on the handle that tightened the rollers.

Brand's expression grew serious. " 'Tis not in the nature of the Dalvahni to lie, but I would caution you not to tell Evie you have been with a thrall." He held up his hand as Ansgar started to speak. "Hear me out. I have come to know Evie in your absence, and I am quite fond of her. She is a gentle, loving soul, but this she would not understand. No more, I think, than you would had she dallied with another male in your absence."

The thought of Evie with someone else made something hot and ugly rise up inside Ansgar. She had no notion of her effect on him, or of her effect on human males. The Peterson human wanted her, for one. He'd noted Trey's interest in Evie in the past few months, the way the man watched her with hunger and yearning in his gaze. It made him want to tear the man's eyes from his head. His restraint stemmed from practicality, not from lack of jealousy. He could not remove the eyes of every man who cast admiring glances Evie's way. To do so would be to blind the entire male population of Hannah.

"The very thought puts me in a killing rage," he admitted. "She is a fever in my blood. But were the cure offered me, I would shun it."

"As would I." Brand clapped him on the shoulder. "Do not look so glum, brother. A solution will present itself. What of the killer? Have you any notion who murdered the Peterson woman?"

"Not a human, I think," Ansgar said, "nor a demon. I felt the creature's presence. It was . . . something else."

"A mutant perhaps, one of the foul offspring of human and djegrali?"

Ansgar nodded. "Aye, that is my suspicion."

"The town is rife with them. How do you propose to ferret out the murderer?"

"I have given the matter some consideration. There is a rout of some sort tonight at a local hall, a celebration linked to the Celtic Samhain. I would like to attend, but only if I can persuade Evangeline to go with me. She has already been attacked once, and I will not leave her alone." He quickly told Brand of the djegrali attack at Evie's home. Her brush with death the day before still made him shudder. "She would have died, I think, if not for the intervention of the fae."

"This is serious indeed. Do you think the attack is related to the Peterson woman's murder?"

"I do not know," Ansgar said. "It is a puzzle."

"I would offer to stay with Evie whilst you investigate the matter," Brand said, "but Adara and I already have plans to attend this dance. It is a masquerade, I believe. Edmuntina is most insistent we be there."

"I am glad to hear it. I will need your eyes and ears and perhaps your sword arm, should the need arise."

"You have it," Brand said.

"My thanks. Now all that remains is to convince Evangeline to go to the dance."

"I will ask Adara to use her influence, and Edmuntina."

"Good," Ansgar said. "She is shy and will be most reluctant, especially in light of what has happened. I will have Meredith speak with her as well."

Brand's brows rose in surprise. "Meredith? The dead woman?"

"The very same. Her shade appeared to us last eve in the gaol."

"Then your quandary is solved! Have the shade name her killer, bring the fiend to justice, and be done with it."

"The shock of Meredith's demise has wiped the events from her mind. She is working with some sort of guide in the afterlife to restore her memory, a shade named Swink. We met him, also."

"By the sword, this is a strange place."

"I concur, brother," Ansgar said. "A very strange place, indeed."

Chapter Seventeen

The yeasty aroma of freshly baked bread and the rich smell of fried bacon and sausage greeted Ansgar when he and Brand stepped into the Sweet Shop. The early-morning breakfast rush was over, but the dining room was still sprinkled with a few stragglers.

Miss Vi waved at them from behind the counter. "Be right with you, gentlemen, soon as I ring these folks up."

While they waited, Ansgar looked around. The eatery had once been a holding unit of some sort. He searched his Dalvahni word bank for the correct term. The Dalvahni had the gift of languages, a necessity in the hunt that took them from place to place, but sometimes the subtle nuances of local speech eluded them. That was particularly true in Hannah, where exaggeration and euphemism seemed to be a matter of pride.

The word he was looking for floated to the surface. *Cotton warehouse: A storehouse for the produce of a small plant that produces balls of fibrous fluff used in the production of clothing.*

Ah, yes. Miss Vi's business had once been a cotton warehouse. The plank walls were covered with a strange assortment of signs and adages. DAIRY FRESH MILK—BEST IN THE LAND! a round red and white sign proclaimed. To the right of the milk sign was a smiling picture of a dark-skinned beauty holding a glass bottle in one hand. Beneath her sandaled feet were the words DRINK PEPSI-COLA! Next to the leggy siren was a narrow tin banner with an image of an elfin boy painted in the

bottom right corner. The lad was dressed in a red cap and flowing scarf. The words *Sing it over and over and over again, Frosty
Morn* trailed behind him. The signs competed with a dizzying
array of printed sayings like, *"If hard work is a virtue, then mos'
folks are living in sin."* There was also the dented backend of a
turquoise automobile and an assortment of rusted farm tools on
the plank walls.

Ansgar's gaze shifted to a blond-haired man sitting alone at a
back table. "Is that not Addy's brother?" he asked Brand, indicating the man.

"Yes, it is. He looks troubled. I must speak with him."

Ansgar followed Brand across the room.

"Shep," Brand said to the man by way of greeting.

Shep pushed his plate of uneaten food aside. "Hey, take a
load off," he said. When Ansgar and Brand exchanged puzzled
glances, he motioned for them to take a seat. "I mean, sit down.
I keep forgetting you two ain't from around here."

Brand and Ansgar seated themselves at the table.

"Haven't seen you in a while," Shep said, eyeing Ansgar.
"You been off chasing boogiemen?"

The question momentarily startled Ansgar until he remembered Shep was in a relationship with the thrall Lenora. She'd
been sent to Hannah a few months earlier by Conall, the captain of the Dalvahni, with orders to see to Ansgar's and Brand's
needs and then return to the House of Perpetual Bliss, the
abode of the thralls.

Lenora had seen to Shep's needs instead.

Even more shocking than her untoward relationship with
the human, Lenora had decided to *stay* in Hannah, an unprece-
dented breach of protocol and tradition. The thralls were
created to service the Dalvahni. Theirs was a symbiotic relationship: the thralls craved emotion, and the Dalvahni provided
it. In that way, the thralls were fed and the Dalvahni maintained
their legendary calm detachment and dedication to the hunt.
This arrangement had satisfied hunter and thrall for thousands
of years.

Until Lenora got her first taste of human emotion. For whatever reason, Conall had decided to turn a blind eye to her unforeseen behavior. Perhaps he considered it an anomaly. Perhaps he hoped Lenora would come to her senses. One seldom knew with Conall. He kept his own counsel.

"What grieves you, Shep?" Brand asked. "Is something amiss?"

"Yeah, you could say that. The Birth Canal's back in town."

"I do not understand," Brand said. "Who is this Birth Canal?"

"Marilee, my ex-wife," Shep said glumly. "She dumped me and the kids for the tennis instructor at the club. The *young* tennis instructor. She and her boy toy are back in Hannah. 'To be near the children.' " He uttered the words in a mocking drawl. "I call bullshit on that one. Seems the little turd she's married has developed a bad case of tennis elbow and can't work. The two lovebirds have moved in with Marilee's mother, and Marilee is looking for a job so she can support him."

"It will be good for the young ones to see their matriarchal unit," Brand said. "I know that William and Lily have missed her."

"Oh, yeah, it'll be great for the kids."

"But not for you?" Ansgar asked.

"My ex-wife is moving back to town, and Lenora doesn't like it."

A thrall jealous? Ansgar was fascinated and somewhat alarmed. Thralls fed on emotion, but they did not have feelings of their own, other than hunger.

"So now I have *three* women riding my ass." Shep's shoulders slumped. "My mother, my ex-wife, and my girlfriend. To top it off, I hate my job."

"I thought you planned to eschew the sepulchral rites," Brand said.

"Yeah, but Mama's dead-set against me giving up the funeral business, 'scuse the pun." Shep stared into his drinking cup. "I've put the word out, but so far nobody's beating down my door to buy Corwin's. The economy sucks, and Hannah ain't exactly crawling with morticians. Until I sell, I got no way to make a living."

"What about your painting?" Brand asked. "Adara has offered numerous times to display your work in her shop. Mayhap you can establish yourself as an artist."

"A starving artist, maybe," Shep said. "I wussed out."

"What is the meaning of this 'wuss'?" Ansgar asked.

"It means I chickened out, that I was scared."

Ansgar filed the term away for future reference.

Shep made a face. "That's something else Lenora's hot about. She thinks I'm ashamed of her."

"Are you?" Ansgar asked.

"God, no! I outkicked my coverage on that one. She's wonderful. What I feel for Lenora is . . . special. I'm just not ready to share that part of my life with people. That's all. Besides, I'm not sure Hannah's ready for my paintings."

"How do you know when you have not tried?" Brand asked.

Brand liked Addy's brother, Ansgar could tell. Ansgar decided he liked Shep, too. And he felt sorry for him. Loving a thrall could not be an easy thing, even without the man's former spousal unit and his interfering, demanding matriarchal vessel complicating matters.

"I think I understand," Ansgar said, spurred by sympathy for the man. "Your feelings for Lenora run deep. She is a lodestar in the dark night of your existence, the distant shining shore you have dreamt of but never hoped to reach, the cool drop of water that soothes the burning heat of your weary soul. She is everything to you, heart's blood and breath. Mere words are inadequate to express your feelings, so you pour your passion for her into your paintings. To show those paintings to others would be to bare your soul to the world. Contempt for your art you could bear. But to have others scorn your love would be intolerable."

A strange heat moved up Ansgar's neck and spread across his cheeks as he realized Brand and Shep were staring at him.

"Or perchance I do not understand at all," he muttered. "Forgive me if I have misspoken."

"No, man, that was *beautiful*. I need to write that shit down before I forget it." Shep grabbed a napkin and motioned to Miss Vi. "Viola, you got a pen I can borrow?"

"Sure thing, sugar." Hurrying over to their table, she gave Shep a writing implement. She handed Brand and Ansgar each a piece of paper that said *Breakfast Menu* on it. Ansgar buried his face in his menu, willing the heat in his face to subside. If this was what humans called embarrassment, it was a most unsettling sensation.

After a moment's study, the strange squiggles on the paper arranged themselves into something intelligible. He studied the words on the paper to avoid looking at Brand. Some items he recognized—eggs, bacon, and sausage, for instance—others he did not. What was Spam? he wondered. And "cathead biscuits" sounded alarming.

"What can I get you fellows today?" Miss Vi asked, pulling a pad of paper from her apron pocket.

"We were sent here to retrieve sustenance and take it back to Adara's establishment," Brand said.

Miss Vi's brown brow wrinkled. "You mean you want a to-go order for the flower shop?"

"Yes, that is the correct term," Brand said. "We want a to-go order."

"For how many?"

"Five."

"That number include you and yo' brother? 'Cause if the answer's yes, that makes a difference. I never seen nobody can eat like you two."

"You know how fond I am of your viands," Brand said, smiling at her. "Rest assured my brother and I will partake."

Miss Vi looked pleased and flustered at the same time. "Viands, is it?" She swatted Brand playfully on the arm. "Go on wid yo' bad self. You talk almost as purty as you look. What kinda viands you wants?"

Brand rattled off a long order from the menu, including a request for something called "grits." Miss Vi wrote it all down and hurried off.

"Now," Shep said once she was gone. "Say that again. It was *good.*"

Ansgar felt his face grow hot again. Fortunately, the bell on the door jingled, distracting Shep.

"Hells bells." Shep slammed his pen on the table. "Here comes Marilee. Dressed for tennis, of course, and loaded for bear, from the looks of her."

There were bears in this demesne? Intrigued, Ansgar turned. A woman headed across the room toward them. She did not appear to be on the hunt, at least not for creatures of the four-legged variety. Her attention seemed to be focused upon Shep. She wore a short skirt that hit her tanned legs mid-thigh, and a sleeveless top. Past the first flush of youth, with short brown hair and doe-like eyes framed by extravagant lashes, she was attractive in an athletic sort of way . . . or would be if she did not look so unhappy.

"We need to talk," she said, addressing Shep without preamble. Her trim body was rigid with tension. "I've got a match in thirty minutes, so I'll get right to the point. I don't want that bimbo girlfriend of yours around my children."

"*Your* children?" Shep raised his brows. "Last time I checked, they were my children, too. I got full custody of them in the divorce decree." He jabbed a finger at her. "You and the douche were fine with it, too, as I recall."

"His name is Parker," she said through her teeth, "and that was before I found out you were shacking up with that woman."

"I'm not shacking up with anybody. Lenora rents Rat Godwin's guesthouse."

"Which is right next door to you." Marilee's mouth turned downward in an unhappy arc. "William and Lily say she's at the house all the time. They say she tucks them in at night and that she's there in the morning to eat breakfast with them. I'm not stupid, Shepton. I know what's going on here. You're screwing that woman, with my children in the house. It's disgusting and I won't have it. I'll take you back to court."

"Good luck with that," Shep said. "Last I heard, you and the Boy Wonder don't even have jobs. How you plan to support them?"

"That won't matter. The judge will give me custody when he finds out you're schtupping that stripper."

Lenora materialized behind Marilee with a high-pitched whine. Ansgar scanned the room and breathed a sigh of relief. No one seemed to have noticed the thrall's abrupt and unconventional appearance.

Like all thralls, Lenora was pleasing to the eye, with a body made for pleasure, skin as smooth as silk, and red, pouting lips. She was modestly dressed, for a thrall, in a garment made out of some kind of clingy material. The dress covered most of her assets, but Lenora exuded sex no matter what she wore.

"Greetings, Sol Vani," she said, acknowledging Ansgar and Brand with the term of respect that meant "most noble lords." She gave Shep an intimate smile. "My love."

Marilee whirled around with an angry little titter. "My goodness, you shouldn't sneak up on a person like that. You're liable to get hurt."

"The same thing could be said of you." Lenora stepped closer to Marilee, her nostrils flaring. The thrall was on the scent. "I detect regret and bitterness, mixed with an unhealthy dose of jealous bile. Normally, I would find such a seething cauldron of emotion alluring, but I fear you would taste sour."

Marilee drew back. "Are you coming onto me, you freak?" She glared at Shep. "Keep her away from my kids, Shep. I mean it. Or you'll both be sorry."

Turning on her heel, Marilee flounced back out the door.

"What is the meaning of this 'bimbo' and 'stripper'?" Lenora demanded of Shep.

He looked as edgy and desperate as a cornered animal. "That's just Marilee letting off steam. It doesn't mean anything."

"I see," Lenora said. She turned to Ansgar. "Sol Van?"

"I cannot be certain," Ansgar said carefully. The thrall knew he would not lie. That did not mean, however, that he was eager to spring the trap on Shep. "But, I believe, the term 'bimbo' connotes a physically attractive woman who lacks intelligence."

"I see. And the term 'stripper'?"

"A woman who performs an erotic dance and removes her clothes, usually for money."

"Thanks, man," Shep said. "You're a big help. Way to throw me under the train."

"She called me names." Lenora spoke without inflection, but her long black hair swirled around her as though stirred by an unseen wind. "She insulted me, and you did nothing."

Shep lifted his hands in a helpless gesture. "Don't mind Marilee, baby. You said it yourself. She's bitter and unhappy."

"I am more than five thousand years old. I am not your *baby*."

Lenora disappeared with an angry *pop*.

"She is gone," Ansgar said. "Unless I am mistaken, she is wroth with you."

Shep glared at him. "No shit, you think?"

"You do not understand. Thralls do not possess emotion. That Lenora feels anything is significant. Momentous, even."

"Ansgar is right," Brand said. "It is most unusual."

"Whatever." Shep jumped to his feet. "I gotta find her and talk to her. Maybe she's down by the river. She likes the river."

He dashed out the door.

There was a loud crash and the sound of breaking glass. Miss Vi stood in the middle of the dining room, a tray of broken dishes and ruined food scattered at her feet.

"Lord have mercy, Jesus," she shrieked. "Did you see that? That woman just up and disappeared. Del, get out here. *Del*."

Several of the other patrons looked stunned as well. Ansgar and Brand exchanged glances. Lenora's sudden disappearance had not gone unnoticed.

"Brother?" Brand said.

"I will handle it."

Ansgar sighed. The Directive Against Conspicuousness had been violated. Again. Memories would have to be adjusted.

'Twas a small enough matter for a demon hunter . . . unless the memories happened to be his own.

Chapter Eighteen

Evie felt a spasm of panic at Muddy's announcement. Trish and Blair were coming to the shop? Oh crap. She was *soooo* not ready to face the Twats.

Trish and Blair had been running buddies of Meredith's. As teenagers, the three of them entertained themselves by making fun of the socially awkward and physically imperfect.

Since Evie was both, she'd always been their favorite target.

Things hadn't changed much since graduation; the Twats still loved to pick on her. Both Trish and Blair had married well—although Blair was newly divorced—and they ran in more elevated circles than Evie, so they had fewer opportunities for torture.

Thank God.

Of all the people Evie dreaded running into today, Trish and Blair were high on the list. Meredith had been their friend, and the women's viciousness would know no bounds.

But if Muddy said Trish and Blair were coming to the shop, they were coming. Muddy had some kind of weird radar. She could tell you who was calling before the telephone rang and who was at the front door before they knocked. She'd cut short her world tour and come home early because she somehow knew Mr. Collier had quit drinking after more than thirty years.

Addy even swore Muddy had a psychic connection to her freezer.

So it was with a feeling of dread that Evie looked out the window. To her relief, the sidewalk was empty.

"I don't see them, Muddy." Evie relaxed. Maybe being engaged at long last to the love of her life had scrambled Muddy's radar.

"They're coming." Muddy took a seat on a stool at the counter. "Get ready. They got their ugly on."

"Huh," Addy said. "What a surprise. They've had their ugly on since 1992."

Addy was right. The Twats had started out as twits at the age of eight and spread.

A minute later, a Cadillac Coupe pulled up to the curb in front of the shop. The doors opened, and Trish and Blair got out.

So much for Muddy's psychic equipment being on the fritz.

Trish and Blair were attractive women in a Southern Slut Barbies with Money kind of way: well groomed and well dressed, nails and hair perfect, makeup expertly applied. Trish was blond and Blair was a brunette. Both women exuded an air of self-satisfied confidence Evie could not begin to understand.

They breezed into the store like they owned the place. Evie looked around for a place to hide, but it was too late. Trish saw her standing by the counter and stopped dead in her tracks, teetering on the five-inch heels of her slinky lace-up boots.

"*Murderer,*" she said in tones of loathing. She pointed a manicured nail at Evie. "You've got a nerve, Blimpo, showing your face in this town after what you've done."

"Yeah, you got a wagonload of nerve," Blair said like a good little sycophant. Blair rarely had a thought of her own. "I hope you get the chair, you fat slug. I hope they fry you till your eyeballs pop out."

Waves of self-righteous hate poured off Trish and Blair. Evie wanted to crawl into a hole and pull the dirt in over her head. And the Twats were the tip of the iceberg. People she'd known all her life were going to point and hiss and talk about her behind her back.

Addy's face went red. Uh-oh, Addy had an ugly bone of her own, and she was fixing to beat the Twats to death with it.

To Evie's surprise, Muddy got there first.

"My, my, aren't you girls a breath of fresh air and Christian charity," Muddy drawled. "If you spent half as much time filling your minds with knowledge as you do filling those blowed-up lips of yours with collagen, you'd know the Yellow Mama's been retired since 2002. We use lethal injection now in the state of Alabama."

Trish made a dismissive gesture. "Whatever."

"A pungent riposte," Muddy said dryly. "With a command of the language like that, you must be scintillating company at the dinner table. I can hardly wait to hear what you have to say next."

"I can." Addy glared at the Twats. "What do you want?"

Blair swished up to the counter on her Manolo Blahnik's. "Now, now, that's not very nice. Especially since we're here to order flowers for Meredith's funeral." She shot Evie a venomous look. "Meredith was our *friend,* in case you didn't know."

"Yes, I seem to recall you two yapping at her skirt tail," Muddy said.

Trish's eyes narrowed. "Why are you being so hateful to *us*? She killed Meredith."

"I didn't kill Meredith," Evie surprised herself by saying. "Somebody put that knife in my car."

Blair rolled her eyes. "Yeah, right. Like anybody's going to believe that."

"If you're here about Meredith's funeral, the arrangements haven't been announced yet," Addy said, returning her attention to her arrangement.

"Yes, we *know*." Trish made a gesture of impatience. "But we're in a hurry and we want to get this over with. We've got better things to think about than some dreary old funeral. Like the dance at the club tonight."

"We want a big arrangement." Blair waved her hands to demonstrate. "Something tasteful, but not too expensive.

Mostly carnations, you know, with a sprinkling of roses. I *hate* spending money on dead people." She shot Trish a coy glance. "Although, in this case I don't mind so much, since it's the Petersons."

"You mean Trey." Muddy nodded wisely. "He's a catch, and that's for sure, although I hear he's got a little dick."

"Oh, Lord Jesus," Addy said.

Muddy gave Blair a wide smile. "Not that it matters. He's got money and looks. Women will be climbing all over one another to get their hooks in him." She paused, her expression thoughtful. "Course, most of them will probably wait until after the funeral. But you're too smart to let something trifling like common decency stop you. So, you go, girl." She made a Z snap in the air. "Jump on that thang before they dump the dirt on Meredith. Never mind she was your friend."

Blair's lips tightened. "Meredith would understand. She'd want Trey to be happy."

"Are we talking about the same Meredith?" Addy said. "'Cause the Meredith I remember wouldn't share jack. She'd snatch you baldheaded over a stick of Juicy Fruit, much less her husband."

"Meredith is *dead*," Blair said. "There's nothing she can do about it."

An ambulance siren wailed in the distance.

"I wouldn't be so sure about that," Evie said, listening to the whine of the siren draw closer. "Meredith was a witch on a broom when she was alive, and death doesn't seem to have changed her all that much." She paused, remembering Leonard Swink. "Of course, she *is* in counseling, so maybe therapy will help."

Evie didn't know who looked more shocked at the sudden emergence of her testicles, Addy or the Twats. Addy stared at her like she didn't know her. To the Twats it must have seemed like their favorite chew toy had grown teeth and bitten them back.

Evie had shocked herself, too. She'd actually talked back to the Twats and called Meredith a witch! Wow. On the scale of zingers maybe it wasn't much, but for her it was huge. So what if she had to wait until Meredith was dead to do it. She did it. The doormat spoke.

The adrenaline rush left her feeling shaky and a little scared by her uncharacteristic temerity. But another part, that brave voice she seldom heard or listened to, the part of her Addy had rubbed off on, shouted *Hell yes, free at last, and about dang time.*

Trish found her voice first. "How dare you talk about Meredith like that, you little worm."

Trish, Evie noticed, made no comment about Meredith being in counseling. Of course, Trish probably didn't know about therapy for the dead or PTDD. Or maybe she thought Evie was a nut job. Probably wasn't a big leap from loser to nut job in the Trish universe.

In any case, it didn't matter what Trish thought. The room got cold, the lights in the shop flickered and went out, and Meredith appeared with a bloodcurdling howl.

Addy and Muddy saw the ghost and Nicole and Frodo, too. Evie could tell, because they looked right at her. Addy's brown eyes grew round, and Muddy had an arrested expression on her face, like seeing a ghost was the coolest thing since the invention of the toaster. As for Nicole and Frodo, Mullet Woman went whiter than a bar of Dove soap and the demon dog snarled, his eyes glowing like fog lights from the depth of his zebra cone.

But the Twats couldn't see Meredith. Evie knew they couldn't, because they looked right at her and kept going, and the Death Starr was not a sight to be ignored. Her eyes bulged and her face distorted into a ghoulish, unrecognizable mask. With a spine-chilling shriek, she rose in the air, her figure assuming a series of twisted shapes in rapid succession as if she was too pissed off to decide which nightmarish form to take.

If this were her first encounter with the ghost, Evie would have been terrified. The spectral show Meredith was putting on was ghastly and fascinating at the same time, a metaphysical train wreck.

Evie couldn't look away. But the Twats could. They looked

everywhere but at Meredith, which confirmed Evie's suspicion they couldn't see her.

Judging from their expressions of terror, they *heard* her, though. They'd have to be deaf not to; Meredith was shrieking like a factory whistle at quitting time. They smelled her, too. The citrusy scent of Meredith's favorite perfume, *Happy,* choked the air, making them gasp and sputter.

Personally, Evie always found Meredith's choice of fragrance ironic. To be fair, they probably didn't make a perfume called *Abject Misery,* which was the emotion the Death Starr had most often aroused while alive.

Dead Meredith had an altogether different effect on the Twats. She scared the pea turkey out of them. Their mouths sagged, they turned pale beneath their tans, and their heavily mascaraed eyes bulged in cartoonish fashion. Evie squelched the urge to laugh because that would be mean.

She didn't want to be a twat.

"Meredith, is that you?" Trish squeaked as a potted plant sailed past her head and crashed against the wall. She raised a shaking arm and pointed at Evie. "If you've come for the Whale, there she is."

That was Trish, self-sacrificing to the end.

"Noooot Ev-i-e-e," Meredith said with a tortured groan.

Meredith was being silly and theatrical, acting like a caricature of movie ghosts. But Meredith had been a total drama queen in life, so why should death be any different?

A bunch of pens and pencils flew out of the metal container on the counter and whizzed through the air at Blair like so much shrapnel. Blair screamed and ducked her head, crying out in pain as she was struck by the zinging missiles.

"What's happening?" Blair shrieked, and covered her head with her arms. "Meredith, it's me, your Care Blair. Why are you doing this?"

The doors of one of the flower coolers flew open and slammed shut. Moisture frosted the glass at the abrupt temperature change, and a message appeared in the condensation.

Stay away from Trey, you tramp, an invisible finger wrote on the glass in Meredith's unmistakable curlicue script.

"Screw this, I'm outta here," Trish said, bolting for the door. Wild eyed, Blair tottered after her. "Trish, wait!"

The bell on the door jangled behind them. A moment later, the Cadillac screeched away from the curb and down the street.

Her narrow face lit with triumph, Meredith watched them leave. "Sluts," she said.

To Evie's relief, Meredith had dropped the *Amityville Horror* routine and returned to her normal size. She looked cool and collected in a ruffled skirt, a pale pink blouse with turn-back cuffs, and snappy red leather platform pumps on her slender feet.

Evie glanced at Addy. Addy's lips were pressed tightly together, and there was an almost panic-stricken look in her eyes. Addy couldn't stand Meredith when she was alive. Dead Meredith seriously freaked Addy out.

"That's kind of like the pot calling the kettle black, isn't it Meredith?" Addy said.

It was so like Addy to play the smartass card. That was how her BFF dealt; she took the world head on. Evie was that way, too, brave and strong and kickass . . . in her imagination.

"Har-dee-har-har." Meredith put her hands on her hips. "I'm trying to think if you're funnier now that I'm dead." She rolled her eyes toward the ceiling as if contemplating. "Nope. You're still lame, Corwin."

"And you're still a toxic bitch," Addy said. "What a surprise."

"I have issues." Meredith shrugged. "But I'm working on them. I want to get better for Trey."

Better for Trey? Oh, dear, Meredith seemed to have a disconnect; she was dead and Trey wasn't.

But Evie wasn't about to tell the Death Starr her relationship with Trey was kaput. Let Swink explain it to her, the poor sap. He had forever, which is what it would take.

"Therapy's working out for you then?" Evie said, hoping to skirt the tricky subject of Meredith's dead-i-tude. "I'm glad."

"Oh, yes, I'm a changed person." Frodo sneezed—probably from the suffocating cloud of Meredith's *Happy* perfume that hung in the room. Meredith turned, her blue gaze narrowing on Nicole. "Saaay," she said, stretching the word out in a contemptuous drawl. "Who's the tacky fat chick in the Chia Pet boots?"

Oh, yeah, Meredith had changed all right. Her outfit, maybe.

"Nice hyena." Meredith floated closer, and Nicole shrank back in her chair. "Who's your hairdresser, tubby, Willie Wonka?"

"Mothertrucker," Nicole wheezed.

Her eyes rolled back in her head and she fainted.

Chapter Nineteen

Nicole oozed out of the chair and onto the floor in a zebra-striped puddle. Frodo tumbled with her. His E-collar snapped open and rolled away. He sprang to his feet, shaking his head at his newfound freedom.

"Nicole, oh, my goodness!" Evie rushed to help the fallen woman, but Frodo lunged at her, driving her back.

The Chihuahua seemed to swell, and Evie could swear he sprouted several more rows of teeth. He stood stiff-legged over his mistress, making a noise like a garbage compactor.

Evie backed away. Frustrated and worried, she rounded on Meredith. "Now look what you've done. Why do you have to be so mean?"

"Me? I didn't do anything to her." Meredith gave a disdainful sniff. "Look at her. She's probably had a heart attack from all the extra tonnage she's hauling around. Or maybe that pink hair dye ate up her brain."

"There you go being mean again," Evie said.

"Boo hoo." Meredith gave her a contemptuous sneer. "Guess you'll have to deal with it, won't you, Whaley? In case you haven't noticed, your boyfriend's not here to back you up."

Something stiffened in the general vicinity of Evie's spine. "Go away," she said. Her voice sounded cold and stern. *Yeah, that's what I'm talking about,* her inner self exulted. "You're not welcome here. Go away and don't come back." She remembered she might need the Death Starr's help to find the killer, and added, "Unless you can be nice."

Addy snorted. "Oh, yeah, that's gonna happen. When Jesus comes back in a pink dress."

"Go suck an egg, Corwin," Meredith said.

Years of frustration, hurt, and resentment, and something like plain old *mad* boiled up inside Evie. "Leave, Meredith. *Now.*"

To her surprise—and Meredith's, too, from the ghost's startled expression—a ball of greenish gold light smacked the ghost and burst like a water balloon.

Meredith's form began to shimmer and weaken. "I'll go, but not because of you," she said as she faded from view. "Later, heifers."

With that tender adieu, she disappeared.

"And your little dog Toto, too," Evie murmured.

"Whew, good riddance." Muddy fanned the air. "Somebody ought to tell Meredith to ease up on the perfume. It smells like a giant grapefruit fart in here."

"Evie, that was ah-mazing." Addy came around the end of the counter and gave her a hug. "You banished the Death Starr."

Evie sighed. "Yeah, but you'll notice she got the last word."

"Doesn't matter," Addy said. "You got rid of her. That glowing ball thingy you shot at her was cool."

"Oh, I didn't do that," Evie said. "The fairies did."

Addy looked around. "Really? Cool. Do you see them?"

"No, but they saved us from Meredith. I'm sure of it."

"Go, fairies," Addy said, doing a little circle dance with her fists.

Evie cast a worried glance at Nicole. The dog's growling had subsided, but his body was draped across his mistress as if to say *Try and touch her. Go on, I dare you.*

"What are we going to do?" Addy asked, following Evie's gaze. "That crazy dog's not going to let us near her."

"I guess we'll have to wait for Ansgar and Brand." Evie worried her bottom lip. "Maybe they can do something."

"Well, I'll be danged," a familiar voice said. "Is that an Alligator Chihuahua? I ain't seen one of them thangs in years."

Evie whirled around. Officer Dan Curtis, one of Hannah's

finest, stood in the doorway looking very official in his blue uniform.

She liked Dan. He went to school with her and Addy. He was a nice guy, attractive in a boyish kind of way, with thick, closely cropped chestnut hair, deep dimples, and hazel eyes.

"Hey, Evie," he said, looking surprised to see her. "You get out of jail?"

"Dan, she's standing in front of you," Addy said gently. "It's obvious she got out of jail."

"Right." He went red in the face. "Sorry. I'm surprised to see her, that's all."

Dan had a major crush on Addy. He was always finding some excuse to visit the flower shop. Brand got all quiet and dangerous whenever Dan came around. But he seemed to tolerate Dan for Addy's sake, which said a lot about Brand's feelings for Addy. Evie didn't know Brand all that well, but he didn't strike her as a holdback kind of guy.

"No problem, Dan," Addy said, smiling at him. "We're glad you're here. We need your help."

Dan blinked for a moment—man, did he ever have it bad for Addy—and seemed to right himself.

"Sure. What's the problem?"

"It's our friend," Evie said, indicating Nicole's limp form. "She's fainted and her dog won't let us near her."

"I think I can fix that." Dan squatted down. "Hey, pup."

Frodo lifted his head and growled, his yellow eyes gleaming like hot embers.

"Watch it, Dan. He's a mean 'un," Addy said.

Dan chuckled. "He's just doing his job, ain't that right, boy?"

"His name is Frodo," Evie said.

"Hey, Frodo." Dan's voice was low and soothing. "This one's for you."

To Evie's surprise, Dan began to sing.

"I'm not here to forget you, I'm here to recall the things we used to say and doooo-ooooh," Officer Curtis crooned.

As voices went, Dan's wasn't bad, a nice baritone without much range. Of course, Evie reflected, she was used to Ansgar the Magnificent. Nobody had a set of pipes like Ansgar. He could sing a nun out of her drawers.

Frodo didn't seem to mind Dan's lack of vocal depth. The dog quivered in response. Evie hoped that was a good thing and not a sign of imminent attack.

"I don't wanna get over you," Dan twanged. *"I don't wanna get over you."*

Frodo's garbage compactor ground to a halt. He whined and rolled over, showing Officer Curtis his belly. Dan lifted the unresisting dog in his arms.

"Good boy," Dan said, getting to his feet. "Liked that, did yah?"

"Dan, that was wonderful," Evie said. "What's that song you were singing?"

" 'The Wurlitzer Prize,' " he said. "My granddaddy had him an Allihuahua when I was a kid, an ornery little ball of mean name of Bob. Allihuahuas are known for their feisty. Bob loved him some Waylon and Willie. Papa wore a copy of *The Outlaws* slap out on that dog."

Throwing Dan a look of gratitude, Evie knelt beside Nicole and patted her on the cheek—no response.

"Stick a shoe in her face," Muddy suggested. "Saw it at a funeral once. A woman fainted in front of the casket, and everybody started running around hollering, *Is there a doctor in the house? Is there a doctor in the house?* This gal in the back took off her high heel and passed it through the crowd. They stuck that shoe over the woman's face, and she come up off the floor like her panties were on fire." She eyed Dan up and down. "Give Evie one of your boots, Dan. They ought to be good and ripe."

He flushed and started to bend over.

"Ignore her, Dan," Addy said. "She's kidding."

"I am not! A stinky shoe's as good as smelling salts."

"Good Lord, Muddy." Addy moistened a paper towel at the sink, wrung it out, and handed it to Evie. "Dab this on her face. If she doesn't come to, I'm calling nine-one-one."

"Thanks." Evie smoothed the damp paper towel over Nicole's cheeks and laid it across her forehead.

"Should have done that already." Dan sounded worried. "The chief will have my hide if he hears I didn't call this in."

"He won't hear it from us," Evie said over her shoulder. "Nicole's going to be fine. She needs to eat, that's all."

Nicole's eyelids fluttered and opened. "What happened?"

"You fainted," Evie said. "Do you think you should go to the hospital? We can call an ambulance, but they have to come all the way from Paulsberg. Dan or I can get you there quicker."

"No, no ambulance." Nicole plucked the paper towel off her forehead and sat up. "Where's Frodo?"

"I got him, ma'am." Dan rubbed the dog's ears. "No need to worry. He's fine. Ain't that right, boy?"

Frodo wagged his tail and barked. It was a happy sound for once, instead of the mating call of a drunken lemur.

A tinge of pink color rose in Nicole's pale cheeks. She rolled to her feet with remarkable grace for someone so short and round. "T-thanks for taking care of him," she said. "Frodo don't usually like strangers, especially men."

"That so?" Dan's gaze lingered for a moment on Nicole's glowing orange cleavage. "Me and him get along just fine." He smiled and handed her the dog. "Maybe it's the uniform."

"Uniform," Nicole repeated, staring at Dan in wonder.

"Nicole, this is Officer Dan Curtis with the Hannah Police Department," Evie said. "Dan sang to Frodo. Did you know your dog's a Waylon Jennings fan?"

"Ulck," Nicole said. She swayed, the color leeching back out of her face.

"She's going again," Evie cried. "Catch her, Dan."

Dan grabbed Nicole by the arm and helped her back to the chair. "Here now, none of that. Sit down. That's an order."

"Yes, ossifer." Nicole gazed up at Dan with a worshipful expression on her plump face. "Whatever you say."

Oh, dear, Nicole and Frodo had a thing for the man in blue, and the man in blue had a thing for Addy. Unrequited love sucked. Big Time.

Are you talking about Dan and Nicole or your own feelings for a certain demon hunter? that sly inner voice whispered. *Sure, he'll take what you offer, but don't think for a moment he could ever have real feelings for you.*

Don't you think I know that? What about throwing it out there and seeing what happens? Evie shot back. *What happened to all your big talk about "nothing to lose" and "having a little fun"?*

Silence. Great. When push came to shove, even her alter ego was a wimp.

With a quiet *pop!* Ansgar and Brand materialized in the shop. The two strapping warriors were an incongruous sight holding large white shopping bags with the Sweet Shop's signature green and pink double "S" on them. The smell of Conecuh sausage mingled in the air with the tangy scent of orange rolls.

Good thing Dan had his back to them and Nicole was too busy gawking at Ossifer Curtis to notice the warriors' sudden and startling appearance, or else somebody would have some 'splaining to do.

Frodo noticed, though, and set up an immediate howl.

Ansgar scowled at Dan. "Who is this human?" he asked in a voice that could have frozen lava.

"His name is Curtis," Brand said, in an equally frigid tone.

Addy gave Brand a warning look. "Dude, don't even think about it."

Evie smothered a giggle. Addy had confided that the Dalvahni could read human thoughts, an ability they could turn on and off at will. Probably a good thing when it came to most people. Talk about your TMI on a cosmic scale.

Dan, for instance, apparently had some pretty randy fantasies about a certain platinum blond florist, and Brand didn't like it. Not one little bit. He controlled himself, most of the time, for Addy's sake. But, every now and then, he'd lose his temper and dump Dan in the river. Fortunately, Dan knew how to swim. Unfortunately, he got regular dunkings. He never remembered *how* he got in the river, which had earned him the nickname Aqua Man down at the station.

From the look on the warriors' faces, poor Dan was headed for another bath, unless she or Addy ran interference.

"You're back." Evie smiled and hurried to take the sacks of food from them. "The food smells good."

"Well . . . uh . . . reckon I'll be moseying along," Dan said, giving Addy a swift glance of longing. He paused at the door. "Almost forgot. The ME has released Meredith's . . . uh . . . I mean, Mrs. Peterson's body. Thought you'd want to know, Addy. The funeral will probably be at the end of next week. You might want to order extra flowers, it being the Petersons and all."

"Thanks, Dan. I appreciate the heads-up," Addy said.

The door closed behind him, and Frodo threw back his head with a mournful yowl. Nicole took one look at the baying dog and burst into tears.

"Nicole," Evie said in alarm. "What on earth's the matter? Are you sick?"

"Chickens," Nicole gulped between sobs.

"Chickens?" Evie tried to sort that one out and failed. "I'm afraid I don't follow."

"Me and Frodo's bad as them dumb old birds," Nicole said, crying harder. "We've done leaped off the Man Hater Bridge and fallen for the Dog Whisperer."

Chapter Twenty

Muddy offered Nicole her shoe since she was still feeling so verklempt. Nicole declined with a watery sniff and accepted a plate of food instead.

There was plenty to eat. Ansgar and Brand had brought waffles and biscuits, a ham and cheese omelet big enough for a lumberjack—or a Dalvahni warrior—a big batch of piping-hot home fries, a quart container of grits loaded with butter and cheese, several rashers of bacon and, of course, Conecuh sausage, and Miss Vi's homemade orange rolls dripping with glaze.

Evie wasn't hungry, but she nibbled on a biscuit to be polite. She had that dull headache again, but she was glad to see Nicole eat something.

Addy seemed to be enjoying her second breakfast. Addy could hit the trough with the best of them, but nothing she ate seemed to stick. Especially now that she was Super Addy the Dalvahni/human mutant, Evie reflected. Sucking in air made Evie gain weight, but Addy could eat enough for three grown men and not gain an ounce.

Evie tried not to resent it too much. But sometimes it was hard having a best friend who was smart, sexy, sassy, *and* eternally svelte—another one of the universe's sick little jokes.

Sometimes, the universe was a mothertrucker.

Nicole still looked a little wan. Evie couldn't tell whether she didn't feel well or if she was still pining for Ossifer Dan. Love sure had a way of catching the heart unawares.

You ought to know, her sneaky inner voice smirked. *Or are you too big a coward to admit you have feelings for a certain demon hunter?*

Oh, shut up, Evie thought crossly. *I'm not talking to you.*

She shoved her uneaten biscuit aside. Ansgar stood on the other side of the room in quiet conversation with Brand. Ansgar seemed to sense her scrutiny and turned his head to look at her. Their gazes collided and *wham!* the room narrowed and fell away. He made her feel that way, like they were the only two people on the planet.

Only they weren't the only two people on the planet. He wasn't even people. He was an immortal demon hunter and she was . . .

She wasn't in his league; that was for sure. Ansgar the Dalvahni Cream Machine could have any woman he wanted, in this dimension or any other. Someone beautiful and exotic. Like Lenora, Shep Corwin's girlfriend. Lenora was tall and curvy with flowing dark hair, a mouth like ripe cherries, and flawless features. Addy didn't much like her brother's new girlfriend, but even Addy had to admit Lenora had it going on in the sex appeal department.

Of course, being sexy was Lenora's job before she met Shep. Addy described her as "an inter-dimensional emotion-stealing hoochie mama." The best Evie could figure, thralls were sex slaves who served the Dalvahni. "An emotionless demon hunter is an efficient demon hunter . . ." Or something like that.

Evie didn't know the particulars. She hadn't had the chance to get to know Lenora better, and Addy avoided the thrall like the plague. Maybe because Addy suspected Brand had availed himself of Lenora's services B. A.—Before Addy.

Lenora was lucky she hadn't ended up in the river. Brand wasn't the only one with a jealous streak. Addy Corwin had a heart of gold, but when it came to a certain handsome demon hunter, she didn't share.

Thinking about the thrall gave Evie an idea. Maybe she'd ask Lenora for some pointers on how to please a man. She stole a nervous glance at Ansgar. Was she seriously contemplating having sex with him? Her heartbeat kicked into overdrive.

Yep, she was seriously thinking about it, had been since the moment she set eyes on him.

Then an awful thought occurred to her. Maybe Lenora knew how to please Ansgar *from personal experience.* Suddenly, Evie understood Addy's animosity toward the thrall. She wanted to scratch Lenora's eyes out.

The door opened and Blake Peterson, Trey's grandfather and the reigning patriarch of the Peterson clan, stepped inside. *Blip!* Ansgar crossed the room to her side before the door had time to swing shut. Evie was glad he was there. Ansgar made her feel safe, and Mr. Peterson gave her the willies. Always had, though she didn't know why. He'd never been anything but unfailingly polite to her the few times she'd seen him at the mill. But there was something about the man that made her skittish.

That went double for today. Blake Peterson was a Big Fish in Hannah's little pond—a big, *rich* fish from one of the oldest families in Behr County—and he thought she'd killed Meredith, his granddaughter by marriage. Evie wanted to crawl under the counter and hide.

Tall and handsome, with silvery blond hair and deep blue eyes, Mr. Peterson was decades younger in appearance than his seventy plus years. Surely, there was a picture of Blake hanging somewhere in the Peterson mansion that was a sagging, wrinkled mess, 'cause he never aged. His wife Clarice was with him today—as much as Clarice was ever "with" anybody. A cloud of perfume enveloped her, something sweet and heavy. Clarice Peterson was the walking dead, a fashionable but lifeless shell compared to her husband's ruthless, restless energy. An almost imperceptible shudder ran through her slender frame when her husband took her by the arm, though the expression on her carefully made-up face remained wooden.

Evie braced herself, expecting them to turn on her in outrage. To her surprise, Mr. Peterson flicked a single, uninterested glance in her direction and moved on. His wife the walking zombie didn't seem to notice her at all.

"We've come to order the blanket for Meredith's casket," he said to Addy in his cultured, honey-and-whiskey drawl.

Evie was born and bred in the South. She had a Southern accent, but she'd never be able to talk like that if she lived to be
a hundred years old. It was the accent of Old Money, entitle-
ment, and privilege, and she was the daughter of a clerk at the
feed and seed store. Blake Peterson wasn't born with a silver
spoon in his mouth. He had the entire place setting.

"I'm so sorry about Meredith, Mr. Peterson," Addy said.

"Thank you," he said, as though she'd complimented him on
his tie. "The coroner has released her body. The funeral will be
Monday."

Addy blinked in surprise. "Monday? As in day after tomorrow? I assumed the funeral would be later next week."

"We want to put this unpleasantness behind us as quickly as
possible. My wife's health is fragile, and Trey needs closure.
Now, about that blanket. It should be something tasteful. Roses,
lilies, and hydrangeas."

Addy nodded and went to her computer. "If you'll give me
a moment, I can give you a price—"

Mr. Peterson held up his hand, silencing her. "Please, let's
not talk about money in this time of grief. It's vulgar. Just send
me the bill. Good day."

Without another word, Blake steered his unresisting wife
back out the door.

"Huh." Addy shook her head. "That was weird."

"It was bizarre-o," Evie said.

Actually, it was anticlimactic. She'd expected them to point
at her and yell *J'accuse!* Instead, she was so invisible to these people she didn't register on their radar, even as the woman suspected of killing their granddaughter-in-law. She should have
been relieved.

Instead, she was ticked, which was pretty weird, too. She
hated confrontation and unpleasantness, and this little scene
could have been both on a major scale.

She realized Addy and Muddy were talking and tuned
back in.

"—wrong with her," Addy was saying. "It's like nobody's
home."

"Clarice hasn't been right since Blake, Junior, died," Muddy said. "You and Evie are probably too young to remember it. He was killed in a freak accident out at the mill more than twenty years ago. A circular saw shattered and split his head in two."

Addy shuddered. "How horrible."

"Yep," Muddy said. "Your daddy like to had a nervous breakdown over that one. It was a closed casket. Shep, Senior, was a fine mortician, but he couldn't fix that one. Poor Clarice didn't utter a syllable for a year after Junior died, just sat in the music room with his piano. He was a talented musician. Played like an angel. Could have been a concert pianist, but Blake wouldn't hear of it. Said it wasn't manly." Muddy shook her head. "People claim he still haunts the Peterson place. Miss Mamie swears she was out walking her dog late one night and heard music coming from the Petersons'. She peeked in the window of the music room and saw Clarice sitting alone. The baby grand was playing all by itself, and Clarice was talking to someone." Muddy's voice lowered dramatically. "Someone not *there*."

"Mothertrucker." Nicole looked appropriately awed. "That is so creepy. Who's Miss Mamie?"

"The town gossip," Muddy said, dropping the *Masterpiece Theater* impression. "She's all up in everybody's business."

"Speaking of business," Addy said to Evie, "I need you and Nicole to deliver this last batch of flower arrangements to the club."

Muddy's expression brightened. "Oh, yes, the big dance is tonight. Evie, you still have the tickets I gave you?"

"Yes, ma'am, but I'm not going."

"Why not?"

"Because. Everybody thinks I killed Meredith. People will stare a-and *talk*."

"Did you kill her?"

"No!"

"Then let them talk," Muddy said. "Somebody's trying to frame you for murder. You got any idea who?"

"No."

"Any idea who killed Meredith?"

"No, ma'am, but I—"

"Then going to the Halloween costume ball is as good a place as any to start. I got one of my feelings. Something's going to happen at that dance tonight, something big. And you need to be there. That's why I gave you those tickets. Had a hunch you'd need 'em."

"I appreciate it, Muddy. It was very kind of you. I'll pay you for the tickets, but I can't go to the dance. Surely, you can understand how uncomfortable that would be."

Walk into a room full of people who thought she was a homicidal maniac or the husband-stealing hoochie from hell? Or both? She could hear the shocked whispers now and feel the weight of their disapproval and condemnation. Uncomfortable didn't begin to describe it.

"Tell you what will be a whole lot more uncomfortable. Going to jail for a murder you didn't commit." Muddy examined her nails. "Did you know Blake Peterson was a major contributor to Frank Horne's campaign?"

"Frank Horne?" Evie processed the name. "You mean *Judge Horne*?"

Muddy nodded. "The very same judge that will be presiding over your murder trial. Blake Peterson owns this county, and he owns Judge Horne. You talk to Amasa today?"

"No, ma'am. I came straight here."

"He'll be calling you any minute with the news."

"What news?" Evie said.

The shop phone rang and Addy answered it. "It's for you," she said, handing the phone to Evie. "It's Mr. C."

A trickle of dread ran down Evie's spine. She had a feeling of her own. Something bad was coming down the pike. There'd been a lot of that lately. She was starting to see a pattern.

She listened to Mr. Collier and hung up the phone.

"What's up?" Addy said, looking at her in concern. "You're white as a sheet."

"My preliminary hearing has been set." Evie swallowed. "And there's talk of convening a special grand jury. The district court judge called Mr. Collier and 'suggested' in the strongest possible terms that he agree to a preliminary hearing this Thursday. Said he wouldn't be happy if the defense was to 'draw this thing out.' " Evie shook her head, the trickle of dread rising to a full-blown flood. "I thought I'd have more time."

"Wake up and smell the coffee, girl." Muddy's tone was sharp. "Blake Peterson owns the district judge, too. You're being rail-roaded. At the rate this thing is snowballing, you'll be indicted before Thanksgiving. You need to be at that ball tonight. It may be your only chance to do some sleuthing in a big crowd."

"Maybe they won't call a special session," Evie said.

Muddy made a noise of disgust. "And maybe a pig's butt ain't pork. Get real. For some reason, the Petersons want this thing over and done with. The Petersons always get their way."

"But, Muddy, I can't—"

"The universe sends us blips, girl," Muddy said, brushing aside her protests. "Most people ignore them. The smart ones don't. Meredith's murder and that knife being found in your car are big-ass King Kong–size blips. The universe is trying to tell you something, and you'd better listen."

"But, Muddy—"

"Ever since that sister of yours died you've tried not to cause trouble. Trouble found you anyway. Being the perfect child didn't keep your sweet mama from getting cancer or your poor daddy from drinking himself to death. Life is trouble and perfect is boring. Grow some balls, Evie. Go to the dance. Maybe you'll find the killer. Maybe not. But at least you'll be doing something."

Ansgar put his arm around her shoulders. "She is right, Evangeline. Not about her reference to growing balls. I assume that is a slang term referring to the generative gland in males, a derivative of the Anglo-Saxon term 'bollocks.' "

"Dude," Addy said. "It's a euphemism."

Ansgar scowled at her. "I am trying to say that I agree with Edmuntina." He looked down at Evie. "My hunter's instincts tell me our quarry will be at this dance. Do not fret about the humans. I will protect you."

"We'll all be there," Muddy said. "We'll have your back." She jerked her chin at Nicole. "You're going, too."

"Me?" Nicole's eyes bugged. "No way. I wouldn't know what to do with myself at no fancy schmancy country club."

"Huh," Muddy said. She sounded just like Addy. Or maybe Addy sounded just like Muddy. Kind of a chicken and egg thing. "Dan Curtis will be there. He's on duty."

"Officer Curtis?" Nicole's eyes lit up. "You reckon Frodo could go, too? I can't leave him alone."

Addy shook her head at Muddy. "Not a good idea. Frodo's not what you'd call a people person. Or maybe he *is* a people person, but in a bad kind of way."

Muddy waved away her concern. "He'll be fine. Nicole can tell people he's a prop."

"I don't know." Nicole wavered. "All those rich folks . . ."

"Come over to my house this afternoon, and I'll help you get ready," Muddy said briskly. "Addy can give you directions. I've got an idea for a costume for you and Frodo that totally rocks. Bring some of Evie's special shampoo and conditioner with you. I don't mean to hurt your feelings, but if you want to get Dan's interest, we've *got* to do something with that hair. It's a cluster fu—"

"No, Muddy," Addy shrieked. "No, *ma'am*."

The violence of Addy's reaction momentarily startled Evie. Granted, it wasn't polite for Muddy to use the Big Bad Word, but it wasn't like Addy had never heard the word before. When they were kids, they used to crawl in Addy's closet and practice their cussing in the dark. They'd whisper bad words and giggle. It felt wicked and good . . . until Bitsy caught them and waled the tar out of them.

She'd have to remember to ask Addy about it later. Right now, she had other things to think about, like how to get out of the dance.

"I can't go," she said, latching on to the perfect excuse with a feeling of triumphant relief. "I don't have a thing to wear."

It was an age-old excuse, one that had stood females in good stead since the first fig leaf had worn out. And it was absolutely true. That was the beauty of it. Evie had scads of baggy dresses but nothing remotely suitable to wear to a Halloween dance at the club.

Muddy widened her eyes. "Didn't I tell you? I've got the very thing for you."

Evie's elation dimmed. Then she thought of the perfect comeback. "Thanks, Muddy, but there's no way I could squeeze into anything of yours."

"Not mine. This dress belonged to my sister Etheline. She was a curvy gal, too. Had nice bazongas, like you."

Evie's face got hot. "Well . . . uh . . . what I mean is, I don't know—"

"Just give it a try," Muddy urged. "The damn thing's been heirloomed and sitting on a shelf for ages. Wait until you see this dress. It's *gorgeous*. I'll have Amasa bring the box to your house this afternoon."

"Yes, ma'am," Evie heard herself say.

She could have kicked herself. She was a doormat, and a doormat couldn't say no—it came with the mat-i-tude.

Holy freaking cow, she was going to the ball.

Chapter Twenty-one

That afternoon, Evie and Nicole delivered the last of the Fright Night table decorations to the club. The day had been stressful. People who came in the shop either ignored her or asked uncomfortable questions. Like, was she was having an affair with Trey Peterson or did she just flip her shit and go homicidal after years of Meredith's abuse? Miss Mamie wanted to know if Sheriff Whitsun strip-searched her before he put her in jail.

"He can search my body cavities any day," the old lady said, waggling her gray brows.

Ugh. Evie was pretty sure Miss Mamie's body cavities pre-dated dirt.

As Evie drove the van back to town, she struggled to find a way out of going to the dance. She tried to picture herself walking into the Collier Grand Ballroom with half the town looking on and failed. She'd rather eat a bee sandwich suspended upside down by a fraying string—over an open latrine. She hated this kind of thing *before* she became Notorious E.

Nicole was over the moon about the dance, especially after she saw the Hannah Country Club, a sprawling white edifice built in the 1920s on 250 acres of land donated by the Petersons. Evie was glad for Nicole, but she wished she'd quit talking about it. Thinking about her imminent demise made her nervous. That's how she thought of tonight. Death by humiliation and shunning. Like Lura Leigh Bledsoe when she quit the Church of the Holy Jump and ran off to Vegas to dance with a pineapple on her head. Or whatever Las Vegas dancers wear.

"And did you see those columns in the ballroom?" Nicole prattled happily from the passenger seat. "Columns" came out *col-yooms* when Nicole said it. Frodo was in her lap. He was wearing his E-collar again. "They go all the way up to the ceiling. Like twenty feet or something. This is gonna be better than prom."

"I never went to prom," Evie said.

Nicole twisted in her seat to stare at her. "Shut up! Me, neither. I had to work. What about you, your boyfriend dump you at the last minute? That's what happened to my friend Piggy Hollingsworth. Piggy loved her some cocktail weenies. Ate them thangs cold right out the bag. Her boyfriend dumped her two days before prom for a girl everybody called BJ." Nicole snorted. "Big surprise there, huh? Men."

Frodo growled in agreement.

"Am I to infer from that cryptic remark that this other female was less discriminating in her sexual favors?" Ansgar asked from the backseat.

Ansgar was riding shotgun. He was a real gentleman and let Nicole sit up front so she could learn her way around town. Even offered to hold the dog, but Nicole said Frodo got car sick if he couldn't look out the window.

Nicole giggled and deepened her voice. "*Am I to infer.* Baby, with a voice like that you can infer anything you like." She giggled again. "You got a voice like sex on silk sheets, Mr. Dalvahni, if you don't mind me saying so."

"Please, call me Ansgar."

"Sure thing, Ansgar. So, Miss Evie, you get dumped right before prom like Piggy?"

"I didn't get dumped. I never got asked."

"No way."

"Way," Evie said, wincing at the memory.

"Sounds to me like the boys in your school had a bad case of the dumbass," Nicole said. "You're gorgeous."

"Yes, she is," Ansgar said. His cool voice sent a ripple of pleasure along Evie's nerve endings. "Although she does not see it."

"Don't get that." Nicole settled back in her seat with Frodo. "All she's gotta do is look in the mirror." She gave a little shriek that pushed the Chihuahua's yap button. "What's that running through the trees?"

Evie slowed down. "What?"

Nicole pointed out the window. "There, the naked guy! He's all white and shiny. See him?"

Evie saw him. She couldn't miss him, because he shot out of the woods directly in front of the van.

She slammed on the brakes to keep from hitting him. Shiny Naked Guy stood in the middle of the road in his altogether. He was actually more silver than white, with the solid, gracefully muscular build of a danseur. A large pair of silver antlers sprang from his head.

Evie stared, and the guy in the road stared back. His gaze made her feel light-headed and floaty. A strange stillness surrounded the van, a bubble of quiet that seemed to separate them from the rest of the world. Even Frodo stopped barking. Shiny Naked Guy gave Evie one last look with his strange, liquid brown eyes, then leaped across the road and disappeared into the woods on the other side.

"Mothertrucker, was that for real?" Nicole said.

"I do not believe he was an apparition, if that is what you mean," Ansgar said.

"Kami kazi chickens, a bitchy ghost, and now Free Willie." Nicole shook her head. "And it's only my first day in Hannah. This is some kind of crazyass town."

"You aren't thinking of moving back to Baldwin County?" Evie asked, dismayed.

"Hell no. This is way more fun than working at the Gas 'N Gulp, right, Frodo?" The dog yipped. "There, you see, it's settled." Nicole beamed. "Frodo says yes."

As soon as they got back to the flower shop, Ansgar pulled Brand aside for a little warrior-to-warrior talk. Evie had a hunch they were talking about Shiny Naked Guy. Both warriors looked stern and forbidding. She couldn't tell whether they were concerned about the guy with the antlers or just being themselves. The Dalvahni weren't known for yucking it up.

Nicole was telling Addy about the man in the woods.

"You say he had antlers?" Addy said, checking the cooler thermostats one last time before closing.

"Yep. Great big ones." Nicole put her hands on her head and wiggled her fingers to demonstrate. "Twelve points, at least. And he was much a man, if you know what I mean."

"Huh."

"Did I mention he was hot?" Nicole asked. "I'm talking Brad Pitt's fine little naked Achilles' butt hot. Normally, I hate movies about old dead people, but I watched *Troy* to see Brad Pitt's tush. Mm mm mm."

Addy and Evie exchanged a look of amusement.

"I seem to recall you saying something about it a time or two," Addy said. Nicole had uttered the word "hot" no less than a dozen times in reference to Shiny Naked Guy. Addy glanced at her watch. "Look at the time. Nicole, you'd better get on to Muddy's. The dance is in three hours."

Nicole's large breasts came dangerously close to giving her a black eye as she bounced up and down with excitement. "Ooh, I can't wait to see what my costume looks like. I never been to a Halloween dance."

Evie's stomach did a funny little roller coaster dip. Oh, God, the dance.

Addy's voice jerked her out of her loop of terror. "Muddy said Nicole should bring a bottle of your shampoo and conditioner, but she didn't say what kind. What do you recommend for Nicole's hair?"

Nicole's hair was a two-tone, dried-out, mangled-up mess with all the texture and shine of a clump of Spanish moss. The hair product didn't exist that could fix such a follicular disaster, although she'd never say so. She wouldn't hurt Nicole's feelings for the world.

She hurried over to her display table and grabbed two bottles of *Fiona Fix-It,* a new line of hair care products she'd created for overprocessed hair. Her palms tingled and the bottles felt warm against her skin. Too much sun. She must remember to move the table farther away from the window.

"Here," she said, setting the shampoo and conditioner on the counter.

Nicole swung her huge purse off her shoulder. "How much do I owe you?"

"Nothing. It's a new line of products. You can be my guinea pig. Just let me know what you think."

"Cool." Nicole flipped open the cap and took a sniff. "Wow, smells great. Kinda clean and woodsy. Frodo's coat is a little dull. I want him to look his best for the dance. Can I use this on him, too, or would that hurt your feelings?"

"Go for it. If it works on Frodo, I may start a doggie line, *Fiona for Fido.*"

"Frodo," Nicole said. "*Fiona for Frodo.* My handsome little man could be your cover cheesecake." She gave the Chihuahua a little squeeze. "You got the guns for it, right, Precious?"

Frodo barked.

"Frodo says yes." Nicole slipped the shampoo and conditioner in her purse, her eyes sparkling with excitement. "I got directions to Miss Muddy's house. See y'all at the dance."

Evie's stomach did another zero gravity roll.

Oh, God, the dance.

Evie sat on the edge of her bed and tried to calm her fractured nerves. Her bedroom was her special retreat, the place where she went to regain her equilibrium. Decorated in shades of cream and sunny yellow, her room was filled with things she loved, things steeped in family memories. The four-poster bed had belonged to her parents, the marble-top nightstand and walnut dresser were handed down from her maternal grandmother, and her mother used to sit in the rocking chair every night as she crocheted in front of the television.

Being in her room calmed and centered her, but not tonight. Tonight none of the usual soothing rituals worked.

She'd soaked in the tub until her fingers and toes were wrinkled, and drank a cup of passionflower tea. No good. The lavender-scented candle on the table by the bed did not soothe her, nor did the cheerful bouquet of purple asters from her garden raise her flagging spirits. Her favorite housecoat, a worn blue cotton robe soft from numerous washings, felt as itchy and uncomfortable as burlap. Even her hair seemed to tingle and crawl with nerves. She piled it on top of her head in a loose knot to get it out of the way. Eating was out of the question, unless she wanted to hurl.

Since leaving the flower shop, she'd formulated and discarded a dozen excuses to stay home. The dance loomed before her like some dreadful, enormous thing waiting to crush her. She tried to think of something else. But she couldn't stop. The harder she tried to forget about tonight, the more her thoughts circled back to it.

She heard the front doorbell ring and the murmur of voices. A moment later, there was a knock on her bedroom door.

"Come in." Her voice sounded small and pathetic, the squeak of a frightened mouse. She cleared her throat and tried again. "Come in."

Better, but still rodent-esque.

Ansgar stepped into the room carrying a large white box. "That was Mr. Collier at the door. He brought your dress. I thought you might like to see it."

Part of her, the cowardly smart part interested in self-preservation, wanted to scream, *What difference does it make what the stupid dress looks like? I'm freaking Hester Prynne and I'm going to the dance and somebody's going to nail a great big 'M' on my chest for murderess.*

Her rational self told her to go to the dance and try to figure out who killed Meredith so she wouldn't spend the rest of her life in a women's prison being somebody's bitch. That same rational self reminded her, quite logically, that it was highly unlikely Ansgar had read *The Scarlet Letter,* so the Hester Prynne reference would be wasted on him anyway.

The female part of her wanted to see the damn dress.

Ansgar being male and, hopefully, less schizophrenic, was unaware of the raging battle within her. He removed the lid from the box, took the dress out with a rustle of tissue paper and silk, and draped the gown across the Queen Anne chair next to the bed.

Evie stared at the dress in disbelief. No one could accuse Edmuntina Fairfax soon-to-be-Collier of not having a sense of humor.

She leaped to her feet. "Is she kidding me? I can't wear that dress!"

The gown was exquisite, an exact replica of the slut dress Rhett made Scarlett wear to Ashley Wilkes's birthday party after she got caught embracing Mr. I-Love-My-Wife-but-I-Wouldn't-Mind-a-Little-Scarlett-Coochie-on-the-Side-Wilkes—yards of deep garnet French silk velvet and a matching butterfly train decorated with hand-sewn Swarovski Austrian crystals. An extravagant ruff of dyed ostrich feather plumes fluttered around the deep neckline and on the hem and bustle of the dress. The box contained shoes, gloves, and hair ornaments to match, and a burgundy net shawl.

"With your hair and eyes, I would prefer to see you in green or gold," Ansgar said slowly, as if not quite sure what all the fuss was about. And why would he? *Gone with the Wind* probably wasn't on the required reading list for the Dalvahni. "The gown is fetching, nonetheless. Why are you distressed?"

"That's freaking Scarlett O'Hara's red dress, that's why!"

"I thought the gown belonged to Muddy's sister."

"It does . . . I mean *did*."

"Then who is Scarlett O'Hara?"

"Only one of the most famous female characters ever written. Strong and gorgeous and a rule breaker. Basically, everything I'm not."

Ansgar took her hands in his. "Listen to me, Sarah Evangeline Douglass, and listen well." His deep, sexy voice sent little shocks of *wowza!* up and down her body. "I do not know this Scarlett, but I have lived a long time, and I have *never* seen a woman more beautiful than you. But, you are not just a lovely shell. You are gentle and warm and kind." He tilted her chin up. "And you are strong and brave, too."

"You're wrong. I'm afraid of everything."

"And yet you persevere in spite of your fear. That is true courage. A weaker woman would have crumbled beneath the trials you have endured."

He thought she was beautiful and strong. He must be on Dalvahni crack. She gazed at the red gown with longing. A dress like that would make a woman unforgettable—if she had the nerve to wear it.

Making an appearance at Fright Night in that dress would be a bold statement, the one-finger salute to the killer, if he or she were there. *I am here. I am not invisible. I will fight.*

Addy would wear the dress. She was bold and fearless. But she wasn't Addy.

She didn't realize she'd voiced her thoughts aloud until Ansgar spoke.

"Your reticence is a cloak you use to hide your true self," he said. "I have always known this about you."

"You've only known me a couple of days."

One day, nine hours, and twelve minutes, to be precise. But who was counting? She was, every glorious second with him.

He hesitated. "Time is of no consequence. I knew you in an instant."

"Thanks for the vote of confidence," Evie said. She didn't bother to hide the bitterness in her voice. "I wish I could believe it."

"Then allow me to convince you," he said.

He pulled her into his arms and kissed her.

She went up like a torch, gasoline to his fiery spark. The nearness of him, the warmth of his touch, the clean, spicy scent and intoxicating taste of him wiped everything else out of her mind. The dance, the dress, her fears . . . all forgotten.

She wanted him with an intensity that shocked her. She'd never allowed herself to want anything before, to hope for anything.

Wanting Ansgar was the height of foolishness, like trying to lasso the moon with a ribbon of silk. She didn't care. He would break her heart. She didn't care about that, either. This was her chance, maybe her one chance, and she was going to take it.

She wrapped her arms around his neck and kissed him back.

Chapter Twenty-two

Ansgar urged Evie's lips apart and dipped his tongue inside the honeyed, warm cavern of her mouth. With a little moan, she pressed her body closer and tasted him, little silken brushes of her tongue that turned his blood to liquid fire and nearly brought him to his knees.

He'd been too long without her. He wanted her too much. The hazy, lust-fogged thought registered over the frenzied pounding of his blood. His hands gentled along her slender back, moving past the enticing curve of her waist to cup her lush bottom. He pulled her closer, nudging the sweet haven between her legs with the bulge of his aching cock.

Sweat trickled down his back and beaded his brow. By the sword, she strained his already-crumbling self-control. He wanted to take her now, plunge inside her with swift, hard strokes. Standing up, on the bed or on the floor, it mattered not. After months of wandering lost, he was starved for her.

But that would not convince her of anything except his rapacious need, a need that she would attribute to animal appetite and nothing more. It would not convince her that she was beautiful and strong. She could see neither. It was up to him to show her, to give her the confidence she needed and deserved.

It took every ounce of his willpower to release her and step back.

She looked up at him, her hazel eyes soft with desire and confusion. "What is it? Did I do something wrong?"

"No. There is something you need to see."

"What?"

"You."

He took her by the shoulders and turned her around. Her eyes widened, and her mouth, still soft and rosy from his kiss, formed an astonished "o" of surprise. She looked back at him from the wall of mirrors. He could almost see the questions fluttering through her mind like so many startled birds. But she was quick witted, his ladylove. She'd seen proof of his powers the day before, when he repaired the damage to her bathing chamber. So, she did not ask him how he'd transformed her bedroom wall into polished glass. She bypassed the tedious "how" and went straight to the heart of the matter.

"Why?" she asked instead.

Standing behind her, he met her questioning gaze. "It is time you abandoned your disguise and unveiled your true self. Remove your robe."

Her cheeks grew pink. Shyness, reluctance, curiosity, arousal, and dismay flitted across her lovely features in rapid succession.

"Now? Like this? I don't think I can."

"Of course you can. Unknot the sash, Evangeline." His pulse quickened in anticipation as her hands crept to her waist and unfolded the twist in the cloth. The garment she wore was simple, plain even, but nothing could diminish her allure. She was a thousand times more comely and captivating than the most provocatively clad thrall. "Good. Now, let it fall."

With a soft swish, the fabric belt dropped to the floor and the robe parted. He caught a tantalizing glimpse of Woman before she grabbed the garment and covered herself.

"But what is this? You regress." He slid his hands down her arms to lightly caress the backs of her fingers. "I want to see you."

She shook her head and closed her eyes, her grip on the fabric tightening. "I can't . . . the mirrors."

He could see her heart thudding through the thin fabric of her robe. His own heart was racing at a gallop. He bent his head and nuzzled the back of her neck. Tonight, she smelled of jasmine and magnolia, sweet, seductive, and sensual, like her.

"Relax," he said softly. A shiver of response ran through her as his lips grazed her ear. "Let go. I will help you."

Slowly, her fingers unfurled, and she stood trembling and uncertain before the glass. The robe slithered open just a bit, giving him another heavenly peek at her creamy, full breasts, smooth thighs, and intimate curls.

His mouth went dry and his body hardened. He wanted to bury himself in her, to lose himself in her sweetness. By the sword, it had been far too long.

"Open your eyes, Evangeline," he murmured against her hair. She was so shy and hesitant. She had no notion of her own power, thank the gods. The woman could lay him waste with a single glance. "I am about to open my present."

She opened her eyes then, his curious, clever siren, and stared back at him. She had beautiful eyes, swirls of golden brown flecked with green, the eyes of a forest nymph, full of mystery and cool, mossy shadows. He could lose himself in their depths.

"Present? What present?"

"This," he said, sliding his hands from her waist to her breasts.

The flimsy robe bunched at the shoulders and gaped open, framing the luscious globes and baring them to his hungry gaze. The thundering of his blood was so loud he could scarcely hear.

"You have lovely breasts, Evangeline. Large, firm, succulently round." He caught the dusky tips between his fingers and gently tugged. "Truly magnificent. A man could love you for your bosom alone."

"Ansgar!"

Her indignation at his chauvinistic remark made him want to chuckle.

"But there is more to you than a fine bosom, much more," he said. "Let me unwrap the rest of my present, and I will show you."

Before she had time to protest, he tugged the robe down her arms and tossed it across the room, leaving her naked for his perusal. A rosy blush stained the creamy satin of her skin, spreading from the tops of her perfect breasts, up the smooth column of her throat, to her lovely face. She quickly covered herself with her arms and would have made a dash for the discarded robe if he had not wrapped his arms around her, stopping her.

"When is the last time you really looked at yourself, Evangeline?" He buried his smile of amusement against the tender skin of her neck, pressing a hot trail of kisses there. She thought to cover herself. Little did she know that the pressure of her folded arms pushed her breasts up, giving him an enticing view of her cleavage.

"I look at myself all the time." She stared at her toes, her arms covering her breasts. She wiggled the fingers of one hand at the small mirror over the dresser. "When I brush my hair and my teeth, and put on my makeup."

"You have a lovely face, sweetling, but no more exquisite than the rest of you."

"You're making fun of me." The uncertainty and self-loathing he heard in her voice tore at his heart. "I'm fat. Whaley Douglass. Thunder Thighs. Bucket o' Lard. That's what they call me."

"I am *not* making fun of you," he said, giving her a little shake. "Furthermore, I should turn you over my knee for suggesting such a thing. As, I believe, I have promised to do if ever you uttered such nonsense in my presence again."

She gasped and pushed against his arms. "You wouldn't dare!"

"Easy, sweetheart," he said, releasing her at once. She stepped away from him and gave him her back, her shoulders heaving. "Meredith and her harpies said those hateful things to you out of jealousy and spite."

She turned to him with an expression of astonishment. "Meredith and her friends, jealous . . . of *me*?"

"Consumed with envy," he said, closing the space between them. "And who can blame them? They are but pale, thin imitations of womanhood, whilst you are desire itself." Cradling her face between his hands, he smiled down at her. "For the last time, Evangeline, you are not fat. You are lush and gloriously curved, thank the gods, but you are not fat."

Unable to resist the sweet temptation of her lips any longer, he gave her a lingering kiss before he spun her around to face the mirror once more. "Look at yourself and see what I see." He cupped her full breasts in his hands, his thumbs grazing her nipples. His face looked strained in the mirror, his tanned skin very dark against her creamy flesh. "Beautiful breasts with nipples that make a man want to taste them." His voice sounded rough to his own ears. He was shaking now, very near the end of his control. His hands moved to the sharp indent above her flaring hips. "See how my hands nearly span your waist? To say that you are fat is absurd." Turning her to one side, he caressed her sweetly rounded ass. "And this luscious bottom? Temptation itself. It makes me want to mount you like a stallion."

The color in her face deepened. "Oh. You shouldn't say such things."

"Why not? It is the truth." Turning her once more toward the glass, he swept his hand across the slight curve of her stomach to the reddish-gold curls at the juncture of her thighs. "And here . . ." His voice dropped to a husky whisper as he brushed his fingers between the sensitive folds. "Here you are beautiful, too, velvet soft, with all the blushing sweetness of a ripe peach. And you know how I love peaches."

He slid his finger inside her and heard her rapid intake of breath. The tiny sound made everything in him tighten another notch. She was damp and ready for him. He groaned aloud. He could not help himself. He wanted her too badly. Her sheath would be slick and hot, and when she came—and he would make sure she did—her pulsing delight would send him hurtling over the edge.

She watched him, wide eyed as a doe, as he played with her. It was an erotic sight beyond his wildest dreams. She, standing naked against his fully clothed body, his hand between her legs bringing her to pleasure. Her cheeks were flushed, and her breasts rose and fell rapidly.

"Evangeline," he said. The words came out a desperate rasp. "How can I make you see? You are beauty and desire, light and laughter to me, a feast for body and soul. I am like a beggar at a banquet, famished for want of you. Let me in before I perish."

She turned to him then, surprising him, and laid a gentle finger across his lips. "I want you, too. Something crazy. We've known each other less than two days, but it feels like I've known you forever. *Wanted* you forever. I don't understand it, but that's the way it is."

He did not burn alone. The knowledge made him want to shout with possessive joy and relief.

"Will you do something for me?"

"Anything," he murmured, placing a hot kiss in the center of her palm.

"Stop talking and make love to me. Please."

Chapter Twenty-three

It was a bold thing to say, totally un-Evie-ish. After a lifetime of being petrified of doing or saying the wrong thing, it was exhilarating to let go and not worry about making a mistake. No matter what happened, Ansgar had given her that, the courage to step away from the prison of herself.

With a muttered curse, he yanked her into his arms and gave her a scorching kiss. Evie clung to him, reveling in the feel of his strong, unyielding body, the raw masculine power barely held in check. She was shameless, but she didn't care. She was on fire for him. Any hotter, and the government would requisition her as a permanent energy source.

Even more amazing, he wanted her, too. The evidence was unmistakable. She could feel the hard length of his erection through his jeans.

He's horny, her wiser self cautioned. *It doesn't mean anything. The guy's majorly gorgeous. He's probably got more girls than Carter has little liver pills.*

Maybe so. But right here and now he was horny for *her,* and that was a great big something in the Evie universe.

It was a big something in his universe, too. Demon hunters weren't supposed to fraternize with human females. There were rules against that sort of thing. Addy said so. The old Evie, the perennial good girl and rule follower, would be worried about that.

The new Evie, the one clinging naked and unabashed to six

feet four inches of hard-muscled male, was throwing the rule book out the window.

Doing the mambo jambo with Ansgar would probably be the biggest mistake of her life, the most *gloriously* wonderful mistake of her boring, little life.

Evie couldn't wait. She put her hands on Ansgar's shoulders and pushed. He released her at once and stepped back. He was breathing hard, and his eyes were so dilated they looked black. His face was taut and strained.

"Take off your shirt," she said.

"What?"

"Take off your shirt. I want to see you."

Heat flared in his eyes. He ripped the shirt off and threw it down. Buttons bounced and rolled across the wooden floor.

"Wow," Evie said, staring at him.

The reality was way better than she expected, and she expected perfection. He was gorgeous, all animal strength and grace, sleek and golden as a mountain lion. Muscles rippled beneath his smooth skin. His powerful chest tapered to a taut, ripped abdomen. The blue jeans he wore rode his lean hips and clung to his strong legs. He was a miracle of power and proportion, the most perfect specimen of the male animal she'd ever seen or could ever imagine.

"You are such a liar," she said, feeling more than a little indignant. "You're a thousand times more beautiful than I am. I mean, geez minnelli, look at you."

"Someone wise once said beauty is in the eye of the beholder." He hooked one hand behind her neck and tugged her close so that they stood skin to skin, her breasts pressed against his bare chest. Heat bloomed between them, hot enough to melt them both. "We could argue about this all night," he said. "But there are other things I would much rather do."

Evie's heart rate tripped up a notch, and she found it hard to breathe. "Like what?"

"Like this."

His hands moved to her breasts, and everything in her coiled

in anticipation. *Nipples that make a man want to taste them* . . .
The hot shivery words thrilled her to the core. She'd been
holding her breath, she realized, wanting his hands on her again.
Wanting his mouth on her.

"Please, Ansgar," she begged. The desperate words slipped
out, beyond her control to stop them. She wanted this, wanted
him too badly to be shy and hesitant any longer. "Please."

"Please what? What do you want, sweetling?" He reached
down and cradled her breasts in his strong hands. Evie almost
swooned with relief. It felt like forever since he'd touched her.
"Tell me."

"Your mouth," she heard herself say. Her boldness shocked
her. Even more shocking, she arched her back. "There."

He bent his head, put his mouth on the aching tip of one
breast, and suckled. The wet pull of his mouth sent a wicked
shock of pleasure to the aching place between her legs. He
shifted his attention to the other breast, and her throbbing
senses spiraled higher. She drifted, panting, on a sea of desire,
and he was her only anchor. She clutched his broad shoulders
and held on.

He raised his head and looked at her, his eyes fever bright,
his beautiful face tight with lust.

"Does that feel good?" He bent his head once more to lick
the tight buds, lazy, teasing strokes of the tongue that made her
twist and squirm in his grasp. "And this?" he asked.

She could hear the satisfaction in his tone. He knew what he
was doing to her, damn him, and he was enjoying it.

Two could play this game.

"It feels wonderful." She straightened and looked up at him,
taking in the glittering eyes, the strong cheekbones and stubborn jaw, the perfect, kissable mouth made for sex and sin.
Good Lord, he was something else. She ran her hands over the
thick muscles of his arms and chest, enjoying his tremble of response. "But now I think it's my turn."

A muscle tightened in his jaw. "Evangeline, I do not think
that is such a good—"

She heard his breath hiss as she trailed her fingers down the muscled ridges of his abdomen and rubbed the hard bulge in his jeans. She suppressed a sigh of longing. He was impressive *there,* too.

"Hmm," she said, reaching for the metal button at the top of his jeans. "Somebody's too big for their britches. Literally."

"Evangeline, I am trying to go slowly." His deep voice sounded hoarse. "But you test my resolve to the limit."

She unfastened his jeans so that his heavy shaft sprang forth. Satin-covered steel, she thought, taking the hot, hard length of him in her hand. It felt good to have her hands on him, natural and right. No shyness, no self-consciousness, for the first time in her life. With him, she was strong and confident and free. The joy of it made her want to weep.

She smiled up at him. "I don't want to go slow. I want you inside me. Now."

The words seemed to demolish the last of his restraint. With a fierce growl, he took her in his arms and kissed her. Any doubt that he desired her ended with that kiss. There was nothing suave or gentle about it. His need was raw and aching, an unquenchable lust and longing. A desire so palpable that she responded to it without thinking. She came alive in his arms, everything in her yearning for him. Energy crackled around them in blues and greens and fiery red, a jagged lightning burst of pure power.

"Evangeline," he muttered, worshipping her with his mouth and hands. "I want you. I need you so much."

"I want you, too, Ansgar." She ran her hands along the corded muscles of his arms and across his wide chest. Every touch set off more sparks, within and without. The nimbus of color around them pulsed and expanded. She rubbed herself against him, desperate to feel him, to be with him, to worship him, too. "Now. Please."

He picked her up and made as if to toss her on the bed, but she stopped him.

"No." She pointed to the floor in front of the mirrors. "There. So I can see."

Something hot and primitive flared in his eyes. He carried

her over to the mirrors and lowered her feet to the floor. She felt something soft beneath her feet and looked down in surprise. The woolen hook rug that covered the hardwood floor in her bedroom was gone, replaced by layer upon layer of luxurious furs.

Dalvahni woo woo, she thought, too hazy and lust drugged to wonder at it.

She dropped to the floor on her knees, offering herself to him. Bold and brazen, perhaps, but she didn't care. She turned her head and saw Ansgar posed behind her, his jeans around his hips. His erection jutted away from his hard, ridged stomach, long and thick. Perfect.

He grasped her hips, his hands bronze against her pale complexion. She liked his hands on her, liked seeing them like this.

"Arch your back, sweetling," he muttered, his hot gaze on her naked bottom.

She obeyed, shuddering as he reached between her legs and stroked her. An expression of fierce satisfaction lit his face when he found her wet and ready for him.

She felt him nudge her with the head of his shaft, and then he was inside, filling her, stroking her. She closed her eyes. The feeling was exquisite, driving her higher toward the edge of something.

His hands tightened on her. "No, open your eyes and look at us. Look what you do to me."

She obeyed. They were connected, flesh to flesh, man and woman.

"Watch," he said, withdrawing slowly.

The slow, deliberate pull of his flesh on hers was delicious. He rocked his hips and entered her again. Her inner muscles contracted, clasping him tighter.

With a groan, he withdrew again and thrust back inside.

"Evie," he said. "You are so sweet, so good. I cannot—"

Impatient, hungry for him, she pushed back, taking him deeper. "It's all right. I love it. I love *you,* Ansgar."

It was true, she thought, torn between panic and elation. She loved him.

With a groan of relief, he plunged harder, faster. She watched them in the glass. She couldn't stop. His head was thrown back, his muscles tensed, his face tight and strained. Her buttocks were firm and white beneath his kneading grasp, her breasts swayed in time with the ancient, thrusting rhythm he set.

It was erotic, amazing. Something built inside her, tingling, golden, and hot. The climax rolled over her in waves. With a shout, Ansgar came, too, spilling his seed inside her. Her greedy body pulsed around him, pulling him deeper into the endless ripples of delight.

It was beautiful.

He was beautiful.

She was beautiful, too.

Chapter Twenty-four

Later that night, Evie was still flying high on post-sex-with-Ansgar pheromones when they left for the dance. To her surprise, the red dress fit, although it was way too tight in her opinion.

"It is not too tight," Ansgar said, giving her a hot look that did funny things to her insides. "You are not used to displaying your curves, and that is why you are uncomfortable. You look magnificent. I will be hard pressed to keep my hands off you at the dance, and so will every other male there." Something dangerous glinted in his silver-gray eyes. "Although they had better."

Evie thought he was pretty darn magnificent, too. Sex walking in black leather warrior garb, was more like it. Black pants, black boots, and a leather vest over a white sleeveless tunic. Silver and leather armbands hugged a pair of biceps fine enough to make the rest of the masculine universe sit down and bawl from feelings of inadequacy. A knife strapped to a muscular thigh and a second one in a sheath around his ankle. Pale blond hair clubbed back with a piece of leather. Bow and quiver of arrows slung over one broad shoulder. Grim, watchful expression on a face carved out of pure gorgeousness.

Scarlett O'Hara and the Demon Hunter, Evie thought with a happy sigh. It sounded like a paranormal romance.

Leaning against him, she stroked the hard plane of his chest. "I don't think I can keep my hands off you, either. What say we skip the dance and stay home?"

Ansgar's eyes grew smoky, and, for a moment, she thought he might yield.

But he shook his head instead. "You are temptation itself, but we are going."

Crappydoodle. So much for that idea.

When she stepped out of the house and onto the porch, there was a new truck sitting in her driveway.

"What's that?" she said, pointing to the gleaming black vehicle. She wondered with a pang how Gussie, her battered Ford Taurus, was faring in the impound yard.

"You do not know? It is called a truck."

"I know what a truck is. Whose is it?"

"Is is mine. It is a Ford Velociraptor Six Hundred, the ballsiest stock pickup ever offered for sale." Ansgar repeated this last with the rote care of someone who's memorized a speech.

"Velociraptor?" Evie said, taking Ansgar's arm as she went down the steps. Walking in the long gown was proving to be a real bitch. "Isn't that the name of that fancy truck in the showroom down at Riverside Ford? The guys at the mill were going on about it. Said there are only a few like it in the state. Talk is Bobby Glenn's wife was mad as a wet hen when she found out he ordered it. Probably afraid he won't be able to sell it."

"Her worries are over. I purchased the truck this afternoon while you were at the shop with Addy. Bobby Glenn seemed most eager to cooperate."

"Cooperate? You didn't . . ."

Ansgar chuckled. "Fear not. I did not compel the human to relinquish the machine. I paid in coin. He seemed surprised."

"You mean you paid *cash*?"

"Yes, that is the correct term."

"Holy cow, I'll bet he was surprised, especially if it cost as much as people are saying."

"It was seventy thousand of your dollars."

"Seventy thousand dollars *for a truck*?" Evie stopped in her tracks to gape at him. "Are you insane? That's more money than most families around here make in a year. Bobby Glenn took you for a ride."

Ansgar guided her toward the black metal behemoth in her drive. "That is correct. He took me for a ride, and afterward I purchased the truck."

"Yes, because he's a car salesman and that's what they do. They talk people into buying cars."

"It is not a car. It is a truck," Ansgar said, as though she were slow. "This truck is special order. It has six hundred and five HP and a Hennessey Performance upgrade. I am not sure what that means or who this Hennessey is. Some kind of magician, I think. No matter. This truck is scary fast. Bobby Glenn says so. It has a muscle-bound body, gargantuan tires, and something called Baja grade suspension. Bobby Glenn says this truck's ass is bad."

Badass. The truck was badass and the subject was closed, Evie reflected as he helped her in the truck and shut the door. Ansgar might be thousands of years old, but when it came right down to it he was just another overgrown boy, delighting in his shiny new toy that went *vroom.*

The truck was very nice, if a little noisy. Ansgar didn't seem to mind. In fact, he seemed to enjoy the loud *wump wump* of the big engine. He drove to the club without hesitation and without the aid of the GPS on the dashboard. Maybe he remembered the way from this afternoon, or maybe he had a good sense of direction. He was a hunter, after all.

"I didn't know you could drive," Evie commented as they headed across the river bridge. She tried not to think about the chickens.

"I observed you when you drove the van this afternoon," Ansgar said. "The Dalvahni learn quickly. I also scanned Bobby Glenn's mind at the automobile store." He shrugged. "Driving is not difficult."

He learned how to drive by scanning Bobby Glenn's mind? Good Lord, her boyfriend was weird.

Her boyfriend; the thought sent her into a swoon of happiness that lasted the rest of the ride.

The club was ablaze with lights. Evie explained the process to Ansgar and he eased the truck up to the sign that said VALET PARKING. They were late and the dance had already started, so there were no cars ahead of them. A teenage boy in a navy blazer and khaki slacks stepped up to the passenger side door.

"Holler, dude. You bought the Velociraptor! That is so cool." The boy grinned from ear to ear. He opened the door and stared at Evie's cleavage. "Whoa, mama, look at you."

In the blink of an eye, Ansgar was around the truck. He scowled at the boy as he helped Evie out of the truck. "She is not your matriarchal unit."

The kid scrambled back with a startled exclamation. "Jeez, mister, I didn't even see you. Where'd you come from?"

Ignoring the question, Ansgar handed the valet some money. "The truck is new. Take good care of it."

The boy's eyes widened when he counted the bills Ansgar gave him. "A hundred dollars? You bet I'll take good care of it, mister. It's a sweet ride."

Ansgar's disgruntlement visibly eased. He gave the truck a satisfied glance. "Yes, it is. Very sweet, indeed. Make sure you park it well away from the other vehicles."

Yep. A man with a new toy, all right.

"You got it." The boy climbed in the truck and wump wumped off.

They stepped inside the lavishly appointed foyer of the club, and Evie heard the faint strains of music coming from the ball- room. The haze of happiness that had enveloped her since mak- ing love with Ansgar evaporated, replaced by a cold wave of panic. This was real. This was happening. In a few minutes, she would walk into a crowded room and be the center of atten- tion. Staring, angry, outraged, scandalized attention.

"Down the hall and to the left," said the vampire bunny who took their tickets.

Evie clutched Ansgar's arm. "I can't do this. I can't."

"Yes, you can," he said. His cool, liquid voice washed over her, soothing her and taking the edge off her panic. "I will be with you."

Stomach fluttering, she walked beside him down the hall. Officer Curtis stood outside the double doors of the Collier Ballroom talking to a short woman with her back to them. The woman wore a strapless cream-colored gown with gold trim and an abundant wig of long, curly brown hair. Dan stopped in midsentence when he saw them.

"Holy shit, Evie, is that you?" Dan blurted. He turned bright red. "I mean, you look great."

The woman whirled around. "Miss Evie! Mothertrucker, you're *gorgeous*."

"Nicole!" Evie exclaimed. Mullet Woman was gone, and in her place stood a stocky little Roman goddess in a sexy floor-length tunic. She held an oversized feather duster under one arm. Maybe she was supposed to be the goddess of cleanliness. "You look gorgeous, too."

Nicole straightened to her full height, which was somewhere around five feet two. "Don't I though? Miss Muddy gave me the gown." She jiggled the feather duster under her arm. "I made Frodo a costume out of a dishcloth so's we'd match."

"Frodo?" The feather duster lifted its head with a familiar snarl, and Evie realized it was the Chihuahua. Frodo looked like the victim of a perm gone tragically wrong. His steel-blue fur sprang in thick, wild curls all over his tiny body. "Good gracious, I didn't recognize him."

"It's that shampoo of yours. It's a flat-out miracle." Nicole fluffed her long wig. "Look what it did to my hair."

"Wait, that's your hair? I thought it was a wig."

"I *know*. I used your *Fiona Fix-it*. Ain't had hair like this since . . . well . . . like *never*."

"But Nicole, that's impossible. No shampoo could do that."

"That's what I told Miss Muddy, but she says you got a gift." Leaning closer, Nicole said in a low voice, "I didn't want to argue with her—she's a real nice lady and been awful good to me, you know—but I'm thinking maybe *he* had something to do with it."

"He?"

"The guy in the woods, Free Willie. I think he put the whammy on us."

"The whammy?"

"You know, magic." Nicole made a whoo-ooo-ooo noise. "I mean, look at the two of us. Girlfriend, we is *hot*. I think Frodo looks hot, too, though he don't seem to appreciate it so much."

And no wonder. Frodo resembled a periwig with teeth. To add to his humiliation, Nicole had pinned a tiny circlet of spray-painted leaves to the puff of gray curls that bushed around his head.

"Um . . . Nicole?" Evie said, upon taking a closer look at the dog. "Frodo's not wearing his E-collar."

"I know. Couldn't get it on over all the hair. He'll be all right."

Yeah, right. Frodo was having a bad hair day. He was one pissed off Allihuahua. Somebody was gonna lose a finger tonight.

At that moment, a man in a bumblebee suit lurched down the hall and swerved into Nicole, almost knocking Frodo out of her arms. The Chihuahua went crazy barking.

"Cute poodle," the bumblebee said with a drunken smile.

"Hey, buddy, watch it," Dan said, steadying Nicole. He reached out and took the snarling dog from her. "You'd better go soak your head. You've had too much to drink."

The bumblebee mumbled something else and staggered off.

Music blared as the doors to the ballroom swung wide and two dashing figures stood posed in the open doorway. Addy was Veronica Lake in *The Blue Dahlia* in a white-pleated gown with a tightly fitted ruched bodice, her platinum hair swinging around her shoulders in a sultry peek-a-boo style. Brand, like Ansgar, was dressed as himself, a dark and dangerous demon hunter in warrior garb. Well, duh. Big surprise there.

"Ah, brother, 'tis you," Brand said. "I thought that I sensed your presence. The festivities began some time ago, and I was growing concerned at your absence. All is well with you?"

Ansgar slid a possessive arm around Evie's waist. "I am sorry for your disquietude. Evangeline and I were . . . delayed."

Heat rushed to Evie's face as Brand arched his dark brows. Oh, geez. He knew what they'd been doing and why they were late. She lifted her chin and looked him in the eye. Brand would have to deal. Tonight with Ansgar was the most wonderful thing that had ever happened to her, and she didn't regret it. Not for a moment.

She forgot her discomfort the next moment as Addy rushed up to her with a happy squeal of excitement. "Oh, my goodness, oh my *goodness,* you look wonderful, Eves! That dress is an absolute dream, and that color red is ah-mazing on you. Who did your hair?"

"I did." Ansgar pressed a lingering kiss on Evie's bare shoulder that sent a shiver of delight to her hot place. "I took great pleasure in the task."

"Huh," Addy said with a knowing look. "I'll just bet you did." She grabbed Evie's hand. "Come on. Muddy's gonna have a whole litter of kittens when she sees you."

She pulled Evie toward the open doors.

Evie hung back. This was it, the moment she'd been dreading. "Wait, Addy. I don't think—"

Too late.

Like her mama and Aunt Muddy, Addy Corwin was an irresistible force. Ignoring Evie's protests, Addy dragged her into the ballroom.

Chapter Twenty-five

The music ground to a halt, and everyone turned and looked at them, men and women in costumes frozen like bizarre statues on the dance floor. A werewolf, a Frankenstein monster, and two she-devils gaped at Evie from the edge of the crowd. The creepy guy from the Burger King ads was dancing with Little Red Riding Hood; he swiveled his smiling, plastic head in her direction. At the far end of the room, Trish and Blair stood on the bandstand with a knot of women. Trish wore a French maid costume that was two sizes too small. Blair was re-living the days of Bitchmas Past in a tiara and an emerald green gown complete with a banner across her chest that said HOME-COMING QUEEN 2000

They were all staring at her, even the members of the band. It was Evie's worst nightmare, the gym locker room in middle school all over again and she just got boobs. She wanted to slink away and hide, but something wouldn't let her.

Maybe it was the dress. Maybe it was the much needed confidence the past few glorious hours in Ansgar's arms had given her. Maybe she was tired of acting like a kicked dog. Whatever the reason, her chin came up, her shoulders straightened, and she leveled what she hoped was a look of haughty disdain at the room full of people.

"Oh, gosh, Evie, I'm sorry," Addy said. "I wasn't thinking. I wanted to show you off. You want me to kick some butt?"

"Yes." Evie took a deep breath and blew it out again. "No. I knew it was going to be like this."

Blip! Ansgar and Brand were beside them in a blur of motion, flanking her and Addy on either side, two perfect bookends of demon hunter badass. Evie heard the low grumble of the Chihuahua's chainsaw growl and knew that Nicole and Frodo had joined them.

"Why's everybody staring at Miss Evie?" Nicole demanded loudly. "Surely these people don't think she murdered nobody? 'Cause that's a bunch of hooey."

"She will be vindicated, you have my word," Ansgar said.

The menace in his tone startled Evie. Her tender, passionate lover of the past few hours was gone, and he was all warrior again, lethal and deadly.

"See, Miss Evie," Nicole said. "We gotcha back. Ain't that right, Precious?"

The Chihuahua chirked like a prairie dog.

"Thanks," Evie said, smiling in spite of herself. "That makes me feel better."

A short, bloated Elvis in a white, sequined jumpsuit waddled out of the crowd, nearly collided with the drunken bee, and headed toward them. Evie's brain did a *WTF* before it registered that Mayor Tunstall was beneath the sideburns and jet-black pompadour. The mayor had his pet possum Priscilla with him on a leash. Priscilla went everywhere with the mayor. The possum looked fetching in a lavender and white princess dress with a matching pointy hat and veil. Priscilla grinned at Frodo, and Frodo grinned back. It was a regular toothfest.

"Evie, my dear, you are a sight to behold in that gown," the mayor said, ogling her bosom. He seemed oblivious to the budding romance between canine and marsupial. "But under the circumstances, I think you'd better leave. The Petersons are here and all the Lalas. Meredith was going to be president of the Lavender League next year, you know, and the Petersons are about to announce a special donation in her memory. This is awkward."

The Petersons were here? She didn't expect that, not with a death in the family. Awkward didn't begin to describe it.

Muddy sailed up on the arm of a giant panda, the picture of

elegance in a black and white 1920s flapper dress and feathered headband.

"Suck it, Eugene," she said. "The gal's not leaving. She has just as much right to be here as anybody." She nudged the panda with her elbow. "Tell him, sugah."

The giant panda removed his head and tucked it in under one arm, revealing Amasa Collier in the furry suit.

"My client is innocent," Mr. Collier said. "Somebody in this town has framed her, and I intend to find out who. Justice will prevail."

The mayor looked uncomfortable. Most folks in Hannah thought Mr. Collier was a few bricks shy of a load because he claimed to see demons. It was obvious that number included the mayor.

"That so?" the mayor said, fidgeting nervously with the veil on the possum's hat. "And how do you propose to do that?"

"With my contrabulator." Mr. Collier whipped a long wire instrument out of his fuzzy sleeve and waved it around. "It's a multipurpose demon-seeking divining rod. If the murderer's a demon or a demonoid and he's here, I'll find 'em with this little baby."

"Demonoids. Really, Amasa?" the mayor said. He looked around. "If you'll excuse me, I have some business to attend to."

Frodo threw back his puffy head with a mournful howl as the mayor wobbled off with Priscilla the possum princess.

"Thank goodness that old sack is gone," Muddy said. She eyed Evie up and down. "I declare, Etheline's dress does look good on you, child. She'd be proud."

Evie smoothed the soft velvet skirt. "It's beautiful, Muddy. I can't thank you enough for letting me borrow it."

"Oh, pooh, it was going to waste sitting on a shelf. I knew it would be breathtaking on you. High time you stopped hiding your light under a bushel basket. Although that green gown you wore to the Grand Goober Ball looked mighty good on you, too."

Green gown? Images flashed through her mind of a different dance floor: Ansgar in a tuxedo and she in his arms. The floor rolled beneath Evie's high heels, and her temples began to throb. Oh, no, she was getting another migraine.

"The Grand Goober?" Dimly, she was aware that the music had started up again. Light shimmered around the whirling dancers, making Evie queasy. She lifted a trembling hand to her brow. "I'm afraid I don't know what you mean."

"Evangeline?" Ansgar put his hand on her shoulder, his deep voice full of concern. The warmth of his palm against her skin comforted and steadied her. "Are you well?"

"Yes, a headache, that's all," Evie said. "I think you must be mistaken, Muddy. I've never gone to the Grand Goober Ball."

"Muddy," Addy said through her teeth.

Muddy looked odd, almost panicked, but that couldn't be right. Nothing ever panicked Muddy Fairfax.

"I'm sure you're right, Evie, dear. Pay no attention to me." Avoiding Evie's gaze, Muddy waved to a caramel-skinned Cleopatra gliding around the dance floor with her burly Roman centurion partner. "Don't Viola and Delmonte look fine? Those ballroom dance lessons in Pensacola are paying off, huh?"

Del and Miss Vi made a handsome couple, but that was beside the point. Muddy had changed the subject.

Evie tried again. "About that green dress, Muddy—"

"So, Friend Collier," Ansgar said, interrupting her. "Have you found anything with your demon sensory device this evening?"

"A few tingles, that's all."

Addy perked up. "You got a tingle? Ooh, does that mean there's a demon here?"

"Nah, no demons," Mr. Collier said, adjusting his contrabulator. "Just some demonoids, but that's nothing new in Hannah. Like fleas on a dog."

"Demonoids?" Addy looked around. "Who?"

"Well, let's see," Mr. Collier said. "Trey Peterson for one."

"What?" Evie yelped, forgetting her headache.

"Oh, pooh." Addy looked disappointed. "I've known about Trey for ages."

"Well, I didn't." Evie gave Addy an indignant look. "He was my boss. Why didn't you tell me?"

"I tried. You wouldn't let me. You said you didn't want to know."

"You're right," Evie said. "You did try to tell me." Trey was a demonoid. Could he have murdered Meredith? Oh, this was horrible. She couldn't live like this, suspicious of everyone she met. "Where is he?"

Ansgar's hand tightened on her shoulder. "Why do you care where he is?" he said, his voice dripping ice.

"Down, Blondy." Addy patted Ansgar on the arm. "She's surprised and embarrassed, that's all. If she was interested in Trey she could've had him months ago. He's been mooning over her for ages."

Evie flushed. "Addy, that's not true. Trey's not interested in me like that."

Addy made a rude noise. "Get a clue, girlfriend. He's interested in you *exactly* like that. Why do you think he put up your bail money?"

Muddy's brows shot up so far they disappeared underneath her feathered headband. "Trey put up Evie's bail money? How . . . interesting."

"He has been repaid with interest," Ansgar said. "Evangeline is my responsibility."

"I am *not* your responsibility," Evie said, unaccountably annoyed.

Whoa, where did that come from? She knew she was overreacting, but she didn't care. Ansgar's responsibility, indeed! Maybe if he loved her. People in love took care of one another. But he didn't love her. He'd had plenty of opportunity to say so tonight. *Up close and personal opportunities.* But he hadn't. And one day—probably one day soon—he would leave and she'd be by herself again. The thought made her feel hollow and empty inside.

"I've been taking care of myself since I was twelve," she said.

"Evangeline."

She heard the warning in Ansgar's tone. Well, he could just get over it. Demon hunters weren't the only ones with pride.

She squared her shoulders and looked him in the eye. "I appreciate what you did, paying Trey back and all, but I *am* going to reimburse you. I'm going down to the bank Monday and take out a second mortgage on my house so I can pay you and Mr. Collier."

"I'm not charging you a fee, Evie," Mr. Collier said. "I told you that from the get-go. I don't need the money. I've known you since you were knee high to a grasshopper, and I'm not about to let you get railroaded. I'm representing you 'cause I want to, so hush."

"I do not want your money, either," Ansgar said. "Money is of no consequence to the Dalvahni."

"It's of consequence to me. I won't be in your debt w-when you leave."

"Evangeline," Ansgar said again. Taking her hands, he looked down at her. Oh, Lord, he had that look in his eyes again, the one that melted her insides and made her heart race. "I am not—"

"Shh," Addy said, nodding toward the front of the room. "I think Trey's about to say something."

Evie turned and saw Trey up on the bandstand, somberly dressed in a dark suit and tie. He was surrounded by the clump of women she'd noticed earlier. He must have been there the whole time, covered in female drapery. They swarmed around him like bees attracted to a piece of overripe fruit. Nothing new there; Trey was tall and good looking and had more money than God. But his appeal was off the charts now that he was Available. These women were acting like maenads, frenzied by the scent of single Male. Trish Russell was flirting with him, and she was married to a doctor in Fairhope—snaked him away from his first wife.

But this was Trey Peterson of *the* Petersons, and he was a widower. It was a blood bath, and Trey didn't stand a chance, demonoid or not.

The drunken bumblebee was buzzing around the steps to the

stage. He and the mayor did a little shuffle dance before the mayor bypassed him and hefted his bulk up the steps, his white polyester jumpsuit straining at the seams. Huffing and puffing, he pushed his way through the cluster of women to the microphone. At his signal, the music wound down.

The mayor tucked Priscilla under one arm. "If I could have your attention for a moment, ladies and gentlemen, Trey Peterson has an announcement."

Maybe her decision to come to the dance tonight wasn't in the best of taste, Evie mused, watching Trey free himself from the tangle of women and join the mayor. She was, after all, *numero uno* on the "who murdered Meredith?" suspect list. But the women clinging to Trey like nylon panties to the top of a dryer drum were downright tacky. Muddy was right. Meredith was hardly cold, and the competition was sniffing at his heels. These chicks were darn lucky Meredith hadn't decided to show up tonight. They'd be scraping ectoplasm off themselves for weeks.

"Thank you, Mayor Tunstall," Trey began. "As you know, my wife—"

A smooth drawl interrupted him.

"Here, son, let me make the announcement," Blake Peterson said, taking the mike out of Trey's hand. "We all know what a strain you've been under."

Trey's complexion went white under his golfer's tan. He shot Blake a startled glance and moved back. Trey seemed smaller and more vulnerable to Evie, like he'd shrunk in the past forty-eight hours. The strain was visible on his face, and he seemed sad, which was only natural given Meredith's death. But he seemed something else, too, something Evie couldn't quite put her finger on.

"As you know, our family has suffered a terrible loss," Blake said. "Our dear Meredith has been taken from us, cut down in the prime of life—"

"Not the way I would have put it," Addy said under her breath.

"—but the Peterson family will pull together and endure this tragedy, as we endured the death of Blake, Junior, lo these many years ago . . ."

"Look at Clarice," Muddy whispered, directing Evie's attention to a thin woman in a knee-length black dress.

Clarice stood at the bottom of the steps, rigid as marble, her gaze fixed on Blake. To Evie's shock, Clarice's eyes blazed with hate and something else, the same "something" revealed on Trey's face.

Fear, Evie realized. Fear was something she knew. She'd lived with the suffocating weight of it most of her life. Fear of saying or doing the wrong thing, of disappointing those she loved or of hurting them. This went way beyond that. Trey was terrified of his grandfather, and Clarice Peterson hated and feared her husband. The Petersons were one big unhappy family.

She returned her attention to Blake.

". . . are making a sizable donation in Meredith's name," he said, "to provide some much needed renovation to Hannah High, Meredith's beloved alma mater. Never fear, Meredith's memory will live on."

Nodding to the mayor and the clapping audience, Blake started toward the steps. He was polished and urbane, but there was something about him that made the hair on the back of her neck stand up.

On impulse, Evie grabbed Mr. Collier by the arm. "Mr. C, point your contrabulator at Blake Peterson. Quick, before he gets off the stage and into the crowd."

Mr. Collier complied. The contrabulator glowed with a sullen orange light and began to vibrate and whine.

"We got ourselves a big one," Mr. Collier cried, hanging on to the shimmying contrabulator with the excited glee of an angler reeling in a wily bass. "This is the real thing. Pure, undiluted e-vil. Hot damn, I think we may have found ourselves the killer."

"Have we indeed?" Ansgar said softly. "Then I would very much like to have a word with this Peterson fellow."

Chapter Twenty-six

Ansgar cursed himself for a fool. He should have suspected Peterson before. Mr. Collier had informed him and Brand months ago of the existence of demonoids, the wretched whelps of demon-possessed humans. The news of the demonoids' existence had sent a ripple of shock and concern through the ranks of the Dalvahni. It was one reason Conall had stationed Brand and Rafe here, to study the situation and report back.

Unlike demonoids, a demon-possessed human was easy to detect. The djegrali were parasites that fed on the essence of the humans they possessed, sapping them physically and spiritually. The human body began to waste away, resulting in an unmistakable stench, a rancid odor that was easily recognizable. Demon-possessed humans also tended to be violent and often engaged in self-destructive or erratic behavior; demons loved excess in food, wine, drugs, and sex.

There was another telltale sign of djegrali possession. The eyes of a demon-possessed human were a sickly, blackish purple, like bruised plums.

Not so their violet-eyed, unnatural offspring. Aside from the sometimes unusual color of their eyes, the demonoids blended in with the populace, passing as humans and living among them. Little was known about them or their powers, thus Conall's concern.

Blake Peterson, urbane, wealthy pillar of Hannah society, was a demonoid. Ansgar chided himself again. Had he been less befuddled by his feelings for Evangeline and fear for her safety, he would have remembered this vital bit of information earlier.

The familiar, icy detachment settled over Ansgar. He welcomed it like an old friend, let it cool his heated blood, calm, and center him. If Blake Peterson was responsible for Evangeline's plight, he would track him down and kill him. Slowly and painfully. He was good at killing. Even among a lethal race, he excelled at it. There would be no mercy for anyone who threatened Evangeline.

Yes, he thought with grim satisfaction, reveling in the return of his dispassion, this was good. A much needed return to control after the fever of desire of the past few hours. The hunt he knew, the hunt he understood, unlike the shifting sands of his feelings for Evangeline. She was everything to him, his own personal kind of madness.

If she were harmed . . .

Steel claws raked his gut at the thought. No, he would not think on it. Reckless rage would not serve his purpose and would give the enemy an edge. He was Dalvahni. He would remain unexcited and detached. Not long ago, the idea of anything less would have been unfathomable. Those days were gone, and there was no going back. The djegrali would delight in his predicament if they but knew: Ansgar, swift arrow of Dalvahni justice, ruthless scourge of their kind, at the mercy of a flame-haired sorceress who was more dangerous and powerful than a thousand demons.

He glanced at her and was swept once more into the maelstrom. That damnable dress, he thought, his gaze lingering on her. The garnet velvet molded to her delectable curves, and the plunging bodice lifted her breasts in a tantalizing display of creamy flesh. Gods, she was lovely. After the long months of hunger and desolation, of aching want and longing, Evangeline's scent, the intoxicating taste and feel of her, the dizzying joy of being with her again, should have been a relief. Instead, his greedy soul, starved of softness, laughter, and light for so many years, hungered for more. He could not get enough. Her teasing, haunting fragrance, the smell of Woman, lingered on his skin. The taste of her on his lips, sweet and succulent as ripe fruit, made him ravenous with need.

Images assailed him, Evangeline, her sweet, beautiful face flush with passion, eyes drowsy with pleasure as he took her.

She'd no notion of her effect on him. Or of her effect on others, he thought sourly, noting the appreciative attention directed at Evangeline by the other males in the room. It made him curse his ability to read human thought. That ability served him well in the hunt for the djegrali, but not tonight. Tonight it made him privy to the lascivious thoughts of every man present. Old, young, married, or unwed, it mattered not. They watched her with hot eyes and fantasized about being with her. He did not blame them, but understanding did nothing to whet his desire to kill them.

He sighed inwardly. Jealousy, another emotion he'd never conceived of until he met Evangeline. He was consumed with it. Had he his way, he would whisk her away and keep her all to himself. Selfish and obsessive, but that was the unvarnished truth. Not that he would get his way. She was a fighter, his Evangeline, soft and sweet on the outside with an inner core of steel. True courage was facing one's greatest fear. She'd done so tonight, with style and aplomb. He would never forget the sight of her standing in the open doorway, all eyes upon her, the air heavy with speculation and self-righteous condemnation. She held her head high, one titian brow lifted in proud disdain.

Magnificent.

She was his, to love and protect. He was a hunter, unsurpassed in tracking skills. He would discover her enemy and crush him. He locked his gaze on the silver-haired man on the stage. Let the hunt begin with Blake Peterson.

Startled by the promise of death in Ansgar's tone, Evie glanced at him and stifled a gasp. His eyes, smoky gray with passion not an hour ago, were pale and unforgiving as the heart of a winter storm. She'd always thought of rage as a fiery emotion, hot, fast, and consuming, but Ansgar's fury was cloaked in ice. The expression on his beautiful face and every line of his powerful body radiated cold, deadly menace.

"Ansgar?"

His glacial gaze did not shift from Blake Peterson's retreating figure. "Stay with Brand until I return," he said. "He will keep you safe in my absence."

"Ansgar, wait!" Evie reached for him, but he was gone.

What had she done? One careless, unthinking act on her part combined with a few wiggles from Mr. Collier's contrabulator—a device that consisted of a couple of wire coat hangers twisted together and nothing more—and Ansgar was in demon hunter mode and on the prowl. Even if Mr. Peterson was bad to the bone, there was no real proof he was the killer. So what if his family wasn't crazy about him? Family dynamics were complicated. He made her uneasy, but that didn't mean anything. Lyle Goodson down at the Chevron station gave her the willies, too. Always staring at her and touching her hand. He was a total creeper, but that didn't make him a murderer, and the fact she didn't like Blake Peterson didn't make him a murderer, either.

Blake Peterson was so elegant and suave, and so darn *rich*. If he wanted Meredith dead, he could hire somebody to do the job. Besides, why would he kill Meredith? She came from one of the "right" families, and, for all her faults, she was crazy about Trey. In her own way, Meredith had been a good wife to him, fitting in with the country club crowd, active in the Lala League and the Episcopal church. It didn't make sense.

"I have to stop Ansgar," she said, starting after him.

Brand stepped in front of her, barring her way. "Stay. You will distract him."

"You saw him." She tried to move around him, but somehow, no matter which way she moved, he was always in front of her. "He's going to kill Blake."

"He will do what is necessary to protect you."

"What if Mr. Peterson is the wrong guy? What if Mr. C's contrabulator doesn't work or is malfunctioning?"

"I'll have you know, my contrabulator's in perfect working order," Mr. Collier said.

Oh, dear, she'd hurt Mr. Collier's feelings.

"I'm sorry, Mr. Collier," Evie said. "I never meant to—"

"Evie, is that you?"

A low whir of titillated excitement buzzed through the people milling about the room as Trey Peterson made his way toward her. Heads turned so hard and so fast you could practically hear the neck bones crack. Murder, scandal, the delicious possibility of a forbidden, torrid affair—heady stuff in a little town.

"Oh, no," Evie said. "Addy?"

"I'm here." Addy took Evie by the hand. "I won't leave."

"What ails Miss Evie?" Nicole asked.

Muddy motioned Nicole closer. "See that man coming toward us?"

"You mean the tall, sandy-haired fellow in the suit looking at Miss Evie like she's dessert?"

"That's the one. He's Meredith's husband—the woman everybody thinks Evie killed. He's got the hots for Evie."

"Mothertrucker," Nicole said.

"Exactly."

The band launched into another number.

Mr. Collier slid his contrabulator up his sleeve and put on his panda head. "Edmuntina, would you like to dance?"

"I'd love to, Amasa."

The giant panda and the elegant flapper swept back onto the dance floor.

"Look at 'em. They're really in love, ain't they?" Nicole sounded wistful.

"Yes, I do believe they are," Evie said, eyeing Trey's approaching figure with dread. She did *not* want to talk to him.

"Love." Nicole heaved a deep sigh. "I can't believe I'm doing this. Come on, Frodo. Let's go flirt with the po-po." She turned to leave and ran headlong into the bumblebee. " 'Scuse me," she said.

She left the ballroom, headed, Evie assumed, to find Dan Curtis. She considered going with her and hiding out in the lobby until Ansgar returned, but it was too late. Trey was already upon her.

"Evie, that dress," he said in a tone of wonder. "Your hair . . ."

"Her boobs." Addy's tone was as dry as a lizard's butt on hot sand. "Go on and say it. You're a guy. We know what you're looking at."

"Addy, please," Evie murmured, embarrassed.

Trey shot Addy a look of dislike. "You're beautiful, Evie," he said, gazing at her in that way that made her want to squirm.

Life was funny. A million years ago in high school, Evie had a secret crush on Trey, along with most of the other girls in town. He was a Big Deal when they were teenagers, the original Golden Boy, quarterback, good looking, popular, and rich. Of course, he never noticed her. Or, if he did, it was to make fun of her, same as Meredith and the other cool kids. Sometimes, she fantasized about what it would be like to date him. Deep down she knew she would hate it. All that attention . . . Meredith and the Twats would have made her life unbearable.

Trey was still a big deal in Hannah, but now she just wished he'd go away.

"Thank you," she said.

Everyone was looking at them. Oh, this was beyond miserable.

Not ten feet away, Yum Yum Truman, who'd come to the dance as Princess Leia from *Star Wars,* was making like the Leaning Tower of Pisa in an effort to listen in on their conversation. If she listed much farther, she'd land on her cinnamon bun hairdo. Mamie Hall tottered closer to them on a pair of four-inch leopard-print platform shoes. She wore silvery thigh-high stockings, a slinky satin dress that was artfully ripped and torn, and a pale peach glamour wig. Evie couldn't decide if Miss Mamie was supposed to be Gwen Stephani at eighty or that creepy, rotting woman from *The Shining.* Either way, she had Evie's vote for scariest costume.

To her horror, Trey grabbed her hand—the one Addy wasn't squeezing the life out of.

"I need to talk to you," he said in throbbing tones. "Alone. It's important."

They were the center of attention, but Trey seemed oblivious. What was the matter with him? Was he totally missing an appropriate valve?

She had to get out of here.

Evie yanked her hands free and bolted for the door. Behind her, she heard Addy call her name, but she kept going. She needed space.

She darted into the hall, passing Nicole and her powder puff Chihuahua, and Officer Dan. Where the heck was the ladies' room, Oklahoma? She'd hide out there until Trey left. Splash a little water on her face, regain her composure. There, at the end of the hall, two doors separated by a water fountain. One door had a sign on it that read BLOSSOMS; the other door's sign read BARK. Good grief, which one was she? She *hated* cutesy names for restrooms.

Blip! Brand appeared in front of her, blocking her way. "Where are you going? I promised Ansgar to keep you safe."

"I'm going in the ladies' room," she said. "Where ladies go to do *lady* things, like powder our noses and freshen our lipstick and *twinkle*."

"Twinkle?" Evie could almost see the Dalvahni translator kicking in. Realization dawned in Brand's eyes, and he took a hasty step back. "I will wait for you here."

"I thought you'd feel that way," Evie said.

With a sense of triumph, she pushed open the door designated BLOSSOMS and stepped inside. Her victory was short-lived.

There was a dead cheerleader in the bathroom.

Chapter Twenty-seven

Ansgar stalked toward the stage, studying his quarry. Though his hair was gray, Peterson carried himself like a much younger man. Much younger. Did the demonoids, like the Dalvahni, escape the ravages of time that cursed the mortals of this frame, living on long after their human friends and family had died? If so, Peterson might have added silver to his hair to disguise the fact that he did not age.

More questions with no answers, Ansgar thought, seething with frustration. Little was known about demonoids. That fact would have to be remedied.

Peterson came off the stage and said something to his wife, who waited near the foot of the steps. Even from a distance, Peterson fairly crackled with pent-up energy, charisma, and something more.

Inhuman power.

Not so the thin woman in the black dress. She seemed ordinary, a dry, brittle husk in comparison to her husband's wicked vitality. Her posture was rigid, her expression as fixed and unbending as her body.

Clarice, Ansgar remembered. Her name was Clarice.

Giving Blake a tight-lipped smile, she turned and made her way ahead of him through the crowd. Their progress was hampered by the many people who stopped to speak to them. Curious to hear their conversation, Ansgar opened his senses.

"—so very sorry about Meredith," a dark-haired woman in

a cat costume said to Clarice. "Guess Greer Whittaker will move up as president of the La Las . . ."

". . . in a better place with Jesus now." A caped man squeezed Blake's shoulder. "If there's anything you need, anything at all—"

"This Monday? My goodness, so soon?" An overweight woman in a butterfly costume shook her head, making her antennas wobble. "I declare, Clarice, I don't know how you're vertical. And to think that Evie Douglass had the *nerve* to come here tonight! She's some kind of tacky. My cousin Tracy works at the courthouse." The woman leaned closer, her large brown eyes widening. "She says Trey put up Evie's bail money. Is it true?"

"Of course it isn't true." Blake took his wife by the arm and gave the fat butterfly a smile that did not reach his eyes. "Enjoy the dance, Babs. I need to get Clarice home. It's time for her medicine."

Ansgar cloaked himself in invisibility and followed the Petersons out of the ballroom. The closer he got to Peterson, the more his instincts jangled in warning. The stench of evil emanating from Blake Peterson was strongly reminiscent of the djegrali and, yet, different.

"Don't touch me," Clarice Peterson said, jerking away from her husband as soon as they reached the hallway.

Peterson looked around, as though checking to see if anyone had overheard. Dan Curtis and Nicole stood at the other end of the passageway near the entrance to the lobby, engrossed in conversation, but no one else was around.

Except me, and Peterson cannot see me, Ansgar thought with grim satisfaction.

"Don't make a scene." Blake's low voice was flat and cold. "You're a Peterson. There are appearances to consider."

"Appearances can be deceiving, as you ought to know." Mrs. Peterson backed away from her husband, her narrow chest heaving. "I wonder what people would say if they knew the truth about you?"

Ah, Ansgar thought, his hunter's instincts sharpening. *Was the female referring to the fact her husband was a demonoid, or something else?*

"Really, Clarice, you grow more tiresome every day." Closing the gap between them, Peterson reached for her. "We both know you aren't going to say anything."

"Don't be so sure of that," Clarice said.

Turning, she scurried down the hall, her heels rapping against the tile floor in a staccato rhythm. She reminded Ansgar of a frightened rabbit in her haste to get away from her husband.

Blake swore savagely and went after her.

Remaining invisible, Ansgar crept into the lobby behind them. He paused when he saw the man in the uniform leaning against the wall near the front doors. So did the Petersons.

"Mr. Peterson," Sheriff Whitsun said, straightening. "I'd like to have a word with you, if I may."

"Not tonight, Sheriff." Blake's lean face, harsh with impatience and disdain not a moment before, assumed an expression of weary sadness. "It's been a long day and my wife is tired."

"It's all right, dear." Clarice's tone was sweet as honey. "I'll wait in the car. Take your time."

Giving Blake a smile that was a thin blade of triumph, she walked out the door.

"Well," Blake said. His expression was bland, but Ansgar sensed the anger boiling just beneath the surface. "What can I do for you, Sheriff?"

Ansgar eased closer, moving without sound. To his surprise, the sheriff's nostrils flared and he glanced around, as though sensing Ansgar's presence. Ansgar went still. How could he have forgotten? Whitsun was something more than human, too.

"There's been a slight complication, I'm afraid," Whitsun said. His sharp gray gaze moved back to Peterson. "The murder weapon has disappeared from the lab in Mobile."

"What?" Peterson's outraged voice rang through the lobby. "This is inexcusable, sheer incompetence. When I find out who is responsible, heads will roll."

"The lab people insist the knife was properly secured. Whoever took that knife broke into the Department of Forensic Sciences and removed it from the evidence locker. And they did it without a key."

Peterson's brows drew together. "Someone forced their way in?"

"No. The locker was undamaged and unopened. Nothing else was missing. Just the knife."

"That doesn't make sense."

"I know, and things that don't make sense bother me, Mr. Peterson. A lot."

Blake took a deep breath, as though struggling to compose himself. "This is most upsetting, Sheriff, but I suppose in the long run it doesn't matter. The blood on the knife matched Meredith's?"

"Don't know yet. The forensics guys took swabs from the knife before it was stolen, but their analysis isn't complete. That's another odd thing. The Department of Forensic Sciences is backlogged with cases, and yet this one was given top priority."

Peterson gave the sheriff a pitying smile. "Not odd at all. I know the director. He moved things along for me."

"Same way the preliminary hearing was pushed to the head of the docket? I hear it's next week. That's mighty fast. You make a few calls to Paulsberg, too?"

"My wife's health is delicate, Sheriff Whitsun, and my grandson is distraught. Did you know Evie Douglass came here tonight, bold as brass, with everybody knowing she's the killer? Why aren't you questioning her? The woman is obviously unhinged. I want this thing resolved quickly and that woman put away, for my family's sake."

"I guess I can understand that. What I can't figure out is the motive. Why would Evie Douglass kill your granddaughter-in-law?"

"The oldest motive in the world—jealousy. Evie Douglass wanted my grandson for herself. She killed Meredith to get her out of the way, poor deluded thing. Trey might screw a girl like that, but he would never marry her. She's nobody. Her father was a drunk who worked in a feed store, for God's sake. Not our kind of people."

A girl like that . . . Some of Ansgar's icy detachment faded. So Evangeline was not good enough. He suppressed the sudden urge to strangle Blake Peterson. Slowly.

"I see," Whitsun said. "So, Miss Douglass killed the victim in a jealous rage and left the bloody knife in her car. Clumsy, to say the least."

"You're the one who found the knife, Sheriff."

"Yes, I did, and that's another thing that sticks in my craw. I searched that car myself first thing yesterday morning, and it was clean. It was like that knife appeared by magic. Or somebody planted it in Miss Douglass's car."

"Good God, Sheriff, you've been watching too much television."

"Something else. I photographed that knife and sent a buddy of mine a picture of it. He says the knife is a Scagel, a real collector's piece with a stacked antler and leather handle and Bakelite spacers. Didn't mean a thing to me, but my friend was mighty excited. He claims that knife is worth twenty thousand dollars." Whitsun rubbed his jaw, looking thoughtful. "So that got me to thinking. Where in the world would Evie Douglass get a twenty-thousand-dollar knife?"

Peterson's gaze shifted. "Maybe it was her father's."

"The drunk who worked in a feed store?" The sheriff shook his head. "I don't think so. I think that knife belongs to somebody with money, lots of money. Someone who collects knives."

"What are you implying?"

"Nothing, just trying to figure things out. You collect knives?"

"I have a knife collection, yes. My father collected many things. He left everything to me."

"He was involved in some kind of unpleasantness back in the sixties, wasn't he?"

Peterson's jaw tightened. There was blackness at the heart of this man. The sheriff had better be careful.

"A woman named June Hammond was murdered. My father was tried and acquitted," Blake said. "Look it up."

"I did. Got the file off microfiche. The victim in that case was murdered in much the same way as your granddaughter-in-law, cut to pieces with a knife."

Peterson's expression grew pained. "Surely you're not suggesting my father killed Meredith? The man's been dead more than twenty years, God rest him."

"Of course not, but what if the person who killed June Hammond—the real killer—is still out there and killed Meredith?"

"You mean like a serial killer?"

"Exactly."

Peterson laughed. It was not a pleasant sound. "June Hammond was murdered in 1967. Your serial killer would be riddled with arthritis by now."

"Maybe, or maybe he was a young man when he murdered Hammond. I've done some research. There have been a number of unsolved murders in Behr County over the past fifty years. Six, to be exact, including June Hammond. They all involve female victims who were stabbed to death."

"Fascinating," Peterson said, striding toward the door. "Now, if you'll excuse me, my wife is waiting."

"How old were you in 1967, Mr. Peterson?"

"Twenty-eight."

"A man in your prime," the sheriff said. "One more thing, Mr. Peterson. Did your father's knife collection include any Scagels?"

Peterson opened the door and looked back. "Scagels, a Frank Richtig, a Nichols blade, several by Bo Randall, and a Bob Loveless. My father loved beautiful things. Come to the house sometime and see for yourself."

"I'll do that. Does Trey have access to your father's knife collection?"

"Yes. So do a number of other people, including me, my wife, and our two daughters."

Peterson stalked out the door and into the night.

Sheriff watched the older man leave, reaching for the device on his belt when it beeped. "Yeah? All right, Willa Dean, try and calm her down. I'm on my way."

He clipped the box back at his waist. "That was dispatch. A woman on County Road Fourteen swears a man tried to kill her Chihuahua. That's the third call like that I've had today." He sighed. "Like I need this craziness in the middle of a murder investigation."

Ansgar looked around. The lobby was empty. To whom was he speaking?

"You might as well show yourself, Mr. Dalvahni," Whitsun said, answering his question. "I know you're here."

With a muttered curse, Ansgar materialized. "How?" he demanded, in no mood to dance around the matter.

Whitsun chuckled. "No need to look so put out. I can smell the leather you're wearing and your cologne . . . and something else. Some kind of wax, maybe?"

Ansgar grunted. "You have a good nose, Sheriff. 'Tis rosin you smell. I use it on my bow."

"A bow hunter, huh? Is that standard demon hunter issue?"

"No, our weapons are a matter of individual taste."

Ansgar considered the man. Most humans were frightened of anything they did not understand and resistant to the idea of the supernatural, to say the least. Yet, this man seemed calm, unnaturally so. Whitsun was an enigma.

"You know what I am?" Ansgar asked finally.

"I'm pretty sure I do. You're in law enforcement, like me, only in your job, the bad guys you round up happen to be demons. The way I figure it, we're in the same line of work. I think of it as damage control."

"Damage control? That is an interesting way of putting it." Ansgar was reluctant to admit it, but he was beginning to admire and like this man. "You are familiar with the djegrali?"

The sheriff seemed to consider the unfamiliar term. "Is that a fancy word for demons?"

"Yes."

"Oh, yeah, then I reckon I know something about them."

"Then be warned, Sheriff. For reasons unbeknownst to us, the djegrali have managed to propagate in Hannah, and their hellish offspring abound in this place. This may come as a surprise to you, but Blake Peterson is a demonoid."

"I'm not surprised at all," the sheriff said. "You see, I'm a demonoid, too."

Ah, Ansgar thought with a surge of satisfaction. Hadn't he always known the sheriff was something out of the ordinary? Then he thought of something else.

"I do not understand," he said, frowning. "Your eyes are gray."

Whitsun chuckled. "I wear contacts, Mr. Dalvahni. Purple eyes are a dead giveaway to other demonoids. Makes my job easier if I stay under the radar."

Chapter Twenty-eight

Evie stared at the ghoul. Meredith lounged on the sofa in the antechamber of the women's restroom. She was wearing her old Hannah High cheerleader uniform, and her blond hair was mussed and scraggly. Black streaks of mascara ran down her face, and she was covered in blood. She looked ghastly, but in a fun, Halloweeny kind of way.

"Nice costume," Evie said. "Glad to see you getting into the spirit of things."

"Is that a crack?" Meredith swung her slender, blood-smeared legs off the couch and floated to her feet. "Because the living impaired have feelings, too, you know." She looked Evie up and down. "What are you supposed to be, the plus-sized madam of a whore house?"

How many times over the years had Meredith called her some version of fat? Too many to count. Evie waited for the familiar hurt and shame to wash over her, drowning her in a sea of self-loathing. Nothing happened. The Death Starr's power over her was broken, thanks to a certain demon hunter.

She gave Meredith a sunny smile. "Actually, I *am* supposed to be a scarlet woman. How clever of you to guess! But, then, you always were good at games."

There was a loud *whoosh* from the other room, and Leonard Swink faded through the metal door of a stall. "Sorry, my EMF must be fluctuating. I had no idea these automatic toilets were so sensitive." He saw Evie and wavered a little in surprise.

"Gracious, you gave me a turn. I didn't realize we had company."

"I don't mean to be rude, Mr. Swink," Evie said, "but I think you're more of a *Bark* than a *Blossom*. This is the ladies' room."

"My client needed my support. She saw her husband for the first time since her Dreadful Demise and became distressed."

"Distressed?" Meredith clenched her fists. "I can't get near Trey for the bitches hanging on him like ticks on a hound dog. I want to tear their hair out."

"Yes, yes, I know," Swink said. "But, as we've discussed, these violent mood swings of yours are detrimental to your recovery. Deathnesia is a serious condition. It can separate you permanently from the light."

"Light, light, light," Meredith said in a singsong voice. "I'm sick to death of hearing about the frigging light. If it's so all-fired great, *you* go to the light, Lenny. I'm staying here with Trey."

"Wait." Evie stared at Meredith in dismay. "Are you saying you still can't remember who killed you?"

"Would I be hanging around this stupid bathroom if I did? Think about it, Chubby."

"This is more of a lounge than a bathroom." Swink looked around the spacious room with an expression of admiration. "Much nicer than the men's room. What is the couch for?"

"Lesbian aerobics, Swink." Meredith rolled her eyes. "Just as you guys always suspected. It's why we never go to the bathroom alone."

"Oh, my." Swink blinked rapidly behind his bifocals.

"It was a joke, dim bulb," Meredith said. "How the hell did you graduate med school?"

Before Swink could respond, the door flew open and Addy and Nicole burst into the room.

"Brand sent us to check on you," Addy said. She sounded breathless. "Are you al—" She saw the ghosts and stopped. "Crappydoodle, there are two of them. Why is an accountant haunting the ladies' room?"

Swink stiffened. "I am not—" Pressing his ruddy lips together in disapproval, he pushed his glasses up the bridge of his nose. "This session is at an end."

Bing! He disappeared.

"Man, am I ever glad he's gone," Nicole said. "I gotta pee and I can't make water with no guy listening. Makes my uvula draw up. 'Scuse me."

She bustled into a stall and slammed the door.

Meredith drifted back onto the couch with a petulant sigh. "This blows."

"What blows?" Evie asked.

"Being a ghost. Most people can't see me, and those who can aren't scared." She glared at Evie and Addy. "Like you two and White Trash Wanda in there."

The toilet flushed and Nicole came out of the stall.

"My name ain't Wanda; it's Nicole. And if it makes you feel any better, you scare me plenty," Nicole said, going to the sink to wash her hands. She dried her hands and plucked a necklace out of the deep cleft between her breasts. "See this?" She waved the pendant on the chain at them. "Number sixteen. That's Greg Biffle's number, and it's pure silver. Silver protects you against haints. And salt. I got me a little snack-size baggie of salt tucked inside my panties and in my purse, for spectral emergencies."

Meredith widened her eyes. "Wow, you mean they make underwear in your size? What do they use, king-size sheets?"

"Ha ha, very funny." Nicole touched up her lipstick. "In my experience, most men like a little cushion for the pushing." She gave Meredith a pitying glance in the mirror. "Your poor husband must've scraped his pecker raw against that bony backbone of yours."

Addy chuckled. "Ooh, burn."

Meredith gasped and turned an unpleasant shade of purple beneath the blood. "Why you . . . you . . ."

Nicole ignored the sputtering ghost. "I left Frodo with Daniel, so I gotta get back." Opening a drawstring pouch that hung from the belt of her toga, she slipped her lipstick back inside and turned to face Evie. "You coming back to the dance, Miss Evie, or are you staying here with Bitchy Boo?"

"Screw you, Wanda," Meredith said, regaining her powers of speech at last.

"I'll go with you," Evie said, making a hasty retreat for the exit.

No way was she going to stay in the ladies' room with Meredith after such an epic smackdown.

Brand waited for them outside the restroom, looking stern and disapproving.

"Oh, brother, that is not a happy face," Nicole said after one look at Brand. "I'll see y'all later. Bye."

With a wave, she scurried off.

"All is well?" Brand asked when Nicole had gone.

"Everything's fine." Addy patted him on the cheek and smiled up at him. "Stop frowning, big guy. You'll give yourself wrinkles. Come on, you owe me a dance."

Addy and Brand were so in love, so *together,* Evie reflected as she followed them down the hallway. She would never have that with Ansgar. Unlike Addy, she was human and would age. But she'd take what she could get and for however long. Something with Ansgar was better than nothing without him.

Deep in thought, Evie didn't notice Trey until he stepped out of the shadows and jerked her into an adjoining passageway. "Evie, I need to talk to you," he said in an urgent tone. "You're in danger."

Blip! Brand the Dalvahni guard dog was there and had Trey pinned to the wall. "You are a most annoying human," he said. "And foolhardy as well. Had my brother returned and found you with Evie, 'twould not be pretty."

"I wasn't *with* Trey," Evie protested. "I was minding my own business, and he came out of nowhere."

Brand looked down his nose at her. "For the first time in his existence, Ansgar is in love," he said, speaking with the care usually reserved for the mentally slow. "Humans toss that word around like so much chaff. Not so the Dalvahni. Duty and the hunt are all Ansgar has known. For eons, nothing has swayed him from his course, until he met you."

"If Ansgar loves me, he should tell me so himself. But he hasn't."

"Give him time, Evie. He will."

He's had plenty of opportunities already, Evie thought, trying to keep her feet on the ground. But it was hard to be sensible when Brand had planted a seed of hope in her heart. What if Ansgar did love her? The very thought made something warm and exciting bloom inside her. Could she and Ansgar have a future together, however brief?

Stranger things had happened. Look at Addy and Brand. Theirs had been a whirlwind courtship. Brand had been placed on permanent assignment here because this one-horse town at the backend of nowhere attracted demons and woo woo like a navy sweater attracts lint. No one knew why Hannah was a demon magnet, but there was no getting around the fact the town was off-the-charts weird.

Weird was good. Weird meant Ansgar might stay. A heavy weight lifted from her heart.

"What of you?" There was a curious, watchful expression in Brand's green eyes. "Do you love Ansgar?"

Evie hesitated, embarrassed to bare her soul to this grim man.

"Yes, I love him," she said at last. "I've never felt like this about anyone before."

"I am glad. It is no easy thing for a Dalvahni warrior to love. Remember that, Evie, and all will be well."

"Hey." Trey said in a strangled voice. "Let go of me. I can't breathe."

Brand released him.

Glaring at Brand, Trey straightened his crumpled shirt and tie. "As I was saying, Evie, there's something I need to tell you. It's about Meredith's murder. You see—"

"Trey? Can you see me, baby? Oh, *please* say you can see me."

"Meredith?" Trey's baritone voice went up several octaves. "Is that you?"

The bloody cheerleader rushed at Trey, arms opened wide. "Your Sweet Stuff is back, Snookems, and she's never gonna leave you again!"

"Holy mother of God," Trey said, and slid to the floor unconscious.

Evie dabbed Trey's forehead with the moistened paper towel Addy had fetched from the ladies' room. Meredith was a big help, fluttering around her fallen husband like an empty plastic bag in a windy parking lot, alternating between cries for help and fits of jealousy because Trey had his head in Evie's lap.

"Oh, for Pete's sake, Meredith, get a clue. Evie is *not* interested in Trey," Addy said, losing patience with the ghost.

Meredith glared at Evie. "Why not? Isn't he good enough for you, Fatty?"

"Much too good for me," Evie said. "I'm nowhere in his league, and I know it."

"Humph," Meredith said, subsiding into disgruntled silence. Trey opened his eyes. "Meredith?"

"Right here, Snooky." Meredith levitated above Trey. "Your Mer-Mer is right here."

"Oh, God." Trey groaned. "I'm losing my mind."

"You're not losing your mind," Evie said. Brand helped Trey to his feet and then her. "I can see her and so can Addy and Brand. Right, Addy?"

"Unfortunately."

Evie shook her crumpled skirts. "See? You're not crazy."

Trey leaned against the wall and raised a shaking hand to his brow. "Can everybody see her?"

"I don't think so," Evie said, remembering Trish and Blair in the flower shop. "I think it's a gift."

"A gift?" Trey's laugh was bitter. "I hope to hell it's returnable."

"Snookems," Meredith cried. "You don't mean that."

"Great." Trey looked a little gray around the edges. Taking a deep breath, he pushed away from the wall. "I'm going home."

Meredith floated closer. "I'll go with you. We have a lot of catching up to do."

"Brand will help you to your car, Trey," Addy suggested. "Won't you, babe?"

"Yes. Wait for me in the ballroom. You will be safer there."

"Hey," Trey yelped as Brand tossed him over one shoulder and disappeared.

"Wait for me," Meredith cried, streaking after them.

Evie shook her head. "I wonder if it's ever occurred to her that Trey may have killed her?"

"Snookems?" Addy said. "No way. Not that I would blame him, mind you, but I don't see him killing anybody with a knife. Trey's too squeamish. Remember how he blew his groceries all over Mrs. Walker's biology lab when we had to dissect a cat?"

"Oh, yeah. I'd forgotten about that."

"What did he want to tell you, anyway?"

"He says I'm in danger."

"Big news flash there. That's why I asked Ansgar to keep an eye on you in the first place."

Ansgar. Evie's stomach did a somersault. She needed to see him, right now. She rushed down the hall toward the sound of the music.

Chapter Twenty-nine

Evie hurried through the doors of the ballroom. To her disappointment, there was no sign of Ansgar. Her giddy excitement faded, replaced by concern. The Dalvahni were powerful, but they weren't completely invulnerable, and Mr. C's contrabulator *had* turned orange, indicating the presence of true evil. What if Ansgar had been ambushed, or was hurt or—

"What's the rush?" Addy said, joining her.

"I was looking for Ansgar. Do you see him?"

Addy surveyed the dance floor and the people mingling in the room. "Nope."

"Shoot." Evie's anxiety level rose. She'd go after him, but she had no idea where to look.

"Stop fretting," Addy said. "Blondy's a big demon hunter. He can take care of himself. You ought to know that by now."

"I should? How? I've known the guy two days."

For some reason, Addy developed a sudden fascination with the color of her toenail polish. "Oh, you know," she said, staring at her feet. "I just meant you've heard me talk about Brand and demon hunters and stuff."

Uh huh. Addy Corwin was good at many things, but she was terrible at lying.

"Fudge," Evie said. "There's something you're not telling me. What is it?"

"Me?" Addy looked a little wild eyed. "I don't know what you're talking about."

An agitated Jackie Kennedy rushed up to them. Good heavens, it was Miss Bitsy, the spitting image of Jackie Kennedy in a hot pink suit with a mandarin collar and a matching pillbox hat.

"Evie, dear, you look lovely in Aunt Ethie's dress," Bitsy said, patting a strand of her perky brunette wig back into place. "I'm proud of you for coming to the dance tonight. That took courage. If anyone says anything ugly to you, you let me know and I'll give them what-for."

"Thank you, Miss Bitsy. Where's the chief?"

"He's working." Bitsy made a frantic little gesture with her hands. "Some maniac has been attacking Chihuahuas. Lucy Saxon's dog was shot with a paintball gun, and Jimmy Wheeler's dog got run over. Lucy was so upset she had to be given oxygen, and Jimmy showed up at the station with his shotgun. Carlee had a time calming him down."

"How awful," Evie said. It sounded like Frodo's dog stalker had come to Hannah. She'd better warn Nicole. "Are the dogs all right?"

"Oh, yes. Gracie—that's Lucy's miniature Chihuahua—was bruised pretty badly, but she'll be okay. And that new vet—what's his name, Addy? Oh, yes, Duncan something or other—was able to save Jimmy's dog."

Addy's color rose. "If somebody ran over Dooley, I'd be after 'em with a gun, too."

Blip! Brand materialized behind Bitsy. Bitsy turned and started when she saw him.

"Gracious, Brand, you gave me a fright," Bitsy said, fanning herself. She looked him up and down. "Who are you supposed to be? I'm dreadful at guessing these character names."

"Brand's a demon hunter, Mama," Addy said.

"A demon hunter, really?" Bitsy's laugh sounded strained. "See, I never would have guessed that. But then I don't watch much television."

Addy rolled her eyes at Evie as if to say *Tell them the truth, for once, and they don't believe yah.*

"Is everything all right, Miss Bitsy?" Brand said. "You seem disquieted."

"I *am* upset. I declare, I don't know whether I'm coming or going." Bitsy fluttered her hands again. "It's Shep. He's here with Lenora, and she's wearing that string dress again. It's a disgrace. You've got to do something with him, Addy."

"Me? What do you expect me to do with him, Mama? Shep's a grownass man."

"Watch your language, young lady, and talk to your brother. *Please.*"

"Why do I have to talk to him? He's your son."

"I have talked to him until I'm blue in the face, but he won't listen." Bitsy assumed a tragic expression. "And why should he? After all, I'm just his mother, the woman who bore him and nursed him and—"

"Oh, for crying in the beer, Mama, don't start," Addy said. "I'll check on him. Although what you expect me to do about Shep's hoochie girlfriend, I have no idea."

"Just try to get Lenora to put on some clothes. Please, before she starts a riot and your brother gets in a common brawl right here in the country club. I think they've had a tiff. Lenora is ignoring him and flirting with every man in sight, and Shep looks positively ferocious. I've never seen him like this."

"Do not be concerned, Mrs. Corwin," Brand said in his calm way. "Adara and I will handle the matter."

Bitsy looked relieved. "Would you do that, Brand? That would be *such* a comfort! I declare, this thing with Shep and Lenora has me turned every which away. He's not acting like himself."

Promising to do what they could, Addy and Brand left Bitsy. Evie went with them. With any luck, she'd find Ansgar. Besides, she really wanted to see the string dress.

"Damn," Addy muttered once they were out of earshot. "I do *not* want to get all up in my big brother's business."

"Do what you can, my love," Brand told Addy as they threaded their way through the people in the ballroom. "I will deal with Lenora."

Evie's heart did a nervous little tap dance as Ansgar materialized in front of them without warning.

"Ansgar," she cried, relieved to see him whole and in one piece. Her imagination had run away with her, and she'd pictured all kinds of horrible things. Gracious, she needed to get hold of herself. He'd only been gone a few minutes.

"Brother," Brand said in greeting. "All is well?"

"I have learned much," Ansgar said. "We will speak of it later."

Brand nodded. "And Peterson? How did you leave him?"

Ansgar put his arm around Evie's waist and drew her close. "Alive, much to my regret."

"That can soon be remedied," Brand said. "In the meantime, we have a situation."

Ansgar gave Brand a questioning look.

"It is Lenora," Brand explained. "I fear she has loosed her powers on the humans, perhaps in a bid to make Shep jealous. It is difficult to discern the motivations of a thrall."

Ansgar swore. "She is out of control. We must stop her. Conall will not be pleased."

"Who's Conall again exactly?" Evie asked. She remembered Ansgar mentioning the name.

Addy rolled her eyes. "Another demon hunter. Some kind of big cheese, apparently."

"He is not cheese, and he is not 'another demon hunter,' " Ansgar said stiffly. "He is our leader and a most bold and valiant warrior."

Taking Evie by the hand, he strode forward. The crowd melted out of their way. He was like a Dalvahni wrecking ball.

"By the sword, 'tis worse than I feared," Ansgar said when he saw the thrall. "Stay here while I try to reason with her. I will return anon."

Giving Evie a quick, hard kiss, he approached the thrall, speaking in his mellifluous voice. Evie caught the words "Directive Against Conspicuousness" among the flow of soothing words. His smooth tone appeared to calm the agitated men that watched the thrall with hot, greedy eyes. But Lenora didn't seem to hear him. She stood with her head thrown back and her eyes closed. Her long, ebony hair and the ribbons of the string dress fluttered around her as though stirred by a mysterious breeze. Evie gaped at her in awe. Lenora was a windblown, mostly naked, centerfold model for Pure Sex with a built-in fan and more curves than a bowl of corkscrew pasta.

Shep, on the other hand, looked ready to murder somebody, *anybody*. He stood nearby, his arms crossed and a scowl as black as an August thundercloud on his face. Evie had never seen Shep like this, and she'd known him all her life. When she and Addy were kids, he took them to Pensacola to the movies and to the Dairy Spin for ice cream. When they turned fifteen, it was Shep who took them to get their permits and taught them how to drive. After her mama died and her daddy started drinking, Shep made it a point to check on her at least once a week. On more than one occasion, he'd shown up at the house unexpectedly, helped her pour her daddy into bed, and left without saying a word. Shep was a nice guy, steady, solid, and reliable. Good to his mama and his sister, crazy about his two kids, and faithful to his wife until she ran off with a younger man.

Evie had never thought of him as sexy or good looking. He was simply Shep, Addy's older, wiser, slightly boring big brother.

So, it was with considerable shock that Evie realized Shep Corwin was a total babe.

There were women in the crowd, and they weren't looking at Lenora. They were looking at Shep. He wasn't wearing a costume, and his blond hair was tousled. It looked like he'd come straight from the house wearing jeans and a long-sleeve cotton Polo. The jeans looked good on him, and the little guy on the horse stretched across a wide chest that was all muscle.

Addy and Brand pushed their way through the packed bodies, joining Evie. Actually, Brand lifted people and set them aside, like so many bowling pins.

"Oh, my God," Addy said when she saw the thrall. "She's like the goddess of hard-ons."

"Lenora is a powerful entity, but when it comes to emotion

she is as a child," Brand said. "I believe she has feelings for Shep. That must be a bewildering thing for a thrall. She has no idea how to deal with emotion."

Evie had expected the thrall to be something out of the or- dinary—and, boy, was she ever!—but what she couldn't get over was the change in Shep.

"Shep looks different," she said to Addy.

"It's the hair. He stopped shellacking it after he and Lenora hooked up. Drives Mama nuts. She says he looks messy."

Velma Lou Pugh elbowed her way in front of them. "He's a mess all right. A hot mess."

Velma was married to a dentist and had three kids in college. She was dressed tonight as a lady pirate. Velma Lou the Pirate looked like she wanted to shanghai Shep and take a ride on his belaying pin.

"Look at those arms and shoulders." The older woman gave Shep a leer that would put Captain Jack Sparrow to shame. "That's a whole bag of uh uh uh. Somebody's been taking their vitamins and working out."

"Good grief," Addy said. "Velma Lou, if you and your vagina would take a step to the right, I need to speak to my brother." Addy pushed past Velma Lou and stepped into the cir- cle. "Oh, my God, look at Roy Van Pelt. He's all red in the face, and his eyes are starting to bulge. Brand, you'd best get Lenora to turn off the tractor beam before somebody's penis ex- plodes."

"Poor Lenora," Evie said with a twinge of sympathy. Love could be a bewildering thing, no matter where you came from. "She must be terrified."

"Oh, yeah, she looks scared to death," Addy said.

Addy was being sarcastic, but she had a point. The thrall didn't look scared. She looked ticked. Lenora exuded a force field of sexual energy, and her face glowed with the cold, white brilliance of a star. She was beautiful and terrifying. She looked hard, fierce. Alien.

A woman dressed as Xena: Warrior Princess shoved past a clump of women and said something to Shep.

"Perfect, Marilee's here," Addy muttered. "I'd better get over there before things break out in ugly."

Shaking her head, Addy hurried over to speak to her brother and ex-sister-in-law. Brand went to help Ansgar with the thrall, leaving Evie alone. Fortunately, no one paid her any mind. The drama playing out in front of them was too fascinating, like something under the Big Top.

See exotic Lenora perform her magical strip tease. Watch her ribbons fly! Will all be revealed or will the grim-faced, dangerous warriors at her side succeed in taming the sultry vixen? Hold your breath as Shep Corwin battles his feelings for Lenora and locks horns with Xena, his two-timing cougar of an ex-wife. Will love triumph or will Shep let loose a bubba thrashing of biblical proportions on the men lusting after his ladylove?

Yep, better than a circus, Evie mused. People would be buzzing about this juicy little business for weeks. Maybe this was the Something Big Muddy had prophesied. Although why Muddy said she needed to be here, Evie couldn't imagine.

"We will dance now," a sonorous voice said in her ear. "Come."

Startled, Evie turned. "Thank you," she said, "but I don't—"

She met the man's luminous, dark gaze, and the polite refusal died on her lips. She was falling, drifting like a leaf on a pool of silence that separated her and the dark-eyed man from the rest of the world. Panic fluttered its wings against her breast and died. It was useless to struggle, a dim voice told her. He was too wise, too old, too powerful.

"Who are you?" she whispered through trembling lips.

"I am Sildhjort," he said, sweeping her into his arms and onto the dance floor.

Or perhaps they were not on the dance floor at all, but spinning beneath a diamond-crusted sky on a cobweb of moonbeams. No, her befuddled brain corrected, she was in a forest under a canopy of trees, sunlight dappling the loamy earth as they danced to the tune of a noisy brook. Faster and faster they twirled, and all the while he held her gaze with his. He was very handsome, her fair-haired captor, with a laughing mouth and eyes as dark as peat. He wore a black frock coat, matching trousers, and a silver vest. The tie at his throat was a splash of color, bright as blood against the dazzling white of his shirt. He moved with the easy, fluid grace of a wild animal as he spun her around the dance floor, and he was strong, very strong, his arms and shoulders taut with muscle beneath the fabric of his long coat.

His form shifted and blurred, and now he was naked and glowing like a star, a shining silver star.

She was dancing with Shiny Naked Guy, Evie realized, the strange, antlered creature she'd almost run over that afternoon. Except that tonight he was Mostly Naked Guy, she amended, noting with dizzy gratitude that he'd donned a loincloth for the occasion. A loincloth made out of something shimmery, like moonbeams.

Out of all the people here, he'd asked her to dance. It didn't make sense. Nothing that had happened in the past two days made sense. But, for some reason, the fact that she'd drawn the notice of this bizarre godlike being with a penchant for going commando and a rack that would make a bull elk give a bugle call of envy bothered her the most.

"Why?" she asked, unable to squeeze more than the one word from her throat. Her body was shaking, and she felt light-headed and out of breath. Muddy was right. Something was coming, something big. She could feel it hovering over her, waiting to pounce.

"You called to me, sweet child. I felt your distress." He dipped his head closer to hers, his hoary antlers sparkling in the light from the chandeliers. "Remember, and come into the fullness of your power."

He kissed her on the cheek, and *wham!*—somebody dropped a piano on her head.

Chapter Thirty

The pain knocked Evie to her knees. Jagged flashes of light pulsed at the edge of her vision. Her stomach churned, and the noise and the smells in the room intensified.

The mother of all migraines, she thought, closing her eyes as pain lanced through her.

Someone called her name. The sound was muffled and hard to hear over the roaring in her ears. Voices and images assaulted her. Ansgar smiling as he loosed her hair the first day they met in the flower shop, chiding her for hiding her fire beneath an ugly gardening hat. Ansgar murmuring words of love and desire in his sorcerer's voice as they had delicious, delirious sex beneath the stars on a clear summer's night.

She shook her head, not caring that it made her head hurt like the devil. No, they hadn't had *sex* in the woods. They'd made love.

. . . love you, Evangeline, he'd said, over and over again. And she, poor stupid, lovesick fool, had believed him. *Love . . . love . . . love . . .*

"No," she said.

Clutching her head, she struggled to her feet, no easy feat in the Scarlett gown. She was winded, gasping for breath like she'd run a marathon. Both shoes were gone.

So was Sildhjort. She was alone on the dance floor surrounded by a sea of shocked, disapproving faces. Lenora watched Evie from the fringe of the crowd, her eyes narrowed thoughtfully. She'd flipped off her come switch and the magic fan, and the string dress was covering her parts. Mostly.

Let them look. Let them *all* look. She was trapped in her own thoughts. The memories rushed over her, shuffling through her brain like playing cards in the hands of a Las Vegas dealer, visions of her and Ansgar in their "before."

She saw them again at the Grand Goober Ball. They were dancing and she was happy, so happy. She wore an exquisite green and gold gown, a gift from *him*. Ansgar, temptation itself in a tuxedo, so handsome he made her teeth ache. The scene switched, and she and Addy cowered beneath a tree in the park, looking on in shocked disbelief as Ansgar and Brand battled creatures out of a nightmare. Felt again the fear that had gripped her, suffocating and paralyzing as the two warriors fought, followed by a floodtide of relief when the demons were defeated. Relived the awful moment and her helpless terror as the wraith rose from the bloody body on the ground and entered her, settling in her bones like cancer.

She remembered her sick certainty that she would never be whole again, not as long as the demon possessed her. That hard as she might fight, she would succumb to evil, her body and soul sucked dry by the demon consuming her from within, a fate worse than death.

She heard herself beg Ansgar to kill her and watched the calm, removed expression settle on his face as he raised his bow and fired. Saw the silver flash of the arrow slicing through the air and felt again the starburst of agony as the arrow pierced her breast.

Falling, falling into nothingness. She'd awakened with a heavy spirit, a curtain between her and the rest of the world and a weight like Stonehenge pressing on her heart. Dragging through the endless, leaden days, alone and bereft and not knowing *why*, without even the comfort of her beloved fairies to ease her suffering. Endless nights of hot, tortured dreams of a man's hands and mouth teasing her flesh, bringing her to the brink of release. Only to have it all vanish when she opened her eyes to face another dreary day.

She remembered. She remembered it all.

"Evangeline?" *Blip!* Ansgar did the demon hunter bop and stood before her, his expression concerned and wary. "Are you well? You were dancing alone. 'Twas the thrall's effect, perhaps?"

Ah, so he hadn't seen Sildhjort. None of them had, she realized. They saw her twirling like a maddened marionette by herself, her feet moving faster and faster until the straps of her heels broke and her shoes sailed across the room. How funny she must have looked, dancing alone. She began to shake. The migraine, no doubt, though her head no longer throbbed and the flashes of light were gone.

"You left me," she said to Ansgar.

"Only for a moment to speak with Lenora. The Directive—"

"You said you loved me, and you left me. Alone, all these months, with nothing but phantom memories of you, like an amputee missing a limb. Only you took my heart instead of an arm or a leg, and you left me here to die without it."

He was getting it now, the fact that she remembered, and his expression was desperate. Good, she'd been desperate since he left, though she hadn't known why.

"I thought it best—"

"You thought it best?!"

She was shouting. She'd never shouted at anyone in her life. Taking a deep breath, she tried to calm down. She was trembling like she had a fever.

"You left me," she repeated. "You told me you loved me, and you left me."

The words echoed in her brain, those magical, wonderful, totally false words. *Love you, love, love . . .*

Liar. She should have known.

He took a step closer. "Evangeline, listen to me. I was wrong. I was a craven fool to leave you. You turned my universe upside down, and I was petrified of the things you made me feel. So, I ran. I told myself I could forget you. But I could not, though the gods know I tried. I volunteered for extra duty, battled and defeated scores of demons, but nothing could defeat my love for you. Not even the emptying embrace of a thrall could erase your memory and I—"

"*What?!*" She was shouting again.

The life-size oil portrait of Mr. Collier's grandfather, Zephaniah John Collier, split down the middle and fell to the floor, and the microphone on the stage flew through the air and crashed against the back wall, narrowly missing the drummer.

"Dude," Addy said, covering her ears. "Ixnay on the all-thray."

Ansgar had sex with someone else? Evie's chest hurt and her heart hurt, and she wanted to smash something. So this was what rage felt like. It felt scary. It felt *good.*

She rubbed the aching spot where the arrow had entered her chest. Ansgar had shot her in the heart. She should be dead, but she wasn't.

He'd saved her, like Brand had saved Addy from the demon. She was no longer human. The world reeled and righted itself. The weeks of not eating without ill effect, her record-setting gorge fests with Ansgar, the sharpening of her senses—deep down she'd known all along that she was different. She'd been too miserable to care, because of *him.*

"You changed me," she said, staring at Ansgar in anger and disbelief. "You changed me and left me here to wither and die without you, while you went off and had your jollies with another woman."

"Not another woman," Ansgar said, "a thrall, to try and forget you, but I—"

"But dying wasn't really an option for me, was it? I'm Dalvahni now. Thanks to you, I can grieve *forever.* And you knew. You took everything when you left, even the fairies. How could you be so cruel?"

He flinched as though she'd hit him. She *wanted* to hit him, to pound her fists on his chest, to make him understand her anguish.

"I know." His mouth twisted with self-loathing. "I hate myself for it, for all of it. But I came back. I was gone but a few weeks. I could not stay away. All these months I have stayed in the shadows, watching you, longing for you—"

Evie didn't want to hear anymore.

"And you," she said, rounding on Addy. "My so-called best friend. You let me walk around like a dead thing for months and didn't tell me. How could you?"

Addy lifted her shoulders in a helpless gesture. "I thought he'd cut and run for good. I didn't want to hurt you. I was so worried. You've been like a zombie." She shook her head. "I was afraid if you remembered, it would be too much, and I—"

"You knew." Evie glared at Muddy and Mr. Collier, Bitsy and Shep. Lenora was there, too, still studying her like she was some kind of bug. Evie ignored her. "You all knew and didn't tell me."

Ansgar had betrayed her and so had her so-called friends, every last one of them. People she loved like family, people she trusted.

The scream boiled out of her, from some angry, hurt place deep inside her. It went on and on, shattering the heavy chandelier and cracking the ornamental medallion on the ceiling.

The storm broke with wind and lightning. It was raining turtles inside the Collier Grand Ballroom. People shrieked and ran for cover. Ansgar remained; Addy and Brand, too. The tempest raged around them. Clothes and hair plastered to their bodies, they stared at Evie in shock.

Ansgar struggled against the gale-force wind, trying to reach her. "Evangeline, wait."

"Don't bother," Evie said. "Whatever it is, I don't want to hear it."

Crack! She disappeared in a blinding flash of light.

The doormat triumphant.

Evie's knees slammed against a hard surface, the ground perhaps. She stretched out her hand and encountered a cool, smooth surface. Not dirt, a wooden floor. How had she gotten here? She remembered an urgent, frenzied desire to get away before she had a complete meltdown, and then a stretching sensation. Granny Moses, she'd destroyed the ballroom at the country club—it was a safe bet she'd never get invited back there again—and then she'd done the demon hunter bop and teleported.

But where was she?

It was dark, the can't-see-your-hand-in-front-of-your-face kind of dark. She smelled cedar and lavender and the faint leathery scent of new shoes. Reaching up, she fumbled around. Her fingers brushed against something silky and soft—fabric. She was in a closet. Perfect.

Taking a deep breath, she began to curse, dredging up every expletive she'd ever heard or read. She started with the mild ones, like *doggone* and *ding dang it* and *darn,* and worked her way up to the big ones, the really foul ones pertaining to bodily functions, sex, and private parts. She reached the end of her list and started over, inventing a few new ones along the way. She was particularly partial to buggerflicking, goathumping, snatherblasted turkey buzzard. For someone who hadn't closet-cussed since middle school, it was good to know she still had the knack.

She was on her third round when the closet door opened and someone turned on the light.

"What are you doing?" Lenora said, surveying her from the doorway.

Evie blinked up at the thrall. "Cussing. What does it look like I'm doing?"

"You are an odd creature. I think I like you."

"Thanks." Evie got to her feet and looked around.

She was in the walk-in closet in her guest bedroom. She hadn't been in this room in months. And now she knew why. The racks and shelves overflowed with clothes, accessories, and shoes, all gifts from Ansgar, an entire wardrobe to celebrate the new Evie.

Then he left and she went back in her shell. But, on a deep subconscious level, she'd known about this closet and its contents and avoided it like the plague. Talk about being in denial.

"I have never liked anyone before," Lenora said. "Except for Shepton and Lily and William, and today I do not like Shepton. Do you like me?"

"I don't know anything about you, except that you're a sex worker from another dimension who likes to wear clothes made out of string."

"Does that mean you cannot like me?"

"No, but we don't have much in common." Lenora looked so disappointed that Evie relented. "Tell you what. I promise to give it a shot." She thought of something and scowled. "Unless you've slept with Ansgar. I don't care if it is your job, if you've slept with Ansgar I can't like you, even if he is a snodcoddling son of a biscuit eater."

"I am not familiar with this term."

"That's 'cause I made it up," Evie said. "I can't say bad words with the light on."

"Why not?"

"I don't know. I just can't."

"How odd. To answer your question, I did not have sex with Ansgar."

"Good."

"Ansgar favors a thrall by the name of Kalia."

"Not good." Evie clenched her fists, the unfamiliar rage building inside her again at the thought of Ansgar with another female.

"Why are you threatened by Kalia? He loves you."

"Oh, yeah, he's eat up with it. That's why he slept with another woman."

"Kalia is not a woman. She is thrall. It is not the same. It was a release, nothing more, an attempt by Ansgar to forget you. It did not work. You heard him. Kalia could not eradicate his memories or his feelings for you." Lenora clasped her hands to her substantial, mostly naked bosom. "The things he said to you tonight, his obvious passion for you . . . It reminded me of a scene from *Loins of Lust*. Do you know it?"

"The soap? I've never watched it."

"It is beautiful." Lenora splayed her fingers across her flat stomach. "Watching *Loins of Lust* makes me feel funny inside."

Good heavens, Shep's emotion-sucking succubus girlfriend was a romantic. This was taking weird to a whole new level.

"What about Shep?" Evie said. "Does he make you feel funny inside?"

Lenora dropped her hands. "I do not wish to speak of Shepton. He is a biscuit eater, too. I am wroth with him."

"You're wroth with Shep and I'm wroth with Ansgar. You wanna get drunk?"

"Kirk Vandergalt got drunk on *Loins of Lust* and fell off a cruise ship. He was never heard from again. They held a lovely ceremony in his memory. It made my eyes leak."

"Probably his contract was up and he wanted off the show."

"Perhaps you are right. His wife Crystal did not mourn him overlong. She married Blane Tarkington four shows later."

"I wouldn't judge Crystal too harshly. Time flows differently on soap operas."

Tilting her head, the thrall seemed to consider this. "I had not thought of that. You are wise. Why do you wish to get drunk?"

"My father drank too much, so I've never been much of a drinker. But, the way I feel tonight, I figure I've got two choices. I either get drunk or I make like Carrie and burn the whole town. Know what I mean?"

"I do not know what you mean. I do not know this Carrie, and I never had a father." The thrall paused. "Or a friend. Will you be my friend, Evie Douglass?"

"Don't rush me. I'm still working on like."

Chapter Thirty-one

She was gone. Ansgar threw back his head with a frustrated howl, uncaring that the rain and wind beat against him. The tempest in the ballroom was nothing compared to the storm of regret in his heart. He should have told her sooner, confessed all. But things had happened too quickly, the murder, the attack by the djegrali, her imprisonment, the sweet delirium of being with her again.

The time had never seemed right. She had so many other worries, so much to cope with. He had been reluctant to burden her with the truth.

Coward, he chided himself. *Admit it. You were being selfish. These past few days with her have been heaven. You did not tell her because you were afraid, you could not risk losing her.*

You left me . . . left me . . . left me.

Her words of rebuke rang in his ears. She was gone. He had to find her, to try to explain, to make her understand. Without warning, the storm blew out the doors, leaving the ballroom a sodden, dripping mess. Someone called his name. Wiping the rain from his eyes, he turned.

Brand helped Addy across the slippery dance floor. They were soaked to the skin and Addy was crying.

"Trifle with thy wench and she shall strike thine codpiece," Brand said. "I warned you how it would be, did I not?"

Ansgar gritted his teeth at the note of amusement in Brand's voice. "Aye, you did, brother."

"Oh, Ansgar, what are we going to do?" Addy sobbed. "Did you see her face? She looked so hurt, so lost. I feel so awful."

In spite of his annoyance with Brand, something twisted inside Ansgar. For all their differences, he knew that Addy loved Evie. It disturbed him to see this feisty, irrepressible woman looking so sad and vulnerable. By the sword, he was becoming maudlin and weepy himself. This would not do.

"You must be distressed," he said, adopting the supercilious tone he knew irritated her. "You remembered my name."

She glared at him. "Well, of course I'm upset. She's my best friend. We've never had a fight before."

"My love, can you not see he goads you apurpose to distract you from your grief?" Brand said. He bowed to Ansgar. "I, too, have grown quite fond of Evie. I am at your service, brother, should you require assistance in the hunt, though I doubt you have need of it. Your tracking skills are without equal."

"I thank you for the offer," Ansgar said, "but 'tis my belief you can better serve our cause here." People were starting to drift back into the ballroom, exclaiming in shock and disbelief at the destruction. "Evangeline has violated the Directive Against Conspicuousness. Can I count on you to set things aright?"

Addy straightened her dripping garment. "What's the big deal? The sprinkler system malfunctioned."

Ansgar gave her a slow grin. "Yes, that will serve. That was quick thinking on your part."

She flushed. "Stop being nice to me and find our girl."

Brand clapped Ansgar on the shoulder and squeezed. "Yes, go after Evie. We will attend to matters here."

With a nod, Ansgar turned to go.

"Wait up, I'm coming with you." Shep strode into the ballroom, his jaw clenched. He held a metal club in one hand. "Lenora's gone, and I've got a notion she's with Evie."

"What in the world makes you say that?" Addy asked. "Evie barely knows Lenora."

Shep jerked his thumb at the door behind him. "*He* told me—that's how. He said he saw Lenora follow Evie."

"Who are you talking about, Shep? You're not making

sense." Addy's eyes widened as a giant white stag trotted into the ballroom on shining hooves. "Holy cow, it's Sid. He's back!"

The stag shimmered and took the shape of a human male with antlers, splendid in form and radiating power.

Addy's face turned red. "*A-a-a-nd* he's not wearing any clothes. Dude, put a sock on Big Jim and the twins before they catch cold."

Sildhjort shimmered, this time assuming the form of a human in modern raiment without the antlers.

"Thank God," Addy muttered.

"Sildhjort," Brand said, acknowledging the god. "What brings you to Hannah?"

Sildhjort shrugged. "I like it here, and I find the girl intriguing."

"The girl?" Ansgar felt the sharp stab of jealousy. "You mean Evangeline?"

"Aye," Sildhjort said. "She is unusual, a tantalizing combination of the shy, winsome beauty of a dryad and the unfocused power of an elemental." He glanced around at the ruined ballroom. "Though she has little control of her abilities, as is most evident." He looked at Ansgar with eyes that were bottomless wells of darkness. "You must find her before the djegrali do. They will be drawn to her, and she is but a fledgling, untrained and ill-equipped to defend herself against them."

Fear swept through Ansgar like a wildfire through dry brush at the thought of Evangeline at the mercy of the djegrali.

No. Think on that and he would go mad. The hunt, he would concentrate on the hunt instead.

He would find her. She would be safe. Anything else was unacceptable.

"I will find her," Ansgar promised. "I shall seek her at home first."

"I wish you good hunting," Sildhjort said. Resuming the shape of a stag, he trotted out the door.

"Let us know something," Addy said. She sounded anxious. "I've already tried calling her house, but my cell phone isn't working. Probably water damage."

Ansgar nodded.

"Hold up," Shep said as Ansgar started to dematerialize. "I'm coming with you."

Ansgar grabbed Shep by the wrist and made the leap through space. They materialized in the back bedroom of Evie's house. The room was dark but for the weak light of a lamp by the bed.

Shep looked around, his expression alert. "I don't think anybody's here."

Ansgar inhaled. He caught a faint whiff of Damascus rose, sweet and mysterious, brightened by a hint of citrus, the perfume Evangeline had dabbed upon her pulse points earlier that evening. Overlaying that, like a rotting carcass in a fragrant garden, was the rancid odor of the djegrali.

"They have gone," he told Shep. "We must hurry. The demons have their scent."

Four hours later, Evie was still sober, and not from lack of trying. She'd consumed enough alcohol to float a jon boat and nothing, nada, not so much as a buzz. Lenora, on the other hand, was pounded. The bars they'd visited seethed with a variety of feelings: anger, envy, hate, lust, loneliness, sadness, depression, to name a few. The thrall had glutted herself on the emotion-rich atmosphere, leaving the patrons in mellow, empty-eyed bliss.

In spite of the glut fest, however, Lenora seemed grumpy and dissatisfied. She kept muttering Shep's name and "snodcoddling" and "biscuit eater" in the same breath.

"I don't understand it," Evie said as they left the third bar. "I've never had more than a glass of wine in my life. I should be knee walking, but I don't feel a thing."

The Coca-Cola thermometer outside the entrance to the bar registered 53 degrees, but Evie didn't mind the chill. In fact, she hardly noticed it. She'd shed the ball gown in favor of a pair of form-fitting jeans, a sexy vee-neck top, and a pair of slinky sandals, selecting her outfit from the overflowing closet in the guest room. Her days of being invisible were over. Old habits were hard to break, but being falsely accused of murder, arrested, talked about by the entire town, attacked by a demon, and deceived by everyone she loved had been a big wake-up call.

The doormat was dead. The woman who'd taken her place was still something of an unknown quantity, but Evie had a feeling she was going to like her.

For one thing, she was done hating her body. No more hiding her figure under baggy dresses and oversized slacks. She was a curvy gal with generous breasts and a caboose. She would never be a size two. So be it. After a lifetime of feeling ugly and uneasy in her own skin, she was at peace with herself. Ansgar had convinced her that she was beautiful and desirable. It was a priceless gift.

A spasm of pain wrenched her heart. *Ansgar.*

No, she would not go there. He left her.

Who was she kidding? He was *all* she thought about. She felt hurt and foolish and disappointed, and she was madder at him than she'd ever been at anybody in her life, but she couldn't stop thinking about him.

She couldn't even drink him out of her mind, *because she couldn't get drunk!*

It was so unfair.

"Why can't I get drunk?" Evie complained. "I don't get it."

"The Dal are impervious to alcohol and drugs." Lenora hiccupped and staggered across the gravel parking lot. "You are Dalvahni now. I do not think you can get drunk."

"What?" Evie grabbed the reeling thrall by the arm. "Why didn't you tell me this before I spent a hundred and twenty dollars on booze?"

Lenora squinted at her through bleary blue eyes. "You said you wanted to get drunk. I wanted your companionship. Besides, we did not know for certain that you cannot get drunk, until now. It was for your own good, a sort of experiment, if you will."

"I *hate* when people tell me they're doing something for my own good. In my experience, that means better for *them*."

"Are we going to another pub?" Lenora asked.

"What's the point if I can't get drunk?" Evie kicked a rock with the side of her shoe. It flew across the parking lot and knocked a chunk out of a tree. *Oops, note to self: new abilities include super strength.* "I'm miserable, and I can't quit thinking about Ansgar." She clenched her fists at her side. "But, I'm mad at him and I don't want to go home."

"I do not want to go home yet, either," Lenora said. Her expression grew distant. "There is another place. It is on the river. Shepton and I went past it once in his boat. When I asked him about it, he said he had never been there, that it is a private club. I cannot recall the name of it, but there was something about it that called to me."

"You don't mean Beck's Bar?" Evie shook her head. "That place has a bad reputation. Even the cops stay away from it."

"Yes," Lenora said. "That is the name! I want to go there."

The old Evie would never go to Beck's. The old Evie was dead. The new Evie was still edgy, antsy, and riled up. And sober.

"If you insist, but I've got a bad feeling about this."

Lenora waved a hand in dismissal. "What can happen? I am thrall and you are Dalvahni. We can take care of ourselves."

"Okay, but you're driving. You know where it is."

Lenora tried to straighten and almost fell over. "As you like."

She grabbed Evie by the hand, and the air shimmered around them. Evie fell through a long tunnel. When she came out the other side, she and Lenora stood on the riverbank. It was dark and quiet except for the slosh of the water and the whisper of the night wind.

"There," Lenora said, pointing.

On the other side of the river, a low, ramshackle building crouched in the mossy arms of a stand of old trees. Moonlight washed the tin roof and weathered wooden walls in shades of pewter, giving the structure an otherworldly glow. A neon sign bled the words BECK'S BAR into the dark. Lanterns shone on the covered porch, and boats bobbed in the water at the end of the pier. The sound of music and voices drifted out the open doors and across the river.

"You missed," Evie said. "The bar's over there."

"This form of travel is draining, and I am weary," Lenora said. "And I would remind you I saw the place but once with Shepton."

And you're drunk as Cooter Brown, Evie thought with a stab of envy. At least one of them was having a good time.

Evie regarded the stretch of muddy water between them and the bar with misgiving. This part of the Devil River appeared deceptively calm and slow, but the water was deep and probably full of critters. As if on cue, something splashed in the river. Something big.

"I can try and get us over there, but I'm new at the warp thing," Evie said. "We might end up in the water."

"Would it not be simpler to take the boat?"

"Huh?"

Lenora indicated a spot a few yards away. Evie saw an aluminum fishing boat partially hidden in the underbrush.

"You want to steal somebody's boat?"

Lenora shrugged. "They are not using it."

"I can't believe I'm doing this," Evie muttered, making her way barefoot down the steep clay bank. "If I step on a snake, I am *not* going to be happy."

"Neither, I suspect, will the snake."

All the supernaturals in the universe and she had to go barhopping with a smartass. It made Evie think of Addy, and that made her sad. And mad at her best friend all over again. She should have told her. About Ansgar. About *everything*. A friend didn't let a friend walk around for months *knowing* she'd changed species and not tell her. It had to be somewhere in the girl handbook. Adara Jean Corwin had some serious explaining to do.

If she ever spoke to her again, and that was a big if.

Chapter Thirty-two

Evie hadn't handled a boat in years, but the current in this part of the river was slow and she still remembered the basics. Five minutes later, they were tied off and climbing up the steps to the landing. Evie eyed the bar at the other end of the dock. She could see people moving back and forth in front of the porch windows, like fleas crawling around a dog's eyes. The buzz of activity should have made her feel better, but it didn't. Beck's looked creepier and more menacing on this side of the river.

She was about to suggest they get back in the boat and leave, when a lean, rough-coated dog trotted up to them. The dog was enormous, and his eyes gleamed in the lantern light. One was golden, the other a darker color. Blue, maybe; hard to tell in the dim light.

"Hey there, big guy," Evie said, giving the dog's shaggy head a friendly rub.

The dog sniffed and trotted off, his tail waving like a flag.

"Guess he's our escort," Evie said, feeling a little better. No place with a dog like that could be all bad.

In spite of the advanced hour, Beck's was still hopping. Beer bottles and plastic Solo cups lined the wooden railing of the porch where people mingled in small groups. In the shadows at the far end of the overhang, a man showed off a baby alligator to a group of squealing women. Through the porch windows, Evie could see the inside of the bar. A band was playing, and people crowded the dance floor. She and Lenora stepped inside to noise and warmth, and the smell of spilled beer and fried food. In the center of the murky room was a circular bar made of clear glass blocks. Inside the bar, lights swam back and forth like schools of brightly colored fish moving restlessly through a glass sea.

Lenora took a deep breath and frowned. "Something is different. Perhaps we should not have come here."

"You have got to be kidding me," Evie said. "We stole a boat to get to this dive. At least let me get a drink. Some of us are still sober."

Leaving Lenora sniffing the air, Evie took a seat at the bar. The blobs of light oozing inside the hollow glass shell reminded her of a giant lava lamp. She thought about what she wanted to drink. There must be *something* she hadn't tried.

Blip! A wiry man with a grizzled ponytail and a long nose appeared in front of her. One eye was hazel, the other one was a glowing purple. He was dressed in a pair of worn jeans and a Buckingham Nicks T-shirt.

"What'll it be?" he said.

The guy had come out of nowhere. Evie rubbed her eyes. She must be tired. She was seeing things.

"You look familiar," she said. "Do I know you?"

"Ever been in Beck's before?"

"Nope."

"Then I don't know you. What's your poison?"

"That's my problem. I don't know." She studied the rows of liquor bottles on the shelves. "There," she said, pointing to a squat, dark decanter with a gold seal. "There's one I haven't tried. What is it?"

The bartender tucked his thumbs in the top of his jeans. "Godiva. It's a chocolate liqueur."

Chocolate. The word seared across Evie's brain. Her mouth watered. She was like Rapunzel's mother, craving the watercress in the witch's garden. She wanted chocolate. Now.

"Chocolate sounds good," she said, trying to curb her impatience. Good was an understatement. Chocolate seemed *essential*. "I'll have the liqueur."

"Polar bear, German Cherry Bomb, or Naked Girl Scout?"

"I beg your pardon?"

He gave a growl of impatience. "What kind of drink you want?"

"Oh," Evie said, flushing at her own ignorance. She handed him a wadded-up ten-dollar bill from her pocket. "Give it to me straight."

"Suit yourself." The man shrugged and poured her a glass of the Godiva on the rocks.

She took a sip and nearly wept it was so good, rich, and creamy; sweet, silken indulgence on the tongue. She drained the glass, closing her eyes momentarily as the chocolate hit her brain. Smiling, she set the shot glass on the bar. To her surprise, the guy with the gray ponytail was gone and a young woman with dark hair stood in his place.

"Where'd he go?" Evie asked, looking around.

"Toby had to get back to the door. He was covering for me while I took care of something."

The woman's voice was as smooth and rich as the liqueur Evie had just finished. Tall and athletically built, she wore her black jeans and a matching scoop-necked tee with a kind of natural elegance. A panther, Evie realized, the woman reminded her of a panther. She was young, early twenties maybe, and wore no makeup. But that only served to emphasize the smooth perfection of her skin and the clean, strong lines of her face. And her eyes . . .

Her eyes were like amethysts.

"So, you like the Godiva?"

With a start, Evie dragged her gaze from the bartender's violet eyes. "Yes, it's delicious," she said. "Best drink I've had all night."

"A shot of liqueur?" The woman's tone was scornful. "There's no artistry in that."

"It doesn't have to be art. It just has to be chocolate."

The bartender gave a rich, throaty chuckle. "Chocoholic, huh?"

"So it would seem. I'm Evie, by the way."

"Nice to meet you. Name's Beck. I own the place."

"Really? You don't look old enough to serve alcohol, much less run a bar."

"Yeah," Beck said. "I get that a lot. Tell you what, if you like chocolate, I've got something that'll knock your socks off." She set a bowl in front of Evie. "Nosh on these while I fix that drink." Her eyes twinkled. "Chocolate Bugles. I think you'll like 'em."

Evie ate a chip. It was the perfect crunchy mixture of salty and sweet. Most important of all, it was *chocolate*. She smiled. Chocolate was wonderful. Chocolate was exhilarating. She felt light and floaty and free.

She ate another one, and another. Delicious.

By the time Beck set the cocktail glass in front of Evie, the bowl was empty.

Beck chuckled again. "I take it you liked the Bugles."

Evie gave her a look of wide-eyed innocence. "What Bugles?"

She went to prop her chin on her fist and missed. Oops, she was tiddly, and on chocolate of all things. All that money spent on alcohol, and she could've gotten snockered on a Hershey's bar.

Now that her memory had been restored, she should have realized the consequences of consuming chocolate. She remembered that Ansgar and Brand had gotten loaded on chocolate pie last summer in the Sweet Shop, and she and Addy had a dickens of a time getting them out of there.

Ansgar. Evie's bottom lip trembled. There he went, invading her thoughts again and making her heart ache.

Maybe you would have remembered about the chocolate sooner if you hadn't been so busy being all pissy with a certain demon hunter, her smarmy inner voice said.

"Oh, go away," Evie said, irritably.

Beck raised her dark brows. "This is my bar. You go away."

Evie blushed. "Sorry, I wasn't talking to you." She inspected the frosted glass on the counter. "What is it?"

"A chocolate martini," Beck said. "Chocolate vodka and crème de cacao. Thought it would be right up your alley."

She shouldn't drink it. She was already drunk on the Godiva and Bugles. But she didn't want to be rude or hurt Beck's feelings, and that martini looked so *good*. One little sip wouldn't hurt.

She paid Beck for the drink and took a swig. The chocolate rush was immediate and intense. She was flying.

She gave Beck a woozy smile. "Hot diggity dog."

Beck grinned. "I thought you might—" She stared across the bar. "Damn, he's back."

Evie was tipsy, but not too tipsy to miss the undercurrent of nervous tension in Beck's husky voice. Beck exuded an air of tough confidence. She ran a dive bar, for Pete's sake. What could make her uneasy?

The back of Evie's neck prickled. She turned to look. A man sat at a table in a far corner of the room, his dark hair and clothes blending in with the shadows. He sat quietly, cloaked in stillness and menace. Predator, she thought with a shiver.

The man's dark gaze did not waver from Beck.

"He's watching you," Evie said.

"I know." Beck lowered her head and made a business of wiping down the countertop. "Third time this week. He comes in, sits at that same table, and stares at me. For hours." She slid a paper coaster under Evie's sweaty glass. "He makes me jumpy, and I don't like being jumpy, especially in my own place. I think it's because I can't figure him out. I know he's not human— he couldn't get past Toby if he was—but he's not kith, either."

"Kith?" Evie took a quick sip of her martini and then another. The chocolate vodka barreled through her bloodstream and shot straight to her brain.

Beck made an impatient gesture. "Half human, half demon, like me. No normals allowed in here."

Evie set down her martini glass with deliberate care. The

chocolate rush had dulled her thinking, but she was pretty sure Beck had just admitted she was a demonoid and that the guy with the gray ponytail was some kind of super bouncer.

A memory stirred. *Purple-eyed whoozits,* that's what Addy called demonoids. She'd never paid much attention to it. Addy was always being funny. Beck had purple eyes . . .

"How exactly does Toby tell if a person is . . . er . . . human?" she asked, trying to sound casual.

Beck tapped the end of her nose with her index finger. "Dog nose. Dogs have a keen sense of smell. Something like a thousand times more sensitive than a human's. He can tell a human from a supernatural a mile off."

The big dog that had inspected them at the end of the pier . . .

Evie's eyes widened. "Are you saying Toby's a *dog*?"

"He's a shifter." Beck gave her a hard stare. "Toby said you checked out. How come you don't know this?"

"I only found out tonight I'm not human. I'm still adjusting."

"Bummer," Beck said. "I've had my whole life to get used to it, and it still sucks ass. So, what are you?"

Evie considered lying, but she was no good at it. "I was an ordinary human until a few months ago when a demon attacked me."

Beck's eyes narrowed, and she wrapped her hand around an empty vodka bottle with a silver pour spout. "You're possessed? You don't stink like one of them."

Something about the way Beck clutched that bottle and said "one of them" made Evie's blood run cold. "No!" Evie said. "I-I was, but this demon hunter saved me."

"A demon hunter, huh? That's a new one on me. Saved you how?"

"He shot me with an arrow. See, if a human dies while possessed, the demon dies, too." Evie fiddled with the stem of her martini glass, not meeting Beck's gaze. "This . . . uh . . . demon hunter shot me in the heart so the demon would leave, and then he healed me." She lifted her shoulders. "And that's why I'm not human anymore."

"Uh huh." To Evie's relief, Beck's grip on the bottle eased. "I don't know from demon hunters, but your boyfriend did a number on you, sweetheart. There are easier ways to extract a demon than—"

"I have decided I like this place," Lenora announced, gliding up to them. She traced the moving lights inside the bar with the tip of one slender finger. "Ooh, pretty. I want to dance."

Blip! She was on top of the bar, the string dress shimmying around her in pornographic splendor. *Whoosh!* People rushed up to the bar, surrounding Evie like a herd of cattle pushing through a crowded pen. Evie heard a collective *ooh* and looked up. Lenora had picked up speed and so had the string dress.

Looking at the thrall and her fluttering dress made Evie light-headed and woozy. The room was hot, and there were too many bodies in close proximity. She felt trapped and claustrophobic. She couldn't breathe. Away, she had to get away from the crush of ecstatic people and the undulating, dizzying figure on the bar before she urped.

Sliding down off the bar stool, she staggered through the crowd and out the screen doors. The porch was empty. Everyone was inside hooting and hollering at Lenora's impromptu 'ho down. The cool breeze off the river felt like heaven after the stuffy bar. Evie wobbled over to the wooden rail and looked out into the night. The blackness pressed against the fuzzy lights along the boardwalk like a heavy woolen blanket. Toby the dog paced at the end of the pier, stopping every so often to sniff the air. A fish hit the water with a dull *plop*. Frogs and crickets *dee-deeped* in steady rhythm in the trees. Moths fluttered around the porch lights. Nearby, Evie heard the insistent buzz of a large insect.

A wave of dizziness swept over her. She closed her eyes. It was a mistake. It made the spinning and the queasiness worse.

She opened her eyes and gasped. The river and woods glistened with drops of light, thousands of fireflies pulsing in the darkness like tiny, living stars.

A dragonfly fluttered in her face, lacy wings whirring. Evie blinked. No, not a dragonfly, she realized with a fierce stab of joy, a fairy. And the fireflies, too. They were all fairies. She could see them again, and they were all around her.

The radiant creature hovering in front of her clapped her tiny hands in annoyance. Pink and gold sparkles flew into the air.

"Take heed, child." The fairy's voice was thin and reedy. "The demons are coming."

Chapter Thirty-three

The tiny messenger darted off in a splash of glitter, and the lights dusting the river and woods winked out.

"Wait, come back," Evie cried, but the fairies were gone.

The frogs and crickets in the woods fell silent. Something was coming. Something bad.

A low growl drew her attention to the pier. Hackles raised, Toby stood at the end of the dock barking at something on the water.

A chill raced down Evie's spine. "Toby, come here, boy," she called. Her voice sounded weak and shaky. She edged away from the railing and closer to the door.

A boat slid out of the darkness and bumped against the pier. Two burly men and a woman climbed out of the vessel, their movements slow and clumsy. Three drunks at a bar, that's what the fairy was warning her about?

The woman paused under a light at the end of the pier. Evie's heart stuttered when she got a good look at the woman's face. Her eyes were black pools of melted licorice above her grinning mouth.

Not drunks, demon-possessed humans.

The dog backed away, still barking. The darkness seemed to fragment as a dozen or more ragged black shapes joined the humans on the dock. Demons, Evie realized with a stab of terror, like the wraith that had attacked her in the bathroom, and there was no one to protect her.

Toby tucked his tail and ran. "Run," he said, shifting into man form as he hit the porch steps.

He grabbed her by the arm and pulled her through the screen doors. Evie caught a flashing impression of heat and moving bodies and the dancing ribbons of the thrall's string dress as they rushed into the bar, before Toby's shout of warning brought Lenora's little party to a screeching halt.

"Demons," Toby said, shoving Evie across the room to where the thrall gyrated on the glass counter.

Lenora stopped shimmying, and everyone turned and looked as the porch door opened and the demon-possessed woman stepped inside. Or what was left of her. In spite of the chill in the air, she wore a grimy sleeveless top, a blue jean skirt that exposed her dirty, knobby knees, and a pair of scuffed flats. She might once have been pretty, but it was hard to tell from the wreckage that was left. Most of her teeth were gone. She was emaciated, a used-up shrunken thing, her features as drawn as a meth addict's. Behind her on the other side of the screen door, Evie saw the swollen outline of the two men on the porch. The djegrali floated behind the two thugs like tattered black scarves.

Evie tried to guess the woman's age and gave up. She could have been twenty, but she looked a hundred. And she *stunk,* like rotting garbage tossed on a burning trash pile. The smell poured off her in waves.

Evie felt sick to her stomach. But for the grace of God and Ansgar, this would have been her, trapped in her own body as the demon consumed her from within, bending her to its evil will.

The demon woman sauntered closer. "Happy Halloween," she said with a toothless smile. "Or maybe I should say trick or treat?"

Beck hefted the vodka bottle in her right hand. "Get out. Your kind's not welcome here."

"We have no quarrel with you." The woman coughed, a horrible rattling sound, and spat a glob of something black, like old blood, on the floor. She pointed a bony finger at Evie. "The morkyn wants her. Give her to us and we will go."

"I don't know any morkyn, and I don't take orders from riffraff in my bar," Beck said.

"Foolish halfling, the morkyn are the oldest and most powerful of our kind." The woman shambled closer. "Drakthal, the morkyn I serve, wants the Douglass woman. You would do well to hand her over. The djegrali have set their sights on this place. You cannot defeat them. Riches are in store for those who aid them. Death awaits those who do not."

"Drakthal can kiss my ass," Beck said. "You won't take Hannah without a fight, and I'm starting with you, bitch." In a swift, fluid movement, Beck leaped across the bar at the woman.

With an evil hiss, the possessed woman morphed into something out of a bad dream. Bones cracked and sinews split as her arms stretched into a pair of grotesque, leathery wings. Her legs lengthened, her feet sprouted talons, and her jaws became a cruel beak.

"Look out," Evie cried as the winged monster attacked. Clutching the vodka bottle in one hand, Beck danced from side to side, avoiding the thing's vicious blows. What did she think she was going to do with an empty bottle? Evie wondered. Bean the thing over the head with it?

A shadow streaked across the room and placed itself between Beck and the monster. It was the grim, dark-haired man from the corner table. Evie had forgotten all about him in the excitement. He was tall and heavily muscled, like Ansgar, and wore the same impassive expression. Unless she was sadly mistaken, Beck's admirer was Dalvahni.

"Stay back," he commanded in a harsh voice. "This is warrior's work." Drawing a short sword, he attacked the winged nightmare.

"Oh, hell no, you don't," Beck said, charging around him to get at the monster.

The doors burst off the hinges, and the rest of the demons poured into the bar. A few patrons hesitated, either high on the sex bomb Lenora had detonated earlier, or eager for a throw down. Most scattered, though, or ran in mindless circles as they tried to find their way out.

The she demon's two goony friends lurched across the bar toward Evie, their Jell-O-pudding eyes wobbling. They moved awkwardly, as though trying to remember how to walk. The demons inside them had sucked their brains dry or fried them on drugs and alcohol, Evie decided, taking in their vacuous expressions.

Or all three. These poor saps would have to go up fifty IQ points to be dumb as a bag of hammers.

A chilling cry made her look up. Three demons circled above her, dementor-like. She screamed and threw her arms over her head as the wraiths dive-bombed her.

Ansgar, she thought with a flash of despair, waiting for the bone-chilling touch of the djegrali or the clammy grasp of one of the goons. *I'll never see him again.*

Nothing happened.

She opened her eyes. A greenish-gold shield enclosed her like a protective bubble. The fairies, Evie thought, blinking back tears of gratitude. She looked around but didn't see them. An angry hiss drew her gaze back to the glowing shield. The wraiths darted above her like angry wasps. One of the goons, his moronic features twisted in frustration, slammed his fist into the barrier. Green fire shot up his arm. He jerked back with a howl of agony and sat down hard on the floor, cradling his injured arm against his chest, a look of stupid surprise on his swollen face.

The second goon shambled up, grasped a heavy wooden table by the leg, and swung it like a mace, hammering the shield with mindless ferocity. The sound was deafening, like being inside a bass drum. He was going to break through, Evie realized with despair. The fairies' shield would not hold.

The goon struck another blow, and the barrier shattered. Evie and the dull creature stared at each other for a moment, and then the goon's drooling mouth stretched in a slack grin.

He reached for her, and Evie screamed. His grin faded, and he staggered back with a grunt of surprise, staring in blank astonishment at the four arrows that protruded from his chest. He groaned and crashed to the floor.

Something dark rose from the body and shattered into black powder. The djegrali, Evie thought, her mind dull with terror and revulsion. The goon's body, freed of the demon, collapsed in on itself and melted into a viscous puddle.

The circling wraiths howled in fury and attacked. Scaly, leprous hands reached for her, and Evie screamed and shrank back. The nearest djegrali fell away, pierced by a shining arrow. A second and a third arrow found their marks. The wraiths wailed and disintegrated into black dust.

Ansgar, Evie thought, shivering with relief.

He materialized before her, his chest heaving and his eyes glowing with silver light. Cold poured off him, harsh and unforgiving as winter. He was furious, she realized, shivering for an entirely different reason.

"You are unharmed?" he asked. His voice was flat, and a white nimbus of power surrounded him.

"Yes," she said. "Ansgar, I'm so glad—"

He picked her up and set her on top of the bar beside the thrall. The air hummed as he muttered something in a strange language.

"I have placed a shield spell around you," he said in the same monotone. "Stay here where it is safe."

"But, Ansgar, I—"

"Not now, Evangeline," he said. "You have tested both my patience and my temper to the limit tonight."

Turning on his heel, he strode back into the fight.

Evie watched him walk off. Of all the nerve. She had tested *his* temper and patience? Was he serious? Mr. Love'em and Leave'em?

"Oh, no, I don't think so," Evie muttered, watching through narrowed eyes as Ansgar fired a rapid volley of silver arrows at the djegrali with deadly accuracy.

He really was a fine shot and utterly magnificent. But that was beside the point.

Evie was still fuming when Shep Corwin strode up, his eyes gleaming with excitement and a nine iron gripped in one hand. He looked bigger, harder, and more dangerous. More *everything*.

"Shep?" Evie said with a yelp of surprise. "What are you doing here?"

"Take care of Lenora for me," Shep said, glancing up at the thrall on the bar. "She's three sheets to the wind."

Blip! He disappeared and reemerged across the room, swinging his club at the swarming wraiths. *Splat!* The club connected with a demon. It disintegrated. *Splat, splat!* Two more wraiths shattered, then another and another. Pieces of demon floated around the room. Toby joined Shep in dog form. Leaping in the air, Toby caught a flying demon in his jaws and shook it. The dog released the demon, and Shep slammed the wraith with his club, finishing it off.

Evie shook her head in disbelief and confusion. Unless she was mistaken, Shep had just done the demon hunter bop and destroyed a bunch of demons. *With a golf club.* He was the valiant little undertaker that could. But that wasn't possible. Shep was the salt of the earth, a regular guy—a good old Southern boy who just happened to have a sexpot succubus girlfriend.

According to Addy, Shep and Lenora had been doing it like bunnies for months, exchanging essences in the old-fashioned way.

Having sex with the thrall must have changed him, because one thing was clear. Shep Corwin was no longer human. She wondered if Lenora had any idea what she'd done. Probably not. She glanced up at Lenora. The thrall's face was slack, and she hummed the theme song to *Loins of Lust*. Lenora was toasted on demonoid funk. As Evie watched, Lenora reached out, plucked a floating piece of djegrali out of the air, and put it in her mouth.

"Gross," Evie said.

Lenora snagged another piece and ate it. "It is not gross. Leftover demon is delicious."

"Shep's here."

"Tell him to go away," Lenora said. "I am angry at him."

"You should tell him how you feel," Evie said. "He's right over there."

"I do not *know* how I feel! I cannot put it into words. It is terrible and consuming and altogether uncomfortable."

Lenora sat down on the glass bar and burst into tears.

The thrall's grief washed over Evie, and she burst into tears, too. She couldn't help it. All the sadness in the world welled up inside her and had to come out, mountains and oceans of it. She heard a mournful howl.

Toby was back in man form. He had his head thrown back, and he was baying like a moon-sick dog.

She looked around. The fight was over, and everybody was crying. The few demonoids that hadn't skedaddled were sobbing. The goony with the burned arm was bawling like a sick calf. Tears streamed down Beck's face as she argued with the stern guy with the sword. Mr. Grimface was crying, too. A tear trickled down Ansgar's cheek, although his expression remained stony.

The air was thick with misery and raw, unharnessed woe. Lenora might be thousands of years old, but when it came to feelings, she was as unpredictable as a teenage girl with PMS, and her moods, good or bad, were contagious.

Shep stepped up to the bar, his face twisted with grief. "Lenora, baby, stop crying," he said hoarsely. "You're killing me."

"I will not stop crying. You are ashamed of me." She wailed louder. "Oh, what is happening to me? Make it stop! This *hurts.*"

"I am *not* ashamed of you," Shep said. "I love you. I've loved you from the first moment I saw you."

"You do?" Lenora hiccupped and looked at Shep, eyes wide. "You love me?"

"Yes." Shep stepped closer to the bar. "And you love me."

Lenora drew herself up. "This I have not told you," she said, haughty as any queen.

"No, you haven't. Believe me, I've noticed. So tell me now. I want to hear it. I *need* to hear it."

The ribbons of the string dress fluttered and hissed in agitation. "I will not. It is unnatural . . . a-an abomination. Thralls do not feel. Thralls do not *love*."

"I see." Shep's shoulders drooped. "I suppose that's why you've slept around so much since you met me, because you don't have feelings for me. I'm nothing special, just another meal." He shook his head. "Hell, I can see how drunk you are. I know what that means. You've probably had sex with a dozen guys tonight."

"I have not! I have not been with anyone else since we met!" Lenora glared at him and then at Evie. "Tell him, Evie."

"She hasn't been with anybody tonight," Evie said. "All she did was dance on the bar."

And send folks into a sexual frenzy, but that was more like a hobby.

Shep gave Lenora a slow smile. "I know you haven't been with anyone else. Even though you were mad and hurting and wanted to hurt me back for being a prize idiot. Know how I know?" Lenora shook her head at him, her expression wary. "Because you love me." He took another step toward the bar. "Say it, Nora. Tell me you love me."

Lenora's magnificent bosom rose and fell in rapid succession, straining the so-called bodice of the string dress. "No, I will not! I am frightened."

"I'm scared too, baby," Shep said. "But, I'm standing here with my heart in my hand telling you I love you. Give a guy a break, won't you? I'm dying here. I need to hear the words."

"But what about *her*? What about your mother, your sister? They hate me."

"They can get over it," Shep said. "I love you, and so do William and Lily. The question is, do you love me?"

"Yes, damn you, I love you!" Lenora's lush mouth trembled. "There, are you happy?"

Shep grinned, and the effect was dazzling. "Ecstatic. Even if I could live without you, I sure as hell don't want to." Tossing the golf club aside, he looked up at Lenora with his heart in his eyes. "Lenora Thralvani, will you marry me? Please."

Chapter Thirty-four

Evie held her breath for Shep. He looked so full of hope, so vulnerable. He deserved some happiness, and he was obviously crazy mad in love with Lenora. But what if she didn't feel the same way? Sure, she *said* she loved him, but what was love to a thrall? Oh, dear, Evie hoped Lenora wasn't about to break Shep's heart.

She needn't have worried. Lenora leaped off the bar and into his arms.

"Yes, Shepton, oh, yes!" she squealed, raining kisses on his face. "I will marry you and most gladly."

"Thank God," Shep said, kissing her.

Fireworks whizzed through the air, and flowers and blooming vines of every description sprang from the floor at Shep's and Lenora's feet. The air grew heavy with the scent of roses, jasmine, hyacinth, gardenia, and lilac. Butterflies and tiny birds with wings like delicate multicolored crystal flitted among the blossoms of golden light starring the air. An unseen chorus sang something in a strange language in voices that were so pure and clear they brought tears of joy to Evie's eyes.

The thrall was happy, really, really happy; Beck, not so much. She stopped arguing with the dark-haired warrior to glare at the two lovebirds.

"Hey, you two get a room," she said. "And take the flowers and the rest of this mushy junk with you. This is a bar, not a freaking Disney movie."

Shep lifted his head and smiled down at Lenora. "An excellent suggestion."

Blip! They disappeared, taking the flora, fauna, and Celtic choir with them, leaving the bar once more a mess. Smashed tables and chairs littered the establishment, and broken glass covered the floor from busted beer bottles. Bits of dead wraith drifted across the room like wisps of black crepe paper, lifted by the night wind blowing through the gaping doors. Evie glanced down at the glass bar she sat on. The exterior appeared undamaged, but the liquid lights inside were bunched at one end, so something wasn't working properly. The goon with the burned arm sat on the floor with his back to the wall, his legs wide open and a vacant look on his broad face. Something had sure poleaxed him but good; maybe the rapid fluctuation in Lenora's emotions or the magic that shimmered in the air from all the supernatural activity.

The few remaining customers drifted out of the bar, headed home, Evie presumed. It was late and the show was over. Ansgar stood next to the pool of dark liquid—all that remained of the she demon—deep in conversation with the dark-haired guy. As she watched, the puddle of demon ooze dried up and blew away. Beck made a face and said something to them. Or tried to—but they were doing the boys' club thing and ignoring her.

As if sensing her regard, Ansgar turned his head and looked at her. His face was stiff and carefully blank, but his eyes shone like beaten silver. He was angry with her.

Evie lifted her chin. So what? He wasn't the only one in a bad mood. She'd been scared half out of her wits tonight for him and for herself. She was still mad at him and woozy on chocolate, and she felt irritable, tense, and jumpy in her own skin.

Beck raised her voice. "But I keep trying to tell you there's another way to do it! You didn't *have* to kill that woman."

"She seems most adamant," Ansgar said in his cool, unruffled way. "Perhaps we should listen to her, Conall."

Evie felt a stab of alarm. Conall? The dark-haired warrior was *Conall,* the leader of the Dalvahni? Why was he here? What if Conall ordered Ansgar to leave? Sent him on a mission and she never saw him again? She was angry at Ansgar, but she didn't want him to go away. Again, she thought darkly.

How was she supposed to make him sorry for what he did if he *left*?

" 'Twas not a woman, 'twas a demon." Conall's voice was harsh, and something like fury flashed in his black eyes. "If not for my intercession the beast would have slain you, little fool. Have you no care for your safety?"

Beck straightened her shoulders. "Look, buddy, I don't know who you think you are, but I can take care of myself." She threw up her hands in disgust. "Oh, what's the use? You're not listening, so I'll *show* you."

"Stay back, woman. The fiend is dangerous," Conall commanded as Beck strode over to the goony on the floor, the bottle still grasped in one hand.

Conall crossed the room in a blur of motion, but Beck was faster. She stabbed the goon in the shoulder with the silver pour spout. The goon's eyes bulged and his hulking body arched. The bottle in Beck's hand darkened and filled with oily smoke. The goony shifted and shrank.

Beck stuck her thumb over the end of the pour spout to keep the demon from escaping. "And that," she said, flashing Conall a cocky grin, "is the proper way to extract a demon."

"By the sword," Ansgar said, staring in astonishment at the rather ordinary looking man sitting on the floor in the goony's place. "She sucked the djegrali out of the human. Astonishing."

"Perhaps he remembers something," Conall said. "Perhaps he can tell us something of the djegrali and their plans."

"Where am I?" The man looked around in bewilderment. His plaid shorts were torn and dirty. "Why does my arm hurt?" He looked down at the blood darkening his shirt. "My shoulder's bleeding. What's going on?"

"You're in a bar in Hannah," Beck said. "Do you remember how you got here?"

"Hannah? What the hell am I doing in Hannah?" Bermuda Shorts looked puzzled. "The last thing I remember was going into the Pink Pony Pub for a beer. My wife and I are staying at the beach with the kids." He scowled. "And then *she* shows up. M'wife's sister. Can't stand that woman. Got a voice like a smoke alarm and never shuts up. That's why I went to get a beer. Had to get away."

"When was that?" Beck asked.

"Fourth of July weekend," he said. "The hottest damn time of the year in Gulf Shores, but that's when Belinda always wants to go. I hate the beach. Hate the heat and the sand and the jellyfish and the damn tourists. I'm telling you, if I had a house at the beach and a home in hell, I'd go home."

"I think that answers your question," Beck said to Conall. "He doesn't remember anything. I'm not surprised. None of them ev—"

"What time is it?" the man demanded, interrupting her. "I gotta get back to the condo."

Beck glanced at her watch. "It's fifteen minutes until three—"

His eyes bulged. "In the morning? Shit, my wife's gonna—"

"—and it's October thirty-first. Halloween morning, to be exact," Beck finished. "You're late, real late. On the plus side, you're not at the beach." Ignoring the flustered, sputtering man, she waved at Toby. "Tobias, why don't you take Rip van Winkle into the office and let him telephone his wife?"

"Sure thing," Toby said.

Staring at Beck in befuddlement, the man allowed Toby to help him to his feet. "The name's Jack," he mumbled.

"Well, Jack, have the little woman take you to the hospital and have that arm and shoulder checked out," Beck said. "And while you're at it, make sure the doc checks you for STDs. No telling where you and your johnson have been since July. You don't want to give the wife a nasty present."

Jack blanched. "Oh, man, Belinda's gonna kill me."

Toby led Jack away.

"And Jack, don't drink," Beck called after them. "It's bad for you."

" 'Tis peculiar advice, coming from the owner of a tavern," Conall said. His deep voice was colorless.

"Yeah, well you don't know anything about me." Walking over to the bar, Beck lifted a loose tile at one end, stuck the end of the spout in the opening, and shook the bottle. Black smoke poured out of the bottle. The wraith turned a sullen, angry red and joined the cluster of lights huddled at one end of the hollow shell. "There," Beck said, slapping the tile back into place with a look of satisfaction. "That's one demon won't be causing any more trouble."

Demons, the pretty little colored lights inside the bar were demons. She was sitting on top of a swarm of them. Evie scampered down off the bar and slammed into Ansgar's shield spell.

Disengaging the spell, Ansgar drew her away from the bar. "Is it wise to keep them thus?" he asked, eyeing the floating demons with an uneasy expression. "Do you not fear they will escape?"

"The glass is too thick," Beck said. "They can't pass through it, for some reason. I got a bunch more in the store room in mason jars."

"You mean, you've been canning demons like . . . like *tomatoes*?" Evie stared at Beck in astonishment. "Holy cow! Can all demonoids do the same thing? Extract demons, I mean."

Beck shrugged. "Maybe. I don't know. We have different talents and varying degrees of ability." She glanced at Conall and stiffened. "Why are you staring at me like that?"

"Like what?" Conall's mouth twisted in a sneer.

"Like I'm something you scraped off the bottom of your shoe."

"You are demon spawn, I am a demon hunter," Conall said. "What else is there to say?"

"I read you loud and clear, buddy. There's nothing else to say. So leave already."

Turning her back on them, Beck attacked the glass on the floor with a broom from behind the bar.

"You must allow me to help you set things right here first," Conall said stiffly.

Beck stopped sweeping and whirled around. "I don't want or

need your help. Get out." She jabbed the broom at the splintered doors. "All of you. Bar's closed."

Evie stepped onto the porch with her two demon hunter escorts. The night was still except for the quiet sound of the river and the steady, rippling call of a whip-poor-will. Hard to believe that, moments before, ugliness and death had marred such a beautiful, serene night. Had things gone differently, right now she'd be dead or at the mercy of demons, a pawn for their evil leader to use God only knew how. The thought made Evie weak. The battle had cleared her head of the chocolate high, but she still felt wound up and jumpy.

She was also more than a little annoyed with Conall and his obvious contempt for Beck.

"She's upset," Evie said to him, not bothering to hide the accusation in her tone. "You hurt her feelings."

"She is demonoid." Conall spit the word out of his mouth, like it was a wad of something nasty.

Demonoid; subject closed. To him maybe, but not to her.

Conall stalked down the steps. After a moment's hesitation, Evie started after him. She couldn't let this one ride.

Ansgar put his hand on her shoulder. "Leave it be, Evangeline," he said. "It is not our affair."

"I'm making it my affair. I have a few things to say to the high and mighty captain of the Dalvahni."

"Evangeline, wait—" Ansgar said.

But she was already down the steps. *Blip!* She caught up with Conall at the end of the pier. She felt, rather than heard, Ansgar come up behind her.

Conall stood at the end of the dock gazing out at the water, his broad, muscled back to them. He radiated power and detachment, and he seemed to draw the night around him like a mantle.

Evie hesitated. She was wasting her time. She hardly knew Conall. He was harsh and intimidating as all get-out, bleak and unapproachable, as hard and unforgiving as a stone. And those were his good points. His mind was obviously made up. He was a demon hunter, implacable in his beliefs, particularly when it came to the djegrali. What made her think she could change his mind?

Evie straightened her shoulders. She had to try. She owed it to Beck.

"The only good demonoid is a dead demonoid, is that it?" Evie said, challenge in her tone.

Conall turned to face her, his eyes dark and swirling with hidden danger like the river behind him. "Yes. She is accursed, the daughter of evil. I should have killed her. 'Twas my duty, yet I stayed my hand."

"You know why?" Evie said. "Because somewhere deep down inside that shriveled-up thing you call a heart, you *know* Beck's not evil. She's a *person,* not a monster. She has a choice, like the rest of us, to do good or bad."

"She is an abomination, the wicked by-blow of unmitigated evil. She is what she is, as am I. There is no choice for either of us."

Evie wanted to shake him. She knew what it was like to be different, to never fit in, to be the object of ridicule and scorn. She didn't know what kind of life Beck had led, but she could imagine. Better than Conall, perfect leader of a perfect race, at any rate.

"Beck can't help who her parents are," she said. "She had no more say-so in how she got here than you or I."

"Why do you defend her?" Conall said. "She is nothing to you."

"Because she helped me tonight, a woman she didn't know. You were there. You saw her. She got between me and that *thing.* If she's so horrible and evil, why'd she do that?"

"I have thought on this," Conall said slowly. "Methinks she is in concert with the djegrali and hopes to lure us into complacency with her beauty and semblance of goodness."

"Or maybe she's exactly what she seems to be," she retorted. "Wouldn't that surprise you?"

"The entire evening has been something of a surprise," Conall said. His brooding gaze moved to the bar. "Quite . . . unexpected."

"Yes, sir," Ansgar said. "If you recall, I stated in my report that Hannah is out of the ordinary."

"Yes, your report was most thorough," Conall said.

"But what about Beck?" Evie persisted.

Conall's dark brows lifted. "What about her?"

"Promise me you won't hurt her."

"You are impertinent." Conall's voice was cold. "I give orders. I do not take them."

"I know, but I want you to promise me anyway."

"Evangeline." Ansgar hooked his arm around her and pulled her close. "You must excuse her. It has been a trying night."

"Yes, it has." Conall's gaze moved once more to the bar. "She has fire and courage, but she is also impetuous and lacks discipline. She needs training." Was he talking about her or Beck? Evie wondered. He seemed to recall himself. He looked at Evie, his expression unreadable. "Since you admitted in your report that you are responsible for this female's . . . er . . . condition, I assign you the task."

"I accept and most gladly," Ansgar said.

Something like amusement glinted in Conall's black eyes. "Somehow, I did not think you would refuse. But I am curious. How do you mean to proceed?"

"After giving the matter much thought, I have decided to marry the chit, sir, and spend the next few thousand years instructing her in the way of the Dalvahni." Ansgar's white teeth flashed in a grin. "Among other things."

"Marry me?" Evie said. "Now wait just a minute. You and I haven't—"

Conall turned his back to them, and the shadows settled deeper around him. "Carry on then."

Ansgar wrapped his arms around her and the pier fell away.

Chapter Thirty-five

Pine needles crunched beneath Evie's feet, and she heard the musical song of tumbling water. She looked around. They were in the woods, the same place Ansgar had taken her the day before, a secluded grotto of trees and moss-covered hills on a quiet finger of the Devil River. The moon peeked at them through the tree branches. A feathery waterfall spilled over a rocky cliff and into the shallow pool below. It was a lovely place, peaceful and serene.

Evie didn't feel peaceful or serene. She was racked by tremors, little shivers of hot and cold. Shock, adrenaline, anger, grief, and terror—too many emotions in one night. She could now add surprise to the list. Ansgar's announcement had gobsmacked her. He wanted to *marry her*? The thought was elating and terrifying. He'd declared his intention in typical alpha male fashion without asking her, she thought indignantly. Like it was a done deal, the arrogant, wonderful jerk, and maybe it was—or would be if she didn't have a murder charge hanging over her head.

"What about Beck?" she asked, latching on to a safer topic. "I'm worried about her. I don't trust your precious Conall."

It was true. She was worried about Beck, and Conall was darkness itself. Who knew what he might do in their absence?

Ansgar closed the space between them. Tension radiated from his big body and an aura of suppressed violence. She wasn't the only one upset, she realized.

"You should be worried for yourself," he said. "You are the one in danger, not Beck."

Yanking her into his arms, he kissed her. Claimed her, like the Viking warlord he resembled, Evie thought, dizzy from his sensuous onslaught. The kiss was hot and needy, a possession that ravaged her mouth and assailed her senses. Murmuring her name, he dragged his hot, open mouth down the tender skin of her throat. Nibbled at her with his lips and tasted her with his tongue, like he couldn't get enough of her. Sensation poured through her and a raging desire that left her trembling and weak. Her breasts tingled, and the place between her legs ached. She was on fire.

"I need you," he said, his voice rough with strain. "Gods, the torture you have put me through, imagining you hurt or . . ." He shuddered and gave her an angry little shake. "Why did you leave me like that when you know you are in danger? You have seen the djegrali with your own eyes. Have you no care for your safety?" His grip on her shoulders tightened. "Do you have any idea how many taverns I tracked you to tonight? Ever one step behind you . . . ever with the foul stench of the djegrali in my nostrils and the taste of death in my mouth. Wondering, always wondering, if I would reach you in time, before . . ." His jaw tightened. "No, I cannot say it. I cannot think on it or I will go mad."

She tore herself free and stepped back, panting. Her skin burned and her brain buzzed. She couldn't think right now. She could only *feel*.

"Then don't say it," she said. "Don't think about it. Take off your clothes."

"What?" He stared at her, his eyes glowing silver in the moonlight.

"Take. Off. Your. Clothes."

"We need to talk. You need to understand that—"

"Later," she said, kicking off her sandals. "Right now, we need to have sex, before I have a come-apart."

She quickly stripped down to her undergarments. The panties and bra she wore were new and sexy, part of the wardrobe from the guest bedroom closet. And they actually *matched*. The bra gave her miles of cleavage, and the panties were especially risqué, a couple of strips of lace and little else. She felt red hot and daring, with "red hot" being the operative term. She wanted Ansgar something fierce.

But he didn't move, just stood there staring at her, his eyes glowing hotter. She frowned. "Why are you looking at me like that? Is something wrong?"

"No. Nothing is wrong. Everything is perfect. You are perfect. Turn around."

Her stomach fluttered. The look in his eyes left her breathless and dialed up the heat a few thousand degrees. It was a wonder she didn't burst into flame. She turned her back to him, giving him a view of her backside in the skimpy panties. He muttered something, his liquid voice harsh with need, and then he was there, behind her, his hands rough and hot, cupping her breasts, stroking and plucking her nipples through the fabric of her bra, making her hotter with every touch. He wanted her as much as she wanted him. She wasn't in this crazy thing alone.

Thank God.

He unhooked her bra, and it slipped down her arms and fell to the ground. Her breasts felt heavy and full. His hands rested lightly at her waist. What was he waiting for? She wanted to scream at him to touch her again and not stop. She'd never wanted anything so much. She held her breath as his hands slid from her waist and back to her breasts. Ah, she thought, arching her back as his thumbs moved back and forth over her tight nipples. The cool air and the heat of his skin were sweet torture. Murmuring her name, he kissed the slope of her shoulder, nipped her, and then eased the sore spot with the flat of his tongue. Everything in her tightened until she thought she would shatter.

Turning in his arms, she pulled his head down and kissed him, memorizing the taste and shape of his beautiful, serious, sensuous mouth, suckling his tongue. She was starved for him, too. With a groan, he grabbed her bottom and tugged her against the hard length of his erection. She rubbed against him, wanting him inside her, hard and thick. When she was with him, everything else went away, everything but her need for him. One look, one touch from him, could undo her completely.

She tore her mouth free. "You're still dressed," she muttered, pushing at the leather vest he wore. "Why are you still dressed?"

"Let me," he said, stilling her restless hands. " 'Twill be faster."

He shrugged out of the vest and pulled the linen shirt over his head.

"Oh, my," Evie breathed, dazed anew by the animal strength and beauty of him. He was all gleaming skin and hard muscle; bulging shoulders and arms, and a wide chest that dipped down to a narrow waist and ripped abdomen. "You are ridiculous."

"Not the reaction a warrior hopes for."

"Ridiculously *gorgeous,* as if you didn't know it."

"If I please you, then I am glad," he said in his haughty way. But she heard the ripple of laughter in his deep voice.

"Oh, yes." Evie's gaze lingered on his slablike pecs. "You please me very much. Any more pleased and I might die of it."

Reaching out, she traced the line of golden hair that ran down the middle of his belly and disappeared into the top of his leather breeches. She fumbled with the ties at his waist, and his erection sprang free. "Beautiful," she whispered, stroking him.

"Evangeline," he said. His voice sounded husky. "I have very little control at the moment. When you say things like that, I—"

"I want to taste you," she said impatiently. "I want you to taste me. I want everything." She stepped out of her panties and rubbed her breasts against his chest. She hardly recognized the wild creature she'd become. She shuddered at the delight of skin-to-skin contact with him, breathing in his heady scent, sweat mixed with cedar and bergamot. "But, right now, I want you inside me."

Somehow, they were on the ground and she was on top of him, straddling him. His leather breeches were open and shoved down around his hips. He took her by the waist and lowered her onto his rigid shaft. She gasped at the pleasure-pain of it. That part of him was big like the rest of him, beautiful and magnificent, but almost too much.

"Easy," he murmured, stroking her breasts. "Lean forward. Let me help you."

She was frantic now with wanting him inside her, but she did as he said, squirming as he took her nipple in his mouth.

"Ansgar," she cried. "I—"

"Shh," he said, suckling and teasing. "No talking. Relax and ride me."

Grasping her thighs, he rose up, impaling her fully. She took him in, all of him, reveling at the miraculous sensation of being joined, at how they fit together like the missing pieces of a puzzle, body-to-body and soul-to-soul. What a clever fellow God was to design them this way. How humbling, how splendid and glorious.

She rose up and came back down again. The pressure and slide were exquisite, pushing her closer to release. Ansgar bucked beneath her, urging her on with rough words of encouragement and entreaty, his beautiful features sharp with passion. She flung her head back and gave herself to him.

The waves of pleasure built. Without warning, she plunged over the edge, shivering around him. With a hoarse shout, Ansgar tumbled headlong after her.

Evie opened her eyes. She felt relaxed and sated. Ansgar held her in his arms, and he was walking, carrying her. He was so strong, she thought, smiling to herself. He made her feel dainty and feminine . . . and safe and sexy and a dozen other things that were just plain wonderful.

"Hmm." She buried her face against his chest and breathed him in. "You smell so good. Where are we going?"

"For a swim."

"*What?*" She struggled in his grasp. Not that it did much good. His arms were like iron bands. "It's October. The water's too cold!"

"Too cold? The days are still balmy, and the first frost has yet to rime the ground." He reached the water and waded in. "The water will be quite pleasant."

"I'm Southern. I've got thin blood. I'll catch my death."

"You are Dalvahni now. We do not get sick, and cold and heat seldom affect us."

"I don't care." She wrapped her arms around his neck and held on. "You're not putting me in that water, Ansgar. No way. *I mean it.* I—"

She shrieked as he stepped under the waterfall, dousing them both.

"Oh," she said, gasping and sputtering as the chilly water pummeled her face and body. "I cannot believe you did that. That was not nice of you. Not nice at all."

"I think we have already established that I am not nice."

He carried her away from the waterfall and into the rocky pool on one side of the cascade. The water wasn't deep—barely waist high on him—and felt quite wonderful now that she was used to it.

Ansgar felt wonderful, too, with his hard chest pressed against her naked breasts. Not that she would admit it to *him,* of course.

"What about snakes?" she asked.

"No snakes," he said. Setting her down on a rocky ledge, he stepped between her thighs. Her eyes widened as she felt the head of his shaft nudge the cleft between her legs. "Not of the reptilian variety, at any rate."

"You're naked!"

"How clever of you to notice. I undressed while you slept."

"I slept?" How embarrassing. Wasn't it usually the guy who passed out after sex? The last thing she remembered was . . . She blushed, remembering how she'd lost herself in his arms. "Uh . . . how long was I out?"

"Quite some time. Mayhap it was the aftereffect of the burn."

"What burn? What are you talking about?"

"Twice tonight, you used your powers," he said. "Once when you became agitated and released that deluge in the ballroom—"

She bristled. "I was not agitated. I was plain old *mad,* mad at

Addy and Muddy and *everybody*. Most of all, I was furious with *you* because you left me. And because you were with that thrall—"

"—and again in the tavern when the demons attacked," he continued in his maddeningly controlled way. "Overpowering sexual desire is a natural result of danger and battle adrenaline, combined with the rush of releasing your powers."

"Wait," Evie said. "You're saying that *I* was responsible for that green bubble thing in the bar tonight? How could I do something like that? I don't understand."

"It seems a small thing in comparison to the maelstrom you released at the dance. Why do you seem surprised? I, for one, am grateful for your ability. I do not like to think what might have happened otherwise."

"I don't know," Evie said, searching for a way to make him understand. Good luck, she thought. *How can you explain it, when you don't understand it yourself?* "So much has happened in the last few days. Losing my temper is bad enough, but this . . . It makes me feel strange, for some reason. Correction. Make that *stranger*. Like I don't know myself."

"*I* know you. I have always known you. Do you remember that first day in the flower shop?"

She smiled up at him. "Yes. You made me so nervous. I couldn't look at you. I remember thinking, *Jeez Louise, look at him! He's so freaking hot he glows!* And then you called me Evangeline and said I was strong. Me, the biggest wimp in the South. I was so shocked. I couldn't say a thing."

"That is not all I said, as I recall. I told you that you are beautiful." He lifted one of her long, wet curls and brought it to his lips. "And you are. You remind me of a wood nymph with your red and gold hair, like autumn leaves." He dropped the damp curl, and Evie shivered as his hands moved to caress her breasts. "And your big eyes . . . so sad and full of shadows. You were shy and skittish as a doe. I remember thinking, *Go gentle with this one, Ansgar, else you will startle her and she will take flight.* Even then, I was terrified of losing you."

"Not too terrified," Evie said. She gasped as he opened her

thighs wider and pushed inside—but not enough. Her greedy body wanted more, wanted it all. She wiggled, trying to get closer to him. To her frustration, he pulled out. Clamping his hands on her legs, he teased her, rubbing the head of his erection along the sensitive folds between her legs. She bit her bottom lip to keep from screaming in frustration. "Y-you left."

"Ah, but I came back." He continued his torturous assault, withdrawing and pushing forward again, entering her without fully sheathing himself, leaving Evie frantic for more. "I could not stay away. I could not forget you. For thousands of years, I have known only duty and the hunt. Nothing of love or tenderness. Imagine my surprise when I discovered I *had* a heart and that I had left it behind with you."

"What about *her*?" she panted, clutching his arms as he slid a little deeper inside her. *Yes, just a little more . . . oh, my God, he is killing me.* She could feel the pressure and the heat building between them, the pleasure. "This Kalia chick you were with?"

"She was as sand poured into the mouth of a man dying of thirst," he said. "She could not ease my torment or make me forget you. Indeed, she only made me more wretched."

"Good," Evie said. "I'm glad. You deserve wretched for leaving me." She arched her pelvis, trying to take more of him in, desperate for him. He chuckled and held her down. "Ansgar," she cried, pummeling his chest with her fists. "Stop teasing me and give me what I want."

He grinned down at her, no more troubled by her blows than by a gnat. "And what is that?"

"You. All of you. Right now."

"You have me." Her eyes drifted shut as he rocked his hips, giving her another slow, maddening stroke and then another. "I am yours, Evangeline, body and soul."

Yes, that was it. A little more, a little harder. Al . . . most . . . there. Everything in her was drawn tight, straining toward him, eager for release.

"Say you are mine." His husky voice made her shiver. He gave her another slow, exquisite nudge, his hardness filling her, taking her to the edge. "I need to hear it."

"Yes, yes." She was almost sobbing now. "You know it's—"

"Say the words. Say them."

Lust drunk and dazed, she opened her eyes. "I'm yours, Ansgar. I love you. I want you. I need you. What more is there to say?"

"But one thing more, sweetling. Say that you will marry me."

"And if I say no?"

"Then I will keep you here until I change your mind."

"I can't marry you," she protested. "Not when there's a murder charge hanging over my head and I could go to prison. That wouldn't be fair."

Tangling his hands in her hair, he tilted her head back. She gazed up at him in surprise. His jaw was clenched, his expression set and stubborn.

"We will go forward with this farce and try to discover the identity of Meredith's killer because I know it is important to you to clear your name. Consequently, that makes it important to *me*," he said. "But, do not imagine—*even for moment*—that I will be separated from you ever again, much less allow you to go to prison. I will whisk you away and keep you safe, by force, if need be." He looked forbidding and determined, and totally irresistible. "I was perfectly content with my lot in life until I met you. But you changed all that. I love you. I cannot live without you, nor am I inclined to try—a circumstance I lay entirely at your door. Now, what are you going to do about it?"

"Oh," she said. "In that case, I guess I'd better marry you."

Chapter Thirty-six

The slow grin Ansgar gave her was blinding, like the sun breaking through a bank of storm clouds. "That was the right answer," he said.

Evie cried out as he thrust inside her. She wrapped her legs around his waist and held on as he began to move, each stroke driving her closer to the edge. The delicious tension built and then uncoiled in a wild rush, taking her and Ansgar once more into bliss.

When she came back to herself, she was in his arms and they were still connected. She smiled, luxuriating in his nearness; being with him felt so right. Even the moon seemed to approve, smiling down at them in their secret lagoon.

Maybe a little too much, Evie thought, squinting as Old Man Moon bore down on them like the headlight on an approaching night train.

"Ah, there you are, brother," a deep, familiar voice said. Evie yelped in surprise and shrank behind Ansgar. Brand stood on the sandy bank, a glowing orb suspended above one upraised hand. He closed his hand, and the shining ball vanished with an audible *pop*. "For a moment, I feared fair Luna had fled the sky," he said. "Then I realized 'twas your backside shining back at me from the river, and not the moon."

"Very amusing." Ansgar turned to face the other warrior, blocking Evie from view. "But, as you can see, Evangeline and I are engaged."

"So I noticed."

Evie blushed at the knowing slyness in Brand's tone. He was enjoying their discomfort. She wished she could say the same. She was horribly embarrassed, and she felt like an idiot huddled naked in a creek behind Ansgar's back. The one time, the *only* time in her life she went skinny-dipping, and she got caught. She thought with longing of her clothes scattered about on the little beach. Ansgar, on the other hand, seemed at ease with his nakedness. He crossed his arms and leaned back, so that he was pressed against her, shielding her from view.

"You misunderstand. Evangeline and I are engaged to be *married,*" he said. "She has consented to be my wife."

"Felicitations," Brand said. "Adara will be delighted when she hears the news. As will her mother." The hint of slyness crept back into his tone. "Bitsy will be in transports when she learns she has yet another wedding to plan. She regards Evie as a second daughter."

"I had not thought of that." The genuine horror in Ansgar's voice made Evie want to giggle. "By the sword, you need not sound so damnably pleased, brother."

"Misery loves company," Brand said. "Take heart. You and I have survived worse. The siege of Rome by the Ostrogoths. Torture. The attack of the winged vairnir upon the City of Light."

" 'Twould be less painful to have my eyeballs plucked out," Ansgar said.

"Do as I do," Brand said. "Tell yourself the woman you love is worth it, and that Bitsy means well."

Evie leaned forward and pressed a kiss on Ansgar's shoulder. "Ask him why he's here," she whispered. "I'm starting to get pruny."

"What brings you here, brother?" Ansgar asked.

"Adara sent me," Brand said. "Evie must come at once. The fabricated residential dwelling unit that Nicole presently calls her abode has succumbed to gravity."

It took Evie a minute to parse Brand-speak. "Oh, my goodness," she said, grasping his meaning at last, "you mean her trailer collapsed? Is she all right?"

"Yes," Brand said, "but she is inconsolable and asking for you. Will you come?"

"Sure." Evie cleared her throat. "But, first, we need to get dressed."

"Of course." Brand bowed. "I will return anon."

Blip! He was gone.

Froggy Bottom was a marshy, low-lying area north of town made up of dilapidated shotgun houses, sagging mobile homes, and abandoned fishing cabins. Nicole's place was located down a dirt drive behind a huddle of mildewed trailers. Sooner or later, everything in Froggy Bottom mildewed due to the proximity of the river, including the people.

The scene when they arrived was bedlam. The police were there and the volunteer fire department. Red and blue emergency lights flashed, illuminating the crowd that had gathered around the wreckage of the prefab home, like hyenas panting around a fallen wildebeest. Yellow police tape, stretched around the perimeter of the weedy lot, held the rubberneckers at bay. Inside the taped-off square, Evie saw officers and firemen moving around in the darkness, trying to assess the damage.

She glanced at her watch. It was 5:30. Not long until sunup. Good gracious, she'd pulled an all-nighter. And what a night! She'd been to her first Halloween ball, had her memory restored by a supernatural ruminant from another dimension, gone on a toot with a succubus, been in a bar fight, had wild gorilla sex in the great outdoors, and received a declaration of love *and* a marriage proposal from the man of her dreams. It was enough to make a girl dizzy.

She found Addy talking with Chief Davis. Addy broke off her conversation when she saw Evie coming up with Ansgar and Brand.

"You're here," Addy said, coming to meet them. Her brown eyes were wide and uncertain. "I was afraid you'd still be too mad at me to come."

"I am still mad at you," Evie said. And she was, but only a

little, although she wasn't ready to tell Addy that yet. "I'm here for Nicole."

"Evie, please." Addy's mouth trembled. "You're my best friend in the whole wide world. I love you. You know I never meant to hurt you. You were so . . . *broken*. I didn't know what to do."

Evie folded. She couldn't stay mad at Addy, not when her hardass BFF looked so contrite and vulnerable.

"You are such a jerk," Evie said, pulling Addy into a tight hug. "I don't know why I put up with you."

"Me, either," Addy said, hugging her back. "But I'm glad you do. And I'm glad you're here. Nicole is so upset. I tried to talk to her, but I think I made things worse. Maybe you can calm her down."

Evie released Addy and stepped back. For some reason, she was crying. It couldn't possibly have anything to do with the fact that she and Addy had made up. No way.

Evie wiped her wet cheeks. "Where is she?"

Addy pointed to a miserable figure across the yard. "Over there."

Nicole stood underneath a mercury light, clad in nothing but a shower curtain and crying as if her heart would break. A large assortment of drooling dogs sat in a semicircle around her. As Evie watched, a mutt with a German shepherd's head on a basset hound body slunk closer.

"Get on," Nicole shrieked, stamping a bare foot at the dog, her face streaked with tears. "I mean it!"

With a startled yelp, the dog retreated just out of leg reach and settled on its haunches. Tongue hanging out of its mouth, the dog gazed at Nicole with longing.

What was with all the dogs? Evie looked closer, but didn't see a Chihuahua. Her heart sank. Oh, dear. Something must have happened to Frodo. That's why Nicole was so upset.

Leaving Ansgar talking to Brand and the chief, she hurried over to the sobbing woman. "What's happened? Is it Frodo?"

"N-no, Frodo's fine." Nicole threw herself at Evie. "But I ain't. Oh, Miss Evie, it was so awful."

Evie wrapped her arms around Nicole to give her a hug, but it was like trying to hold on to a buttered eel. "Nicole, why are you so slippery and what is that *smell*?"

"Bacon grease." Nicole stepped back, her chin quivering. "D-Daniel said bacon was the perfect food, so I invited him to my place after the dance for a BLT."

Bacon grease—Nicole *reeked* of it. Granny Moses, she was a walking, talking bacon-flavored treat. No wonder she'd attracted every dog in the neighborhood. It was a miracle she hadn't been mauled to death.

"After we ate, Daniel and me talked." Nicole hiccupped and grabbed the shower curtain as it started to slide south under the twin influences of gravity and lard. "One thing led to another, and the next thing you know, I'd done rubbed myself down with bacon fat and broke out the old pole."

"Pole?" Evie repeated blankly. It was hard to concentrate. Nicole's plastic sarong had started a downward trek again, like a glacier inching over mountainous terrain, and Evie expected the whole thing to hit the ground at any moment.

"I used to be an exotic dancer at the Booby Trap in Pensacola," Nicole said, sniffling. "That's where I met my first husband, Travis the Louse. I gave up dancing, but I kept the stripper pole for old time's sake. I was doing a cradle spin, when the whole dang trailer busted, because . . ." Her round face crumpled and she began to wail. "Because I'm so fat!"

Evie patted Nicole's greasy shoulder. "Don't say that. This is not your fault. That trailer should have been condemned years ago. Cousin Ick ought to be ashamed, letting family live in a dump like that."

"He's not blood kin. He's Travis's cousin. I shoulda known better than to trust a Eubanks." Nicole gave Evie a watery smile. "Thanks for coming, Miss Evie. I've been beside myself."

"Please, call me Evie. 'Miss Evie' makes me feel like an old maid schoolteacher."

Nicole gave a halfhearted chuckle. "Right, that's why you got such a fine-looking man sniffing around you, on account of you's an old maid." Her mouth trembled and she burst into tears again. "Dan ain't gonna have nothing to do with me again, not after this. Not if I wear a bacon *dress*. I gotta get out of here."

"Nicole, wait. I wouldn't make any sudden moves if I were—"

Too late. Nicole took off at a run, clutching the shower curtain around her. The pack of dogs howled and streaked after her. Nicole shrieked and darted around a patrol car, the dogs in hot pursuit.

Bacon, bacon, bacon— Evie could almost hear the dogs panting the battle cry.

"For a chunky gal, she sure can move," a man wearing overalls and no shirt observed.

Evie glared at him. After a lifetime of fat jokes, she *hated* that kind of remark. Who was he to talk, anyway? He had back boobs and a belly like a pregnant hippo.

"Save me, Jesus," Nicole yelped. "Save me!"

A beagle snarled and latched on to the back of the shower curtain. Nicole picked up the pace, trailing the beagle behind her like a banner as she circled the police car for a second time.

"Nicole, get on top of the car," Evie shouted as the snarling dogs closed the gap. "They can't get you there."

"I can't!" Nicole cried. "I'm too slicky!"

"Oh, my goodness," Evie said. "Help! Somebody help!"

Blip! Ansgar was there lifting Nicole out of harm's way. He rumbled deep in his chest, and the dogs scattered and slunk away.

He set Nicole down in a plastic lawn chair. Her chest heaved and her eyelids fluttered.

"There," he said. "Do not be affrighted. The hounds will trouble you no more. You are safe now."

"Holy Moses." Nicole was gasping for breath. "Thought I was a goner. Thought them dawgs was gonna eat me for sure. And then you come out of nowhere, like the Flash or something. It was amazing."

"Not at all," Ansgar said.

"Oh, no." Nicole went pale. "I think I see Daniel coming

this way." She gave Ansgar a pleading look. "Don't tell him about the dogs. Please. He already thinks I broke the trailer."

"What dogs?" Ansgar said. "I do not see any dogs."

Nicole's eyes filled with tears. "Bless you, Mr. Dalvahni."

Dan strode up with Frodo under one arm. "You all right, Nikki?" he asked.

"Course." Nicole adjusted her shower curtain, her color high. "Why wouldn't I be?"

" 'Cause somebody sabotaged your trailer, that's why," Dan said. "I've been talking to the firemen. Whoever did this crawled under your trailer and weakened every last one of the supports. That's why it collapsed. And the culprit left this." He brandished an evidence bag at Nicole. "It's a toy animal, a stuffed Chihuahua. Frodo found it, isn't that right, boy?" Dan patted the dog's mini Afro. "He's got a heck of a snoot on him. He could be a SAR dog. Went crazy when he found it, snarling and snapping to beat the band. There's a note attached. It says 'die demon dog' on it."

Nicole shrieked and slumped back in the chair. "It's the dog stalker. Lord have mercy Jesus, he's done tracked us to Hannah. We ain't never gonna be safe again."

"We're going to catch this guy, Nikki," Dan said. His jaw was set and he looked determined. "That's our job." He set the Chihuahua in her lap. "Now, if you'll excuse me, I need to show this evidence to the chief. We've had a rash of dog attacks in the past few days, and this could be related." He started to walk off and turned around. "Here," he said. Removing his uniform jacket, he draped it around Nicole's bare shoulders. "It's kind of chilly out. Should've offered it to you sooner, but I get tunnel vision when I'm working."

He winked at Nicole and walked off.

Nicole watched him depart with a stunned expression. "Did you see that? He winked at me and then he give me his jacket. And me smelling like bacon." A tear dripped down her cheek. "That's the most r-romantical thing anyone's ever done for me."

"You like him, don't you?" Evie asked.

"He's a prince," Nicole said with a blissful sigh. She shifted uncomfortably in the chair. "When you reckon the police gonna let me back in my place? This shower curtain is starting to chafe."

A shout drew their attention to the trailer. Several firemen leaped back as the trailer roof fell in and the walls buckled.

"I'm afraid you won't be getting anything much out of that trailer," Evie said, shaking her head. "It's toast."

Nicole started to cry again. "Everything me and Frodo had was in there. What am I going to do? I can't go around in no shower curtain for the rest of my life."

"I'll tell you what you're going to do," Evie said. "You're coming home with me. I've got a guest bedroom that's empty. We'll find you some clothes and get you fixed up right."

"You're my guardian angel," Nicole declared. "I knowed it the first time I laid eyes on you." She swiped her wet cheeks with the back of her hand. "But it wouldn't be right, me bumming off you and me with no job."

"What? You mean to say Addy *fired* you? I can't believe it."

"No, she ain't fired me yet, but she will." Nicole looked down at the dog in her lap. "She ain't gonna want no ex-stripper working in her nice shop, 'specially no ex-stripper with a crazy dog stalker after her."

"Miss Corwin is not going to fire you," Evie said firmly. "Meredith Peterson's funeral is tomorrow, remember? We've got a ton of flowers to deliver."

Nicole perked up. "That's right, I forgot about that." Her brows drew together. "I sure hope that bitchy haint don't show up. She makes my butt wanna suck a lemon and spit the seeds."

"An interesting visual," Ansgar said. " 'Tis to be hoped the expression is figurative and not literal."

"Huh?" Nicole said.

"Don't pay any attention to him," Evie said. "He has an odd sense of humor. As for Meredith, I can't imagine her missing her big day." She helped Nicole struggle out of the plastic chair. "Let's go home. I'm tired and hungry."

Ansgar wrapped his arms around Evie. "I am not surprised," he said. He nuzzled the back of her neck, sending shivers of delight up and down her spine. "You have not eaten since yesterday at midday. When we get to your abode, I will cook omelets, if you like."

"I like very much," Evie said. She leaned against him with a happy sigh. "But hold the bacon, please."

Chapter Thirty-seven

Two hours later, sleepless but refreshed by a shower and a hot breakfast, Evie rumbled down Main Street in Ansgar's spiffy new truck. Driving the Raptor was fun and exciting. Heads turned as the brawny Ford cruised down the street. She could almost hear the buzz of speculation following in their wake. Evie loved her beat-up old Taurus. It was familiar and dependable and totally unexciting, like her former self. But handling the sleek, powerful Raptor was a thrill.

Kind of like handling Ansgar, she thought with a mental giggle, sneaking a peek at the hunk sitting in the passenger seat. Yep, big and muscular and sexy as hell, like his truck, with an engine built for power and endurance.

She turned down a narrow lane and pulled into the empty lot behind Flowers by Adara. It was 7:30 a.m. and they were the first ones to arrive; the shop didn't open for another half hour.

Evie eased the truck into a parking space, cut off the motor, and unfastened her seat belt. "Thanks for letting me drive," she said. "It was a rush."

She glanced over at Ansgar to find him studying her legs with wolfish hunger. The knee-length skirt she wore had ridden up during the drive from her house, exposing her bare thighs. A flush of lust swept through her, leaving her feeling hot and achy. He made her feel womanly and desirable. She wanted him with an intensity that was scary. Right here, right now, in front of God and his sister and anybody else that happened along. This wouldn't do. She needed to get a firm grip on her hoochitude. She would *not* have sex with Ansgar in the parking lot of the flower shop. No matter how much her inner wild woman complained.

She reached down to tug the skirt back into place. *Pfft!* Ansgar was out of his seat belt and across the seat, his hand covering hers.

"I have missed you," he said, his voice a low, sexy throb.

Her heartbeat ratcheted up a notch as his strong fingers caressed the sensitive flesh of her thigh, and her inner slut purred in anticipation.

"Missed me?" She gasped as his hand slid up her skirt and higher. "What do you mean? I haven't gone anywhere."

"No," he said, "but I have missed this."

He kissed her, and she forgot everything but the hot delight of being in his arms and having his hands on her. She'd missed him, too. It seemed like hours since he'd touched her. She wanted to climb him like a trellis. The thought had barely registered when she was in his lap, her skirt hiked around her waist, kissing him for all she was worth.

So much for her self-control. *Ding!* Round one to the hussy.

Ansgar groaned her name as she reached between them and undid the top button of his jeans. The hard length of his erection pushed against the palm of her hand. A tug on his zipper and he'd be inside her. It was outrageous and reckless, scandalous and wonderful, and she couldn't wait.

A loud rap on the truck window interrupted them.

"Hey, you kids, get off my lawn," Addy said. "This is a no hump zone."

Evie scrambled off Ansgar's lap. "Gracious, Addy, you startled me." Avoiding her friend's gaze, Evie got out of the truck and straightened her twisted skirt. "You're early."

"Huh." Addy eyed Ansgar with hostility as he exited the Ford with pantherish grace. "The way you two were going at it, I'd say I was just in time. Blondy was just about to insert tab 'A' into slot 'B.' "

"Addy, the things you say," Evie said, her cheeks flaming.

Addy tilted her head and surveyed the Raptor. "Nice truck. Whose is it?"

"Mine," Ansgar said. "Did Brand not tell you?"

"No, he did not." Addy thumped him on the chest with her finger. "All right, bub, that's my best peep you had your hands all over. What are your intentions? Enquiring minds want to know."

Ansgar shut the truck door and leaned against it. A smile played at the corners of his fine mouth. "You mean to say Brand did not tell you that, either? How remiss of him."

Evie saw Addy's jaw tighten; Ansgar really knew how to push her buttons. "What are you talking about?"

"Evangeline and I have plighted our troth."

"What?" Addy screeched. She grabbed Evie, and they danced around the truck, laughing and crying and squealing at the top of their lungs.

"I'm so happy for you," Addy said once they'd quit doing the ring-around-the-rosy in the parking lot. Ansgar still leaned against the truck, arms folded across his broad chest. He was trying to act cool and unaffected by their excitement, but a flush rode his high cheekbones. Addy gave him a look of re-crimination over her shoulder as she punched in the security code on the back door. "If *somebody* had come to his senses earlier, we could have had a double wedding," she said. "I love Muddy, but you *are* my best friend, Evie, and my sister from another mother. It would have been so perfect if the four of us could have gotten married together."

"I know." Evie followed Addy into the back of the store with Ansgar at her heels. "But you'll come to our wedding, won't you?"

"Well, duh." Addy strode between the neatly lined shelves of floral products in the storage room. "Wild horses couldn't keep me away."

Flinging open the store room door, Addy flipped on the lights in the main part of the shop and froze.

"Holy shit," she said.

"What is it?" Evie stepped into the business area of the flower shop, Ansgar hovering protectively at her side, and gasped in astonishment.

The shop had been transformed into a makeshift art gallery. Dozens of paintings covered the walls. More paintings were displayed in the shop window and propped on tables and against the foot of the service counter. Some of the canvases were framed—most were not. There were several magnificent oils of the Devil River; a pen and ink drawing of the Trammell Bridge; a sketch of Jebidiah Hannah, Spanish American war hero and founder of their small town; and a fabulous painting of a white buck with silver antlers, graceful head bent as it drank from a forest pool.

The vast majority of the paintings, though, were nudes—lush, sensual, stirring—and all of them were portraits of Lenora.

"It's official," Addy said. "My big brother has lost his ever-loving mind. I've been begging him for months to let me display some of his work—*some* of his work, not all of it. I suggested we start with something simple. You know, a land-scape or two, to get people used to the idea that Shep Corwin, local undertaker, paints. And what does he do? He sneaks in here and fills my shop with nekked pictures of his girlfriend. He didn't come out of the closet. He busted down the damn door."

"Shep did these?" Evie examined one of the paintings. It was boldly signed *S. Corwin.* "You said he could paint, but I had no idea he was this good."

"Oh, my God, he's signed them," Addy said, noticing the signature on one of the oils. "He's gone from being shy and *I'm not sure I want to share this part of me with people* to putting it all out there. Mama's going to have a cow. She has no idea."

"She knows Shep paints," Evie said. "I've heard you two talking about it."

"Oh, yeah, but she doesn't take it seriously. She doesn't take anything seriously that doesn't fit into her version of the uni-verse. And this definitely doesn't fit, so she ignores it." Addy pointed to one of the nudes. "What do you think she's going to do when she sees *Homage to Lenora's Boobs?*" She jabbed her finger at a picture of a voluptuous, ebon-haired Athena rising from the river. "Or *Succubus on a Half Shell?*" Turning, she gave a little shriek. "And can you *imagine* what she's going to say about *this?*" She picked up a canvas and brandished it at them. It was a portrait of the thrall lying naked on a couch. "Shep Corwin has put a picture in my shop of Lenora petting her petunia! If that ain't a sign he's lost his marbles, what is it?"

Evie thought about it. "I think this is Shep's way of declaring himself and his love for Lenora, sort of an early wedding present."

"He could have given me a blender, for Pete's sake."

"Not *your* wedding present, Addy," Evie said. "Lenora's . . . and his, too, if you think about it. Shep has asked her to marry him."

"What?"

Evie winced as the plate glass window rattled and the clock on the wall chinged and chimed. Super Addy had a voice that shattered glass when she got excited.

"Oh, yeah," Evie said. "I forgot to tell you about that."

"When? Where? And how come I'm just now finding out about this?"

"Lenora and I hung out together last night."

Addy's expression soured. "I heard."

"We went drinking, only I couldn't get drunk and we wound up at Beck's Bar and—"

"Hold the phone. You went *where?*"

"Beck's Bar," Evie repeated patiently.

"Damn. I've heard about that place. What was it like?"

"Seemed like a regular bar to me, except for the demonoids. I think the scary rep is to keep normals away."

"Whoa, it's a demonoid bar?"

"Yeah, the owner's name is Beck, and she sucks demons out of people with one of those little metal thingies on the end of a liquor bottle and she keeps them in a glass jar."

"Shut your mouth," Addy exclaimed. "And you went there without me? Girlfriend, we are in a *fight*."

Evie held up her hand. "True story. Anyhoo, Lenora was dancing on the bar and I had this great chocolate martini and got a little tiddly—*finally*. Oh, and Beck keeps these chocolate Bugles on the bar that are the bomb." Evie smiled in ecstasy at the memory. "They are so good, Addy, but *do not buy them*. They will change your life. They should come with a warning on the package that says DANGER: DO NOT EAT. Those Bugles are *world* shifting."

"I get the picture," Addy said. "You really liked the Bugles."

Evie opened her eyes wide. "Like? They will expand your universe and your thighs." She shook her head. "Anyway, while we were there, this demon chick comes in with these two scary guys, and there was a big fight. Shep shows up swinging a golf club and puts a beat down on some of the demons and then he asked Lenora to marry him, and she said yes."

Addy dropped the painting to the floor and staggered over to a stool. "Holy mother of criminy Christmas. That inter-dimensional super hussy is going to be my sister-in-law?"

"She loves him," Evie said, "and Shep loves her. You should be happy for them."

"But what happens when he gets old and she leaves him?" Addy shook her head. "What kind of a future do they have?"

"I do not believe Shep's age will be an issue," Ansgar said.

Addy lifted her head to glare at him. "Oh, yeah? How do you figure that, Blondy, when she's immortal and he's not?"

Ansgar raised his brows. "Have you not noticed the changes in your brother?"

Addy's eyes widened. "Oh, my God, you're right. I thought it was the hair, but it's more than that, isn't he? He is different." She frowned. "But how?"

"I cannot say for certain, but I believe it is related to Shep having sexual congress with the thrall." Ansgar cleared his throat. "Repeatedly."

Evie chuckled. "I guess you could say she rubbed off on him."

Addy wrinkled her nose. "Ew, do you mind? This is my big brother we're talking about here."

"Lenora has feelings for Shep," Ansgar said. "Somehow, she has changed him."

"And Shep has changed her," Evie added, growing serious. "She's crazy about him, Adds. Really."

The front door rattled, and they looked up to find Nicole peering through the glass at them. Frodo peeked over her shoulder from a velour carrying pouch, his eyes glowing like coals amid the wild mass of curls on his head. With his pointy nose and the crazy hair, he was a canine King Charles II of England. Standing behind Nicole and Frodo were Muddy and Mr. C.

"I'll get it," Evie said, hurrying to let them in.

"I would have come through the back, but I forgot the code. Am I late?" Nicole said as she entered the shop. From the pouch on her back, Frodo chortled at them in greeting like a frizzy-haired miniature T. rex.

Nicole wore one of Evie's old dresses. The garment hit her at the ankles—Nicole was a good four inches shorter than Evie—and was too tight across the bosom. "It took me two showers and some of Evie's special kitchen soap to cut through the bacon grease. I like to never got the shower clean. It was slicker than a rat's ass in a Crisco factory." She stopped in her tracks, looking around at the paintings in awe. "Man, oh man," she said. "If this ain't something like."

"Quite magnificent," Mr. Collier agreed. "Who's the artist?"

Addy straightened on the stool. "Shep," she said in a tone that dared them to criticize her brother.

Mr. Collier gave a low whistle. "You don't say? He has real talent."

Muddy had put on her glasses to better inspect one of the nudes. "Does your mother know your brother paints dirty pictures?"

"No, ma'am," Addy said.

"Oh, goody," Muddy said. "I want to be here when she finds out. This is going to be fun."

"Oh, yeah," Addy mumbled. "In the same way jabbing a piece of glass in your eye or setting yourself on fire is fun."

Nicole's chin quivered. "They're beautiful. Every last one of 'em. Makes me want to burn my stuff and start over."

"You're an artist?" Mr. Collier asked.

Nicole turned red. "Nah, I ain't no artist. I fool around a bit, that's all. I ain't never had lessons or nothing like that. We was always too poor."

"I'd love to see some of your work," Mr. Collier persisted. "Have you got anything with you?"

Nicole hung her head and scuffed her shoe on the floor. "Most of it was in the trailer, but I got a few things in my truck. Nothing as fine as these here paintings, mind you. I make my stuff out of whatever I find laying around."

"You're an eco-artist," Mr. Collier exclaimed. "I am, too! I create sculpture out of copper wire, coat hangers, and scrap metal. What do you use?"

"Pop tops and bottle caps, old bottles and rubber tires, tin cans." Nicole shrugged. "But mostly I use cigarette butts."

"Fascinating. Now I *must* see something of yours." Mr. Collier looked at Addy. "That is, if you don't mind, my dear. I know y'all have work to do."

Nicole shot Addy a nervous look. "That's okay. Some other time, maybe."

"Oh, for crying in the beer." Addy waved her hand at the door. "Go."

"You sure?" Nicole said.

"*Go.*"

Nicole scooted outside, returning in record time carrying a large rectangular package wrapped in butcher paper. She tore off the paper, revealing the canvas underneath.

Evie caught her breath, and not because of the faint smell of tobacco and ashes that rose from the picture. "Why, Nicole, it's beautiful."

Frodo yowled in agreement.

It was a primitive painting of an old woman sitting in a rocking chair on the porch of a weathered farmhouse. Nicole had added texture to the picture using the paper and tobacco from the cigarettes, giving a three-dimensional effect. The woman on the porch had her head bent, and she was shelling peas into a bowl. The portrait was so vivid, so loving, that Evie could almost feel the breeze that pressed the woman's worn cotton shift against her legs and lifted the stray pieces of gray hair that had escaped her bun.

"I know that house." Mr. Collier drew closer, an odd expression on his face. "Know the woman, too. That's Ima Faye Smelley. She was married to my mother's cousin, Luke Smelley, over McCullough way."

"Luke Smelley was my pop pop," Nicole said, her voice rising with excitement.

Mr. Collier beamed at her. "How 'bout that? We're kin."

Nicole's mouth sagged in surprise. "No way."

"My mother and your great-granddaddy were first cousins," Mr. Collier said, "which means—if I'm figuring this right, and don't hold me to it—you and I are third cousins once removed."

"Oh." Nicole looked somewhat deflated. Frodo seemed to sense her disappointment and stuck his snoot against her neck. That or he was getting ready to eat her. "That ain't so much then."

"Nonsense." Mr. Collier's tone was brisk. "Once a Smelley, always a Smelley, that's what my mama used to say."

Muddy clapped her hands. "Amasa, darling, I have the most wonderful idea. You've been talking for ages about opening an art gallery in the old five and dime building. Well, this is the cosmos telling you to do it! It will be the perfect place to show your work, and Shep and Nicole's, too."

"Thank you, Jesus," Addy said. "I love my brother, but I'd like my shop back."

"By golly, Edmuntina, you're right," Mr. Collier said, his eyes alight.

Muddy's mouth turned up in a cat-got-the-canary smile. "And, as an added bonus, it will pearl Bitsy's onions to have Shep's dirty pictures on public display."

"Muddy, you are positively wicked," Addy said.

"Speak of the devil," Evie said as Bitsy bustled through the front door, looking the picture of funereal perfection in a little black dress and matching bolero jacket.

"Dressed for the Peterson shindig already, Mama?" Addy asked. "It's a little early to be wearing your planting duds, isn't it? The service isn't until two o'clock."

"Don't be vulgar, Adara Jean. It is a funeral, not a shindig, and I do not wear 'planting duds.' " Bitsy's hands flew in the air like birds, a sure sign she was upset. "I am beside myself. Shep called me a few minutes ago. Said he and Lenora are getting married. *Married,* can you believe it? And all this time, I thought they were having a fling."

"The way I see it, that's a good thing, Hibiscus," Muddy said. "Means you didn't raise the boy to be a dick whittler."

"She's nothing like Marilee," Bitsy continued, appearing not to notice her aunt's crudity. Goodness, she *was* upset. "Different as chalk and cheese. What kind of a wife will she be for my boy? Where's she from and who are her people? We don't know anything about her. And what kind of mother will she be to my grandchildren? I mean, goodness, did you see her last night at the club in that string dress?" Bitsy shuddered. "Scandalous."

Addy set down the length of ribbon she was working on for a bouquet. "Shep's not a boy, Mama. He's a man. And he's a fine father. You know he would never do anything to hurt Lily and William. He loves Lenora, and she makes him happy. That's good enough for me."

"But how do you know he loves her, Adara Jean?" Bitsy wrung her hands. "How can you be sure this isn't about the s-e-x?"

"Open your eyes, Mama, and look around. This is Shep Corwin saying *I love Lenora* to the whole world, and saying it loud and clear."

Bitsy turned her head, her eyes widening when she saw the paintings. "Merciful heavens," she said.

"Told you it would pearl her onions," Muddy said as Bitsy went pale with shock.

"There she goes," Evie cried. "Quick, Ansgar."

Blip! Ansgar crossed the room, catching Bitsy as she fell.

Chapter Thirty-eight

Ansgar surveyed the Peterson home from the opposite side of the shady street. The dwelling was impressive, three stories of mellow brick with rows of narrow, gleaming windows. Ansgar breathed deeply. It was good to get away from the flower shop and the unceasing activity and noise there. He'd been itching to be at the hunt all morning, but caution and concern for Evangeline had made him wait for Brand to arrive.

"Where have you been?" he'd demanded earlier that morning when Brand had finally made an appearance at the shop. Like Ansgar, Brand was dressed in the modern raiment that humans called jeans and a T-shirt. "I have been waiting for you."

Brand's dark brows had risen at Ansgar's brusque tone. "I had a meeting with Conall."

Evangeline, busy behind the counter with a customer, gave them a curious look. Reining in his temper, Ansgar had drawn Brand aside.

"And?" he'd said more quietly.

"He does not want Blake Peterson killed, not until we see how things unfold. He suspects the demonoids may be in league with the djegrali, and he would very much like to know their plans. Blake Peterson has money, position, and power. As such, he is a natural leader among the demonoids and may be in bed with the demons. Conall thinks he bears watching."

Ansgar swore. "Evangeline is my only concern. I will do what I must to protect her, Conall and the consequences be damned."

"I understand, brother. Were I in your place, I would feel the same." Brand put his hand on Ansgar's shoulder. "Console yourself with the knowledge that Evie is in little danger with a Dalvahni warrior at her side."

"Aye, that is true enough. The Dalvahni have ever been a match for the cursed djegrali." Ansgar frowned. "What do you make of Conall's sudden interest in Hannah?"

"From the first, he has suspected there is more at work here than ordinary demon mischief. Of late, though, his interest seems to have taken a more . . . personal turn."

"There is something I must do," Ansgar had said. "Will you stay with Evangeline until I return? I dare not leave her alone for fear of the djegrali."

"Certainly, but where are you going?"

"To pay Blake Peterson a visit."

"Curb your spleen, brother. I know you are anxious to clear Evie's name, but remember Conall's orders."

"Conall said not to kill the man," Ansgar had said with a shrug. "He did not say I could not question him."

Satisfied that Evangeline would be safe in Brand's care, Ansgar had left the shop and traveled here, to the Peterson home. He studied the property more closely. The gardens were lush and extensive. The entranceway at the front of the house was decorated with hay bales and pumpkins. A wreath of colorful leaves, berries, and pinecones hung from the tall front door. Workmen were busy on the grounds, lining flowerbeds with straw and trimming and carrying away dead limbs. Ansgar became invisible and walked around the side of the house. A pair of arched doors opened onto an inviting outdoor space with tables and chairs and an outdoor oven. The side entrance was barred, but that presented no hindrance to a Dal. Ansgar put his hand on the metal handle and heard the lock snick. He eased the door open and stepped inside.

He was in a music room of some sort. A sweet, almost suffocating odor permeated the space. A wooden instrument with three legs, a black and white keyboard, and a horizontal harp-shaped frame stood open. As Ansgar paused to get his bearings, the ghost of a slim, blond-haired man materialized on the bench in front of the instrument and began to play a lively tune.

"Don't play that boogie woogie, Junior," a woman said. "Play something restful."

Ansgar turned his head. Clarice Peterson sat in a winged-back chair on the far side of the room, her head bent over the needlework in her lap. It was her cloying perfume he smelled, he realized. He scrutinized the frail, older woman. She seemed detached and removed, untouchable. It was impossible to tell what swam beneath the surface of that calm water.

"He's having a bad day," she said, "and your music is the only thing that soothes him."

The ghost complied, and the music became softer. An unusual household, Ansgar thought, shaking his head. The ghost looked up at him and smiled as though reading his thoughts, his pale eyes full of gentle humor.

By the sword, he can see me, Ansgar realized with a sense of unease. This was a new experience; never before had a shade been able to penetrate his cloak of invisibility. Once again, things were different in Hannah. But why so? Conall was right. There was more to Hannah than demon mischief, though there was that, too, and aplenty.

The ghostly musician halted, and Ansgar heard the distant sound of masculine voices in another part of the house.

"Don't stop, Junior," Clarice said. "You know how he loves your music."

He? Of whom did she speak? Another shade perhaps? Ansgar shrugged away the thought. It did not matter.

The ghost gave Ansgar another beatific smile and tilted his head in the direction of an interior door before launching into another melody. Leaving the odd pair to their music, Ansgar strode quietly out. To his frustration, he found Blake Peterson already in conference with Sheriff Whitsun in a room at the end of a hall. The chamber was large with a high ceiling and gleaming paneled walls of dark wood. Lighted glass cabinets held an impressive collection of knives, and more knives were displayed on brackets on the walls. Blake Peterson sat behind a marble-topped writing desk listening to Sheriff Whitsun.

"—curious about that missing knife in your collection," the sheriff was saying. He walked over to a lighted case full of knives and pointed to an empty bracket. "There's an impression in the felt backing that's the same size and shape as the handle on the murder weapon."

"And how could you possibly know that, Sheriff?" Blake Peterson asked in a bored voice.

"I told you last night that I took a photograph of the knife before I sent it to forensics." Whitsun pulled a piece of paper from his pocket, unfolded it, and held it to the glass. It was a picture of a knife. "See? The dent in the felt matches the ridges and the shape of the horn handle." He put his finger on the glass. "And right there is the ring the brass quillion made on the cloth. How do you explain that?"

"It's very simple," Peterson said. He leaned back in his chair and offered the sheriff a cool smile. "I'm a rich man. I have several knives with horn handles in my collection. The knife missing from that case is at the appraiser's."

"I'll need the name of that appraiser, sir."

Peterson slammed his hand on the desk. "Have you no sense of decency, man? We've had a death in the family, and we are all very upset. Why are you in my home harassing me on the day we're burying my grandson's wife? We already know who killed Meredith, and it wasn't me."

"I don't think Evie Douglass killed Ms. Peterson," Whitsun said.

"I don't give a damn what you think, Sheriff." Peterson rose. "What matters is what the grand jury thinks. Now, if you'll excuse me, I have a funeral to attend."

He strode out of the room without another word.

"Learn anything, Mr. Dalvahni?" the sheriff said.

Whitsun and his infernally sharp senses were becoming a nuisance.

Irritated, Ansgar removed his shield. "Nothing I did not already know. You think Peterson killed Meredith."

"Yes, I do, and then he planted the knife in Ms. Douglass's car to frame her for the murder," Whitsun said. "But the collector in him couldn't bear to let the knife go, so he broke into the evidence lab in Mobile and stole it back without setting off the alarms, something only a demonoid could do. Or a demon hunter." He stuck the piece of paper back in his pocket. "One thing bothers me, though, and that's the motive. I don't know *why* Blake Peterson killed Meredith." He shrugged. "I'm still working on that one."

"What if you found the missing knife, Sheriff?"

"Which one, the murder weapon or the knife that's missing from Peterson's collection?"

"What if they turn out to be one and the same?" Ansgar said.

"Well, then, I reckon we'd have us a new suspect. You know anything about the whereabouts of this knife?"

"No, but I know someone who may be able to find it."

"Really, who's that?"

"His name is Collier, and he uses a tracking device similar to a divining rod called a contrabulator."

Whitsun rubbed his jaw. "You don't say? I'd like to meet this fellow."

Ansgar smiled. "That can be arranged."

By the time Addy closed shop at one thirty that afternoon, Evie was exhausted. The activity at the flower shop had been nonstop, and her nerves were worked by the stress of the last-minute orders and the snide, sometimes downright ugly remarks made by customers. Evie didn't blame folks. She was a suspected murderess—an already convicted murderess in many people's minds—out on bail. But that didn't make dealing with the venom any easier.

She bit her tongue and didn't say anything to them or Addy. Addy would have flown off the handle and clean into next week if she'd heard some of the hateful things people had said to her that morning. Between filling orders and fielding the endless, excited questions about Shep's scandalous artwork,

Addy had her hands full. The last thing Evie wanted to do was add to her problems.

She stayed out of the way at the funeral home, watching the memorial service on a monitor in Bitsy's office, then helped Nicole and Addy haul the last of the flowers out to the van for transport to the gravesite. Normally, Addy's job ended when she delivered the flowers to Corwin's, but the Peterson funeral was such a big event that she'd agreed to give Shep and Bitsy a hand. And a good thing, too— Shep's engagement and his impromptu artistic debut had pretty much fried Bitsy to a crispy, crackly crunch. She walked around with a stiff smile on her face and a blank look in her eyes.

They pulled into River Oaks Cemetery and began to unload. People had gone all out to show their support of one of Hannah's leading families, and the Peterson plot overflowed with flowers.

"There." Nicole set down a funeral spray of red and white carnations decorated with a crimson sash hand-printed with the words SAY HELLO TO THE BEAR FOR US. Reaching over her shoulder, she patted the Chihuahua riding on her back in the pet pouch. "That's the last one. Ain't that right, Frodo?"

The Chihuahua grumbled in response.

"Just in time," Addy said. "Here they come."

The Petersons' cemetery lot stood at the crest of a gentle hill guarded by three tall oaks. Evie looked down the slope. The two police cars at the head of the funeral procession made a sharp turn, blocking the road, their blue lights flashing. In the distance, a groundskeeper was tooling around on his four-wheeler near the front gate of the cemetery. He halted, idling his motor as the hearse turned onto the white gravel drive that wound through the cemetery. A line of cars with their headlights on crept down the highway and into the cemetery behind the hearse, like a long, lighted tail. Two more police cars brought up the rear. Hannah's finest were out in force today.

"I'll move the van and wait for y'all over yonder," Evie said, pointing to one of the trees. The temperature was in the low seventies, but it still got hot in the van sitting in the sun.

"I will go with you," Brand said.

Brand had been on her like a duck on a June bug all morning since Ansgar had vamoosed without a word.

"You don't have to do that," Evie told Brand. "I'll be fine."

"I insist."

Evie sighed. "I thought you'd say that. Where did you say Ansgar went?"

"He had business to attend to. He asked me to protect you in his absence."

Sweet, but unnerving, like having a 250-pound pit bull glued to your butt cheeks.

She parked the Pepto-Bismol pink van under the tree and waited, wishing she could get closer. The whole town had turned out for Meredith's funeral, and it was the perfect opportunity to do a little spying on the mourners to try to figure out who killed Meredith. Evie's stomach clenched. Mr. Collier had stopped by the shop this morning to confirm that the preliminary hearing was, indeed, set for this Thursday—three days from now. Time was running out.

Ansgar appeared in the back of the van without warning. "All is well?" he asked Brand.

"Yes," Brand said, and vanished.

"My, people come and go so quickly here," Evie muttered.

"He cannot bear to be away from Addy for very long," Ansgar said. "I think he is addicted." In a blur of motion, Ansgar moved to the front seat and pulled her into his lap. "As am I."

She sighed and leaned against him. "You smell nice."

He nuzzled her neck. "You smell nice, too. What is this fragrance you are wearing?"

"Kudzu flower. It's a new scent I'm trying at the shop. You like?"

"Yes."

"Where did you go?" she asked. "I missed you."

"I have been speaking with Sheriff Whitsun. Come, we must attend the sepulchral service."

"I can't," Evie protested. "It would be too awkward. Not to mention tacky."

"It will not be awkward. No one will know we are there."

Ansgar wrapped his arms around her. Evie felt the now familiar pulling sensation, and they were out of the van and standing in the middle of the crowd gathered around the large canvas tent that had been erected over the gravesite.

"Be at ease," Ansgar said in her ear. "We are shielded from human eyes and ears."

The family members were seated in cloth-covered chairs under the navy blue tent. Trey, Clarice, and Blake sat on the front row along with Meredith's parents, Brenda and George Starr, and her brother, Joey, an insurance salesman. Father Ben, the Episcopal priest, was reading from the *Book of Common Prayer* to the accompanying drone of the four-wheeler. Rude; somebody ought to tell the guy to park that thing during a funeral.

Mayor Tunstall stood at the priest's elbow, his Bible at the ready and Priscilla the possum on her jeweled leash. Mayor Tunstall always prayed over dead folks. He liked to say that praying his constituents into the hereafter was his sacred duty as mayor. Evie suspected he mumbled over the dead because he enjoyed the attention and because it got him votes. Who wouldn't vote for the man who read the Good Book over Aunt Bertha Mae and Cud'n Floyd? Why, he was practically family.

Tunstall kept shooting the priest anxious little looks, like the *Book of Common Prayer* made him nervous or something, which it probably did. Mayor Tunstall was a Hard Shell Baptist.

Shep and Bitsy stood at a respectful distance, looking calm and professional. Or at least Shep looked calm. Bitsy looked sucker punched. Muddy and Mr. C were somewhere in the crowd, too. Addy, Brand, and Nicole were at the edge of the tent just outside the awning. Frodo kept sticking his head out of the pooch pouch to leer at Priscilla. Priscilla, for her part, was playing hard to get. Maybe she wasn't into guys with curly hair.

And standing by the gargantuan granite Peterson crypt were Meredith and Leonard Swink.

Meredith looked smashing in a vee-neck black sheath dress with a wide band of white trim at the neckline and hem, a chunky white bead necklace, black heels, and a big brimmed black hat trimmed with yards of black netting and a matching bow.

Meredith had her head down, as if overcome with emotion. She appeared to be listening to Swink, whose lips were moving. Then she lifted her head, and Evie saw the look in her eyes.

Uh-oh. Meredith was emotional, all right. She was *pissed*.

"I think Meredith can see us," Evie whispered to Ansgar. "She's staring right at us, and something has ticked her toodle." She looked around. A few people cast nervous glances toward the mausoleum. But, by and large, those assembled seemed unaware that Meredith was attending her own funeral. "Let's go talk to her."

"Surely you jest. Why you would seek out that fishwife apurpose, I cannot fathom."

"Maybe she remembers who killed her and the murderer is here pretending to be sorry she's dead. I know that would make me mad."

"I confess I had not thought of that," Ansgar admitted. "Although it seems to me not many mourn her loss."

He had a point. Meredith's parents seemed distraught, and Trish and Blair were shedding crocodile tears, but few other people were crying. Blair kept sidling closer to the tent and Trey. Any closer and she'd be in his lap. Trey didn't seem to notice. He looked more tired and shell shocked than sad. Probably had something to do with Mer Mer returning from the Great Beyond and attaching herself to him like a tick, poor guy.

Blip! Ansgar bopped them out of the crowd and over to the Peterson mausoleum.

"Hey, Meredith, how are you doing?" Evie asked.

"How do you think I'm doing, Fatback? I'm *dead*, and that trout-mouthed bitch Blair Woodson has her twat aimed at my husband."

"Now, now, Mrs. Peterson, remember our mantra. Composure, control, and contentment. *A placid ghost is a happy ghost,*" Swink said.

"Stick a cork in it, pudgy," Meredith told Swink. "I don't do placid."

Evie cleared her throat. "Ansgar and I were hoping you might have remembered who killed you. It's important. The preliminary hearing is in three days, and I could go to jail."

Meredith lifted her gaze heavenward, and she tapped her cheek with one finger. "Hmm, let's see. I'm thinking . . ." She dropped her hand and glared at Evie. "Nope, still don't give a shit about you or your pathetic little problems." She pointed to the canvas tent. "See that? That's me, being stuck in a hole in the ground like the family dog instead of inside the crypt with the rest of the Petersons." She pointed a red-tipped nail at the stainless steel box resting on the casket placer. "And they've put me in a powder blue casket. My nana used to beat me with a house shoe. Powder blue and fuzzy. I *hate* powder blue. Clarice knows it. She did it on purpose."

"Trey didn't stop her?" Evie asked.

"Trey's a guy," Meredith said. "He wouldn't know powder blue if it bit him on the ass. And you want to know what really boils my oil?"

"Uh, sure," Evie lied.

"That 'big' donation the Petersons announced night before last, the one to Hannah High in my name?"

"What is it, a new wing?"

"Hah, I wish." Meredith's red lips twisted in a sneer. "They're redoing the girls' restroom in my memory."

"Oh, that's nice," Evie said, not sure what else to say. "You spent a lot of time in there."

"The Meredith Starr Peterson Memorial *Toilet*? Are you kidding me?" Meredith said with a screech. A gust of wind blew out of nowhere that rattled the tent and lifted Harold Cohn's toupee. "This stinks out loud. This is not the way it was supposed to be."

"Now, now, Mrs. Peterson," Swink said. "You cannot reach

ghost actualization as long as you continue to indulge in these temper tantrums."

"Stick it where the sun don't shine, Swink." Meredith's head snapped up in irritation as the grinding of a motor grew louder. "What *is* that gardener doing? This is a funeral. Has he no couth at all?"

The four-wheeler topped the rise at full speed with a giant bumblebee at the wheel. It was the drunk from the dance; had to be the same guy. How many bumblebee costumes could there be in a town the size of Hannah? The cart swerved on two wheels, righted itself, and headed straight for the funeral tent.

People screamed and scattered. So did Priscilla the possum.

"Priscilla, come back," Mayor Tunstall said, waddling after Priscilla as the startled possum yanked the leash out of his hand and took off.

"I've got you now, demon dog," the man on the four-wheeler shouted. With a crazed cackle, he chased the terrified animal in circles around the gravesite. "All. Chihuahuas. Must. Die."

"It's him! It's him," Nicole cried, throwing up her hands in terror. "Run, Frodo. Run!"

But, instead of fleeing, Frodo leaped out of the pet pouch with a savage growl and gave chase. *Blip!* He caught up with the four-wheeler and sunk his teeth into the back left wheel. The tire blew, and the cart careened into the tent, scattering the chairs and knocking the casket off the rack. With a loud crash, the four-wheeler landed nose-down in the grave.

A mist rose out of the hole in the ground and solidified into the form of a man in a bumblebee suit.

"What happened?" The ghost looked around in obvious confusion. "Where am I?"

"You've dented my casket and ruined my funeral, you jack-ass," Meredith said. "Just for that, I hope you spend the rest of eternity in that ridiculous outfit."

"Mrs. Peterson, please," Swink said. "You've already said you hate the color of the casket. Let it go. We cannot concern ourselves with earthly matters. We are beyond that now."

The ghost in the bee suit looked down at the figure in the crumpled cart. "Why is my neck at that funny angle? What the hell's going on here?"

"I think you may have another client, Mr. Swink," Evie said.

"Right." Swink pulled out his pen and notepad. "Name?"

"I'm not certain because I've never met him, but I'm pretty sure that's Sylvester Snippet," Evie said. "The dog stalker."

Chapter Thirty-nine

Sylvester Snippet's sister arrived on Tuesday and took his body back to Baldwin County to be buried. Things in Hannah settled back down, and the business at the flower shop slowed. But time didn't slow for Evie. She was on a high-speed train headed for Thursday and the preliminary hearing in district court. Every time she thought about it her stomach did a swan dive, and she thought about it a lot. Ansgar was up to something. All of a sudden, he and Sheriff Whitsun were best buds. Whatever they'd cooked up, Mr. Collier was involved, too. He walked around with an excited gleam in his eyes, rubbing his hands together and mumbling to himself. But he wouldn't talk to Muddy about it.

"Police business," he would say, puffing out his chest when she questioned him. This made Muddy nuts, which tickled the stew out of Mr. C.

Something happened on Tuesday afternoon that got Evie's mind off of her troubles, if only temporarily. Jeannine Mitchell from the Kut 'N Kurl came into the flower shop with a business proposition.

Nodding and smiling at Nicole, Jeannine had said, "I met Nicole at the dance Saturday night and was admiring her hair."

"Yeah." Nicole grinned. "I told her all about that hair crack of yours and what it done for me and Frodo. She wouldn't believe it until I showed her my driver's license picture. I just got it renewed a few weeks back." She rustled around in her purse, found her wallet, and pulled out her ID. Mullet Woman smiled back at them from the photograph with her pink and yellow nightmare of a hairdo. Nicole fluffed her now luxurious brown locks. "Me and Frodo got a new lease on life and hair that's pimping fine thanks to *Fiona Fix-it*." Her hand stilled. "Say, that 'ud make a good slogan. But don't put it on your girl fuzz. You'll be so super fluffy down there you won't be able to get your britches on."

"I'll be sure and put that on a warning label," Evie had said with a straight face.

Jeannine had ordered a case of *Fiona Fix-it* with a promise to order more if her customers liked it. Evie had the promise of a new career on the horizon . . . if she didn't spend the next umpteen years in jail.

The preliminary hearing arrived before Evie was ready for it. Like you could ever get ready for a thing like that. As she waited in the courtroom Thursday morning for the proceedings to commence, she was DUI: Decidedly Under the Influence of Ansgar. He'd made sure she had something else to think about the night before, like him and his wonderful hands and his hot mouth and hard body.

Some of her euphoria wore off as she took her place at the defendant's table with Mr. Collier. She was wearing a conservative navy suit with a notch collar jacket and three-quarterlength sleeves and no jewelry, as suggested by Mr. Collier.

"Don't wear anything slinky or too flashy," he'd told her several days before. "No short skirts or cleavage and no open-toed shoes. You want to come across as approachable and sympathetic. Wear something nice, like you'd wear to church, but no polka dots. Judge Ward's ex-wife loved polka dots. She cleaned his clock, and he loses his grip now when he sees them."

Mr. Collier sat beside Evie humming to himself as they waited for their case to be called. He looked very handsome and professional in a dark pin-striped suit, starched white shirt, and silk tie. He seemed unconcerned by the upcoming proceedings. Evie wished she could say the same. She was starting to wonder if Mr. C was operating on all cylinders, not a good feeling to have about your lawyer.

She glanced around the courtroom. Nicole was minding the shop so Addy could be here. Bitsy and Muddy were here, too. Evie felt a surge of affection for them, her surrogate family. They had been with her through the horror of Savannah's disappearance and the deaths of her parents. They would stand by her in this, too, no matter what.

Brand was here, and Ansgar. They sat on one of the high-backed wooden benches on either side of Addy like a pair of matched archangel bookends, one dark and one light. Their otherworldly good looks and the aura of danger they exuded had created quite a stir. The door to the courtroom kept opening and closing as word of the newcomers spread and folks sneaked inside to take a look. The deadly menace the two warriors oozed kept people away, leaving Addy, her mom, and aunt in a vacuum of empty space.

The Petersons sat on the opposite side of the room with Meredith's family, along with a good number of folks from Hannah. Some were there to show their support of Hannah's premier family, some for the Starrs. Others had come out of idle curiosity. Trish and Blair were there making googly eyes at Trey, although they didn't sit beside him. And a good thing, too, because Meredith was next to him, looking cool and elegant in a knit boat neck dress in a pale citron color, with three-quarter-length sleeves. She'd topped off the ensemble with a wide taupe belt and matching heels.

Trey's grandmother, Clarice, wore a blue sheath dress and coordinating duster. Her hair was carefully arranged, her expression more so. She sat between her husband and Trey, as stiff and lifeless as a doll. If she realized Meredith was there, she was ignoring her. Blake Peterson radiated confidence and power, as usual, in a suit that probably cost more than most people's cars. He stared straight ahead at the judge's bench, looking neither to the right nor the left. Trey was wearing a navy blazer and khaki slacks. He looked pale and tired, and seemed as jumpy as a rabbit in a coyote den. From the way he was acting, you'd think *he* was the one on trial, not Evie.

Evie's pulse rate jumped as a door opened in the mahogany-paneled wall at the back of the courtroom and a man in a black robe entered.

"All rise," the bailiff said as the district court judge took his place behind the bench.

Evie got to her feet.

"Try to look scared or depressed," Mr. Collier whispered. "Judge Ward hates a happy defendant."

Scared was no problem, Evie thought as the courtroom was called to order.

"Sarah Evangeline Douglass." Hearing the bailiff call her name was like a dash of cold water. "Charge, first-degree murder of Meredith Starr Peterson."

The last vestiges of Evie's calm evaporated. Nothing like a little first-degree murder charge to get a girl's blood pumping first thing in the morning. *OhGodohGodohGod.*

The silence in the courtroom stretched as District Court Judge Silas Ward, a droopy-eyed man with a face like a beagle, shuffled some papers around behind the bench. He looked up. His dark eyes were flat behind his bifocals.

Shark eyes, Evie thought with a shiver.

"I see the defendant has filed a waiver of arraignment and plea of not guilty," the judge said. "We will proceed, then. Call you first witness, Mr. Dean."

The ADA, a pleasant-faced man with glasses and a receding hairline, cleared his throat. "The State calls Mamie Louise Hall to the stand."

Dismay washed over Evie. Miss Mamie was the biggest gossip in three counties.

Miss Mamie was sworn in and took the stand, describing in vivid detail the scene in the flower shop a few days before Meredith's murder.

". . . and Meredith came in to the shop and she seemed really upset," Miss Mamie said, smiling at the ADA. "She was all red in the face, and she had this little fleck of spit right here." The old lady pointed to her bottom lip. "I remember thinking, *She's so mad, she's foaming at the mouth.* It reminded me of that rabid dog in *To Kill a Mockingbird*." She smiled to the ADA. "You ever read that book?"

"Yes, ma'am, in the ninth grade." Mr. Dean was looking a little glassy-eyed. "Do you know why Mrs. Peterson was upset?"

Miss Mamie scooted to the edge of the chair. "Meredith accused Evie of having an affair with Trey. Told her she'd better stay away from her husband, if she knew what was good for her."

Miss Mamie giggled.

"Why is that funny?" Mr. Dean asked.

"Because Evie Douglass is the office manager at Peterson Mills, and Trey is her boss." Miss Mamie's eyes shone. "They *work* together. Real close, if you know what I mean."

"And then a few days after this disagreement, Mrs. Peterson was found brutally murdered in Evie Douglass's office," the prosecutor said. "That will be all, Miss Hall."

Evie closed her eyes. He made it sound so sordid, so damning.

"Chin up, my dear," Mr. Collier said in a low voice. "We've just begun. Circumstantial evidence. Not to worry."

"Yes, but what about the knife?" she whispered. "That's not circumstantial."

Mr. Collier patted her on the hand. "Let's cross that bridge when we get to it, shall we?" He rose and approached the stand. "Do you have any personal knowledge that Trey Peterson and Evie Douglass were having an affair?"

"Well, Rose Austin told Maddy Gordon that—"

"*Personal* knowledge, Mamie Louise."

Miss Mamie sat back. "If you mean did I ever see them myself, well, no. But that doesn't mean it wasn't so." She folded her hands in her lap. "If there's one thing I've learned in eighty-two years, Amasa, it's that people canoodle. Take Dusty Smitherman and Ronald Ledbetter. Dusty's husband came home for lunch and caught them doing it under the front porch."

Miss Mamie was excused and Sheriff Whitsun was called to

the stand. His lean jaw was set, his eyes hard and unreadable. In a clipped, emotionless voice, he told the court about Evie's call to 911, the scene he and his men found at the mill, and the bloody knife that he found in her car.

"Has the knife you found in the defendant's car been positively identified as the murder weapon?" Mr. Dean asked.

"Not yet. We're still waiting on the results from forensics. We sent the knife to Mobile for testing."

"Thank you," the ADA said, and sat down.

"Does the Alabama Department of Forensic Sciences still have the knife, Sheriff Whitsun?" Mr. Collier asked, getting to his feet once again.

"No, the knife was stolen out of the evidence locker at the lab."

"So the knife is missing?"

"*Was* missing," Sheriff Whitsun said. "We recovered the knife late yesterday inside a locker in the men's room of the Hannah Country Club."

"Whose locker did you find the knife in, Sheriff?"

"Cole Peterson's locker. He's been dead for more than twenty years, or so I've been told. But, for some reason, his old locker was never reassigned. Sentiment, maybe, since he was one of the founders of the club. The manager used his master key to open the locker. The knife was inside an old golf bag."

"How can you be sure it's the same knife?" Mr. Collier asked.

"Aside from the fact that it's a handmade Scagel worth twenty thousand dollars, whoever stole it from the Department of Forensic Sciences didn't bother to remove the evidence tag."

"Were you surprised to find the knife in Cole Peterson's locker?"

"No," the sheriff said.

"Why not?"

"There aren't many folks around here can afford a twenty-thousand-dollar knife. Cole Peterson was a rich man. It's common knowledge he was a knife collector, and that he was partial to fancy knives, like that Scagel. When Cole died, his son Blake inherited his knife collection. I know this for a fact, because Blake Peterson told me as much, and I've been in his home and seen them myself."

Trey jumped to his feet. "I did it," he said in a loud voice.

Evie turned in her seat to stare at him in astonishment. So did everyone else in the room.

Blake Peterson yanked him by the arm. "Sit down, Trey."

Trey jerked free of his grandfather's grasp. His chest heaved and sweat ran down his face. "No. I did it."

Judge Ward gave Trey a mournful look over the edge of his bifocals. "You did what, Mr. Peterson?"

"I killed her. I killed Meredith."

The courtroom erupted as everyone began to talk at once.

"Shut up, Trey," Blake Peterson shouted over the ruckus. "Don't say another word until we talk to a lawyer. You're crazy with grief. You don't know what you're saying."

Judge Ward pounded his gavel. "Bailiff, clear the court-room."

The courtroom was cleared of spectators. Evie caught a whiff of cedar and bergamot; Ansgar had remained, although he'd made himself invisible. Meredith stayed, too, of course, there not being a ghost bailiff on hand.

The judge glared at Trey. "Mr. Peterson, I do not appreciate such antics in my courtroom. I recommend you listen to your grandfather and seek the advice of counsel."

"I don't want an attorney. And I want it on the record that I'm not crazy and I'm not drunk or on drugs. I know what I'm doing. I killed Meredith and planted the knife in Evie's car." He looked at Evie. "I'm sorry, Evie. I panicked. I love you. I never meant to hurt you. " Straightening his shoulders, he looked at the judge. "I stole the knife out of the evidence locker because it was one of my grandfather's favorites, and I knew he would miss it and start asking questions. And I was afraid the sheriff would trace it back to my grandfather's collection. I couldn't take it back to the house. That was the first place the police would look. So I hid it in Great Granddaddy Cole's locker at the club. I figured it would be safe there. I'll make a statement now and sign it."

Evie stared at him in confusion. Something was wrong. Something did not feel right. "Why, Trey?" she blurted, unable to make sense of it. "Why did you kill Meredith?"

"You do not have to answer that, Mr. Peterson," the judge said. "Again, I advise you to remain silent until you speak with an attorney."

"Goddamn it, Trey, listen to him," Blake said.

Trey shook his head. "Meredith and I had a fight. We used to fight a lot, but this was a real knock-down drag-out. We haven't been getting along for ages, but Thursday night she went nuts on me and accused me of having an affair with Evie. I told her there was nothing between me and Evie, although I wanted there to be. She went ballistic when she found out I had feelings for Evie. I told her I wanted a divorce, but she refused. I lost my temper and killed her."

Brenda Starr screamed and burst into tears. "Oh, Trey, how could you?"

Her husband George put his arms around her and tried to comfort her.

Blake Peterson was red in the face. "Preposterous. He's made all of this up to protect that woman, Judge."

"I'm not making it up," Trey said without looking at his grandfather. "I killed Meredith." He glanced around, his expression frantic. "Sheriff, where are you? I want to make a statement right now."

"Hold your horses, Mr. Peterson," Judge Ward said. "We'll get to you in a minute, but first there's something I want to ask the sheriff."

"Yes, Judge?" Whitsun said.

"How did you know where to look for the knife?"

Mr. Collier, Evie noticed, didn't look at the sheriff. All of a sudden he seemed mighty interested in making notes on his legal pad. Huh.

"Just a hunch," the sheriff said.

"Did you have a warrant for this search?"

"Didn't think I needed one, Judge. A dead man has no expectation of privacy and neither do the Petersons. The locker's not theirs. No one has paid the dues on that locker since the old man died. It's been unused all these years."

"This morning has been something of a surprise," the judge said, his beagle face growing longer. "I don't like surprises. Remember that in the future, Whitsun, and you and I will get along." He shook his head. "Very well, let him make his statement. But, for God's sake, make sure you inform the fool of his rights."

"Yes, Your Honor."

Taking Trey by the arm, the sheriff escorted him out of the courtroom. Evie glanced back at Meredith. Her lips were curved in a smile of pure, unholy satisfaction.

Chapter Forty

Two hours later, it was over. The Peterson family attorney, a high-powered, $350-an-hour muckety muck from Mobile, made a mad dash to Paulsberg at Blake's insistence, but Trey had refused to talk to him. After being advised of his rights more than once and signing a waiver form, he'd made a statement to the sheriff and confessed to murdering Meredith. The judge, with obvious distaste for the whole kit and caboodle of them, dismissed the case against Evie and she was free to go.

"OhmahGod, ohmahGod, ohmahGod," Addy shrieked when Evie walked out of the courtroom with Mr. Collier, and then she promptly burst into tears.

Ansgar materialized in the hall. "Why all the leakage?" he demanded, looking down his nose at Addy. "Is it your aspiration to become a watering pot? Evangeline was never in any danger. I would not permit it."

"Watering pot?" Addy bowed up at once. "Why, you pompous ass, I oughta—"

Brand pulled her into his arms. "Thank you, brother. You have taken her mind off her distress." He smiled at Evie. "I am happy for you, too, though I dare not cry, for fear of earning Ansgar's reprobation."

Evie was hugged all around and oohed and ahhed over by Bitsy and Muddy.

"And *you*." Wiping her cheeks and blowing her nose into a lace handkerchief, Muddy glared at Mr. Collier. "I know what you've been up to now, you old rascal. You used your contra-bulator to find that knife, didn't you?"

"Shh." Mr. Collier glanced around the hall. "That's not something I want advertised. The ADA might get the wrong idea, like maybe I planted that knife there to get my client off."

"You're a hero," Muddy said. "Folks ought to know."

Evie kissed Mr. Collier on the cheek. "You're my hero. Thank you, Mr. C."

Mr. Collier looked proud enough to pop. "That's good enough for me," he declared.

As they filed down the hall to exit the courthouse, Evie pulled back.

"There's something I have to do," she told Ansgar. "You go on ahead, if you like. It won't take long."

"No. I stay with you."

She smiled up at him, loving his concern for her, loving *him*. "Notice I'm not arguing? I know it would be a waste of time."

"Yes, it would."

They waved good-bye to the others and retraced their steps through the courthouse, crossing the magnificent domed lobby. Going down the stairs into the bowels of the building, they pushed open the door to the Behr County Sheriff's Department. Willa Dean Mooneyham sat behind the receptionist's desk, looking as formidable and intimidating as ever. She could give a Dalvahni warrior a lesson in grim.

"Hey, Miz Mooneyham, how you doing?" Evie asked.

"I sit behind a desk all day and deal with idiots," Willa Dean said. "How do you think I'm doing?"

"Oh." Evie mustered a bright smile. Willa Dean's fuchsia lip-stick was crooked, like she'd put it on without looking in a mir-ror. Her lips were skinny and she'd missed. The result was scary, so Evie stared at Willa Dean's smokestack of gray hair instead. "Would you tell Sheriff Whitsun that Evie Douglass would like to speak to him, please?"

"Humph," Willa Dean said, jabbing a button on the phone with the eraser end of a pencil.

Evie decided it was more of a general principle "humph"

than a "humph" based on any personal animosity. At least, she
hoped so. Willa Dean was one scary broad, especially when she
was channeling the Joker, like now. A part of Evie, the suicidal
part, wanted to tell Willa Dean that her lipstick was crooked.
Fortunately, the suicidal part of Evie was the size of a gnat's behind. The rest of her wanted to run out the door and come
back in a few years when Willa Dean had either retired or nas-
tied away.

"Sheriff, there's someone to see you," Willa Dean barked
into the receiver.

Sheriff Whitsun came out of the back a few minutes later.
"Miss Douglass." He nodded at Ansgar and they did the male
grunt thing. "Let me guess," the sheriff said. "Now that the
charges have been dropped, you want your car back. The paperwork will take a few days, but we'll get it out of impound."

"Uh, no . . . I mean, yes, I want my car back, but that's not
why I'm here." Evie took a deep breath. "I'd like to speak to
Trey Peterson."

The temperature turned frigid. Uh-oh, the big guy was
miffed.

"No," Ansgar said.

"I know you don't like him," Evie told him, "but I have to
talk to him . . . to thank him for what he did. In a way, he saved
my life." She turned to the sheriff. "So, is it possible? Is he allowed visitors?"

"I don't see why not. His grandfather pulled some strings,
and his bail's already been set and posted, by you-can-guess-
who. But Peterson won't go. Insists he belongs in jail. Begged
me to let him stay." The sheriff shrugged. "Maybe he's afraid of
what his in-laws might do."

Evie and Ansgar followed him through the swinging door,
past the office section of the department, and into the jail. Once
again the metal door slammed shut behind her with awful fi-
nality. She shivered, resisting the urge to run screaming back
the way she'd come. This time, though, things were different.
She didn't have a murder rap hanging over her head—thanks to
Trey. Ansgar was with her, like before, only this time he wasn't

invisible. They stopped a few feet away from the door to a private cell.

"I figured I'd better keep him segregated," Sheriff Whitsun said in a low voice. "Pretty boys don't do well in here, especially rich pretty boys."

Trey was sitting on a cot. He looked so lost and alone that Evie's heart twisted for him. She knew what alone felt like. He looked up when the sheriff unlocked the door.

"Evie," Trey said, getting to his feet. "What are you doing here?"

"We need to talk," Evie said.

The sheriff motioned to Ansgar. "Come on, let's you and me give them some privacy. We can wait down the hall."

"No." Ansgar's jaw tightened. "This I cannot allow. I will stay with you."

Shades of Brand, Evie thought, swallowing a smile. How many times had she heard Brand say that very thing to Addy, especially when she was about to do something dangerous?

She put her hand on Ansgar's broad chest. "This is something I need to do. For myself. *By myself.* Nothing is going to happen to me. I'll be fifteen feet away if I need you. I have to talk to him. To thank him . . . to try and understand. It's important."

He swore under his breath and stalked a few feet away from the door. "I will wait for you here. See that you do not tarry long."

Whew, bossy. Evie nodded and entered the cell.

Trey gave her a crushing hug as soon as she walked in. He was shaking. "Evie, my God, Evie. I'm so sorry I put you through this. I should have done something sooner, but I'm a coward."

"You're not a coward," Evie said, stepping back. "You did the right thing. I think you're incredibly brave." She gazed at him, noting his pallor and his eyes, red with unshed tears. "You *did* do the right thing, didn't you, Trey?"

He looked away. "Of course. I couldn't let you go to prison for a crime you didn't commit."

"I see," she said slowly. "But what about you? Are you going to prison for a crime you didn't commit?"

Trey walked back to the cot and sat down. "I don't know what you're talking about."

"Meredith was stabbed to death. You can't stand the sight of blood. I don't think you're capable of killing someone with a knife."

"You've known Meredith since grammar school. You know what she's like. There's an old saying. *No matter how beautiful she is, someone . . . somewhere is tired of her shit.*" He lifted his shoulders. "Maybe I got tired of her shit."

"Or maybe you're covering up for somebody," Evie said. She perched on the edge of the cot beside him. "Who are you protecting? Who killed Meredith?"

Meredith materialized on the other side of Trey. "Butt out, you walrus," she said, giving Evie a hateful look. "Trey's better off where he is."

"Better off," Evie repeated. "Not 'I want him to rot in prison for killing me.' That would be the Meredith I know and dislike. Instead, you say he's better off in jail. Trey didn't murder you, did he?"

Meredith gave her a look that said *duh*. "Of course not, you moron. I'd be haunting the shit out of him if he did."

"Like you're doing now, you mean," Trey muttered.

"There, there, Snookems." Meredith patted Trey on the hand, and he jerked his hand away like he'd been stung. "We've talked about this already. We decided this is what's best for you. You'll be safer here."

Evie gave Trey a sharp look. "Safer? Safer from whom?"

"Oh, for God's sake, you queen-size pain in the ass, mind your own business," Meredith said.

Something inside of Evie snapped. "Shut up, Meredith, or, so help me God, I'll have Ansgar put you back in the bottle."

Meredith wavered and shrank in size. "No, you can't do that. I hate it in there."

"Then be quiet. Not another word. I mean it." Evie realized she was on her feet and her hands were clenched into fists.

Slowly, she took a deep breath and opened her fingers. "Now, what are you afraid of, Trey? Tell me."

"I can't. He made me promise not to tell." He was trembling, and his complexion was gray. He sounded like a little boy, not a grown man. "He said he'd put me in the barker or throw me on the circular saw, just like he—"

He swallowed and shook his head.

"Like he did what?" Evie urged gently.

"I can't," he said. "I'm scared."

Something Muddy had said drifted through Evie's mind. *Blake, Junior . . . killed more than twenty years ago in a freak accident at the mill. A circular saw shattered and split his head in two.*

Twenty years ago, Trey would have been a young boy.

"Your father's death wasn't an accident, was it?" Evie said, taking a stab in the dark. "Somebody murdered him."

"Bingo, tits for brains," Meredith said. "You ain't as dumb as you look. But, then, how could you be?"

Evie narrowed her eyes at the ghost. "Bottle, Mer Mer."

"Okay, okay," Meredith said, holding up her hands in surrender.

"Who killed your daddy, Trey?" Evie asked. "You can tell me. We're friends."

Trey's head drooped. "My grandfather." A long shudder racked his body. "He hated my father because he thought he was weak. He despised him for it. *My son, the pansy ass musician,* he would say. He was always after Daddy to do what he called 'man' things, like hunting. He wanted him to take more of an interest in the mill. But Daddy just wanted to play his music." He raised his head. "He was a wonderful pianist, my dad. I remember standing at his knee when I was little, watching him play. I could feel his music in my bones. I thought he was magic. And he was gentle and kind. Nothing like—like *him*."

Tears streamed down Trey's face. "He killed my daddy in front of me and made me watch. He's strong, Evie, and he has power. And I'm not talking about money and influence. He can *do* things."

"Because he's a demonoid," Evie said.

Trey's eyes widened. "Yes. He picked up Daddy and threw him on that saw like he was so much meat. His own son. Said he'd do the same thing to me if I disappointed him. If I was *weak*."

"Oh, my God." Evie ached for that terrified little boy. "And your mother left you with him and took your sister to live at the beach?"

"That's right," Trey said. "Grandfather convinced her that I should stay with him as the *heir apparent*. And Mama let him have his way, for the money. But, the truth is, he didn't dare let me out of his sight, in case I told." His mouth twisted. "Like anybody would believe me."

"I believe you." Evie turned to Meredith. "But, eventually, Trey told you, and that's why Blake killed you."

"Something like that," Meredith said.

"Why go to prison for a murder you didn't commit?" Evie asked Trey. "Why not testify against your grandfather? He should pay for what he's done."

"*No.*" Trey got to his feet. "I can't. You don't understand what he's like. What he *is*. I'm safer this way."

"Your grandfather's not the only one with abilities. Ansgar and Brand are powerful warriors. They can protect you from him."

"Leave it alone, Evie." He dropped back on the cot as though his legs would no longer support him. "Even if I testified against him, there's not a jail in the world that will hold him. I'm hoping, this way, that he won't come after me. That he'll let it alone and be happy that I'm taking the rap for him."

Evie gave Meredith an imploring look. "Tell him, Meredith. Tell him he doesn't have to do this. You don't want Trey to spend years in prison for something he didn't do. If you love him, you'll want what's best for him."

Meredith hovered closer to Trey. "This is what's best for him, and for me, too. I died a horrible death. I deserve something wonderful after all I've been through. This will be a fresh start for us, a second chance at happiness. We're going to spend the next however many years together in prison working on

our problems. He'll never be lonely or alone. I'll see to that."
She patted his hand again, making him jump. "Isn't that right,
Snookems? Death and prison are the best things that ever hap-
pened to our marriage."

Bing! Leonard Swink appeared.

Meredith bounced off the cot to greet him. "Here he is now!
Swinky's going to give us marriage counseling. Isn't that right?"

Swink cleared his throat. "That is correct."

"So beat it, Cheese Hog," Meredith said, turning to Evie.
"This is a private session."

"Are you sure, Trey?" Evie asked. "This isn't your only
choice."

"Yes, it is." Trey's shoulders sagged in defeat, and he waved
his hand toward the door. "Go on. Get out of here, Evie. Live
your life and be happy. It will give me something to think about
besides"—he glanced at Meredith, who was busy chatting with
Swink—"about . . . how things didn't work out so good for me."

"Good-bye, Trey," Evie said, her mouth trembling.

It didn't have to end like this. It couldn't. There must be
some way to help him. It went against everything in her to remain silent and let an innocent man go to jail. But what if he
was right and his grandfather came after him for testifying
against him? He thought he was safer in jail, but that was only
an illusion. She suspected that Blake Peterson was in league
with the demons. She remembered the smoky figure that had
leaked through her bathroom window, and shivered. Trey
would be helpless in jail if the djegrali attacked, with no one to
come to his aid but Meredith.

Meredith. Evie wondered how long she'd had her memory
back, the selfish, deceitful little witch. She'd probably convinced Trey to confess, preying on his fear of his grandfather to
get her way. Meredith had gotten what she wanted, in death if
not in life—Trey's undivided attention, without the threat of
other females. How could she be so conniving and mean?

Evie rushed out of the cell in tears.

"Evangeline?" Ansgar took her in his arms. "Why are you
crying?"

She was very aware of Sheriff Whitsun watching her. She had to be careful or she'd give Trey away, and she didn't want to do that. Not yet. Not until she was sure it was the right thing to do and that Trey wouldn't get hurt.

She buried her face against Ansgar's hard chest to hide her expression from the sheriff. Lobo was on the prowl again, and he had the scent of something in the wind.

"I'm too upset to talk about it right now," she said in a muffled voice. "I'd like to leave. It's been a really hard day."

"I'll walk you two out," Whitsun said. "I want to see this fancy truck of yours that everybody's talking about."

"I would be most happy to show it to you," Ansgar said. Oh, boy. Evie could hear the male pride in his voice. Men and their toys. "It is a piping hot ride."

"Smoking hot," Whitsun said, his eyes twinkling. "Piping hot refers to food."

Ansgar's expression became distracted, as if he were checking this information against his Dalvahni translator.

"Ah, yes," Ansgar said. "My mistake. It is so smoking hot it will erupt your mind."

The two guys were still talking truck when they stepped through the front door of the courthouse and they were attacked. Evie screamed as a black knife arched through the air and plunged into Ansgar's chest. Blood spurted from the terrible wound and spread across the front of his starched blue shirt.

"Ansgar," she cried.

He groaned and fell to his knees, the light in his silver eyes fading. "Run, Evangeline. *Run,*" he said hoarsely.

She threw herself onto the steps beside him. "No, I won't leave you. Let me help you."

Invisible arms closed around her, lifting her away from Ansgar. "Let me go," she screamed, kicking her legs and reaching for him. *"Ansgar."*

Their unseen assailant shoved a cloth over her face. She smelled paint thinner and cocoa, and everything went black.

Chapter Forty-one

Evie coughed and sat up. Ansgar was dead. No one could survive a wound like that. She'd seen the knife sink into his chest and his expression of undisguised fear. Not for himself, for her. And the blood, so much of it, pumping out of the gaping hole and staining his shirt.

She was dizzy and queasy and her head felt like it was going to split, but she didn't care.

He was dead. Nothing else mattered.

"Ah, so you are awake."

Evie lifted her head, her vision blurred with tears. She sat on the floor of a richly appointed room with a high ceiling, arched, floor-length windows, and dark-paneled walls. Hundreds of knives in all shapes and sizes glittered in glass front cases. Blake Peterson sat on the other side of an enormous mahogany double pedestal desk with a leather inlaid top. He wore a look of smug satisfaction. Now would be a really good time to do the demon hunter bop, like she'd done the night of the Halloween ball. But she was too sick and weak from whatever evil cocktail Peterson had drugged her with to hold her head up, much less teleport.

"Feel bad, do you? Could have been the ether. I remember when I had my tonsils out. I threw up my toenails." He paused. "I've heard, of course, that drugs don't affect the Dalvahni. Don't know if I envy them or pity them for that. Imagine my surprise when I learned that an innocent little thing like chocolate gets them intoxicated. I decided not to take any chances, though, so I mixed ether with pure cocoa, just in case some part of you is still human."

"Cocoa?" Evie stared at him in dull incomprehension. Ansgar was dead. She should have made him understand how much she loved him when she had the chance, should have told him she forgave him for leaving, for everything. A dull weight pressed against her heart. There were so many things she wanted to say. Now she'd never have the chance.

"I put the word out that I'd pay for information about the Dalvahni," he said. "Someone saw you at the bar the other night and noticed you got plastered on chocolate." He chuckled. "Money is power, Miss Douglass, and I have a lot of money, thanks to dear old Dad. If there's one thing I've learned, it's that anything can be bought, for a price."

Evie lifted a shaking hand to her brow. "Wait, how do you know that I'm—"

"Dalvahni?" He gave her a cold smile. He reminded her of a snake, with his smooth elegance and coiled watchfulness. "You are a silly piece. I noticed the change in you right away. You always were a pretty bit of goods, with that red hair and those big eyes and smooth skin. Nice tits, too. I like my women with meat on their bones." His gaze drifted to her breasts and stayed there. "But after that demon hunter boyfriend of yours changed you, you practically glowed. Trey's had his dick in a knot over you for months. You must have something mighty special between your legs. I've had a lot of poontang in my time, but none worth going to prison for."

"You killed Meredith," Evie said.

"Sorry, I can't take credit for that one, though I'm not saying I didn't think about it. Meredith was, shall we say . . . challenging." Rising, he walked over to one of the cabinets and removed a wicked-looking hunting knife from one of the brackets. "I enjoy killing, Miss Douglass. I'm quite good at it. I enjoy the hunt and the feeling of power that comes from wielding death. Nothing else like it. The Dalvahni and I have that in common, I think, the joy of the hunt."

"Ansgar is nothing like you, you sick bastard."

Was. Oh, God, Ansgar.

Peterson vanished in front of her. Evie gasped as she was grabbed by the hair and the knife was pressed against her throat. She smelled something sweet and fruity with woody undertones and, beneath that, the stench of something rotten.

Blake Peterson spoke in her ear, his voice honey smooth and deadly. "I'm a god, Miss Douglass. Your god because I hold your life in my hands. Do not despise a god." The tip of the knife pierced her skin. "Have I mentioned that I like blood?" Evie shuddered as she felt the wet length of his tongue lap at the blood on her throat. "The demon in me likes the taste and smell of it, craves it. That's why I kill." To her surprise, he released her. Reappearing back at his desk, he opened a drawer and began to clean the knife with loving care. "Pity I can't kill you. I would enjoy it. I'm extremely annoyed with you, you know. You've cost me my only grandson. He was a fool to take the fall for you."

"You were there, in the office with me when I found Meredith. I recognize your scent. It's frankincense."

"Frankincense was used by the ancient Egyptians to embalm the dead. Did you know that? It was also used as a fumigant and it's wonderful at masking odors." He walked over and put the knife back in the case. "Yes, I was in the office with you that morning. As I'm sure you've noticed, I can make myself invisible. I was trying to figure out what to do when you so conveniently showed up." He waved at one of the leather chairs that littered the room. "But, I forget my manners. Please, take a seat."

"No, thank you. I'm leaving."

"I'm afraid that's not possible," Blake said. He looked up as the door opened and Clarice stepped into the room on a heavy cloud of perfume. She was carrying a tray with glasses and a pitcher of iced tea. "There you are, my dear. Offer our guest some refreshment."

Clarice waited until Evie rose with some difficulty from the floor and wobbled over to a leather chair.

With a vacuous smile, she offered the tray to Evie. "Tea?"

"No thank you," Evie said. She wanted nothing to do with anyone or anything in this house. Blake Peterson was a psychotic mad man, and his wife wasn't dealing with a full deck, either. Trey's mother should be horsewhipped for leaving her son with these horrible people.

Blake strode back to the desk and sat down. "Have a seat, Clarice. Evie and I were just talking about Meredith's murder. She seems to be under the misapprehension that *I* killed her. Why don't you enlighten her?" Clarice remained where she was, her wooden expression unchanged. "No? Allow me, then." He folded his hands on leather inlay. "You see, my wife killed Meredith. Some misguided notion of getting revenge on me, I suppose. She blames me for the death of our useless son."

"Not so very misguided," Evie said. "You did kill him. Trey told me. He saw you."

Crappydoodle, she'd just outted Trey. Evie could have bitten her tongue.

"Trey told you this?" Clarice stared at Evie and then at her husband. "It's true then. Just as I always thought. You killed Junior."

"Not now, Clarice." Blake shook his head. "She's such a whiner. I'd have slit her throat years ago, but she has her uses." He paused. "Now where was I? Oh, yes, Clarice used the Scagel because she knew the police would trace it back to me. She was trying to frame me, the naughty thing. I overheard her ask Meredith to meet her at the mill early Friday morning to plan a surprise birthday party for Trey. Totally unlike Clarice— she hasn't shown interest in anything since Junior died—so I knew she was up to something. I followed her. Imagine my surprise and delight when I discovered my dull little stick of a wife had murdered Meredith and in such spectacular fashion. Clarice was magnificent." He gave his wife a beatific smile. Merciful God, he was proud of what she'd done, Evie realized with a shudder. "And all these years I thought we had nothing in common," Blake said. "After she left, I pulled my knife out of Meredith's chest and replaced it with your letter opener."

"And later you put the knife in my car," Evie said. *And stole the knife from the lab in Mobile using your creeper powers,* she added mentally.

"Yes. Meredith told me Trey had asked her for a divorce because he was in love with you. I couldn't care less if he screwed you—a man is entitled to a little on the side—but I couldn't have *that*. So, I planted the knife in your car. In hindsight, perhaps, it wasn't the smartest of moves, but at the time it seemed like a way to get rid of you. Kill two birds with one stone, so to speak." He shrugged. "It was the excitement of the kill, I suppose. The blood lust does that to you, exhilarates you and makes you careless. Isn't that right, Clarice?"

Clarice stood. Her posture and expression were as frozen as a mannequin's. "I'm going to check on Papa."

Blake waved his hand. "Yes, yes, do that. Your devotion to him is the only reason I keep you around."

Moving like an automaton, Clarice walked behind Blake's massive desk and pushed a piece of scrollwork in the wood. A door slid soundlessly open and she disappeared inside, closing it behind her.

"Every family has its little secrets," Blake said. He tilted his head, examining her. "I'm surprised you haven't asked me why you're here."

"You're going to kill me. That's what you do, right? Kill people."

"It is something of a hobby of mine. I particularly enjoy killing women." His hungry gaze moved over her from head to foot. "They're so soft and they squeak so prettily, the little mice." His eyes narrowed to slits. "But you don't seem too disturbed by the notion. I must say, that's unsporting of you. Tasting your victim's fear is half the fun."

Evie lifted her chin and glared at him, refusing to let him see her fear. "There are worse things than death."

"How noble and dramatic of you," he said. "I suppose next you'll say life has lost all meaning now that your boyfriend is dead. Please. You'll get over it and sooner than you expect."

Opening a drawer in the desk, he unfolded a length of felt and removed a knife. "Ugly, isn't it?" He held the weapon aloft.

"Deer antler handle and a simple stone blade. Crude and un-wieldy. Very little workmanship. Nothing sleek or elegant about it, but this knife is worth more than my entire collection. In fact, I daresay this knife is more valuable than everything I own. Do you know why?"

"No," Evie said dully. Ansgar was dead. The slashing pain in her chest made it difficult to breathe.

He laughed. "No, of course you don't. This knife, Miss Douglass, is my ticket to power and riches. This knife killed your precious demon hunter, and I know where and how to get more. Enough for an army. Think about it, Miss Douglass. Think what this knife represents, a weapon to defeat the Dal-vahni. Give the djegrali such a weapon, and anything I want is mine. Anything at all. My father's so-called accomplishments will pale in comparison."

Anger and grief rose up in Evie, choking her. "Bastard," she said.

The rage boiled out of her. She raised her hand, wanting to strike at Peterson, to hurt him. To her surpise and satisfaction, a ball of green light flew from her fingertips and hit Peterson in the face. It stuck there like slimy pudding. He staggered away from the desk with a howl of anguish.

"It burns," he screamed, clawing at his face. "Get it off. Get if off."

Evie pushed out of the chair and staggered toward the door. A misty malformed shape barred her way. The demon bent down and flowed into the room on clawed feet, towering over her and filling the room with the chilling presence of evil and the smell of rotting meat. More than a score of demon wraiths flowed into the study behind him, rubbing against his scaly legs like a cluster of affectionate cats.

"Is this the one?" The harsh voice that grated out of the nightmare made Evie shrivel inside.

"Yes, Drakthal." Sobbing in pain, Blake snatched up the piece of cloth that had been around the knife and scrubbed at his face. Bits of flesh rolled off onto the felt. He shrieked. "Look! The bitch has burned me."

Drakthal. The name sounded familiar. Evie tried to think, but her brain was sluggish with terror.

Memories of the bar fight came back to her. *The morkyn . . . the oldest and most powerful of our kind.* That's what the possessed woman in Beck's had said, right before she turned into a monster.

Drakthal was a super demon. Evie remembered her hopeless terror a few months earlier when she'd been possessed. The wraith had risen out of the dead man in the park and entered her body, pushing the essence of Evie into a place of deep despair from which she could never escape.

And this demon was much stronger.

"Cease your whining, halfling," Drakthal said to Blake. "You will be recompensed for your pain."

The demon reached for her, and Evie cringed.

Something brushed past her ear, so close that it stirred her hair. A silver arrow sank into the morkyn's knobby abdomen. The demon bellowed in pain. One, two, three more arrows found their mark, and Drakthal shattered into black dust.

Evie whirled around, relief, joy, and disbelief surging through her. "Ansgar!"

He was alive. Covered in blood and obviously still wounded and weakened by Peterson's attack, but he was *alive.*

"Get out of the way, Evangeline," he said, his lips drawn back in a snarl.

Shrieking with rage, the cluster of wraiths attacked. Evie scrambled behind the desk, her attention focused on Ansgar as he sent arrow after arrow whizzing through the air at the demons. He was outnumbered and he was hurt. There were too many of them.

A giant black wolf leaped through one of the windows. Shaking the shattered glass from its fur, the wolf looked right at her. Something passed between them. Evie's jaw sagged in surprise. Whitsun, the wolf was Sheriff Whitsun. Crazy, but she was sure of it. He must have recognized Peterson's scent and followed them here.

The wolf joined the fray. Leaping into the air, the beast caught and tore the wraiths to pieces with its powerful jaws.

Evie began to relax. It was going to be all right. She would not lose Ansgar again.

A draft of cool air blew her skirt against the back of her legs. She caught a whiff of frankincense and was yanked backward through the opening in the wall. The door in the paneling closed, and the sounds of battle faded.

It was not going to be all right. She was trapped inside a hidden passage in the Peterson insane asylum with the biggest nutball in the joint.

Chapter Forty-two

Blake Peterson dragged Evie along a dimly lit hall, flung open a door, and threw her down a flight of stairs. He was extremely strong. She rolled, end over end, and hit her head on the wall at the bottom. Dazed, she looked up. Blake stalked down the steps. His face was cracked and swollen, his eyelids were puffy, and strips of flesh dangled from his chin.

"Tsk, tsk, my dear," he said. "You should be more careful. You could hurt yourself." He jerked her to her feet. "Come along. There's someone I want you to meet."

Evie pulled back. "Let me go, and maybe Ansgar won't kill you."

"He can't kill me if he can't find me, and he can't find us here." He led her down a winding brick tunnel. "My father made his first fortune during Prohibition running bootleg whiskey. This was a speakeasy. There was a nightclub and rooms for gambling and sex. People used to come here from miles around to dance and eat and party. We still use the original furnace to heat the house." He stopped in front of an entrance in the brick. "Here we are."

He opened the door. A horrible odor rolled out of the chamber, a smell so strong and overpowering that Evie gagged. Something inside that room was dead, maybe several somethings. She drew back.

Peterson gripped her arm. "Filthy smell, isn't it? Breathe through your mouth. I'd say you get used to it, but you don't."

He shoved her inside. Evie expected a scene out of a horror

movie—rotting body parts, bloated corpses, blood, decay, and filth. Instead, the room was tidy, spacious, and elegantly furnished. Framed photographs and tasteful artwork hung on the brick walls, and a Persian carpet covered the floor. A flat-screen television on an antique sideboard faced a large four-poster bed. There was a large custom-built glass display case on one wall, empty except for a curved dagger. More room for Blake's growing collection of weaponry, no doubt. Clarice Peterson sat in an armchair in one corner of the room doing needlework. She seemed oblivious to the stench, but then she always seemed oblivious.

Blake shut and locked the door. Evie's heart sank. She was well and truly trapped.

"Mrs. Peterson, help me," she said. "Please."

Clarice gave her a blank look. No help there.

"Daddy, you have a visitor," Blake said.

Clarice put down her needlework and rose from her chair.

That's when Evie noticed the figure on the bed, and the horror movie really started to roll. It was a man. Or maybe what *used* to be a man. Evie couldn't be sure. The thing on the bed was a twisted, gnarled lump and it *stunk,* like spoiled meat, charred fat, boiled cabbage, offal, and fish guts rolled into one. The oily, putrid smell crawled over Evie in waves. Anything that came within fifty feet of Creeper Dude was bound to stink, too. No wonder Blake used frankincense to disguise the odor and Clarice bathed herself in perfume.

Blake grabbed her elbow and dragged her closer to the four-poster. "This is Evie Douglass, Daddy," he said. "Miss Douglass, meet my father, William Coleman Peterson."

"Cole Peterson?" Evie said. "He died when I was little."

"Yes, we had a funeral and everything, but Daddy didn't die. He can't, not for a very long time. He just keeps getting more and more like this." Blake waved a hand at the thing on the bed. "He was possessed by a demon when he was in his thirties. Most humans don't survive long after they are taken. A couple of months, a few years at most, before the demon sucks them dry. But not my daddy." There was pride in Blake's voice.

"Cole Peterson was a match for that old demon. Latched on to it and wouldn't let go. Daddy liked the power the demon gave him. Used it to build him an empire. By the time that old devil got tired and wanted to move on, it was too late. Cole Peterson and the djegrali had somehow merged. And now they're stuck with one another. If Daddy dies, the demon dies, so the demon keeps him alive. Sort of. You can see why we had to fake his death, although Daddy still helps me run the business from down here. Uses his powers to give us an edge on the competition, right, Daddy?"

The thing turned its head. The skull was hairless and brown—it reminded Evie of a big pecan—and its eyes were withered raisins in the sockets.

Why have you brought this woman into my presence? Take your plaything and leave.

The voice sounded in the room although the lump on the bed didn't speak. It couldn't. There was nothing recognizable as a mouth left.

"It's not like that, Daddy." Blake sounded petulant. "She's not my mistress, and I haven't killed anyone around here in years."

See that you don't. I am done cleaning up your little messes. I have not forgotten June Hammond.

"You still mad about that? That was ages ago," Blake said. "Listen, Daddy, this is different. This is *big*. Remember that story you used to tell me, the one about the Dalvahni warrior?"

Kell, Creeper Dude whispered. *In the form of a giant. I beheaded him and took his knife as a remembrance.*

"Yes, yes, Daddy, the knife in the new case I had built here in your room."

"You never told me you had a Dalvahni knife," Clarice said. Her voice startled Evie. Clarice was so quiet Evie had forgotten she was there. "Their weapons kill demons, don't they?"

"Shut up, Clarice," Blake said, dismissing her. "I'm talking to Daddy. Anyway, this woman I've brought you is Dalvahni."

This cannot be so. The Dalvahni are male.

"She was human, but a Dalvahni warrior changed her. *Made* her Dalvahni. But she's still weak. She hasn't been trained, and she hasn't had time to develop her powers." Blake touched his swollen face. "Fully, at any rate."

Creeper Dude was silent.

"Don't you see, Daddy? We can use her to bargain with the morkyn. They want her. Imagine what a demon could do with a Dalvahni body, even if it is only female. They'll give us anything we want. Money. Women. Power. We'll be kings."

No. I want her.

"You do? But, I don't think you can—"

Don't be a fool, Blaketon. You will cut me into pieces and feed me to her. Every last bit.

Evie's stomach lurched. "No," she said, stepping back.

Blake grabbed her. "Do you think that'll work?"

I have no idea. It has never been done. But then few other djegrali have slain a Dalvahni warrior. I will make it work.

"No." Blake's hand bit into Evie's arm. "If you could promise me it would work, then I'd do it, but I'm not going to waste her on a 'maybe.' You've had your time, now it's mine. I've got plans. Big plans and I—"

Blake screamed and staggered back. Creeper Dude's blind pecan head swiveled.

What is happening?

Evie whirled around. Clarice held the Dalvahni dagger in her hand. It was dripping with blood.

"That's for all the mistresses and for screwing the maid and my best friend," she said. Blake grunted in pain as Clarice stabbed him again. "And that's for all the beatings I've taken from you over the years." She drew her arm back, her eyes blazing. "And this is for killing my son, you son of a bitch."

Clarice drove the dagger deep into Blake's belly. He dropped to his knees and looked up at his wife in shock and surprise, like his favorite hound had bitten him.

Clarice shoved a key in Evie's hand. "Go. Get out of this house now, if you want to live. Tell the sheriff he can find my signed confession to Meredith's murder in my safe–deposit box at the bank."

Evie took the key, unlocked the door, and ran down the

labyrinthine hallway. In the distance, she heard a roaring sound. It was Ansgar calling her name.

"Here," she shouted, running faster. "I'm here."

He came around a bend in the tunnel and snatched her into his arms. His eyes were wild, and there were white lines of strain around his mouth.

"Evangeline, are you—"

"I'm fine. Just get us out of here. Where's the sheriff?"

"Searching the grounds for you in case he took you that way."

"Good. Get us out of here. Now. And use your woo woo."

He wrapped his arms around her, and a second later they were standing on the Peterson lawn. Sheriff Whitsun came striding up. Evie wondered where his clothes went when he shape-shifted, but didn't ask, 'cause that would be rude.

"Well met, Devlin," Ansgar said, surprising Evie by calling the sheriff by his given name. They must be big buds now. "I thank you for your help."

"Glad to do it," Whitsun said. He nodded, indicating Ansgar's bloody shirt. "How bad is your wound?"

Ansgar rubbed his chest. "It pains me still, but it will heal."

"Good," Whitsun said. "I see you found Miss Douglass."

"Yes, though just barely." Ansgar's mouth tightened with anger. "Stay here, Evangeline. I'm going back for Peterson. He must pay for what he has done."

She grabbed his arm. "No, he's dead. Clarice killed him." A low rumbling sound came from underground, followed by an enormous explosion. Servants poured out of the house. "And I'm pretty sure she just blew up the furnace."

Whitsun made a quick call on his radio. "Fire department's on its way, though I don't know what they can do." His nose twitched. "From the size of that blast, I'd say she used explosives."

"Oh, Sheriff," Evie said, remembering. Her brain was whirling, but this was important. "Mrs. Peterson killed Meredith. She said you can find her confession in her safe-deposit box in the bank."

Whitsun grunted. "Not surprised. My nose told me Trey was lying. With Blake Peterson dead, I assume Trey inherits the family fortune?"

"Most of it, I guess," Evie said.

"In my experience, money does not bring out the best in humans," Ansgar said.

"Poor guy might be safer in jail," Whitsun said. "He's got all that money, and now he's a widower. Women will be killing each other over him."

Meredith might have something to say about that, Evie thought. She lifted her head, listening. "What's that?"

"Siren," Whitsun said. "Fire Department is on its way. 'Scuse me, I see Chief Davis. I need to speak to him."

He strode off.

"I hear music." Evie started toward the burning building. "Someone's still in there."

Ansgar grabbed her. "Someone *is* in there, but he is not alive. It is the shade of the one called Junior."

"Trey's daddy? Show me."

"Very well," Ansgar said.

The Peterson mansion was engulfed in flames, and, though the fire department had arrived and was valiantly trying to put out the fire, it was pretty much a done deal. Shielded from sight in Ansgar's arms, Evie stood on the east side of the house and stared into the burning music room. Blond head bent, a man played the piano amidst the flames. The tune was wild and lonely and, yes, utterly haunting.

"I do not see her," Ansgar muttered. He sounded troubled.

"Who?"

"Clarice Peterson. She loved her son's music. I thought she would stay with him."

"She did stay with him," Evie said. "Far longer than most people would have done."

Junior played on.

Epilogue

Two weeks later

Evie and Addy stood quietly together in the narthex of the Trinity Episcopal Church waiting for the wedding to start. This would be the second double wedding in Hannah since Halloween, and the town was abuzz with the excitement of it, though *technically* only one of the weddings had taken place locally. Two days after the Big Fire—the local name for the conflagration that had burned the Peterson place to the ground—Muddy and Mr. Collier had eloped to Disney World. And so did Shep and Lenora. Muddy had a premonition there'd be a last-minute cancellation, and the two couples had gotten married in the Disney Wedding Pavilion. Afterward, Muddy and Mr. Collier left for his place on Cape San Blas, and Shep and Lenora got a room at the Grand Floridian—another one of Muddy's hunches. Several days later, they'd picked up Lily and William at the Orlando airport, and the new family had spent five happy days vacationing with the Mouse. The kids were ecstatic, Lenora was lit up like a Christmas tree when she came home, and Marilee's liver was permanently curled.

Initially, Bitsy had been taken aback by Muddy's defection. But, in typical dynamo fashion, she made a speedy recovery. A few adjustments here and there that included a new bride and groom, a rapid consultation with Tweedy Gibbs down at Tompkins about tuxedos for exceptionally tall and bodacious men, and a hurried trip to Mobile to find a wedding dress for Evie, and it was on. Piece of cake for a pro like the Bitser.

The windows in the nave were decorated with candles, greenery, and flowers; the pews were bedecked with satin bows; and the church parking lot overflowed. Not one single person had regretted.

"Not that they would have anyway, mind you," Bitsy had chattered happily over supper a few days before, "but now that Evie and Ansgar are *celebrities* because of the thing with the You Know Whos, no one will want to miss it."

Voldemort had nothing on the Petersons now that Clarice's confession had come to light. People in Paulsberg thirty miles away swore they could see Hannah glowing in the distance like a gi-normous lightning bug because of all the excitement and gossip generated by the revelations in that letter. And it was some letter. Clarice aired the Peterson dirty laundry big time. But she was smart about it. She didn't say anything about magic or whoozits or demons. Nope, people would've thought she was a nutter and dismissed her out of hand, unless they were demonoids— and they would have been ticked. It was an artfully woven tale of cruelty, greed, corruption, lust, and murder, and people sopped it up, savoring every last drop.

Nah, that was for regular old ordinary run-of-the-mill gossip. People kept *this* tucked between teeth and gums like a jaw-breaker or a chaw of tobacco, so they could suck on it a long time. Like forever.

Trey was released from jail and immediately faced with planning some kind of memorial service for his grandparents and for the great-grandfather everybody had thought was dead and buried. And was—now. Poor Trey was a basket case. His mother and sister bailed on him—no surprise there—and his two aunts claimed they couldn't get away from their obligations in Atlanta and Birmingham long enough to bury their parents. So Bitsy had stepped in to help. The service was short and simple, but everybody came, including Meredith, Swink, and Junior Peterson, though most people didn't seem to notice them.

Just another weird day in Hannah, supernatural suck hole of the universe.

Due to the vagaries of human nature, Evie went from pariah to pop star princess overnight. People stopped her on the street to shake her hand and to assure her that they never, *for a minute,* thought she killed Meredith. *No sirree bobtail,* such an encounter typically went, *I told my wife Ellen, Ellen, says I, I no more believe that tale about Evie Douglass than a man in the moon.* The names and the gender of the speaker might change, but the drift of the conversation stayed the same.

It made her extremely uncomfortable, but she was learning to deal. After the things she'd been through, it would take a lot to rattle her cage from now on.

And now it was here, the Big Day, and Evie and Ansgar and Addy and Brand were getting married in the double wedding of the century—no, the *millennium*—and Evie was so happy she thought she might burst. She didn't say so, of course. Not in front of Bitsy, anyway. Ladies don't say things like burst, or pop, or blow up—rule number fifteen in the *Rules of Lady-tude Handbook* by Hibiscus Hamilton Corwin. The *ROLH* was only in Bitsy's *head,* mind you, but that didn't make it any less real.

Evie saw Addy's cousin Bernadette raise her hand. "This is it, Adds. You're on. I'll be right behind you."

Addy flung her arms around Evie's neck. "Oh, Evie, I'm so happy we're having a double wedding. I love you so much."

"I love you, too," Evie said. "You make a beautiful bride."

"You're both beautiful." Muddy hurried up. "Come on, Addy, before your mama pops like a zit right here in the middle of God's house."

"Don't say pop, Aunt Muddy," Addy said automatically, stepping forward.

She didn't know what she was saying, of course, Evie reflected, watching with tears in her eyes as Addy walked toward the open doors of the nave in her white, one-shoulder, A-line wedding dress of organza and satin, with asymmetric layers of lace and an elegant sweep train. Evie had learned *a lot* about dresses during her shopping trip to Mobile with Bitsy. But the

ROLH was pretty much engraved in Addy's DNA. Hers, too, come to think of it.

Bouquets in hand, Evie's matron of honor fluttered up, looking very pretty in her ivory dress of tulle and organza that coordinated with Evie's wedding gown. "You so look like a fairy-tale princess in that dress, Evie," Nicole said.

"Thank you." Evie smiled, her heart overflowing with happiness. She felt beautiful and loved. Oh, so very loved. She smoothed her hand over the flowing ivory skirts of her strapless tulle and organza ball gown with embellished lace. An organza ribbon sash encircled her waist. "You will, too. It's the way every woman should feel on her wedding day."

Nicole blushed. "Daniel's got me moved out of 'never' to living in 'we'll see.' Miss Muddy says to come on. They're playing your song. Though how the heck you're supposed to know it's your song beats the tar out of me. Did you know you can't play sexual music in the 'Piscopal church? They got some rule against 'Here Comes the Bride.' "

"Secular music," Evie said. Merciful heavens, Bach was rolling in his grave right about now. "Yes, I did know that."

She took her bouquet from Nicole, an exquisite arrangement of white roses, sweet peas, ranunculus, and tiny lily-of-the-valley that Addy had designed, and glided across the narthex.

Shep smiled down at her. "Ready?"

Evie looked through the open doors and down the aisle at Ansgar. He stood at the altar next to Addy and Brand, waiting for her. He wasn't hard to miss. He'd always been gorgeous, but in a tux he took her breath away. She was going to need an inhaler to live with this man. *Her* man.

Her love.

The glorious strains of "Jesu Joy of Man's Desiring" floated down from the choir loft above the nave. Junior Peterson really was a brilliant musician. The cellist and the violinist hired for the wedding joined in, clueless, along with Bitsy and most of those present, that the guest organist Evie had requested was a ghost.

Evie smiled back at Shep and nodded, her soul lifting with

joy. She walked through the doors and into the nave on Shep's arm. Everyone was looking at her, but she didn't care. She saw only Ansgar. He watched her come down the aisle. His look of hungry yearning and his fierce expression of pride and possessiveness, of eager longing, gave her feet wings. He loved her. It was written in every line of his beautiful face, and it was in his eyes. It poured out of him like light.

She loved him every bit as much.

Oh, yes, she was ready.

Trey sat in his car outside the church. He'd parked down the street under a tree, close enough to hear but not be noticed. The gossips would have a field day if they saw him, lurking in the shadows like a pathetic lovesick loser.

The organ music swelled; the wedding had begun.

Evie. Oh, God, Evie.

She'd gotten her happy ending, leaving him with nothing but the ashes of his former life and bitter regret.

And Meredith.

He laughed at the thought. Yes, he still had Meredith, although God knows he didn't want her. He glanced around, half expecting her to appear, breathing a sigh of relief when she didn't.

Maybe she was with Swink the Shrink. Trey didn't care where she was as long as she wasn't with him.

She hardly ever left him alone anymore. He'd kill himself, but Meredith would only follow him into the afterlife. She'd never stop hounding him. He needed to get rid of her, but he didn't know how.

Father Ben might help him, but he was reluctant to go to him with his peculiar little "problem." What if Father Ben couldn't see Meredith and thought Trey was crazy? There'd been more than enough talk about the Petersons already.

His hands tightened on the steering wheel. Since the fire and the shocking revelations in his grandmother's letter, everything had changed. He still had money, but people treated him differently. People he'd once considered beneath him didn't show him the same respect, like the scandal had knocked him down to their level somehow.

As for his peers at the country club, they either greeted him with tight-lipped reserve or gave him the cold shoulder.

Was it his fault his granddaddy was a psychopath? Hadn't he suffered enough because of that man?

If he couldn't have Evie, at least he could have his old life back. There had to be a way to prove to himself and everybody in Hannah that the Petersons were still a force to be reckoned with.

Something moved in the gloom, startling him. A man flowed out of the shadows like some dark genie responding to Trey's desperate wish. The stranger was young and handsome, but much too thin, with sooty, artfully messy hair and a full-lipped, sensuous mouth. He wore jeans and scuffed black boots with chains at the heels, a torn white T-shirt, and a black leather jacket. A thin silver tooth dangled from one ear, and his eyebrow and bottom lip were pierced.

The stranger tapped on the driver's side glass. "Trey Peterson?"

Trey rolled down the window. "Yes?"

"I represent a consortium interested in making a deal with you."

"What sort of deal?" Trey said, frowning.

The guy looked more like a drug dealer than a businessman, and he was wearing eye liner, for God's sake.

"The kind that could make you a lot of money—"

"Money I've got," Trey said, starting to roll the window back up.

"—and make you a very powerful man."

Trey's finger stilled on the power button. "I'm listening."

"Your grandfather had a knife."

Trey's interest faded. Another collector. "My grandfather had lots of knives. They were destroyed in a fire."

"This was a very special knife. My . . . uh . . . employers are most eager to obtain another one like it. They know about the fire, but are wondering if, perhaps, your grandfather left some information about the provenance of this knife someplace else. A safe-deposit box, perhaps. Give them what they're looking for, and you can name your own price."

Name his own price, huh? Maybe they'd be interested in buying the mill. He hated the damn place. Nothing but bad memories there now Evie was gone. He'd never have to set foot there again. And selling the mill would make Old Blake spin in his grave, an added bonus.

He could start fresh. He could be free for the first time in his life. Of course, he'd still have Meredith to deal with, but maybe she wouldn't want to leave Hannah. Maybe she *couldn't* leave Hannah.

He'd never thought of that.

Trey drummed his fingers on the steering wheel, thinking. His grandfather had been a cagey old bastard. It would be like him to stash important papers and other items in several different banks.

"I could look," he said.

The stranger's eyes flared with excitement, shining purple orbs in the darkness. A trickle of dread crept down Trey's spine.

"Excellent," the stranger said. "The consortium will be happy to hear this. We look forward to doing business with you, Mr. Peterson."

The man with the glowing eyes smiled.

Did you miss DEMON HUNTING IN DIXIE, the first book in Lexi's hilarious series?

A warrior, a demon, and the girl next door . . .

Looking for Trouble

Addy Corwin is a florist with an attitude. A bad attitude, or so her mama says, 'cause she's not looking for a man. Mama's wrong. Addy has looked. There's just not much to choose from in Hannah, her small Alabama hometown. Until Brand Dalvahni shows up, a supernaturally sexy, breathtakingly well built hunk of a warrior from—well, not from around here, that's for sure. Mama thinks he might be European or maybe even a Yankee. Brand says he's from another dimension.

Addy couldn't care less where he's from. He's gorgeous. Serious muscles. Disturbing green eyes. Brand really gets her going. Too bad he's a whack job. Says he's come to rescue her from a demon. Puh-lease. But right after Brand shows up, strange things start to happen. Dogs talk and reanimated corpses stalk the quiet streets of Hannah. Her mortal enemy, Meredith, otherwise known as the Death Starr, breaks out in a severe and inexplicable case of butt boils. Addy might not know what's going on, but she definitely wants a certain sexy demon hunter by her side when it all goes down. . . .